CIRCLES
OF CHAOS

THE AURELIUS ARCHIVES: BOOK TWO

NYX NYGHTINGALE

Circles of Chaos

Content Warning: This book contains explicit sex.

Cover Art by Linda Bulickova | Noeran

Cover Lettering/Design by Nyx Nyghtingale

Scene Break Image by Freepik

ISBN 979-8-9923715-2-9 (Print Edition)

ISBN 979-8-9923715-3-6 (eBook)

www.nyxnyghtingale.com

CONTENTS

I

A WEEK LATER

Amara stared at the inside of her wing. The bony frame, the deep red skin that stretched between it, the way it twitched when she repositioned. Pitch-black darkness enveloped her, courtesy of the mountain of blankets piled on top of the bed, but ever since Halloween, she'd developed impeccable night vision.

It was impossible to bury what she'd become.

She was lying on her side, the blankets pulled completely over her head, which sat in a small pocket of space under her wing. One hand rested under her cheek, the other clutched her phone tight against her chest. It buzzed in her hand, and she immediately unlocked it before reading the notification. Seeing who it was from, she sighed and rolled her eyes. She dismissed the text, but not before seeing how many unread messages sat waiting for her: 57 from Nick, 21 from Tessa, 6 from Chloé.

None from Vee.

How many times had Amara texted her? Dozens, easily. Were they even going through? She wouldn't blame Vee for blocking her, not after what happened, after she'd almost—

Shut up Amara. You didn't, doesn't that matter?

She threw her phone to the bed, then buried her face in her hands and pulled her knees to her chest.

But I almost did. I can still feel her blood.

Pulling back, she closely inspected her hands. Her skin was smooth, warm to the touch, and completely unblemished despite inflicting so much carnage that night. What had they become? She'd only ever used her shapeshifting to turn into other people, but could she alter her own body? What other explanation was there?

Her curiosity urged her to try, but she couldn't bring herself to do it. Even if she wanted to, she didn't have the energy; it had been more than a week since she'd last had sex. Food had long ago lost its flavor, and she couldn't remember the last time she'd slept for more than an hour or two.

11 AM

She reluctantly left bed to use the bathroom.

12 PM

Two more messages from Nick. She ignored both.

1 PM

Grabbing her phone, she opened her most recent tab. The local newspaper's website stared back at her, and she read the article in its entirety, despite having the whole thing memorized.

—

STUDENT INJURED IN HALLOWEEN FIRE

A local Halloween celebration ended in disaster last night when the site of the party unexpectedly caught fire. Although most students were evacuated safely, one student was injured in the blaze.

Emergency services were dispatched at approximately 12:30 a.m. after being automatically notified when the building's fire alarm activated.

The residence in question, commonly referred to by local students as The Jade Palace, had long ago been converted into a Chapter House for Sigma Alpha Upsilon (ΣAY), a local fraternity. As part of the renovation, a full fire suppression system was installed.

Authorities are still uncertain as to the cause of the fire. While students on scene confirmed that the sprinklers had activated, the fire was able to consume the building despite this countermeasure.

Foul play is not suspected at this time, although the investigation is ongoing.

—

What if I turned myself in? No, they'd want to know how I did it. It's not like I can tell them I'm a demon.

I'll bet arsonists can burn down buildings without beating their friends half to death.

Amara flinched as she recalled her last moments with Vee, seeing her utterly convinced she was about to die. The image had been seared into Amara's brain, haunting her every time she closed her eyes.

She wanted to cry, but had run out of tears days ago. Her body retched and shook as it attempted anyways.

The hours kept passing. Amara did nothing but turn to her other side, which took nearly half an hour given the size of her wings. Her phone occasionally pinged with texts from Nick and Tessa, but she continued ignoring them. It was almost four in the afternoon when she heard a knock at her bedroom door.

"Amara?" Nick asked, "I know you're in there."

"Go away!"

"Not this time, Amara. When's the last time you left the house? Ate something?" He paused for a moment, then awkwardly mumbled, "Had sex?"

"Is that why you're here? Need a slut to get your rocks off?" Amara hissed.

"C'mon, that's not fair. We both know that if you're not having sex, your body shuts down. I just want to help."

"Maybe you should help yourself, and leave me alone!" Amara threw the comforter off, shouting at Nick through the door. "How do you know I won't snap? That I won't go berserk and murder you?!"

A different voice spoke up next, alerting Amara to the fact that Nick wasn't alone. "Vee attacked you, what choice did you have? You were defending yourself!"

"You know why she attacked me, Tessa? Because I lied to her! Because you told me to! Still think that was the right call?"

"Of course I do! The instant she found out, she ambushed you and tried to cast you into Hell! What did I say about those Church idiots? To them, you're just a monster, that's all you'll ever be. You really think a literal fuckin' angel is going to give you a pass because you used to do each other's makeup?"

Amara pulled the covers over her head again, burying her face in a pillow without saying anything. Another few seconds passed before Tessa spoke again.

"Amara? Great, real mature. Just ignore us, I'm sure that'll fix everything."

"C'mon Tess, don't make this worse."

"She's the one ignoring me!"

The two continued bickering for a while, but Amara tuned them out. She screamed into her pillow again, sighing with relief when they eventually left. After a few minutes, someone walked back inside, and a quiet voice traveled through the door.

"Um, Amara?" Chloé asked, her voice barely audible.

"Oh, Chloé, I... didn't know you were here too." Amara crawled out from under the covers, moving closer to her bedroom door. She readjusted her zip-up hoodie, which mostly rested on her hips due to her wings. "Did you... hear any of that?"

"No, I was waiting outside. How are you feeling?"

Amara paused, unsure what to say. "What did they tell you?"

"Well, they said you and Vee were talking at the party, and didn't get out in time when the fire started, and she got hurt."

"That's... yeah, that's about right." Amara sat down, leaning against the wall near the door. "Here to tell me it's not my fault?"

Chloé paused for a moment. "I'm not a therapist, I don't think... that's not why I'm here. I just... I miss you, is all. I miss eating lunch with you, talking about our projects, telling you about what I'm playing. You're great company, and we both know I can't say the same about Tessa."

"Nick's still around," Amara muttered.

"He's a boy! It's not the same!"

A weak chuckle caught Amara by surprise. "Alright, well, how's your charity thing going?"

"We're gonna launch this week!"

"Shit, really? Chloé, that's great!"

"Well, the whole point is to make fundraising easier and more transparent, and now we've got the perfect excuse to launch. We're gonna raise money for the fire relief."

Amara froze, a response escaping her. Another minute passed in silence before Chloé spoke up again.

"I know you're in a rough spot, but I was kinda hoping you would help?"

"Oh, I don't... I'm not much of a charity person."

The exact opposite, in fact.

"Well, you said before we could maybe work together, that you could help with the social media side of things? Plus, I know you're really into photography, and we could really use some high quality pictures for our campaign."

Chloé remembers that? I feel like that was ages ago... though, her life hasn't been as hectic as mine has recently.

Amara glanced over at her closet, thinking of her photography stuff still packed away inside. It had been one of her first passions and was the reason she decided to get into marketing in the first place. She had figured the two skills would pair really well, giving her a lot to offer when searching for a job. In the chaos surrounding her transformation, she'd completely forgotten about it.

"Gimme a sec?" Amara asked. She heard a muffled response from the other side of the door, and got up.

Digging through her closet, she pulled out her camera bag. She looked through all her different lenses, carefully laying them out one by one, smiling at the memories. When she finally took hold of her camera, she remembered how good it felt in her hands. She turned it on and began flicking through the old pictures stored on her memory card.

She found pictures of Nick, mostly headshots she'd taken so he could have something to put on resumes. There were a few of Tessa, sometimes with her partners, sometimes flicking her off when she realized Amara was taking pictures.

In one of Tessa's pictures, she was winking at the camera while angling the lens up her skirt. That definitely wasn't one of Amara's shots.

There were also pictures of Chloé out in the quad, leaning up against a tree while sketching in her notebook. Whenever Amara had captured her by surprise, she'd always looked incredible. After the first few, however, she'd hidden her face behind her notebook.

She stopped when she found her first picture of Vee. It was a simple profile, her face slightly illuminated by the sunlight bouncing off a building behind her.

Vee had always been the most supportive of her photography. Unlike the others, she was eager to pose, and Amara had plenty of pictures of Vee smiling, but also of her goofing off. Scrolling through the pictures, she remembered the day she took them, smiling at the memories.

Eventually, Vee had insisted that they switch, that Amara be the subject for once. The next batch of pictures had been taken by Vee, with Amara struggling to find good angles for herself. She'd always been more comfortable behind the camera, but Vee had walked her through some tricks, and she'd ended up enjoying herself. The shots Vee had taken that day were still some of her favorite pictures of herself.

The last picture was the two of them laughing. It was horribly off-center, blurry, and angled heavily to the right, but that was Vee's fault for trying to take a selfie with something other than a phone. It was, without question, the worst picture on the camera, and yet it was so evocative.

Amara couldn't look away. As she stared at the picture, her mind warped the image. Vee's face grew sharper and the blur vanished, only to be replaced with blood. The soft, warm light grew more intense, flickering as flames surrounded them, threatening to collapse the Palace. Tears fell from her face, which was begging Amara not to continue, yet utterly convinced that she would. Blood dripped down Amara's clawed hands, tightening slowly around Vee's neck until—

I DIDN'T DO IT! I STOPPED MYSELF!

"Amara?" Chloé asked, her voice tense.

There were fresh tears on her face, apparently. Had Chloé heard her crying? She looked down at her camera, no longer in her hands, which lay on its side on the floor.

She took a deep breath, her body shaking.

Photos. Human Amara loved that, she was great at it.

"I-I'm still here." Amara said, crawling closer to the door. She wiped her eyes, brushing away the tears as she thought about Chloé's question.

"I'll do it." She finally whispered.

"Yay! I'd hug you if I could!" Chloé cheered.

"I appreciate the thought, though..." Amara looked back at her tail and her wings, "I'm not really decent at the moment. Tell you what, I'll join you for dinner tonight, and we'll talk everything over."

"That's awesome! I'll put together all our fundraising material, and we can look through it!"

"Oh, and Chloé?" Amara asked, "Can you send Nick in on your way out? I need his help with something."

In the time it took for Nick to say goodbye to everyone, Amara had half-heartedly picked up her room. It was still leagues beneath her typical standards, but she was more than willing to settle for mediocrity today. She was mid-yawn, half-buried in a pile of tangled bedsheets, when Nick entered.

"So... talking with Chloé helped?" he asked.

"Look, I know you want to ask a million questions, but can we not? I'm gonna focus on what's in front of me, one step at a time. Which means, well..." Amara flexed her wings, "I need your help putting these away."

Nick started to say something, then stopped. When he finally spoke, his words were soft and cautious. "Of course. Did you have anything in mind?"

She paused, the awkwardness of the situation staring her in the face. "Obviously I need to do this, but there's a lot I haven't shaken off. A distraction would be nice, would you want to put something on? Got any favorite pornos?"

The thought clearly seemed to catch Nick by surprise. "Uh, yeah, we can do that. What do you like?"

Amara lazily undressed as she cast her thoughts back to her porn watching days. Her sweatpants came off easily, especially with the help of her tail, and she threw her hoodie to the floor after unzipping it. "What about... something with anal in it. That was my go-to for a while."

Without saying anything, Nick pulled up his phone and started scrolling through a porn site. While he looked, Amara had an idea and ran back to her closet, where she started to dig through her photography equipment. After a moment, she found what she was looking for: a ring light on a tripod, with a phone mount in the middle. She'd bought it during her first semester of college to help with her marketing projects, though it had been forgotten in the chaos of her transformation.

"Wait, we're not filming this, are we?" Nick asked, finally looking up.

"Absolutely not! I just figured we need a place to put your phone so we can both see it." Amara set up the stand at the foot of her bed, then grabbed Nick's phone. She snapped it into place, then turned the mount to landscape and hit play. "So, what did you find?"

"I don't really have any favorites, but I found a video from an amateur couple I've seen before," Nick said, unbuckling his pants.

Amara stared at Nick as he finally started undressing, but hesitated when she thought about crawling closer. She looked up, caught Nick awkwardly staring back at her, then sighed. "Alright, look, this isn't gonna be the world's best fuck. I just need you to cum, and I'll get what I need. How about you get behind me, get yourself excited, and just... I dunno, go for it."

Amara turned away, facing Nick's phone, then fell forward onto her stomach. He shifted into place behind her, then began gently massaging her ass. She had a feeling he was going to try and make this enjoyable for her, though she didn't know if that would be possible.

In front of her, the girl in the video was showing off her bikini, bending over and spreading her legs to show how little it covered. Amara tried to lose herself in the video, hoping that the scantily clad model would get her excited, but all she could focus on was the cinematography. The unseen male model was holding the camera too close, and he was much too eager to zoom in on specific parts of the girl rather than appreciate her figure as a whole.

Nick reached between her legs, his fingers gently running up and down her pussy before settling on her clit. He started making small circles, and after a few moments, his other hand carefully pushed a finger inside her. Surprisingly, it felt better than expected, and she spread her legs further to give him better access.

They stayed like this for a few minutes. Amara began to enjoy the laid-back finger-fucking, and she'd even managed to start enjoying the video. The amateur actress was on her knees now, eagerly gagging on the thick cock of whoever was manning the camera. As she pushed herself further down, the camera catching every detail, Nick pushed another finger into Amara.

She moaned, pleasantly surprised that Nick had coaxed some pleasure out of her. She laid her head down and started teasing Nick with her tail. She ran it up and down his legs, eventually wrapping it around his cock, slowly stroking it. As they weren't in a rush, she tried to experiment with her tail; its dexterity still caught her off guard sometimes. She practiced stroking him up and down, then wrapped her tail entirely around his shaft and tried to flex the hundreds of tiny muscles that traveled the length of her demonic appendage. His aura smelled sweeter with each passing second, and once he started moaning, his pleasure was potent enough to feed on.

Eventually, the slow pace grew annoying, and Amara wrapped her tail around his waist to pull him closer. Getting the hint, he lined himself up and pushed inside of her.

Nick moaned softly as his aura blossomed even brighter, and she continued pulling energy from it. The lethargy that had been hanging over her head since Halloween began to thin; her aches faded, her senses sharpened, and the world seemed to snap into focus. Looking back at the video, she saw the couple had switched positions. The girl was now lying on her back, holding her legs in a split, as the cameraman pushed his cock deep inside her ass.

Although frustrated that she'd missed her favorite part, the sight was more than enough to heighten her own arousal. She tensed her legs, meeting Nick's thrusts with her own as she tried to bring him closer to orgasm. His aura had grown even brighter, and she was eager for his final burst of energy to shake away the rest of her malaise.

Turning away from the video, she looked over her shoulder to better read his aura. He seemed ready to cum, and she threw herself back onto his cock with ever-increasing fervor to push him over the edge. He grabbed her ass, squeezing it hard as he buried his cock deep inside her, and seconds later he froze up entirely. He groaned with pleasure, and energy from his aura poured into Amara at a much greater rate than his thick load. Her own body tingled with excitement, growing hotter as its inner fire began roaring with vitality. The combined sensations over-whelmed her, and despite her earlier skepticism, she began to cum.

Her orgasm was nowhere near as spontaneous as Nick's, but she was pleased to have one at all. Slow, powerful waves of pleasure washed over her, dispelling the last of her aches and pains. While she shuddered with orgasmic bliss, she made sure to temper her inner fire to avoid any accidental burns.

By the time she finished, and had caught her breath, she noticed that Nick's orgasm had long since passed. She released her tail's hold on Nick as he pulled out of her, then took a deep breath as he fell back. They both took several minutes to rest and catch their breath.

"Well, I won't say I feel better, but... I certainly don't feel as bad." Amara muttered, panting into the covers.

Once he'd caught his breath, Nick moved to the edge of the bed and pulled his phone from the mount. "Glad you got something out of it. Other than your energy back, I mean. I heard you're gonna meet Chloé for dinner?"

"That's the plan. She's gonna show me her charity plans and... and I'm gonna see what I can do to help."

She readjusted, swinging her legs to the floor as she watched Nick stand up. He seemed about to say something, then bit his tongue and stayed quiet. Happy that he wasn't continuing to pry, Amara turned her attention elsewhere. Her morbid curiosity had returned, and she stared at the back of her hands, slowly flexing them.

I have to know.

She connected with her inner fire, pausing for a moment as she let herself bask in its warmth. She'd been without it for so long, she'd forgotten how comforting it was, though now it was tinged with fear and uncertainty. She tapped into that strength, directing it at her hands as she tried to alter them. It was a slow process, and it required thinking about what they looked like before, but she fought through the painful memories.

A collection of bony ridges began to grow on the back of her hands. They were pitch black, hard to the touch, and seemed nearly identical to whatever material her horns and wingtips were made of. The ridges were nowhere near as smooth as her horns, however, and examining it reminded her of an insect's exoskeleton. Flexing her hand once more, she watched as the various plates seamlessly layered over each other, allowing her complete freedom of movement despite their rigidity.

"Whoa, that's really something." Nick was halfway through putting his pants on, but paused to stare at Amara's hands.

She jumped in surprise, having forgotten he was there, and shook her hands to return them to normal. "It's nothing, I shouldn't have... just forget about it." Amara stood up and, with a small flurry of embers, got rid of her demonic features.

"I'm jumping in the shower. Just do whatever you want." She took a few steps into the hall, paused, then doubled back. "And... I'm sorry about earlier."

Nick simply nodded, quietly smiling at Amara. She forced one of her own, then left.

After a long, lukewarm shower, Amara got dressed and left the house for the first time since the party. Loathe as she was to admit it, locking herself inside probably hadn't been the best idea. She did her best to smile, to laugh with her friends and enjoy dinner, but her actions felt shallow and performative.

The pain and guilt crashed in and out like the tide. Sometimes she found it difficult to talk, and other times she caught herself nearly hyperventilating without reason. As much as she tried to hide it, her friends obviously noticed. Still, they seemed willing to leave the matter alone, and Amara appreciated it.

They spent most of the dinner listening to Chloé's plans, including a run-down of how her platform worked. It seemed to focus on two main ideas: keeping the finances transparent, and providing exposure to everyone raising money for the charity. As Chloé explained it, anyone that wanted to contribute to a specific charity could link their efforts through the platform. Then, people that wanted to donate money could scroll through everyone listed and look for products or creators that appealed to them.

Ideally, she explained, creators would be incentivized to advertise their services, while potential donors would have more reasons to donate other than the goodness of their heart.

Amara was thoroughly impressed with everything she heard, and eventually took over the conversation as she explained how she could help manage the social media side of things. She explained peak traffic hours, which content would work best on different platforms, and tried to help set reasonable expectations when it came to setting donation goals.

After spending considerably more time talking than she'd imagined she would, and eating her first real meal in over a week, Amara's exhaustion finally caught up with her. She hugged each of her friends tight, thanking Chloé in particular, and went home to finally get some sleep.

It was dark, the only light coming from the occasional streetlamp. One flew by every few seconds, whizzing past the car at incredible speeds. She checked the dashboard and saw she was driving much faster than the speed limit. Laughter filled her ears, and she realized she wasn't alone. To her right, a woman sat in the passenger seat, her phone illuminating her face.

A tight miniskirt left her legs completely on display, the sight of them driving her crazy. She reached out, grabbing the woman's thigh before sliding her hand higher. It was playfully slapped away, and the passenger smirked as she said something, but the words were muddled, almost as if she were underwater.

Without a woman's body to enjoy, Amara instead reached for the drink in the cupholder. The beer was starting to warm, and she finished it off before throwing the can in the backseat.

A scream filled her ears, and when she looked back at the road, she found it had vanished. The car rattled as it veered into the grass, smashing through a small barrier. It left the ground suddenly, jumping into the air before angling down and crashing into a river.

She lurched forward, gasping as a wall of water—

Amara sat up in a panic, her body shaking. Sweat dripped down her face, and her sharpened hands clutched tattered bedsheets. She looked around the room, nervous and disoriented, as she tried to catch her breath.

"What the fuck?"

2

HEATING UP

"—and then, when I woke up, my claws were back, and I'd ripped through my sheets!"

"I mean, kinda just sounds like a bad dream. Everyone has them."

"But why drunk driving? Why do I remember it so vividly?" Amara asked, shoving her hands into her pockets.

"Didn't you say you can't get drunk anymore? Maybe it's combining that with your feelings about the party?"

"That's a stretch, Nick, even by my standards."

"Hey, I'm an architect. If you seriously want someone to examine your dreams, go ask Tessa or something. Isn't she super into tarot reading?" Nick shrugged as he pushed the crosswalk button, waiting for traffic to stop.

The two continued bickering, trying to guess if Tessa seemed the type to read into dreams, as they continued their walk. It was early in the afternoon, and Amara's hair fluttered in the light autumn breeze. She wore black shorts, her legs visible through the heavily distressed denim, and a loose red shirt hung off one shoulder. All the students they passed wore sweaters, jackets, and other appropriately warm items, but Amara's body was incapable of feeling cold. Her camera bag hung at her side, its weight comforting her as they turned the final corner, The Jade Palace now in sight.

At least, what remained of it.

The blackened skeleton of the house's frame still stood, for the most part. One wall had collapsed, and now lay in pieces amongst the ashes, but the others had managed to stay up. Bits of plumbing were visible, iron veins that had long ago stopped pumping, and Amara also saw hints of electrical wiring amongst the damage. The rest of the lot was covered by a thick blanket of charred remains, still awaiting a proper burial.

The debris wasn't completely undisturbed. Several sets of tracks led in and out of the ashes, likely from curious students eager for a thrill. A few larger pieces had also been tossed around, probably by someone looking for anything salvageable, though Amara doubted there was anything of value left.

She paused, her knuckles white as she clutched the strap of her bag. Closing her eyes, she tried to fight back the intrusive memories by taking deep breaths; in for two, out for four. Before she had a chance to lose that battle, Nick spoke up.

"Hey, we can still turn back. Chloé will understand if- -"

"No," Amara said quickly. "I need to do this."

Opening her eyes, she took her first steps towards the building. Thin strips of yellow tape fluttered in the light breeze, hastily wrapped around poles embedded around the ruins, but no one stood watch to enforce their words of caution. Over the last week, Amara had hyperfixated on the aftermath, desperate for any scrap of news regarding the future of the Palace, but she'd unearthed nothing but rumors. Some claimed the insurance wasn't up to date, others thought the building didn't actually have an owner; the only concrete fact was that cleanup had yet to begin.

That's why I'm here. Chloé needs these pictures to help with the fundraising.

Setting her bag down, Amara began setting up her camera. She double and triple checked each step of the process, cursing her jittery hands under her breath. After a few test shots, she stepped closer and ducked under the caution tape.

When she finally mustered the courage to look at the building, she found herself staring at the back entrance. At least, what remained of it. The door lay in pieces just past the frame, shattered from her panicked rush to escape. She flinched as she remembered how the door had snapped under her shoulder and looked to the lawn beside her. The grass still held impressions from where she'd landed with Vee, traces of blood mixed in among the ashen green blades. Her nose twitched as she detected a faint hint of iron, then smoke began drifting off the burning house. Sirens screeched in the distance, the noise punctuated by the sickening sound of lumber snapping nearby. She locked eyes with Vee, bloodied and bruised on the ground, her face—

Shut up! It's over!

Amara shook her head, the smoke and sirens vanishing as she grabbed her camera. She raised it higher, between herself and her memories, then snapped her first pictures.

CLICK

The memories locked away, she began circling the house. Just past the frame, she found the centerpiece of the Palace, the large living room with the previously bright green wall. The furniture, while warped and blackened by the fire, was still recognizable, and the railing from the loft jutted out from a pile of rubble. She remembered kicking it to the floor, grinning madly as she smothered the exits in hellfire. Waves of heat began drifting off the destroyed loft, the fire spreading in tandem with her rage. It was a part of her, a living, breathing weapon that longed to consume everything it—

CLICK

Another deep breath, another batch of pictures.

The fire's gone. Keep moving.

Stepping towards the front of the house, she kicked aside small piles of discarded cups and bottles, abandoned in the rush to escape disaster. The excitement of the party returned, the joy of showing everyone her true form, of reveling in their adoration. Eager hands caressed her tail, her horns, the more inebriated students attempting to touch her exposed legs and ass. She'd never felt so desired before, yet somehow it had felt so right.

CLICK

She raised the camera higher, looking into the kitchen. The breakfast bar still stood, which was impressive given the destruction everywhere else. Hints of alcohol danced across her lips, every drink graciously donated by a horny co-ed eager for her company. The more she drank, the more she noticed the absence of inebriation, which had only intensified her desire to feed.

CLICK

I'm more than that. I have to be.

Amara pushed onward, locking her memories away behind her pictures. She was close to finishing, and she quickly glanced back at Nick before moving on.

The last side of the building had surprisingly little fire damage, all things considered. The bulk of the fire had been in the main room, as the flames hadn't spread until after they'd left the bedroom. Most of the drywall here had been destroyed, and she saw that some sections of the floor had collapsed. Through the gaps, she saw the room Vee had pulled her into.

She had replayed her conversation with Vee thousands of times. She'd learned so little, they'd barely spent any time talking, but there was so much she wanted to know.

"Stop fucking lying to me!"

Amara winced, the stinging pain from Vee's hand still fresh in her mind. The pain from the magic, the Enochian assaulting her very essence, had paled in comparison to the look on Vee's face. She moved her hand to her cheek, recalling the last words they'd said to each other before giving up on a peaceful resolution.

When she pulled her hand away, it was unexpectedly wet.

CLICK

She moved her camera to her hip, letting the straps hold it aloft, then brought her hands to her face. Taking a deep breath, she brushed away the rest of her tears.

I'm so sorry, Vee.

A hand appeared on her shoulder, pulling her back to her senses. She looked over at Nick, who said nothing as he held her camera bag open. No doubt her eyes were red and swollen, but thankfully he stayed silent as he helped pack her camera away.

Several minutes passed before Amara spoke up.

"Hellfire."

Nick gave her a questioning look.

"My flames, they're hellfire."

He paused, likely choosing his words carefully. "How do you figure?"

"I don't entirely know. Maybe Vee said something while we were... y'know, but it could've been something else. There's still so much I don't know about myself, maybe demons just know this shit innately."

She zipped up her bag, slinging it over her shoulder again before turning to leave the lot. Ducking under the caution tape, her and Nick began the walk back to campus.

"You ever practice with it?" Nick asked.

"Practice? After what happened?" She gestured back at the remains of the Palace, huffing as she picked up her pace. "I'm better off forgetting about it completely."

Nick jogged after her, matching her stride before changing the topic to something else. Amara was more than happy to leave any talk of hellfire, as well as the Palace, behind her.

As cathartic as visiting the Palace had been, Amara was far less enthused about returning to classes. Assignments were piling up, and while most of her teachers had been willing to give her extensions, she only had so much good will to burn. This was the second time she'd spontaneously taken a week off school, after all: she'd previously been forced to stay home when her wings had first appeared. She still remembered why she enjoyed her field of study, but it was growing difficult to focus on the mundanity of school with everything else happening around her. Trying to channel Nick, she pushed herself to stay optimistic; perhaps the extra challenge would serve as a distraction from her own thoughts.

She was currently attempting to engage with a U.S. history lecture. They had recently started a multi-week unit entirely focused on World War II, and were exploring its origins towards the end of the 1930's.

"—and even though the Anschluss was a direct violation of international treaties that had been established after World War I, Germany faced no consequences. I mentioned earlier the idea of Appeasement, and this is a prime example. In their eagerness to avoid another great war, major players on the international stage—"

Amara yawned as the professor kept talking. She wasn't entirely uninterested in history, but she much preferred classes with more practical applications. She shifted in her seat, rolling her neck and absentmindedly gazing at the other students around her.

Quite a few of them were sweating. Students with extra layers, like sweatshirts and jackets, had uniformly removed them, and many others were using notebooks to fan themselves. Even Professor McKenney had removed his blazer, and he'd rolled up the sleeves of his wrinkled undershirt.

As the lecture continued, it became clear that the heat was only getting worse. The thick smell of sweat threatened to overwhelm Amara's senses, and she was shocked no one else seemed perturbed by it. Class even paused momentarily so they could open all the windows, which were old and stubborn. The professor also clarified that the school was aware of the problem but had no timeline on when it would be fixed. A thought popped into Amara's head, and she pulled out her phone.

Amara: You have any classes in Brandt today?

Tessa: nah, skipped em

Tessa: why?

Amara: Everyone here is sweating like crazy, and the teacher says the heat's busted.

Tessa: so? im not a plumber

Amara: What if it's a circle? You said the one in Lysander made things really cold, so what if this is like that? But with heat?

Amara: Also plumbers aren't for heating

Tessa: dam, thats a good idea. count me in

Tessa: tonite? after dinner?

Tessa: electrician watever idc

Amara rolled her eyes, unsure if Tessa was joking or not. Thankfully, the heat didn't affect her; if anything, she found it rather comfortable. The smell of sweat, however, only got worse as time went on, but mercifully the lecture ended soon after. She packed away her notes, zipped up her backpack, and headed for the door. Her eyes were glued to her phone as she walked; in a conversation with Tessa, she was explaining that electricians weren't responsible for furnaces, but she was also texting Chloé to discuss charity details. As she left the lecture hall, she accidentally ran into another student, knocking a pile of books to the floor.

"Shit, sorry!" Amara said, shoving her phone in her pocket before kneeling to help clean up.

"Well, what are the odds? Second time now you haven't watched what you're stepping into, Amara."

She froze, finally looking up at who she'd bumped into. Brandon smiled back at her, his insufferable smirk bringing back painful memories. Her breath quickened as she narrowed her eyes, and she pulled her hands away from the books on the floor, no longer interested in helping.

"What, here for payback?" she asked quietly.

"I just want to talk, nothing more." He slowly picked up his books, keeping his voice down as he placed them in his backpack.

Amara fought to hold back her anger, fully aware that they were surrounded by other students. Standing up, she began walking to the exit before looking back at him. "Five minutes."

He picked up the pace, now matching her stride as they left the building. "I owe you an apology. What I did was wrong, and I accept that."

"Likely story. You're just upset I escaped."

"On the contrary, I'm glad you did. It made me reexamine myself, and I realized I didn't like who I was becoming."

"And all it took was attempting to enslave a fellow student? Truly your empathy knows no bounds," Amara snapped. She turned off the main path, hoping to avoid accidental eavesdropping as they kept talking.

"Except you're not just a student, we both know that. You're so much more, yet you continue to waste your time with classes and schoolwork!"

Amara glared at him, the true meaning of his words hitting her. "So you're following me?"

"We go to the same college, and we happened to cross paths a few times. Not that weird." Brandon cleared his throat, pausing for a second. "Why bother with school? You've got power that most people can only dream of."

"Can we cut the bullshit? Tell me why you're here, we both know it's not just to get to know me."

"Alright, fine, I'm not just here to apologize. Though, for what it's worth, getting to know each other would be nice." Amara glared at him, refusing to acknowledge his statement. A moment passed before he finally started talking again. "I think we can help each other out."

"Please, what could you possibly do for me?"

"I can find you people to feed on. People who don't deserve their souls."

Amara stopped in her tracks, shocked at his offer. His eyes were deathly serious, and she grew sick to her stomach even thinking about it. "I don't do that."

"C'mon, you're a demon! Without souls, you'll wither away. Think of how many people on campus deserve to be punished. You have the power to balance the scales! What happens the next time you get hungry and the only students nearby are good people?"

"What, you're an expert on demons now?"

"I've done my homework, and everything I've read says the same thing. Your body is wired differently, and there's no fighting biology; sooner or later, you'll give in to those instincts. Don't act like it hasn't already happened."

"You don't know anything about me!" Amara hissed.

"People show their true colors when they're backed into a corner. You're a succubus, right? You didn't hesitate to strip down when you needed an edge over me. I saw how easy it was for you to get on your knees, to beg for my—"

Amara grabbed his shirt, shoving him against a nearby building. Her eyes flared as she pinned him to the wall. "Finish that sentence and you'll regret it."

"I'm offering you a way out, a way to take control of what you are!"

In the corner of her vision, Amara realized that several students had slowed down, watching the heated exchange between her and Brandon. She scared them off with a glare, then turned back to the matter at hand. "I don't know what sick fantasy you're dreaming up, but you can forget it. I'll make this easy; if you come near me or my friends again, you'll regret it. You have no idea what I'm capable of."

Without giving him a chance to respond, Amara released her grip and turned away. This time, thankfully, Brandon let her leave.

I just wish I did.

Dinner passed slowly and uneventfully, for better or for worse. Amara found it hard to concentrate on eating, on talking with her friends, when so much else was happening. Still, the distraction was nice, and anything was better than the stuff she'd forced down when she'd lost her taste. Once finished, she left the cafeteria with Tessa and started walking to Brandt Hall.

Although classes had mostly wrapped up for the day, it would be a few more hours before the building locked up for the night. They had almost approached the entrance when Amara finally spoke up, her fear and curiosity overpowering her desire to not freak Tessa out.

"Have you felt any different since we started sleeping together?"

"Like, do I regret it? Are you forgetting how great the sex is?"

"That's not what I mean! I want to know if you've noticed any changes. Weird mood swings, apathy, stuff like that."

"Nah, I'm the same loveable bitch I've always been." Tessa smirked as they walked, the two of them wandering the first floor as they looked for the basement. "What's this really about?"

A few moments passed before Amara responded. "I ran into Brandon today." She saw Tessa's eyes narrow in anger, then quickly added, "He just wanted to talk, I'm fine."

"What did that little cretin want?"

"At first he just wanted to apologize, which I didn't buy for a second, but then he... offered to find me people to fuck. Like he was offering them up as sacrifices or something."

"Blech, fucking gross. That's just like him, though. He probably thinks he can use you to get revenge on everyone he doesn't like. I trust you turned him down?"

"Of course! I feel gross even thinking about it. But still, he kept going on and on about how I'm a demon, that I need souls to survive, and I just... can't shake the idea. What if I've been taking bits of soul every time I fuck?" Amara's voice grew quiet, scared to even think it, let alone say it.

"You're scared I'm losing my humanity?"

"I mean... a little, yeah. Aren't you?"

Tessa shrugged. "Eh, we all die eventually."

At this point, the girls finally found the door to the basement and started down the stairs. Amara reflexively reached for her fire to light the way, then hesitated. Thoughts of the Palace's charred exterior returned, and she shivered. Instead, she pulled out her phone and turned on the flashlight. "But what about the afterlife? My existence proves it's real, aren't you worried about... y'know."

"You think fucking a demon is gonna keep me out of Heaven? Please. I'm a witch, I'm sure they made up their minds the instant I first used magic."

Walking out of the staircase, Amara found herself staring at a familiar sight. While she'd never been down here before, it bore an uncanny resemblance to the basement under the Science Building. Unlike there, however, the classrooms in front of them appeared to see regular use. The hallways clearly had updated, functioning lights, even though most of them were off at the moment, leaving only the occasional emergency light to cast a pale glow amidst the darkness.

Definitely plenty of places to hide a magic circle.

After picking a direction and starting out, Tessa continued talking. "I still can't fucking believe Vee. She didn't even try talking to you! Nooo we've got to jump right to banishing your best friend just because they're different."

"It's not like I didn't provoke her," Amara said bitterly. "Repeatedly."

"Okay, but banishment? Murder? She gave you, like, a minute to state your case, and when it wasn't exactly what she wanted to hear, too bad! Do you think she knew I was a witch? It's not like I keep my tattoos hidden, even if the design hides them a bit."

Before Amara had a chance to respond, something strange caught her attention. She heard a low murmur from further down the hallway, though she couldn't pinpoint what its source might be.

"Maybe angels think they're too high and mighty to bother with witches. Wouldn't that be wild? Saved purely because she thinks I'm beneath her. I bet she doesn't even—"

"Shh!"

"Look, I know you're still upse—"

Amara jumped forward, pushing her hand against Tessa's mouth. The witch glared back before relenting, rolling her eyes slowly. Now able to focus, Amara confirmed her suspicions; there were people up ahead, and they were moving closer.

"We need to hide, now!" Amara pulled Tessa with her, backing down the hallway until they were outside a classroom. Trying the door, she found it locked and cursed under her breath. Taking a step back, she rammed her shoulder into the door and snapped the lock, opening a path for them to run inside. Closing the door as best she could, Amara pushed them both against the wall so they couldn't be seen from the window. In the hallway, the low murmur grew louder, and soon Amara was able to hear the conversation.

"—just don't let it happen again, okay? People were complaining all day, and we don't need that kind of attention. He's still pissed about the cafeteria; do you know how much that cost?"

"I told you, that wasn't me! The modification went fine, then I covered up the circle. When I left, there wasn't a vine in sight."

The voices were both masculine. One was deeper, and slightly breathy, while the other had more youthful energy. They walked slowly, the conversation continuing as Amara and Tessa locked eyes, both surprised by what they were hearing.

"I don't give a shit about your excuses, just get your act together. Everything will be ready in a few weeks, and the fewer excuses he has to yell at us, the better."

"Tch, fine. Sometimes I don't know why I bother." The younger man paused to clear his throat, then continued talking. "You hear we might be switching to a new online grading system? I guess the school got some new tech grant, and—"

The conversation grew more distant, and significantly less interesting, as the two men walked further away from the classroom the girls were hiding in. Tessa stood to try and leave the classroom, but Amara held her back. She closed her eyes, focusing on the footsteps in the hall, and waited until the strangers had entered the staircase. She sighed, the tension leaving her shoulders as Tessa walked out of the classroom.

"Did you hear that? Did you fucking hear that?!"

"I'm just glad they didn't see us, that would have been bad."

"Bad? You're a fucking demon! You fought an angel and won! I bet you could've wiped the floor with those bozos and then gotten them to spill their secrets!"

"Tess, we know nothing about them! Can they do magic? If so, how powerful is it? And what if they'd seen you? Do you think you could take other witches in a fight?"

"Ugh, this is stupid! We finally get a chance to score some real answers, and all we have now are more questions." Tessa pushed past Amara, walking deeper into the basement. "And what's happening in a few weeks? Do we have a fucking time limit now?"

Amara ran after Tessa, matching her pace as they continued talking. "We have more information, and that's never a bad thing. They're definitely planning something, and now we know we need to pick up the pace."

Tessa's tattoos lit up, and she started tracing her hand across the wall as she walked. Every few moments she would pause, tap a few bricks, then move forward. Amara could tell she was still frustrated, but didn't know what she could say to smooth things over, so she joined the search for an illusory wall.

Minutes passed, the silence only broken by them testing different lengths of wall. After a few minutes of silent searching, Tessa spoke up. "Did one of those voices sound familiar to you? The younger one?"

Amara paused her search, replaying the conversation in her head. "No, I don't think so. It sounded like they were teachers, though."

"Teachers... teachers..." Tessa mumbled to herself, lost in thought as she continued tapping on the new section of wall she'd just gotten to. After a few seconds, the wall started glowing, magical runes forming in the light. Tessa seemed completely oblivious, her focus turned inward as she tried to place the stranger's voice.

"Um, Tess?"

The witch shook her head briefly then looked back at Amara, who was pointing at the glowing wall. "Oh shit! We found it!"

"Hey, you found it. I'm just the bodyguard, remember?"

Tessa refocused her attention on the wall, finishing the process of dispelling the illusion. When the wall finally vanished, they were able to see the room it was hiding. It resembled the rest of the basement, with gray concrete floor covering the entire length, though it was obviously less trafficked. The back wall, instead of a more modern white brick design, was instead covered by old, red bricks, their age made apparent by the crumbling mortar holding them up. The room was quite compact, and likely designed for one specific purpose: to hide the large magic circle that was now visible on the floor.

"Whew, you feel that?" Tessa asked, fanning herself with her shirt.

Amara shook her head. "Living hellfire, remember?"

"Right, you're too hot for your own good. Always forget that. Well, keep watch or whatever, we don't want those morons coming back." The witch moved into the room, carefully tracing the outside of the circle as she took it in. After her first lap, she pulled out her notebook and started jotting down notes, likely making her own copy of the circle as well. As she worked, she continued mumbling to herself about what she was seeing.

While this happened, Amara continued searching up and down the hall, looking for any possible clues about the strangers that had passed them earlier. Other than a cozy studying area and a few more classrooms, nothing stuck out to her as particularly interesting. As she slowly wandered back to her friend, she realized that she hadn't manifested any of her demonic aspects. She instinctively began to reach for them, but just like in the staircase, she hesitated.

Can I distance myself from them? Do I even want to?

After a moment, she decided to pull out her tail. Although she no longer needed to physically wrap it around her waist and under sweaters, which caused uncomfortable cramps, she'd started noticing strange feelings of discomfort when her demonic aspects stayed hidden for too long. Poking her head back inside the alcove with the circle, she saw Tessa still buried in her notebook, sketching and muttering. Past experience told Amara she had quite a bit of time to kill while Tessa worked.

Amara leaned against one of the walls opposite the room they'd discovered and slid down to the floor. She pulled out her phone and checked her socials, but knew there wasn't much to see. The fire at the Palace was still the talk of the town, and Chloé's charity didn't need any work at the moment. Pocketing her phone, she instead found herself staring at her hands again, her thoughts drifting back to her new shapeshifting abilities. With nothing else to do, her curiosity won out.

She flexed her fingers, connecting with her inner hellfire as she urged the strange, bony ridges to return. Her knuckles grew sharp and rigid, the low light revealing soft red undertones in the blackened substance. She pushed the chitinous material further, covering her fingers entirely before extending it out to create claws. She lightly dragged them across her arm to get a feel for how sharp they were.

How much can I change?

Pulling her tail closer, Amara laid it in her lap and studied the tip. Focusing once more, she tried to manifest the same exoskeleton here as well. The practice seemed to be paying off, and soon her tail sported the same bony material as her hands. She molded the material into a point, watching as an impressively long barb grew from the tip of her tail. With another thought, the chitin shifted until one long edge had sharpened, forming a makeshift blade. She playfully swiped her tail through the air, smirking at the satisfying swish it made, then angled her new knife-tail towards one of her palms. She was curious how sharp this strange material could be, and tested it by running the blade across her hand. It effortlessly cut into her skin, catching her by surprise, and she quickly pulled her tail back to stop the experiment.

Droplets of blood formed along the cut, slowly dripping down her palm. Not prepared for a mess, Amara began digging through her backpack to try and find some kind of tissue. It only took her a few moments to find some, but when she looked back at her palm, the cut had vanished. Surprised, she hesitated for a moment before slowly cleaning her hand with the tissue.

I guess that explains why I healed so fast after Halloween. Fuck, didn't Vee stab me? I remember the sword pushing completely through my shoulder, but it hasn't hurt at all since then. How did I forget that?

After cleaning the blood off her hand, she crumpled the tissue up and glanced back up at Tessa. Her friend was loosely holding her notebook, eyebrows furrowed as she stared directly at Amara.

"Oh, you're finished?" Amara asked.

"Not quite, I got distracted by... what exactly are you doing? 'Cuz it looked like you turned your tail into a knife and stabbed yourself. Since when can you do that?"

"Since now, apparently. I was just trying to figure out what my shapeshifting limits are, but then I didn't know how sharp this weird exoskeleton could get, so I—look, it's nothing. What have you learned about the circle?"

Tessa hesitated, giving Amara a concerned look before finally speaking up. "Nothing groundbreaking, sadly. I found the modifications they made, it's pretty similar to the circle under the cafeteria, but no new information." She closed her notebook after making a few last-second marks, then walked back into the hallway to restore the illusion.

"Dang, I was hoping this time would be different." Amara stood up, removing all the chitin from her body before demanifesting her tail.

"How am I supposed to focus on classes now that we know there's, like, some kind of cult running around? I have no idea what to do next!" Tessa grumbled as the illusory wall reappeared. With a huff, she threw her backpack around her shoulder and joined Amara in heading for the exit.

"You? Focus on classes? I didn't know you were capable of such a thing." Amara chuckled under her breath, ignoring the dirty look from Tessa. "What are you skipping tomorrow?"

"Psych and Chem in the morning, English after lunch, and then I'm—" Tessa suddenly froze, her eyes wide.

"Tess? Y'alright?"

"The voice from earlier! That was my English teacher!"

"Shit, really? That's a huge lead!"

"This is perfect! We barge into his office, you scare his pants off, and he tells us everything he knows!" Tessa punctuated her sentence by punching the inside of her palm, clearly excited by the idea.

"Absolutely not!"

"C'mon, you're a demon! What could possibly go wrong?"

"Everything! What if he attacks me? Then I have to fight back, and risk losing control in the middle of school. Plus, I don't even know if I'd win; we still don't know if he has any magic!"

Tessa groaned as she pushed open the door to the stairwell. "What do we do then? Ask nicely?"

Amara went quiet, thinking about their options. "We have the element of surprise. They don't know we're onto them, and they don't know what we are. We should try to hold onto that advantage as long as possible. You said you have English tomorrow? I'll come with, maybe we can learn something by watching or tailing him."

"Really Amara? *Tail* him?" the witch said, rolling her eyes.

Amara chuckled. The pun had been entirely accidental, but she was happy to roll with it. "With a good plan, I bet I could make his life a living Hell. Unless you'd rather I wing it?"

"Ugh, I can't believe we're friends."

The girls spent the rest of the walk speculating what the cult might be up to. Despite living on opposite ends of campus, Amara refused to let Tessa walk home alone, and she had a feeling the witch appreciated it. She stayed for a few minutes, happily taking time to catch up with Tessa's partners.

Sydney was trying to throw together a decent meal from the scraps of food in the fridge—apparently Tessa had forgotten to go grocery shopping—and Riley was over as well. Strangely, Amara didn't see Raine anywhere, but when she tried to ask about them, Sydney cut her off in a panic, heavily insinuating that talking about Raine in front of Tessa was a bad idea. Confused, but not wanting to poke the hornet's nest that was Tessa's dating life, Amara politely said her goodbyes and left to return home.

With night having fallen, the campus was much quieter than usual. Amara's thoughts raced from Chloé's charity to the strange events from earlier, but eventually her better judgment failed her. She thought of the Palace, of Vee, of their fight, and felt herself starting to spiral. She picked up the pace as her emotions swelled, eager not to cause a scene in public. After making it home and closing the door, she pushed her forehead against the entrance, her breath panicked and irregular. She squeezed her eyes tight, hoping to fight back her tears, but she couldn't stop them all. She stayed there for several minutes before managing to pull herself together.

Slowly getting undressed, Amara set an alarm for the morning, but hesitated before turning it off. She opened her message history with Vee, scrolling through the dozens of texts that had gone unanswered, refreshing the page in desperate hope of seeing a response. When nothing appeared, she spent the next half hour drafting another text.

Amara: I'm sorry.

Plugging in her phone, she crawled under the covers and tried to get some sleep. It took several hours, and she had to flip the pillow to avoid sleeping on fresh tear stains, but eventually the night took her.

Amara leaned in, pushing her lips against her girlfriend's before eagerly grabbing her ass. The two made out for several minutes, slowly grinding against each other, before breaking apart. They whispered for a moment, planning to go somewhere more private to have some real fun, then got in the car. As the sounds of the party faded into nothing, she pulled onto the main street and floored it. Her car was top of the line, the best money could buy, and she loved showing off what it could do.

Soon the only light around them came from the occasional streetlamp. She loved counting how long it took to pass each one, the power of her car thrumming under her control. In the passenger seat, her girlfriend laughed as she opened her camera. She adjusted her hair, checked her eyeliner, and generously reapplied her lipstick; they both knew how much Amara loved watching it come off.

She reached over, resting a hand on her date's leg. She gripped it tight, savoring the feel of her soft skin under her fingers. She massaged her thigh slowly, watching as her girlfriend opened her legs ever so slightly, her bright red thong visible each time they passed a light. Her hand moved higher, squeezing and massaging the delicate skin, before they brushed against the silky fabric of her date's panties. She gasped, the touch exciting her, before suddenly slapping Amara's hands away, though not without a playful smirk.

When she spoke, the words were far away, garbled and incomprehensible.

Amara sighed, knowing they'd be home soon and the real fun could begin. She grabbed her drink, a half empty can of beer in the cupholder, and slammed the rest of it. She couldn't taste it much anymore, the mixed drinks from earlier made sure of that, but it kept her primed and eager for the coming romp. She threw the can behind her, hearing it rattle as it landed amongst the others.

The road suddenly started shaking, and she assumed she must have hit a rumble strip. Without warning, however, her girlfriend screamed and grabbed the handle above her. Amara looked back at the road, but it was nowhere to be seen. A sea of grass and gravel stretched in front of her and she tried to slam the breaks, but an unexpected ditch disoriented her for a moment. The car slammed into the edge of a protective barrier, and that's when the rattling stopped. It flew into the air, just for a second, as Amara realized they were headed directly into a river.

The front of the car slammed into the water, throwing Amara forward as the airbag erupted. Instead of hitting it, however, her momentum continued. She flew through the airbag, flinching as she approached the windshield, but she harmlessly passed through that as well. She flipped forward, spinning briefly before coming to a stop a few feet above the surface of the river. When she turned to face her car, she saw it was starting to sink into the river, and she thought she could make out two shapes in the front seats.

Despite only being a few feet away from the vehicle, Amara felt like she was seeing it through a lens of some kind. It seemed so distant, the entire scene more like a painting than the late-night tragedy she'd just been living. The edges of her vision started to blur, and she shook her head in confusion.

It wasn't her vision that was blurring, it was the ground and the sky around her. She looked up and watched as the night sky slowly shifted away from its midnight hues. It grew lighter, streaks of gray and white filtering in as she watched, and she felt herself floating higher and higher. The strange colors of the world above continued to blur, to pull her closer as an endless landscape of grayish void called to her.

A strange static filled her ears, starting with a small hum before building to something more recognizable. It almost sounded like rain; a storm off in the distance, with the occasional low rumble of thunder confirming her suspicions. Why did this sound so familiar? She reached for the sky, eager to answer its call as the sounds of rain grew louder, and just as she touched it, everything around her vanished.

Her eyes opened, the dim light of dawn already peeking through the blinds. She groaned, pulling her pillow close in an attempt to go back to sleep, but she knew it was pointless. After a moment of defiance, she relented and began stretching out her arms to wake them up. A loud scraping sound caught her attention, and when she looked to her side, she saw her wingtip had gouged another hole in the wall.

My wings are out? How? I didn't go to sleep like this...

She flexed her tail, and sure enough, it rose out of the covers to greet her. She pushed her hands through her hair, confirming her horns were also present.

I've never manifested my true form in my sleep before. Is this natural? Is this the demon equivalent of wetting the bed? I guess it's better than accidentally burning my covers to a crisp.

Amara groaned, pulling herself up before sliding to the edge of her bed. She reached for her phone, almost scared to check the time, when she paused. Her phone was exactly where she'd left it, plugged in on her nightstand, but it was making noise. Specifically, the app she'd downloaded to play thunderstorm sounds while she slept. She picked it up, increasing the volume as she listened, and realized it matched the noises in her dream exactly.

3
AFFAIRS & ASPIRATIONS

Amara looked around the barren classroom as Tessa flicked the lights on. Rows upon rows of empty seats sat ready, perfectly positioned to give everyone a clear view of the front of the class. The floor escalated just past the first seats, each step containing another row, until ending at the back wall. Tall beams of sunlight poured in through large windows nestled in the back wall, though the sun itself was nowhere to be seen; it was just past noon, and the sun was too high to be visible.

The girls shared a glance before heading towards the back corner. They wanted to avoid unnecessary attention, though Amara had a feeling that Tessa would have chosen the same spot regardless of cult activity.

The witch was wearing a pair of black, baggy cargo pants, as well as her usual combat boots. A red tank top hugged her curves, bearing the distressed logo of some band Amara had never heard of. A black jacket that was several sizes too big completed the outfit, though it only properly sat on one shoulder, the other side bunched around her elbow as she sat down.

Amara had put considerably more effort into her outfit. When her tail and horns had first appeared, she'd been forced to spend several weeks in large, unflattering sweaters. Now, with her shapeshifting under control, she took every chance she could get to show off her wardrobe. Dark blue jeans clung tightly to her legs, ending just above beige ankle booties. A gray, low-cut shirt offering tantalizing hints of her impressive cleavage, though much of the shirt was itself hidden by a deep orange cardigan that ended around her thighs. She opted not to join Tessa in sitting down, and instead wandered the classroom while her friend opened her journal.

"I'm so fucking sick of these circles. I was hoping that finding more would make it easier to figure them out, but I've got nothing," Tessa griped. They had decided to get to Tessa's English class early, hoping to spend as much time as they could hunting for potential clues. In the meantime, since no one was present, she poured over her diagrams of the various magic circles they'd discovered.

"Well, what do we know? What are easy assumptions we can make?" Amara slowly wandered around the room, looking at all the different seats as she meandered towards the front of the class.

"I'm like, ninety percent sure each one is tied to a different plane. That's the simplest way to explain why all the circles act differently. The most obvious was the circle under the cafeteria, which is definitely connected to The Wilds."

"The Wilds?"

"That's what witches tend to call it, but it's got a lot of names. It's all about ground, plants, and wildlife. Think lots of heavy forests, thick jungles, winding rivers, stuff like that. It's home to a lot of magical creatures, too: werewolves, fairies, dryads, tons of others. If there's a cryptid on our plane, it's likely from there."

"Y'know, I'd briefly forgotten how weird my life had gotten, so thanks for the reminder." Amara tried to picture everything she'd just heard. "Fairies? Really?"

"Welcome to the World of Magic! Population: everything and anything you've ever heard of. You're a succubus, just be thankful you have a way to fight back. Learning about magic means you're fair game to a lot of creatures, and not everyone has that kind of safety net."

"I'm going to get attacked just because I know about magic?" Amara asked, looking back at her friend.

"Alright, well, it's not quite that cut and dry. A lot of things, people and creatures alike, greatly benefit from magic being underground, and there's an unspoken rule that we should try to keep it that way. However, once someone knows about magic, you can fuck with them without breaking that rule." Tessa took a deep breath, her eyes briefly staring into the distance. "But it's more than that. This world, Amara? Magic? It's a giant fucking curse. For some reason, things always seem to go wrong once people join it."

Amara leaned against the main desk at the front of the classroom. Those last words rattled around in her head, and her thoughts drifted back to Halloween. She felt herself starting to spiral, then shook her head to stay in the moment. "Right, so each circle is tied to a plane. What else?"

"That's honestly my only good guess. These things are complicated as hell."

"What about the Science Building? You said it was keeping things out?"

"Even if I'm right about that one, I have no idea if the other circles were built the same way. If they are, why was that one hidden the way it was? Why not use illusory walls like the other circles? Why are there so many?" Tessa groaned again, sliding back in her chair as she threw her head back.

Amara, unsure what else to say, instead circled behind the teacher's desk and started rummaging through its drawers. Most were filled with insignificant office supplies, but she dutifully looked through every nook and cranny just to be safe. In the end, the most interesting thing she'd found was a small bag of chocolates. She happily swiped a few, returning to Tessa in the back of the classroom and handing her some sweets.

"So what's the plan? Are you seriously just gonna watch him teach?" Tessa unwrapped a chocolate and popped it into her mouth.

"Yes, actually. Why is that so weird?"

"It's just so boring! If I had your powers, I'd only need five minutes alone with him and we'd get all the answers we wanted." The witch's tattoos lit up, and her pen started hovering over her notebook. "Look at this, how am I supposed to threaten someone with mild levitation?"

"Tess, when I first saw you do magic, you threw someone across a room."

"That was a fluke! And I shouldn't have done it in the first place, I overexerted myself and had a headache for days."

A sound in the hallway caught Amara's attention, likely a crowd of students nearing the classroom. She reached out and pushed Tessa's pen back to the desk just as the door opened, then whispered, "Well, let's be thankful that I'm the demon here, not you."

Tessa rolled her eyes but dropped the topic without a fuss. She reached into her backpack, pulling out her notebooks for the English class that was about to start, and sighed heavily.

Amara, on the other hand, pulled out a pair of stylish sunglasses. She felt a little silly putting them on, but she figured the worst-case scenario would be strangers thinking she was hung over. In truth, she was hoping to study the auras of everyone in class. The events at the Halloween party, coupled with her recently discovered night vision, had been a reminder that her body was still changing.

With her eyes safely covered, she let them flare and began looking around the room. A young man in the hallway hugged his girlfriend goodbye, and they'd clearly fucked this morning. A minute later, a smaller girl with a tight black braid walked in with a vibrant aura, but there were no traces of a second person; she'd definitely just finished masturbating. An incredibly fit boy in a varsity jacket in the front row was pining for a tall, brown-haired boy that had just entered. The taller boy either didn't share those feelings or hadn't noticed the athlete, instead staying glued to his phone while he pulled his books out.

Everything she learned fascinated her, it was incredible seeing such intimate details out in the open like this. Still, other than a chance to flex her improved senses, she didn't see anything noteworthy.

Students continued wandering in, and the classroom gradually filled until most of the seats were taken. Every few seconds she'd catch someone stealing a glance at her, complete with small pulses in their auras, which she found surprising. She was no stranger to that kind of attention, but she swore it was happening more than it had in the past. The only other explanation was that people were always checking her out, and she'd simply never noticed until she had supernatural senses to make it easier to detect.

One aura in particular stood out to her, both due to its relative intensity and the fact that its owner was walking straight towards her.

"Amara! Hey, what's up?" the student asked. "Are you transferring into this class?"

Quickly dulling her eyes, Amara pulled her sunglasses off and looked up. Now that she wasn't focusing on how horny everyone was, she actually recognized the guy talking to her. His name was Alex, and he was one of Nick's athletic friends from back in his wrestling days.

"No, I'm afraid not," Amara replied. "I had some time to kill, and Tessa needs all the help she can get staying awake during lecture. Isn't that right, Tess?"

Amara playfully jabbed an elbow into Tessa's arm, who awkwardly stumbled over her words as she tried to act natural. "Uh, yeah, you know me. It's a miracle I'm here at all, right?"

"Well, that's a shame. I certainly wouldn't object to seeing you around more frequently. Oh! You know what could be fun? You should join Nick and I at the gym sometime, I finally talked him into giving freerunning a shot! Just throw on some activewear and I can show you both the basics!" Alex's words seemed nice enough, though Amara sensed a noticeable pulse in his aura as he suggested Amara dress for the occasion.

Probably just wants an excuse to see me sweaty and half-naked. He's flirted with me before, but has it always been this obvious?

"Maybe some other time, Alex. I've got a lot on my plate, sadly," Amara said, forcing a smile.

"That's cool, not a problem," Alex said, nodding his head enthusiastically. "Well, hope you enjoy the class! And try to keep Tessa awake, will you? She already looks a little bored!"

Once Alex had left to find an open seat, thankfully one further away from them, Amara looked back at Tessa just in time to catch her rolling her eyes. They shared a mutual look of understanding, then Amara donned her sunglasses to continue surveying the class. Strangely, despite all the students sitting at the ready, the teacher was nowhere to be seen.

"Where's Mr. Luxnor?" Amara whispered.

"He's always a little late," Tessa replied. "I think he's got office hours right before this class, sometimes he gets here with a student or two."

As if on cue, the door opened. Professor Luxnor hurried inside, but not before holding the door open for the last student. Amara vaguely recognized the girl walking in behind him, a tall redhead in a green, low-cut top. Her simple leather jacket clearly wasn't trying to hide her ample cleavage, and her posture implied that she was used to being the center of attention. A small handful of students grew noticeably excited at her entrance, though Amara was far more interested in the aura of this new student.

"Who's the redhead? She looks familiar," Amara asked.

"Kylie? You danced with her at the Halloween party. I remember 'cuz I was really fucking jealous."

"Oh, I don't think it's me you should be jealous of."

"What? Who?" Tessa leaned closer, but Amara didn't say anything. She simply gave a knowing look towards the teacher. "Mr. Luxnor?! Shut the fuck up!"

"Their auras are perfectly in sync; I'd say they finished within the last half hour or so."

"I can't fucking believe it! First the cult, but now he's hooking up with a student? Man, he used to be one of my favorite teachers too..."

"You're missing the silver lining here, Tessa." Amara smirked, letting her eyes return to normal as she put her sunglasses away. "We can use this against him."

Professor Luxnor's class dragged on much longer than Amara would have liked, though it was thankfully not the longest lecture she'd ever attended. Once it had finished, and she'd parted ways with Tessa, she found herself with nothing to do for the rest of the day. Nick's Tuesday schedule was packed full, and he wouldn't be free until close to dinner. She thought about returning to her apartment to work on some homework, but being alone didn't sound all that appealing. Instead, she pulled up Chloé's number and shot her a text.

Amara: What's up? Still in classes?

Chloé: Nope! I just finished up lunch and I'm handing at home

Chloé: Hanging*

Amara: Can I come over? Got nothing going on

Chloé: That sounds awesome!

Chloé: I'll meet you at the entrance :)

Sighing in relief, Amara redoubled her pace and turned towards the housing south of the quad. Chloé was the only one of her friends that lived in a dorm, which meant the walk was enjoyably brief. She did her best to enjoy the feel of the sun on her face, but its rays kept getting swept away by the cool autumn breeze. As happy as she was to be immune to the changing weather, she was still vaguely aware that it was getting colder.

As she approached the building, she saw her friend leaning against the wall in the main lobby. She moved closer, opened the door, and the two hiked back up to the third floor.

It felt like ages since Amara had been at Chloé's place. She hadn't been here since she'd accidentally snapped at Chloé back during Nick's week away from school. Guilt weighed her down as she walked up the steps, both from the memory of her harsh tone but also as she realized just how long it had been since they'd last hung out. She loved spending time with Chloé, but in the chaos of her demonic transformation, it had been growing harder to find time to visit. Thankfully, the trepidation creeping at the edge of her thoughts vanished as soon as she stepped inside Chloé's room. Everything looked unchanged, as if nothing had happened over the last few weeks.

Chloé jumped on her bed and picked up her controller, happily crossing her legs as she unpaused her game. Amara quickly ran to the other side of the room—she'd learned recently that walking in front of a TV was a gaming faux-paus—and sat down next to Chloé. Before she could settle in, she needed to rearrange a few plushies, and mentally said hello to everyone as she moved them around. She ended up using a large shark named Finnster as a pillow while resting her feet in Chloé's lap.

"So, what's on the agenda for today?" Amara asked.

"Not much, to be honest. I've got a few things I'm waiting on for the charity, and I can't really do much until those finish up. Until then, the day is mine! I was probably just gonna play games, eat dinner at some point, nothing much." Chloé leaned back, resting against the wall as she talked.

Amara pulled out her phone, half-heartedly scrolling through various sites as she kept talking. "Hey, whatever happened with that guy you were into? Did you ever make a move?"

Chloé blushed, stammering for a few seconds before managing to speak. "N-no... nothing yet. We still talk somewhat regularly, but every time I try to say something, I freeze up!"

"Girl, you just gotta go for it! Put yourself out there!"

"We talked at the Halloween party! I almost asked him to dance, but I froze up and couldn't think of what to say. Plus, later I saw him dancing with some other girl, and she was super pretty..."

"So? I danced with a bunch of people, even kissed some, but I'm not dating any of them. There's a big difference between letting loose at a party and actually looking for a partner." Amara playfully jabbed Chloé with her foot, "And how many times do I have to tell you how cute you are? You can't keep comparing yourself to other girls like this!"

"Well, yeah, but... It's not..." Chloé buried her nose in her sweater, blushing profusely as she failed to think of anything to say. Amara was used to these kinds of pep talks, and she knew from experience that trying to push further wouldn't do any good. Instead, she decided to change the conversation and ask about the game she was playing.

Chloé's mood immediately shifted. She loved video games, and loved talking about them almost as much. The change in her demeanor was so drastic it was almost comical, and she now spoke with unparalleled confidence as she explained the various intricacies of her game. Amara couldn't help but smile at the enthusiasm. When they'd first met, Chloé had been terrified of oversharing and dominating the conversation, but months of encouragement had gotten her to open up. Now, Chloé had fully internalized that Amara genuinely loved listening.

In Amara's opinion, everyone had a spark inside of them. A passion that burned brighter than the sun under the right conditions. Sometimes it was food, sometimes music, movies, or games; everyone had something that truly made them come alive. Finding that spark, and encouraging people to share it, was consistently her favorite thing about photography. When she was on her game, she knew how to ask the right questions, pick the perfect angle, and time her shots to capture that joy before immortalizing it in a picture. In many ways, it was Amara's own game, an intricate puzzle that gave her the chance to see people at their best.

Today, Chloé was playing a game about farming. She'd inherited a dilapidated farm from her grandpa, and needed to restore it to working order while slowly integrating with the seaside town nearby. Amara had first thought it was an older game, as its heavily pixelated graphics seemed out of date, but Chloé assured her it was purely an aesthetic choice.

After an hour or so of relaxing, while Chloé was in the middle of harvesting a batch of blueberries, her phone went off. She paused the game with unusual urgency, grabbed her phone, then gasped in excitement.

"Amara!"

"Everything okay?"

"It got delivered! Quick, we have to go see it!"

"That... doesn't exactly answer my question." Amara pulled her feet out of the way as Chloé jumped off the bed, sliding on her shoes before throwing on her deep blue peacoat. Amara followed suit, and soon the two of them were rushing down the hallway.

After a quick jog down the stairs, they left the building. Amara had expected this to be the end of the journey, but she didn't see any sort of package or delivery. Instead, Chloé kept walking. She stared at her phone, frantically texting, and Amara had to steer her away from other students a few times as their mysterious journey continued. It took another ten minutes or so for Amara to realize where they were heading, and she did her best to steel her nerves.

The Jade Palace.

"Amara, look! There it is!" Chloé said excitedly.

With their destination now in sight, Amara finally saw what had Chloé so excited. The Palace, a charred and blackened monument to Amara's guilt, was no longer the only feature of note on the lot. Off to the side, sitting in the middle of the overgrown driveway, sat a massive green dumpster. Its deep green finish had countless dents and scratches, revealing the heavily weather-worn metal underneath, and was nearly the size of a small bus. Chloé ran closer, approaching the latch on the short end, and attempted to pull it open. The door was clearly too large for her, and Amara joined in to help. She pulled the door open with ease, barely even registering its size.

"Thanks Amara!" Chloé said, gasping for air. "This thing is huge! It's just what we need!"

"What happens now?"

"We can begin cleanup! It's gonna take a lot of time, and we'll need a lot of help, but I already have that planned out. We can start recruiting volunteers now, designate specific cleaning hours so everything stays supervised, stuff like that. I just need to check in with some of the other members—"

Chloé continued talking, and Amara quickly realized she wasn't a part of this conversation; her friend was likely talking to herself just to keep her thoughts in order. Instead, Amara wandered closer to the burnt remains of the old party house, staring at the destroyed lumber and drywall. She knew she would be at the cleanup, taking pictures of the volunteer efforts, but it didn't feel like enough. She closed her eyes, a deep breath filling her lungs, and flinched as the embers from that night brushed across her face again. She heard the house groaning and snapping, threatening to collapse on top of her. Her claws squeezed tight, Vee's blood running down her—

No. That's not who I am.

She shook her head, pushing the memories away as she wiped a tear from her face. Another deep breath, this one sending tremors through her body, and she turned to face Chloé. "Why can't we start now?"

"What?" Chloé asked, her thought process interrupted by Amara's question.

"The cleanup. We're here, why can't we start now?"

"Oh! Well, we don't have any of the materials. Obviously we'll need protective gear; safety glasses, gloves, hardhats, all that, but we're also not dressed for it. Look at your clothes, you'd ruin them!" Chloé paused, examining the remains of the Palace before continuing. "Plus, even if we had all that, I doubt I'm going to be much help. I lost a lot of muscle after I started hormones."

"Right, silly question. I guess I'm just... I want to help." Amara stepped closer to her friend, then pulled her in for a hug. "You're a good person Chloé. Thanks for putting this together."

"You're already doing so much!" Chloé eagerly returned the hug, then stepped back. "Want to help put together a schedule?"

Amara laughed, then politely declined. She was about to turn her attention back to the ruins of the Palace when she noticed a car pulling up beside the lot. The bulky SUV had heavily tinted windows, and after it crawled to a stop, the back door clicked open. A tall, imposing figure stepped out of the vehicle, a simple black suit perfectly tailored to his broad shoulders. Everything about him seemed unnaturally sharp and angular; his chin, his jaw, even the eyes underneath his thick sunglasses. He sneered in disgust as he looked around the ashen lot, quickly turning to mutter something to the driver.

The instant he removed his glasses, Amara recognized him. Although she'd only ever seen pictures of him, those pictures had managed to perfectly capture the sheer contempt this man held for the world around him.

This was Sebastian Wellington, the head of the school's Board of Directors.

"You there!" Mr. Wellington called out, cautiously skirting around the debris as he walked towards Amara and Chloé. Once he was close enough, he gestured to the large dumpster sitting behind the Palace. "What's the meaning of this? I didn't sign off on any relief efforts here."

Chloé shuffled closer to Amara, burying her gaze in the dirt. "U-um, well, this lot isn't on school property, Sir..."

Mr. Wellington scoffed. "Tch. It hosts a school fraternity, and I can state with absolute certainty they haven't approached me about funding this. Are you in charge of this travesty?" His attention broke away from Chloé the instant she nodded, and he began typing on his phone as he continued to survey the plot.

With Mr. Wellington ignoring them for the moment, Amara leaned over to Chloé. "He can't shut this down, can he?"

"I-I mean, technically no, but..." Chloé muttered, digging her heel into the dirt.

Amara knew exactly what Chloé meant. Mr. Wellington had a reputation around campus for being extremely stingy with school resources. Quite a few smaller organizations had been shut down under his direct orders, and despite ostensibly being one person of many on the School Board, they caved to his desires suspiciously frequently.

When Amara looked back, she saw that he'd already started a conversation with someone else over the phone.

"I don't care why no one told me, I just want— No, that's not good enough. What do you mean, all the permits have been correctly filed? Wait, back up, you mentioned fundraising." He looked back to Chloé as he angled the phone away from his face. "Is this a charity thing?"

Chloé slowly nodded, but before she could say anything, Mr. Wellington resumed his other conversation.

"Well, why didn't anyone tell me?! Fuck, I don't know why I bother with you people. Okay, listen up, because I'm only going to say this once. You're going to email Stevenson, and he's going to review this quarter's budget and put together projections for—"

Amara failed to catch any more of Mr. Wellington's conversation, as he'd turned away to walk back to his car. He angrily tapped the window twice before getting in, then his voice vanished completely as soon as the door closed. Within seconds, the vehicle had veered away from The Jade Palace and disappeared around the corner.

"Stupid School Board..." Chloé muttered, kicking a clump of dirt.

Amara forced a smile and gently rubbed Chloé's shoulder. "Hey, like you said, we're outside school property. Mr. Wellington might be an asshole, but his influence only extends so far. Plus, since this is a charity effort, he'll catch some serious blowback if he tries to shut this down."

"I guess there's not much we can do at this point. Let's just hope he doesn't pick a fight with us."

"Hey, don't you think the rest of the charity would want to see the dumpster? It could be a great thing to post as we prepare for the first cleanup!" Amara said, forcing a smile to try and cheer Chloé up.

"You think so? Okay, yeah! Let's do that!" Chloé said, a hint of energy returning to her voice.

After snapping a picture of the dumpster, Chloé signaled she was ready to leave. Heading back towards campus, Amara began asking detailed questions about the charity to keep Chloé distracted from Mr. Wellington's ominous appearance. They went over their finances, optimal social media strategies, and tried to brainstorm other ways they might drum up interest. Before leaving the lot completely, Amara turned to look back at the destroyed house, her thoughts lingering on the impending cleanup.

Chloé's charity efforts lingered in Amara's thoughts for the rest of the day. Even after meeting up with Nick and heading back to her place, she found herself distracted. Seeing the dumpster, hearing Chloé talk about the fundraising, the reality of it all had finally sunk in. The cleanup wasn't just a glint in Chloé's eye anymore; it was ready to begin and just needed people willing to help. Nick led most of the conversation on the way home, and while he obviously noticed, he didn't say anything.

Amara wasn't completely silent, of course. She updated Nick about the circle under Brandt Hall, discovering Professor Luxnor's involvement, and then sitting in on his class and learning of his affair with Kylie. Nick was just as shocked as Tessa had been. He'd never had Luxnor as a teacher, but had always heard nothing but praise for him.

"What if it's all connected?" Nick asked.

"What do you mean? You think Kylie's a part of this cult too?"

"No, but what if he wants her to be? Or what if he's trying to set her up to be some kind of sacrifice? There's already a huge power imbalance at play here, and he has a great excuse to invite her to secret locations without her asking why."

Amara gagged slightly just thinking about the idea. "Fuck, I hadn't thought about that. Guess it's a good thing Tessa and I are picking up the pace."

"Are you sure there's nothing I can do to help?" Nick asked, concern in his voice. "I know this is way outside my wheelhouse, but it's frustrating knowing what's going on and sitting on the sidelines."

"You're going to stay put and stay safe. We have no idea what these people are trying to do, and you're just a squishy human," Amara said, poking Nick's arm to accentuate her point. "Tessa's got magic, she's the only one that can read the circles, and I recently confirmed that I've got super-healing. We can hold our own."

"Wait, did you get hurt again?"

"I was testing a shapeshifting thing and cut my hand a bit, no big deal. Especially since it healed in seconds. Plus," Amara pulled the shoulder of her shirt down, "Vee stabbed me right here, the blade went completely through, and there's not a hint of it there. That sword was Enochian, too."

Nick paused for a moment before responding, his face twisting in concern. "I... didn't know that. At least it healed, right?"

His surprise reminded Amara that she'd never fully explained the events of the Halloween party. Eager to shut everything out, especially the more painful memories, she'd purposely dodged the question every time Nick had brought it up. Still, it was easy to forget that Nick didn't actually know everything about her. They exchanged awkward glances for a moment, then Amara nodded sheepishly and looked away, spurring Nick to change the subject.

"Well, if I'm gonna be on the sidelines for this, I think I deserve a snack." He grabbed his backpack from behind the couch and opened it up. "Make us some popcorn?"

"Do you actually have any? Or is this a setup for a terrible joke?" Amara watched as her friend pulled out a bag of microwave popcorn, then tossed it to her. "Shit, you were serious, alright then."

The two of them were sitting on the couch, Nick on one end, Amara lying on the other with her feet in his lap. She started to stand up when he grabbed her legs, preventing her from leaving. "Ah ah, no cheating," he said, waggling his finger.

"Do you want popcorn or not? The microwave isn't about to grow legs and walk over here."

"You're not going to use the microwave," he said sternly.

She stared at Nick for a few moments before the meaning of his words hit her. "No. Absolutely not!"

"You can't just ignore who you are, Amara."

"Says who? This stupid hellfire can't hurt anyone if I never use it!"

"And how are you going to do that? Can you honestly say you're never going to get mad again for the rest of your life? What happens if a fight breaks out when you confront this cult?"

"I-I'll figure something out!" Amara stammered.

"I'm sorry, but that's not going to cut it. This fire is a part of you; it fuels your shapeshifting, your ability to sleep and enjoy food. It's going to come out at some point, whether you want it to or not. When that happens, do you want to be scared of it? Or would you rather have the understanding to control it?"

Amara couldn't bring herself to respond, but her thoughts drifted back to last night. In her sleep, without realizing it, she'd manifested her true form. Who's to say the same couldn't happen with her fire?

She sighed, reluctantly meeting Nick's eyes. "...Fine."

He released her legs, letting her swing forward and plant her feet on the floor. She grabbed the bag, tore off the plastic, and held it in her palm.

Alright Amara. An open flame would be too much, right? I need heat without fire, which I know I can do; I did it with Tessa when I was breaking through the Enochian seal.

Closing her eyes, Amara focused on her inner fire. It responded eagerly to her touch, dancing and flickering inside of her. Reaching out, she pulled it into her palm and tried to release a tiny fraction of energy. For a moment, she didn't feel much of anything. She stared at the bag of popcorn, wondering if anything was going to happen, and eventually decided to push a little more. Within seconds, her hand, and then the bag, caught fire.

"Shit!"

She moved her other hand over the popcorn, shifting her focus to putting the fire out. She felt the flames underneath her fingers, the warmth calling to her, and fought to exert her own will over them. Soon enough, the color turned as she regained control, and she extinguished the fire. There was a blackened hole in the middle of the bag, the kernels now visible, and Amara found a single piece of popcorn.

"Um... bon appétit?" Amara said, throwing the popcorn at Nick.

He stared at it blankly before looking back at her. "I think you can do better than that."

"Well, I ruined the bag, so I guess we'll have to try another time. Oh well." She sighed dramatically, glad the experiment was over.

Nick, on the other hand, reached into his backpack and pulled out another bag, throwing it at her. "Sorry, you're not getting off that easy. Try it again."

"What am I supposed to do? I can't feel heat the way you do! By the time I register anything, I've already created flames." Amara grumbled as she opened the bag of popcorn, throwing the wrapper on the floor in frustration. Nick said nothing, his eyes on hers as he waited for another attempt.

Grumbling, she repositioned on the couch. Instead of grabbing the bag of popcorn, she let it sit in her lap while she looked at her hands. With her palms up, she summoned small flames in each of them, trying to focus on what they felt like. The heat was comforting, the small flames skipping across her hands, but she knew it was too strong. Despite her hesitations, she remembered when she first gained control over her fire, how she'd giggled and called it cute, and she tried to focus on that feeling rather than her fear. Concentrating on the flames, she tried to slowly pull energy away from them, urging them to grow smaller. It took more effort than she'd expected, but eventually she managed to snuff out the fire while keeping the connection alive.

Focusing on that feeling, she quickly grabbed the popcorn and placed it on her hand. She stared intently at the bag, remembering that popcorn normally took a couple minutes to cook. A count began in her head, slow and steady, as she continued focusing. The seconds ticked on, each one an eternity as she fought to keep the bag from igniting, but eventually she heard a familiar popping sound.

The bag jumped in Amara's hand, causing her to flinch. Thankfully, she didn't drop the popcorn, and she moved her other hand on top of the bag to keep it steady as more and more kernels popped. Over the next minute or so, the bag continued inflating until the popping sounds grew less frequent, and she severed the connection entirely.

"Well?" Nick asked.

Amara waited a few seconds, then nervously pulled the bag open. To her delight, a fragrant, buttery smell washed over her. "I think it worked! Want some hellfire popcorn?"

The two of them took turns testing the food, and although they found a small handful of blackened popcorn, quite a bit of it was edible.

"Not bad for a second attempt!" Nick said, playfully ruffling Amara's hair. "Ready for the midterm?"

"What, there's more?"

"If you recall, Amara, we haven't eaten yet."

"Ugh, what's for dinner? More schemes?" Amara asked playfully, her mouth full of popcorn.

Nick pulled Amara off the couch, bringing her to the kitchen before opening the fridge. He'd apparently gone grocery shopping at some point, and a considerable amount of food now sat at the ready. Picking a relatively simple meal, they got to work.

She started by boiling a pot of water, but this time she didn't hold it in her hands. She kept it on the stove and summoned a small fire underneath it. She focused on this exclusively for a few minutes, testing how far she could move away from the fire while keeping the heat consistent. Just like under the cafeteria with Tessa, it took more effort the further away she was, but she was happy to have any control at all. Once the water boiled, Nick put in some spaghetti and prepped the next step.

He placed a frying pan on the stove, next to the boiling water, and set two pieces of chicken inside. After a deep breath, Amara summoned a second flame under the pan, doing her best not to lose concentration on the first. This proved much more difficult, and the water boiled over a few times when her focus slipped, but thankfully Nick stood at the ready. He had taken charge of setting timers, flipping the chicken when appropriate, and cleaning up when needed.

Soon enough, the spaghetti was finished, and Amara moved on to the last piece of dinner. While still focusing on the flame under the frying pan, she held a piece of store-bought garlic bread in her hand and started cooking it. This proved to be the most difficult step; previously she'd had two open flames, but now she kept one flame alive while purposely snuffing the other.

At the end of the whole ordeal, the chicken had been slightly overcooked, and Amara had accidentally burnt three of their five pieces of garlic bread, but she was happy with everything they'd put together. She grabbed their drinks, sat down at the counter, and sighed in relief.

"Alright, I'll admit it. This was a really good idea," Amara said, biting into a piece of bread. "Honestly, it was kind of fun too. I've never been much of a chef, but maybe it's something to look into."

"You seem more put together, if you don't mind me saying."

Amara paused, finishing her bite slowly before responding. "It... comes and goes. It still hurts, and I desperately wish Vee would respond, but at least I feel like I have a way forward now. You really have the patience of a saint, you know that?"

"What can I say? I hate seeing you down in the dumps."

"Oh! Want to see something cool?" Amara manifested her tail, then moved the tip next to her plate. Focusing on her tail, she manifested the familiar, chitinous exoskeleton. She altered the edge, and soon had a razor-sharp knife once more. "This is what I was telling you about earlier, with my shapeshifting!"

Nick watched in surprise as Amara started cutting up her chicken with her knife-tail. "Dang, that's pretty sharp. Are you sure it's clean? Where does this stuff even come from?"

Amara kept eating as she examined her tail. "Ooh that's a good question. Is it a part of me? Am I summoning it from elsewhere?"

The two friends continued eating their dinner as they discussed theories about Amara's shapeshifting. Nick was curious how Amara's exoskeleton might compare to an insect's, but she adamantly refused to break pieces of herself off for study. They eventually decided that, since magic was clearly involved, they were unlikely to get any real answers anytime soon.

Cleaning up the kitchen was a relatively quick affair, as Nick had been keeping things tidy while she'd been focusing on cooking. After they finished, he moved back to the couch and sighed in content while he sank into the cushions. Amara, on the other hand, wasn't interested in relaxing quite yet.

"Alright, time for second dinner!" She said, tying her hair back.

"What? You can't possibly still be hungry."

She smirked, then fell to her knees in front of Nick. "Little slow on the uptake, are we?" They locked eyes, Nick's aura starting to swell as understanding hit him.

"So, what will it be today?" Amara continued, "Tits out or in? Slow and sensual or hard and fast? Horns? Tail?"

"We just ate, so I think something slower will be nice." Nick began undoing his pants as they talked, and Amara eagerly began helping. Soon enough, he was leaning back with his legs spread to give her space.

Moving in, Amara ran her hands up his legs as she watched his cock start to twitch. Kissing his thighs, she took plenty of time to tease him as she drew closer. After each kiss, she playfully licked his leg, finally stopping only inches from his throbbing member. Her hands continued to massage his legs while her tail, no longer a bladed weapon, moved in and wrapped around his shaft. She held it high, slowly stroking it while she leaned in and began teasing his balls, her tongue moving in circles as she pulled them into her mouth.

She moaned, remembering how much Nick liked her vocalizations, then pushed her hands higher. She massaged his chest next, enjoying the feeling of his muscled body as he tensed in pleasure. Her tail loosened its grip, sliding up until it held only the tip of his cock. Amara moved with it, her tongue reaching for the base of his shaft as she slowly kissed it. She turned her head sideways, lips eagerly sucking his length, as she began moving up and down Nick's cock.

The feel of her lips seemed to be the turning point for Nick, and his aura was finally strong enough for her to begin feeding. Strength and vitality filled her senses, restoring her energy that had been spent cooking dinner. Last time they'd fucked she'd simply fed out of necessity, and she hadn't bothered taking more than she needed. Now, although her confidence was still shaken, she felt comfortable enough with her abilities to try and top off her reserves once more.

Deciding that Nick had been teased long enough, she pulled her tail off his cock completely and replaced it with her lips. She kissed the tip, a long, drawn-out affair that pushed Nick to squirm in anticipation. Her tongue teased his cock-head, slowly pushing in and out of her mouth as she continued sucking. When she pushed her head down, pulling his cock further inside, his moans filled the apartment as he tried to thrust deeper still. She wouldn't let him, and moved with his hips to keep his cock only halfway in her mouth. He tried again, eager for more, her throat more than capable of taking his length, and yet she continued to refuse.

When her tail wrapped around his neck and playfully slapped his cheek, he finally got the hint and stopped trying. He settled for running his hands through Amara's hair, softly playing with it as she happily bobbed up and down on roughly half of his length.

It only took a few more minutes for her to decide that he'd waited long enough. With a deep breath, she pushed down again and felt his cock push against her throat. She gagged loudly, not out of reflex, but because she knew he loved it. Her tongue massaged his shaft as she stayed at that depth, his cock continually testing the entrance to her throat. She gagged playfully, over and over, before meeting Nick's eyes with her own. Even were she not reading his aura, it was obvious how much he was enjoying himself.

Amara pulled back one last time, teasing the tip of Nick's cock before pushing down and opening up her throat. Her lips planted on his crotch as she successfully took the entire shaft, her tongue reaching for his balls and eagerly massaging them.

She began moving up and down his length, from tip to base, in purposely slow strokes to drive Nick crazy. His aura grew stronger with each pass, each push into Amara's throat, and she felt her inner fire roaring with renewed vigor. As she picked up the pace, knowing he likely didn't have much time left, his hands tightened in her hair. She let him guide her, surrendering her control to make sure he had the strongest orgasm possible. It only took another few seconds before Nick pulled her completely down, his cock twitching before unloading into her.

Nick unexpectedly pulled her back, his first load shooting into her mouth before her lips left him completely. He continued cumming, covering her face while she focused on drawing energy from his aura, now at its most potent. She playfully pushed her tongue out, the cum in her mouth dripping down onto her chin while his cock shot its last spurt on her cheek.

Soon enough, Nick's breathing began to calm down. She stayed connected to his aura as long as possible, the energy of his climax filling every fiber of her being with infectious giddiness. Her senses expanded, her body twitched with anticipation, and she felt lighter than ever. Unfortunately, the moment passed quickly as Nick reached the end of his orgasm.

"Fucking... wow," Nick panted, "That was amazing, Amara."

"You're the one doing me a favor, remember? Your orgasm is a lucky coincidence, that's all." Amara smirked, her sarcasm eliciting a chuckle from her best friend. When his laughter broke, he looked down at Amara just in time to see her pushing his cum into her mouth.

"Do you actually get anything from that?"

"Eating cum? I do, actually. It's not as potent as feeding directly from the source, but it absolutely has traces of your aura." She swallowed the last of it, then licked her lips clean and stood up again. "Plus, I hear guys love it. You're a bunch of perverts."

Amara hopped back on the couch, grabbing her phone as she curled her tail around her legs. Nick, having finally caught his breath, took the time to get dressed while she checked her various socials. In particular, she was looking into Chloé's charity and the numbers it was getting. They were in a good spot at the moment, but the campaign was still in its early stages. The true test would be keeping momentum after the initial excitement, something Amara considered herself responsible for.

By the time Nick was fully dressed, she'd already made a few notes for herself regarding posting ideas. He joined her on the couch, pulling her in for a hug as he pulled out his own phone. "So, what's the plan for the rest of the night?"

"Eh, it's already pretty late. Throw on some TV?"

Nick nodded in agreement, searching through their various streaming apps before settling on an old sci-fi show. Amara wasn't as interested, but it was nice to have something on in the background that she didn't feel obligated to pay attention to. The rest of the night passed uneventfully, the two friends happy to have a quiet evening, and soon enough Nick left to return home.

Amara took a long shower to ground herself, hoping her various soaps and lotions would keep her from lingering on unpleasant thoughts. She was pretty sure no water would ever be hot enough for her, but it was still nice to feel pampered.

Now alone in her bedroom, she set up her white noise app, double checked that her demonic features were absent, and fell asleep the instant she hit the pillow.

Amara reached over, resting a hand on her date's leg. She gripped it tight, savoring the feel of her soft skin under her fingers. She massaged her thigh slowly, watching as her girlfriend opened her legs ever so slightly, her bright red thong visible each time they passed a light. Her hand moved higher, squeezing and massaging the delicate skin, before they brushed against the silky fabric of her date's panties. She gasped, the touch exciting her, before suddenly slapping Amara's hand away, though not without a playful smirk.

"Alright, hands to yourself mister! Just a few more minutes and you can bend me over anything you'd like."

Amara sighed, knowing they'd be home soon. She grabbed her drink, a half empty can of beer in the cupholder, and slammed the rest of it. She couldn't taste it much anymore, the mixed drinks from earlier made sure of that, but it kept her primed and eager for the coming romp. She threw the can behind her, hearing it rattle as it landed amongst the others.

The road suddenly started shaking, and she assumed she must have hit a rumble strip. Without warning, however, her girlfriend screamed and grabbed the handle above her. Amara looked back at the road, but it was nowhere to be seen. A sea of grass and gravel stretched in front of her and she tried to slam the breaks, but an unexpected ditch disoriented her for a moment. The car slammed into the edge of a protective barrier, and that's when the rattling stopped. It flew into the air, just for a second, as Amara realized they were headed directly into a river.

The front of the car slammed into the water, throwing Amara forward as the airbag erupted in front of her. The force of the impact threatened to knock her out, but after a few seconds she regained her senses and looked around.

Water pooled in the bottom of the car, its icy grip already creeping into her feet. In a panic, she undid her seat belt, pushed open the door and scrambled out of the driver's seat. She fell into the water, no idea how deep it was, and desperately swam back to shore. Her clothes were soaked, and it took everything she had to keep breathing, but she collapsed with relief once she made it to land.

After giving herself a few seconds to catch her breath, she began looking around. Where was her girlfriend? Had she made it out? She shot back to her feet just in time to see the rear bumper of the car disappear beneath the river.

"Steph?! Steph!!" Amara screamed, her voice unusually deep. She wanted to run, to dive in after the car to try and save her girlfriend, but she couldn't move. Her entire body locked up in fear, she could only think of one thing to do. Her hand reached into her pocket, grabbing her phone, and she prayed it still worked. Against all odds, she was able to turn it on and dial out. After the first few rings, someone finally answered.

"Do you have any idea what time it is?" The voice on the other line snarled, its contempt obvious.

"Dad, the car, I—"

"What did you do to my Bentley?"

"Fuck the car! It's Steph, she... I can't..."

The voice paused, sighing in frustration. "Ugh, just tell me what happened, Derek."

Amara shot forward, her covers a tangled mess around her tail. She gasped in panic, and she didn't even register that her wings had torn out more chunks of drywall. The reality of what she'd just seen finally hit her, and everything clicked into place.

"They're not my dreams!"

4

UNDERCOVER

The revelation that Amara's recent nightmares weren't actually hers kept her distracted for the entirety of the next morning. On the one hand, the dreams had been quite troubling, and she was relieved to know that she wasn't repressing any horrible memories or seeing grim portents of a possible future. On the other, it meant dealing with yet another new ability, and the intangibility of this one meant testing it would be difficult.

All her other developments had been delightfully straightforward. She could touch her tail and her wings, and she could manifest fire whenever she wanted. How was she supposed to practice dreamwalking?

Should I even call it dreamwalking? I don't know if I'm physically traveling to Derek's dreams, or if I'm picking up on his thoughts like some kind of dream television. Do I need to be asleep to do this? Maybe I should let Nick sleep at my place and try to jump into his dreams...

Her morning lectures did nothing to distract her. In fact, she even saw a student nodding off in the back row, and she was tempted to amplify her vision to look for hints of his dreams, but decided against it.

Soon enough, the professor let everyone go, and Amara eagerly headed for the athletic campus. She hadn't visited it since the night her wings first appeared, and today she was planning on meeting up with Nick. Even though he didn't wrestle anymore, he frequently joined his friends for exercise and pickup games. It kept him in shape, which Amara certainly appreciated, and it gave him a chance to spend time with his more athletic friend group.

They eventually met up behind the Gymnastics building. The back wall faced away from campus, and held a large field dotted with trees and bushes. Nick had mentioned a few times that this was a great spot to relax, and due to the morning hours, they were the only people present. She found Nick leaning against the bricks of the building, sitting in the grass with his backpack open beside him. Black gym shorts showed off his muscular legs, and a tight green shirt flattered his torso in much the same way.

"Good workout?" Amara asked, setting down her bag and sitting across from Nick.

"It was great! Alex finally talked me into freerunning. He's been trying to teach me some of the basics, and it's pretty tough. I swear I used to be able to keep up with him, but he must have amped up his workout routine or something, that guy's a beast now. What's going on with you?"

"Ugh, you know the answer to that."

"Derek's dreams?" Nick asked.

"Yes! What does it mean? Am I seeing them for a reason?" Amara fell backwards onto the grass, groaning loudly.

"There's always a chance it means nothing. Does he live near you? Maybe you're picking up his dreams because he's down the hall or something."

"But every night? There have got to be other people dreaming around me."

Nick went quiet, then pulled out his phone after a minute of thought. "You said the dreams are the same every time?"

"They're similar, but sometimes I see different parts. And there was the time I floated away from everything, which I don't know was part of his dream or my own powers acting up."

After another few moments of silence, Amara looked over at Nick to see why he wasn't responding. Before she could ask, however, he finally spoke up.

"Isn't it weird that he's having the same dream, night after night? I doubt that's happening for no reason, especially when it's such a realistic nightmare. What if this actually happened?"

Amara sat up, sliding closer to Nick while he continued his online sleuthing. "Shit, that's a good idea! Maybe this is something we can use to our advantage!" She pulled out her own phone, deciding she may as well try to help. It took another few minutes before Nick spoke up again.

"Anything yet?" he asked.

"Nothing," Amara sighed. "Well, I guess technically I'm finding a lot, but it's all mindless fluff pieces about how great he is. He's America's next great entrepreneur, he's valedictorian of his graduating class, blah blah blah. I feel like I'm reading obsessive fanfic that his dad paid people to publish. What about you?"

"Mostly the same, but also a lot of stuff about his dad's rise to wealth. Supposedly he's a modern-day rags to riches story; he amassed a huge fortune practically overnight."

"What did he do? Win the lottery?"

"That's the weird thing, I can't find any answers. I'm seeing a lot of vague references to playing the stock market, but nothing tangible. The only thing I can tell for sure is he didn't inherit it; his parents were relative nobodies." Nick sighed, pinching the bridge of his nose before rubbing his eyes. "Maybe we're coming at this from the wrong angle. What was his girlfriend's name? Stacy?"

"He called her Steph, so probably Stephanie. What are you thinking?"

"Well, I think it's safe to assume that everything we find online is going to be heavily curated. What if we find news that's not about him?" Nick shifted on the ground, leaning back against the brick wall. After another few minutes, Amara groaned and gave up. She hated this type of research, choosing to instead stand up and stretch out her back.

"Got it!" Nick pumped his fist in victory, waiting for Amara to look over before he started reading the article aloud. "'A student was found dead early this morning after officials pulled a car out of a local river. The girl was identified by the local coroner's office as Stephanie Peterson, 18, a senior at Jefferson High. Stephanie had been drinking with friends late last night and attempted to drive home at approximately 2:15 AM. The last person to see Stephanie was her boyfriend, who let her borrow his car to return home. He was unaware that she'd been drinking and reported her missing early this morning.'"

As Nick continued reading, Amara began pacing across the grass. Each word he spoke infuriated her further, and she squeezed her hands into fists as she began breathing heavier. The full scope of Derek's actions were now obvious, and she was having trouble thinking straight.

"He blamed her? He murdered his girlfriend and blamed HER?!"

"Hey, deep breaths Amara, don't—"

"That FUCKING. **ASSHOLE!!**" A chitinous gauntlet suddenly encased Amara's hand, and she lunged at the nearby wall. With a furious scream, she smashed a small hole in the brickwork, dust and mortar scattering across the nearby grass. Her vision blurred, her panicked breathing now more akin to demonic growling. A second later, she locked eyes with Nick and immediately recognized the look on his face.

Fear.

Her vision sharpened again, her panting returning to normal as she shifted the chitin off her fist. She fell to her knees next to Nick, gently grabbing his arm in a panic. "Nick! Please, it's okay, I'm so sorry! I don't know what came over me! Are you okay? I didn't hurt you, did I?"

Nick took a few deep breaths, his shock quickly fading as he held up a hand. "I'm okay, nothing hit me. I just... I don't think I've ever seen that side of you."

Amara leaned in, pulling Nick into a tight hug as she continued whispering apologies in his ear. They stayed there for several moments before Nick finally whispered back.

"That's what happened at the party, isn't it?"

The two separated, Amara nervously wringing her hands. "Y-yeah, but a lot worse. I'm sorry you had to see me like that."

Nick forced a smile. "Well, at least you're angry at someone who deserves it this time, right? I'm not going to take it out on this wall, but I understand how you feel." The two of them looked at the nearby bricks and saw that a noticeable chunk of the wall had been destroyed.

Amara crawled over to the debris, brushing it towards the base of the building to hide the evidence of her outburst. Looking around, she also saw a circle of discolored grass centered on where she'd been standing moments earlier.

"Does the article say anything else?"

"Doesn't look like it, but I think it's pretty obvious what happened. His dad must have bribed the police to pin the blame on Stephanie."

"There's got to be a way we can use this against him, right?"

Nick paused for a moment, then said, "Not with conventional methods."

Their eyes met again, and Amara gasped. "But, with my powers, I might be able to do something! All those books we read about succubi, a bunch of them mentioned that we can control dreams!"

"If he's having nightmares about this every time he goes to sleep, he's got to be torn up about it. If you can push him further—"

"—I might be able to force him to come clean! Nick, you're a genius!" Amara jumped up in excitement and began pacing the grass once more. She'd been eager to do something about Derek ever since he'd attacked her, and this was the perfect opportunity.

"Think you're up for it?" Nick asked, smiling at her excitement.

"Well, I'll need to learn how to control my dreamwalking. Want to sleep over tonight?"

"Nah, tonight won't work." Nick grabbed his backpack, pulling out a small agenda. "What about tomorrow?"

Amara did the same, though her schedule was on her phone. "That should work. I figure we'll hook up right before bed, then I'll try to jump into your dreams. If I can't do it while I'm awake, I'll go to sleep and hope something happens."

"Great! It's been a while since I've crashed at your place. Maybe we'll do some more cooking while we're at it?"

"I love it! Think of what you want, and I'll do my best not to burn it." Amara chuckled, but stopped when an alarm on her phone went off. "Oh! Shit! I've got to get going, office hours are starting."

"Office hours?" Nick asked. "You never care about—"

"See ya!" Amara said, rushing away.

She grabbed her bag and threw it over her shoulder as she ran back to the main campus. Taking a quick detour to her apartment, she overhauled her appearance to prepare for the next stage of her plan. A change of clothes, a long jacket to hide everything, and a quick look in the mirror to assess her shapeshifting abilities. The trek across campus was tense—memories of her last impersonation attempt lurked in the back of her mind—but thankfully the journey passed without incident. She took a deep breath, looked up at Lysander Hall, then opened the door.

Amara sighed in relief as she approached Mr. Luxnor's office. Most classes had already started by now, which meant the halls were devoid of students. Once she confirmed that no one else was taking advantage of office hours, she flicked her phone's selfie camera on for one final inspection.

Deep, emerald green eyes stared back at her behind a curtain of bright red hair. Her makeup was the perfect mix of slutty and sexy, though she added a bit more lipstick just to be safe. With a deep breath, she moved in and knocked on the door.

"Professor?" she asked.

Mr. Luxnor looked up, clearly surprised by her arrival. "Ms. Donoghue? What brings you by at this hour?"

Up close, Amara finally got a good look at the professor. His deep brown hair was naturally wavy, and it was long enough to frame the sides of his face quite elegantly. His eyes, a similar shade of brown, clearly stole a look at her figure as she entered the office, and the smell of arousal began to tickle her senses. Well-manicured stubble accentuated his soft jawline, and as he leaned back in his chair, Amara got a better look at his outfit. A simple black blazer helped define his shoulders, and the blue button-down shirt he wore underneath flattered his figure just as well.

Amara took one last look down the hallway before stepping into the office, leaning against the door as she played with its handle. "Well, I'm just really nervous about class. I'm worried my grades are slipping..."

"Kylie, we went over everything yesterday. At this point, you couldn't fail even if you wanted to." Confusion crossed the teacher's face as they continued talking.

"I'm not sure you understand, Professor." Amara slowly pushed the office door closed, locking it as she turned to face Mr. Luxnor. Her hands moved to her jacket, which she slowly unbuttoned to reveal the outfit underneath. A black push-up bra accentuated her generous cleavage, while also being more than visible itself from underneath the thin white blouse that she'd tied to show off her taut midriff. A red plaid skirt sat high on her hips, accentuating her legs while leaving little to the imagination, and the tiny straps of her cherry red thong crested over the top of the skirt. "I *really* think I need more extra credit."

Mr. Luxnor's aura grew impressively fast, and his desire to toss composure to the wind was obvious. "Well, now that you mention it, I did just finish grading your last test. I must say, I was very disappointed with your results."

Amara smirked, thrilled that her plan was working so well.

Men are so predictable. Still, he's young and cute, no reason I can't enjoy myself while I'm here...

She placed her jacket on the chair across from the professor's desk, followed by her purse. After a quick glance at the man behind her, she bent at the waist to show off her bright red panties. His aura confirmed how distracted he was, and she took a quick second to readjust her purse one final time. With everything ready, she turned towards her target and walked closer.

"Is there anything I can do to make it up? To show you how much this class means to me?"

"Oh, I think you know the answer to that, Ms. Donoghue. Assume the position."

Shit, I was worried about this. That could mean anything! Does he want me bent over? On my knees? On his lap? Ugh, focus Amara! Commit to the roleplay!

"Why, whatever do you mean, Professor?" Amara playfully bit her finger, hoping she could pretend that her ignorance was all part of the game. Thankfully, a devious smirk on Mr. Luxnor's face assuaged her fears.

"My, you've forgotten so much of the curriculum already. Perhaps you just need a strong hand to get you straightened out." The teacher stood up and moved towards her, his hand lacing into her hair before grabbing tight. He pushed down, his firm grip bringing her to her knees in front of him. His hand moved to her cheek, and he pushed his thumb into her mouth, which she dutifully sucked deeper. His other hand moved to his pants, undoing them while he continued playing with her lips.

Soon enough, he managed to grab his shaft and pull it free. An impressively thick cock now pointed at her mouth, and she locked eyes with Mr. Luxnor as he pulled his thumb from her lips.

"Time for your first lesson, Ms. Donoghue. Open wide, tongue out."

Amara did as she was asked, opening her mouth as wide as possible before pushing out her tongue. She made sure to leave a fair amount of spit on it before it left her mouth, letting it drip down her chin and onto her cleavage. The teacher grinned, slowly stroking his length while taking in the sight of this eager college slut on her knees. Stepping closer, he slapped his cock on her tongue several times, then moved his hands back to her hair. Holding tight, he pushed forward.

The tip of his cock slid down her tongue, entering her mouth slowly. Amara reacted by wrapping her lips around his shaft, but was surprised when Mr. Luxnor lightly slapped the side of her face.

"Ah ah ah, we've talked about this. Mouth stays open until I say so."

Amara nodded, doing just as he wanted. With her mouth open once again, he pulled her head closer and moaned as his cock caused her to gag softly. He couldn't push as deep this way, but she had a feeling that wasn't the goal. He began pulling her head up and down, and each time a small gag escaped her lips. His aura indicated that, like Nick, he seemed to love the sounds she made, so she did her best to make them louder.

Over the next few minutes, she made a few attempts to do more for Mr. Luxnor, and each time he reprimanded her. He didn't want her tongue to swirl around his shaft, he didn't want her to move her own head, and he didn't want his cock to go any deeper.

He wanted nothing more than a submissive toy.

It was a strange sensation, as Amara had grown used to being extremely active during sex. Nick loved to see her enthusiasm, and recently she'd begun to enjoy holding him down while they fucked. Tessa loved to be dominated, and always appreciated the extra attention Amara's tail could bring. Even Brandon, as much as she hated him, had clearly enjoyed her faux desperation. In this office, however, she was simply an object of desire.

Another few minutes passed before Mr. Luxnor spoke again. "Next lesson, Ms. Donoghue. Close your mouth, and prepare to take this cock as deep as you can."

Amara nodded, finally letting her lips wrap tight around his shaft. She was fairly sure she could take all of his cock; the length definitely wouldn't be an issue, but the girth would certainly be a new sensation. He continued to hold her tight, and once her lips closed, he began guiding her head once more. His first couple thrusts were slow, he seemed to be testing her limits, but she could tell he wanted more. She'd been connected to his aura ever since getting on her knees, so she was intimately aware of everything he was feeling. She kept her eyes locked on his, and couldn't help but notice that he seemed more interested in watching his cock pump in and out of her lips.

With another thrust, he tried to reach deeper into her throat. She gagged reflexively, still adjusting to his size, but by the time he'd thrust again she was ready for him. The tip of his cock pushed into her throat, just for a second, and he involuntarily let out a quiet moan.

"That's a good girl, just like that..." Mr. Luxnor whispered.

He continued thrusting into her mouth, slowly and deliberately, as he kept pushing her limits. Each time his cock entered her throat, his aura pulsed with excitement, giving Amara a mouthful in more ways than one. It only took a few more minutes before he had what he wanted: a slutty schoolgirl's lips pressed against the base of his cock. He stayed there, rocking her head back and forth as he savored the feeling of her tight throat. When he pulled out, Amara made sure plenty of spit was visible.

"Fuckin' hell, you're getting better at this!"

"Do I have enough extra credit to pass the class yet?" Amara asked, pitching up her voice to sound playfully innocent.

"Oh, not even close. Open up."

Amara nodded, and soon Mr. Luxnor was slowly fucking her face again. He moved her back and forth, meeting her head with his own thrusts, as his cock repeatedly bottomed out. She made sure to keep the throatfucking as wet as possible, both for her own sake and to coat her tits in spit to enhance the view. It only took a few more minutes for his movements to grow faster, more erratic, as he reveled in the feeling of her throat. She was unfamiliar with how much control he had over himself, but his aura seemed to indicate he was close to cumming. The facefucking grew relentless, his cock hammering into her throat as his grip tightened, but he stopped without warning just before his orgasm overtook him.

She watched his cock leave her mouth, gasping heavily as she took a deep breath. Her tits were soaked, the thin fabric of her shirt completely see-through at this point.

"I'd say we're almost there, Ms. Donoghue. Are you ready for your final?" Mr. Luxnor asked.

"Yes please, Mr. Luxnor. I want to show you what a good girl I can be!" Amara smirked, playfully biting one of her fingers as she waited for a hint of what to do next.

"Panties off, bend over my desk," he said sternly.

Without hesitation, Amara rose to her feet before moving towards the desk. She leaned forward, hooked her thumbs into her panties, and slowly pulled them to the floor while trying to give the teacher the best show she could. Once they were off, she tossed them at Mr. Luxnor, spread her legs, and bent forward over his desk.

She felt him move behind her, and soon his fingers had found her pussy. He slid them over her entrance, causing her legs to tremble, and they stopped moving once they found her clit. He rubbed slowly, making small circles that drove her crazy, and she found herself moaning out in pleasure.

Without warning, she felt Mr. Luxnor lean forward, his weight pushing her harder against the desk, and his free hand pushed her panties into her mouth. "You'd better stay quiet if you want that A, Ms. Donoghue."

Amara couldn't respond, not with her mouth full and her clit being played with. She instead gave a barely audible whimper of approval, which the professor seemed to appreciate.

"Now, last time, I seem to recall you got quite a lot of attention. I think we can skip that today, hm?" Mr. Luxnor stood up straight again, his hand pushing against her back to keep her in position. He tapped the inside of her ankle with his foot, and she quickly pushed her legs further apart to accommodate him. Now completely exposed, the teacher pushed his cock against her pussy, which was already incredibly wet. The tip teased her entrance, repeatedly taunting her, until finally he gave in.

She immediately noticed how different his cock felt from Nick's. Her best friend wasn't likely to be starring in any pornos soon, but he still had a respectable size that had delivered dozens of orgasms over the last few months. The cock now entering her, which she briefly remembered was only the second she'd ever taken, was much thicker. Amara had never been a size queen—all of her toys were quite conservative—but as her pussy stretched open she began to see the appeal. Each inch that pushed inside opened her up further, and it took every ounce of restraint she had to hold back her moans of ecstasy.

"Fuck, every time we do this, I forget how tight you are. You're a good little slut, aren't you Ms. Donoghue?" Mr. Luxnor muttered. When he finally bottomed out inside of her, his weight pushing her into the desk, there was another surge in his aura. The hand holding her down moved, and the teacher grabbed her hips tight. He pulled back slowly, his cock threatening to leave her entirely, then he slammed back inside her again. Her body trembled, and her legs shook from the overwhelming pleasure. She bit down on the panties in her mouth, doing everything she could to avoid making noise, knowing that both of their plans would be ruined if they got caught now. With another powerful thrust, he began fucking her in earnest, his iron grip on her hips refusing to let her move.

Amara was still eagerly feeding off his aura, the taste of his pleasure mixing with her own body's sensations to heighten the entire experience. For the first time since Halloween, she decided to push her own limits, to see how much energy she could take in. After everything she'd talked about with Nick last night, wondering if Kylie might get pulled into this cult business, and the recent revelation about Derek, her resolve had hardened. She knew she'd need the energy to really make a difference.

Her train of thought derailed, however, as her first orgasm caught her off guard. Her entire body tensed, and her pussy squeezed Mr. Luxnor's cock tight as he continued pounding her. She couldn't stop herself from moaning quietly as she shook with pleasure, the teacher's sexual energy racing through her body. She grabbed the sides of the desk, doing everything she could to avoid making noise, but she kept moaning as she came. Her eyes rolled back in her head, her back arched, and her hips bucked wildly against the professor's iron grip.

She was practically vibrating with pleasure, and Mr. Luxnor continued to hold her tight as he fucked her through her orgasm. It was impressive, his own pace continued increasing, yet he took great care to not make any noise. Every time his cock hammered into her, she expected to hear the sounds of his body meeting hers, but it never happened. Her ass shook hard with each thrust, despite his impressive self-control, and her pussy had long ago started dripping down her legs.

Mr. Luxnor's grip changed, his nails now digging into her hips. The sensation caught her off guard, and when his cock pushed inside her again, her legs finally gave out. She was now supported completely by his desk, her body still nothing more than a toy for him to get off with. He leaned forward, one hand grabbing her hair as the weight of his body pushed her harder against the desk. He pulled her head back, the slight pain joining with his harsh grip on her hips, and she felt something shift. Until now, he'd been enjoying himself, but it was obvious he'd been taking his time. Now, with her body completely under his control, he was determined to cum.

His aura grew more excited, twitching and pulsing as he slowly lost control of himself. His body shook, his breath grew panicked, and he leaned forward to whisper into Amara's ear. "You're my fucking slut, you know that? I'm going to cum deep in your fucking pussy, and there's nothing you can do about it."

Amara moaned in agreement, eager to pull everything she could from the teacher. She wanted his cum, and she wanted to continue feeding so she could keep pushing her limits. Another orgasm stirred inside of her, spurred on by the feeling of being pinned against a desk. When it finally arrived, her entire body twitched once more, and her pussy clamped tight around Mr. Luxnor's cock. He kept thrusting faster and faster, no doubt spurred on by her orgasm, and soon enough he got what he wanted.

His thick cock began to twitch, filling Amara with cum as he buried his entire shaft inside of her. His aura, which had already been impressively strong, swelled to even greater heights as she kept pulling energy from it. She had a good sense of her usual limits, and had previously tried to keep herself in check, but this time she ignored all of them. She pulled as much energy as she could from the teacher, and a familiar feeling began to creep into her body. Her senses started to expand, a connection forming with the world around her as her own orgasm continued running circuits through her body.

Soon enough, Mr. Luxnor's orgasm ended, leaving her to lament how short male orgasms were. Her own ended soon after, and she became aware of how heavily the teacher was panting behind her. He released his grip on her hair, pulled his cock out of her, and took a step back. He sighed heavily before moving to rummage through a drawer, but Amara was much more focused on herself.

There was something different about the office, but she couldn't figure out what. It was like the colors had been adjusted, while the air itself shook and vibrated, almost as if a heat wave had set upon the office. Previously, when she'd felt her senses expand like this, they'd reverted shortly after she stopped feeding, but that hadn't happened this time. She was about to look back at the professor, to see what he was doing, when she caught her eyes in the middle of flaring. She closed them tight, urging them to dim, and sighed in relief when they did as she asked.

"Here, you'll need this, Kylie," Professor Luxnor said. Amara saw a small hand towel land on the desk next to her, and she jumped at the chance to clean herself up. As she pushed off the desk, the teacher continued talking. "So, what was this about? We normally only meet once a week."

Smiling, Amara tried to put on her best impersonation of her classmate. "Oh, I was just in the mood, and I thought you'd enjoy it. Don't go thinking this is a new weekly meetup!"

"That's probably for the best. I don't think anyone's noticed, but we can never be too safe." The teacher checked the clock as he started dressing himself, "And speaking of safe, you might want to get going. The hallways are going to be pretty crowded in another ten minutes or so."

It barely took any time for Amara to get dressed again, a happy side effect of wearing so little to begin with. She threw her jacket over her schoolgirl costume, her purse over that, then moved to the door. "Thanks for the lesson, professor!"

She watched Mr. Luxnor fall back into his chair, smirking at her, then took her leave. Moving quickly, she decided it would be best to get back home as soon as she could. As she headed for the exit, however, she felt her eyes flare up again. The feeling from back in the office returned, and she had to grab a nearby railing to steady herself as the strange sensations returned.

Once more, the colors around her seemed to shift slightly, like someone was messing with the saturation filter. The air above her shimmered unnaturally, the strange vibrations moving incredibly fast. Strange patterns formed in the walls, racing from side to side faster than she could follow, and ambient chatter from nearby classrooms suddenly sounded as loud as a landing plane. Nervous about being seen, and not entirely sure what she looked like, she pulled out her phone again to check her appearance.

She was still Kylie, and while her makeup had definitely seen better days, she was much more worried about her eyes. Her bright green irises were practically on fire, thrumming with energy as they tried to show Amara parts of the world she couldn't yet understand. After grabbing a tissue from her bag, and using it to clean herself up, she tucked it back in her purse. Her hand brushed against the camera inside, and she realized it was still recording, so she quickly turned it off before leaving the building.

Outside, soft glowing sunlight illuminated the campus through a thin blanket of clouds. She headed straight for her apartment, eager to change out of her costume, when she noticed another strange shimmer in the air in front of her. It seemed to connect with the phone in her hand, and before she had time to guess what was happening, her phone vibrated. She'd just gotten a text from Nick.

She barely even registered what he'd said, something about asking if her grades were slipping, and she was much more interested in testing her theory. She typed up a quick response, made sure her eyes were still engaged, and clicked send. Sure enough, as soon as the message departed, another strange vibration traveled through the air, this time originating from her phone.

The rest of the day passed painfully slowly. Her amplified senses, which she assumed were somehow showing her electrical signals, faded roughly an hour after she left Mr. Luxnor's office. While disappointed, the excess energy from her illicit affair made it impossible to relax. She felt as if she were crawling from class to class, and it seemed like the clocks had all joined a conspiracy to move at half their usual speed.

When she joined her friends for dinner, it barely took them five minutes to realize that she couldn't sit still. Her legs were bouncing, she kept drumming her fingers on the table, and she'd long ago exhausted all the new updates on her socials. Tessa offered to help her burn off the extra energy, but Amara had assured her that would only make the problem worse.

Thankfully, after what seemed like an eternity, she made it to the end of the day. Her true form manifested the instant she closed the front door, and she began looking around the apartment for something to keep herself busy.

Ultimately, she decided the entire apartment needed to be cleaned. While the kitchen was up to par, thanks mostly to Nick, the rest of the apartment was in sorry shape. After her wings had first appeared, but before she'd figured out how to hide them, she'd accidentally damaged nearly every wall and ceiling in the apartment. She also felt more comfortable summoning and controlling her hellfire—something she was quite proud of—but her inability to properly detect heat still caused problems. Among other, more localized spots of heat damage, she'd taken to playing with her hellfire while watching TV. This had led to her partially melting her remote, as she'd forgotten to extinguish her hands before attempting to switch shows.

Over the next few hours, Amara did her best to restore her apartment to a halfway respectable state. She vacuumed every room at least twice, reorganized all her clothes, and even took time to wash all the walls. Without the proper materials, she couldn't fill in the gouges from her wings or restore the heat damage, but she felt better knowing she'd done everything she could. Unfortunately, her energy had barely waned over the course of her impromptu cleaning session.

Her next attempt to burn off her energy was much more literal. The fridge was still full of Nick's groceries, and she decided to cook an elaborate dinner. She used her tail to cut up the ingredients, which let her practice both her shapeshifting and her tail's dexterity, and she used her hellfire to cook everything. The finished product certainly wasn't high cuisine, and she knew she could stand to learn more about cooking, but she enjoyed it nonetheless.

After dinner, while she attempted to find something to watch for the evening, she opened a package of cookie dough for her next experiment. She pulled off pieces of the dough and balanced them on her tail, doing her best to try and make cookies. She saw about as much success as when she'd made garlic bread, and barely a third of the cookies were anything close to edible. However, it was impossible to deny that her control was improving, and the more cookies she made, the fewer she burned. Before long, she'd finished the entire packet of cookie dough and finally decided it was time for her next experiment.

As she brushed her teeth and got ready for bed, her mind raced with ideas. She was hoping to enter Derek's dream again, and she wished she had a better way of making it happen. She thought of what she might be able to do if she gained control, and what might push Derek to finally confess his misdeeds.

Sadly, the excitement that had permeated her body all day now refused to let her fall asleep. She tossed and turned, her body unable to get comfortable as she tried, and failed, to wrestle her excited mind into submission.

She continued like this for the better part of an hour, alternating between counting the cracks in her ceiling and imagining nightmares she might be able to inflict on Derek. She tried her best to avoid checking the time, to focus on the ambient rain noises that normally helped her sleep, but nothing worked. Her thoughts unexpectedly returned to Chloé's charity, which gave her an idea for all this energy.

After rummaging through her freshly organized closet, grabbing old clothes she didn't mind ruining, she reverted to her human form and left her apartment. The campus was cloaked in soft moonlight, and the night breeze felt wonderful as it danced through her hair. The sky seemed heavy tonight, and the humidity hinted at rain in the near future, but a bit of harsh weather didn't affect her plans. She caught herself staring up at the sky, watching the clouds as they periodically covered up the moon, but she knew it wouldn't be safe to fly up to meet them.

Instead, she crossed campus to a building that was growing increasingly familiar to her. The smell of ashes and burnt lumber filled her senses, and she stared at the empty lot of The Jade Palace, now with an empty dumpster just waiting to start making things right.

She looked around, thankful that the property was somewhat isolated, and opened the large metal door to the dumpster. It was still empty, as Chloé was planning to start the cleanup effort this weekend, but Amara had been itching to come back here ever since she'd last hung out with Chloé. She tore the caution tape, freeing up a path to the burnt remains of the party house, and cracked her knuckles as she moved closer.

While Chloé and the rest of the volunteers needed protective gear to keep themselves safe, Amara had no such disadvantage. She manifested her chitinous exoskeleton, watching as it covered her hands, and decided to do the same with her legs as well. Even if she sustained any cuts, she was sure she'd be able to bounce back quickly.

With the logistics taken care of, she dove into the wreckage and went to work. She immediately noticed how light everything felt; even larger pieces of lumber felt as light as cheap plastic in her hands. She tossed piece after piece into the dumpster, learning quickly that her muscle memory needed to adapt to her new level of strength. As she worked, she tried to envision a group of regular volunteers tackling this cleanup, and immediately recognized how much faster she was able to move on her own. Many of the larger pieces, that she easily handled by herself, would likely require two or three people to move, and the need for caution would grind all relief efforts to a crawl.

In just under an hour, a large chunk of the plot had been cleared of its bulkiest pieces. Amara wiped some sweat from her brow as she looked around, wondering what to tackle next, when her focus landed on the two walls that had managed to stay upright. Moving closer, the rain she'd predicted earlier finally arrived, a moderate shower accompanied by the low rumble of thunder in the distance.

She circled the building until she'd positioned herself out of view of the street. Tossing her shirt aside, she manifested her wings and pulled them close. Connecting with her inner fire, she tried to recreate the same chitinous plating that protected her hands. It took longer than expected, mostly due to the amount of blackened carapace she needed to create. When she finished, she immediately noticed how much heavier her wings were. After making a note to never try this while flying, she stepped up the first wall and prepared to strike. After taking a deep breath and hopping side to side to hype herself up, she lunged at the wall, knocking down its supports with her fists.

She broke through surprisingly easily, quickly wrapping her wings around herself to act as a shield. The already damaged walls collapsed quickly, scorched detritus and debris bouncing off her impromptu demonic fortress, and seconds later everything came to rest.

As Amara unwrapped her wings, she saw a flash of light out of the corner of her eye. She immediately looked skyward, wondering if the storm was picking up, but nearby trees were blocking her view of the heaviest clouds. Thunder continued rumbling above, the rain ebbing and flowing, but it still wasn't enough to deter her.

She repeated her maneuver with the second wall, which took a little more convincing before it was ready to come down. Soon enough, there were no more freestanding structures, and a quick look inside the dumpster revealed it was already half full. It took another hour of labor before she'd moved the rest of the larger pieces into the dumpster, and around the same time she finally felt her boundless excitement start to wane.

She closed the door to the dumpster, locking it tight, when suddenly an idea popped into her head. An idle curiosity that she'd been able to ignore in the past, but now had no reason not to indulge. She squatted down, grabbed the bottom of the dumpster, and tried to lift it off the ground.

Her breathing intensified, and her muscles strained as she attempted to move the massive structure in front of her. She even engaged her inner fire, wondering if it might be able to enhance her strength, but it was hard to tell if anything was changing. In the end, she gave up after a minute or so.

Well, I might not be strong enough to lift cars yet, but this was one hell of a night.

Amara reverted to her human form, grabbed her shirt, and started the trek back to her apartment. Before leaving the lot, she looked back and felt an unexpected sense of pride as she reviewed her progress. She may have been the cause of this disaster, but this felt like proof her abilities could be used for something other than destruction.

The walk home took longer than expected, the activity of the night finally catching up to her as she opened her front door. She collapsed on her bed, completely and utterly exhausted, and fell asleep within seconds.

5
NIGHTMARES

MISSED CALL: Chloé

  MISSED CALL: Chloé

  Chloé: AMARA ARE YOU UP??

  Chloé: SOMETHING CRAZY HAIRBRUSH

  Chloé: AND I NEED YOU TO POST ABOUT IT!!

  Chloé: HAPPENED*

  MISSED CALL: Chloé

  Chloé: Okay I couldn't wait

  Chloé: I need you to look over the post I made

  Chloé: Text me when you wake up!

Somehow, Amara had managed to sleep through Chloé's barrage of notifications. After a split second of panic, she realized nothing was wrong and finally returned her friend's calls.

"Chloé? Hey, I'm up, what's going on?" Amara yawned, still not entirely awake.

"Amara! Okay, so you know Connie? From the charity? Wait, shoot, I don't think you two have met yet. You'd love her, she's great! She's always posting really pretty pictures of herself, I think she might have a fancy camera too?" Chloé said, talking a mile a minute.

"Chloé..."

"Sorry, that's not important. Anyways, so Connie has this friend that lives off campus, right? Connie is over there all the time, and honestly I think they're dating but don't want to say anything yet, 'cuz she seems to spend the night pretty frequently."

"Chloé!"

"Right, sorry. Sorry! So Connie, she spent last night with her friend, and she's walking home this morning, when she sees that a huge chunk of the Palace has been cleaned up! Like, the remaining walls are down, a bunch of the bigger pieces are in the dumpster, it's crazy! I had to call the waste management people to schedule a pickup, and we technically haven't even started yet!"

By the time Chloé had finished talking, Amara had already moved to the kitchen. Her tail held her phone, which left her hands free to start the coffee. "So, did anyone see who did this?" she asked nervously.

"That's the weirdest part! No one saw anything, it must have happened in the dead of night. But, I mean, who would do that? We've already been advertising the scheduled clean-up hours, why would they do this in secret?"

Amara chuckled at the irony of the situation, wishing she could tell Chloé the truth. "Honestly? It might be better that we don't know. If this stays a secret, there's a good chance people will speculate about what really happened, which translates to a bunch of free publicity for your charity!"

"Ooooh, see, this is why I wanted to work with you on this! You understand all the marketing nonsense!" Chloé paused, her initial excitement having faded somewhat. "Are you able to check my post? I'm sure I didn't use the right buzzwords or whatever."

"Don't worry, I'm sure you did fine. I'll talk to you later, okay? I gotta start my day."

The girls said their goodbyes and hung up, leaving Amara alone in her apartment once more. She tackled her morning routine at a leisurely pace, getting dressed, doing her makeup, and eventually setting up her laptop on the kitchen counter. She curled her tail around her coffee mug, took a long sip, and got to work.

Opening her editing software, she plugged in her smaller camera and watched the content slowly transfer. Editing photos was a comfortable, familiar routine, but she hardly ever worked with video content.

Thankfully, she didn't need to do anything complicated with yesterday's video. The important footage was only the fifteen or so minutes in the middle, and cutting out the useless footage on either end was simple. Her biggest concern was that she might have accidentally flashed her demonic abilities; after all, she didn't fully understand what those might look like to an outside observer. To be safe, she watched the video in its entirety.

It was a surreal experience. This was her very first sex tape, yet she wasn't actually in it. She did her best to focus on the important parts, watching her eyes, looking for hints of hellfire, and she was pleasantly surprised when she found nothing. While watching it made her incredibly horny, she knew she couldn't afford to be distracted at the moment. Plus, Nick and Tessa were busy with classes.

After uploading a copy to her phone, she began packing up the rest of the day's classwork. Her thoughts lingered on Mr. Luxnor, on this strange cult he was a part of. What did they want? What was this all leading to?

She tried to think back to all the magic circles she'd been exploring with Tessa. While she didn't understand the technical side of things, she wondered if there had been any other clues she might have missed. Right now, they knew about the one under Lysander Hall, the Cafeteria, the Science Building, and Brandt Hall. Many of them hidden in different ways, none exactly the same.

Unfortunately, her curiosity didn't amount to anything. In the end, she simply didn't understand the magic. Her strengths were more tactile, and she was hoping this lead with Mr. Luxnor would pan out.

Thinking back on all the circles, however, brought up memories of Vee. If Amara hadn't been investigating these circles with Tessa, she might never have left the house while shapeshifted. Would that have changed things? Derek would never have accused Vee of attacking him, but how did she know she didn't scare him off in the process?

Of course, Vee probably could have taken him. At the time, I thought I might have indirectly helped her avoid an attack of her own, but she's an angel! She could probably take him out with both hands tied behind her back! I still have no idea how I didn't lose that fight... am I really stronger than her? Is there more I'm not seeing?

Memories of Halloween began trickling into her thoughts. Flashes of pain, her body changing and warping, the house falling to pieces around them. The hatred in Vee's eyes, the utter contempt for everything Amara was. Those same eyes, bloodied and tearstained, begging for mercy before—

Stay focused Amara. You can't change the past, and you've already done so much to try and help.

She shook her head, grounding herself in the moment as she calmed her panicked breathing. Pulling out her phone, she opened Vee's contact and stared at it for a while, hoping she might manifest a response.

Predictably, nothing appeared.

Amara: I hope you're planning on finishing the semester. I miss you.

She wiped a tear off her cheek, gathered the rest of her things, and left for class.

Amara was thrilled that her energy levels had returned to normal. While the new abilities had been fun to play with, and she was determined to explore them further, she hadn't enjoyed bouncing off the walls all night. If nothing else, she was proud of everything she'd accomplished in the end.

Every so often, she heard students talking about the mystery of The Jade Palace. The event hadn't necessarily gone viral, but there was a healthy amount of buzz that Amara appreciated. She'd simply been trying to burn off energy and atone for her actions, and hadn't even considered that she might be drumming up interest for the charity. With the official cleanup scheduled to start this weekend, she hoped this interest would lead to a decent turnout.

She was in between classes, walking out of Brandt Hall, when Alex happened to run into her. It seemed they were both heading in the same direction, and they struck up a conversation while they walked.

"Oh, did Nick tell you about the other day?" Alex asked, a goofy grin on his face.

"You mean the freerunning? Yeah! He seemed to enjoy it, but he said it was pretty tough. He tends to favor short bursts of activity rather than endurance stuff."

"It's a shame you couldn't make it," Alex said, playfully jostling Amara's shoulder. "I bet you would've had a blast! Say, even if it's not your thing, maybe you could bring your camera stuff? I bet it would be a great place to practice getting some action shots!"

Amara tensed up slightly as Alex touched her. "Uh, yeah, I'll think about it. I'm pretty busy helping out the charity, though, so I won't be free for a while."

"Aww. Well, lucky them, am I right?"

Forcing a smile, Amara was thankful to see that it was finally time for them to part ways. As she started down a side hallway, she politely said, "I'll catch you around, Alex."

He waved goodbye, and Amara was free to return to her classes. While time seemed to slow as Amara watched the clock, soon enough the teacher dismissed them, which meant it was time for the next phase of her plan. She retraced her steps from yesterday, as Amara this time, and soon found herself standing outside Mr. Luxnor's office. It was fortunate that he kept consistent office hours, and even luckier that the building was relatively quiet during them.

Still, she had to wait for a few minutes while the teacher finished helping another student. Amara sat outside while they talked, and she did her best to focus on what was happening inside. Thankfully, it seemed like nothing scandalous, though it struck her as odd that she was able to hear everything so clearly.

Has my hearing improved? I know my eyesight has, even apart from the night vision. Come to think of it, I was able to hear the teachers under Brandt Hall even though Tessa was talking, and she didn't notice anything until I pointed it out...

Her train of thought was derailed when the office door opened, and another student walked out. She had dark skin and incredibly curly black hair, the ends of which she'd dyed a deep shade of burgundy. A loose, flowing green blouse hung off her shoulders, and she briefly waved at Amara as she walked past. Amara didn't recognize her, but she waved back anyways before standing up. Her attention returned to Mr. Luxnor when she heard him close a drawer, and she turned to enter the office.

Showtime, Amara.

The professor looked up with a warm smile as she entered. "Hi there! Are you a student of mine? I must admit, I don't recognize you."

Amara closed the door behind her, refusing to acknowledge the question. As she fell into the chair opposite the teacher, she kicked her feet up on his desk and playfully leaned back. She rocked back and forth on the chair, the front legs no longer touching the ground, as she let her gaze wander through his office. Atop his desk sat a small plaque with the teacher's full name: Professor Garrett Luxnor.

"I'd rather you kept your feet off my desk, if that's alright. Can I help you?" he asked, growing frustrated.

She let a few moments pass as they continued looking at each other, then pulled out her phone. "I want to know about this cult of yours. What's their plan?"

A mix of emotions appeared on Mr. Luxnor's face, surprise the most obvious. "I think you have me confused with someone else, Miss. If you're just here to make baseless accusations, perhaps you'd better leave."

Amara didn't justify his denial with a response. Instead, she turned her phone sideways, increased the volume, and hit play. Her voice, as Kylie, soon filled the office.

"Is there anything I can do to make it up? To show you how much this class means to me?"

Mr. Luxnor's eyes went wide, darting to the phone. His breathing quickened, and he swallowed nervously. Another few seconds passed, and it became more than obvious what he was listening to. "Where... How did you get that?"

"Does it matter?" Amara asked. "I have it, and it's backed up in multiple places. If you want this to stay private, you might want to start talking."

The professor glared at her, but quickly yielded. "Fine. What do you want to know?"

"There's a good boy." Amara smirked, letting the video continue as she talked. "What's the endgame? You're tracking down all these magic circles, and making alterations, but why?"

"I don't suppose you're going to tell me how you learned all this?" he asked. When Amara didn't say anything, he sighed and continued talking. "I don't entirely know. He's been vague about many of his plans. He's given us all tiny bits of magic, and he's promised a lot more if we help him."

"Magic? What can you do?"

"Nothing flashy, mostly improvements to our bodies. I'm faster, stronger, and more alert. Supposedly he's getting us ready for the main event, but again, he won't say what it is."

"And who is he? This mysterious cult leader that you're stupid enough to follow?"

Mr. Luxnor laughed, a touch of ego coming through in his words. "You think I'm stupid? I've seen what he can do, how far he's come. Mr. Wellington has proven time and time again that he's not lying to us."

Mr. Wellington? Seriously?

"So why fuck with the circles?" Amara asked.

"He says they're in his way. They've sealed up the magic, and he can't take what he needs until we weaken them. We've been at it for a while, though, and it's too late to reverse anything. He's going to start delivering on his promises next weekend, in fact."

The sound from the video picked up, and Amara now heard muffled moans from when she'd been bent over the teacher's desk. "When and where?"

"There's a small complex under the quad, one of the original structures from the founding of the campus. The only way to reach it is through the elevator in Lysander Hall; there's a secret button hidden by an illusion. We're meeting at three in the morning, next Sunday."

"How does Kylie fit into this? Human sacrifice? Part of the cult?" she asked, narrowing her eyes.

"I'm not a monster, though I don't expect you to believe me. Kylie has nothing to do with this; she needed help with classwork, and one thing led to another. No one is being forced, we're just two adults enjoying each other's company."

"Easy for you to say, you're the one with all the control. I think it goes without saying that, if something happens to her, this video is front page news the very next day."

"I happen to care for her, and frankly I'm insulted you think I'm capable of hurting her," Mr. Luxnor protested. "Why do you even care about any of this? Who are you?"

Amara pulled her feet off the desk, letting the chair fall back to the floor before she stood up. She leaned forward, placing her phone down to emphasize its contents. "I'm no one you want to get comfortable with. How do I know you're telling the truth about Kylie? About the cult? You could be making up a bunch of nonsense just to placate me."

Mr. Luxnor leaned forward himself, matching her stern glare. "Because it doesn't matter. Somehow, you've stumbled into some magic knowledge, and you're convinced you're going to be the hero who takes down the big bad cult. I've seen students like you before, utterly convinced that you're invincible, that you can change the world with a can-do attitude, but that's not how this works. This is bigger than you, and if you were smart, you'd drop this whole thing."

"You'd like that, wouldn't you?" Amara moved away from the desk, turning off her phone and pocketing it to get ready to leave. "Do yourself a favor, and don't go to this meeting next Sunday. If you do, the video leaks."

Turning to leave, Amara moved the chair out of her way before reaching for the door. As it opened, however, the teacher behind her continued talking. "Threaten me all you want, but I'm not scared of you. I've seen what he's capable of, and when I tell him some punk student is trying to disrupt his plans, I'll be rewarded."

Amara paused, the door partially ajar, her hand grasping the handle tight.

Fuck. I was hoping the blackmail would be enough, but he's really all-in on this stupid cult. What else can I do?

Echoes of Tessa's voice crept into her mind, and as much as she hated to admit it, her friend might have been right all along.

"If I had your powers, I'd only need 5 minutes alone with him and we'd get all the answers we wanted."

"All you have are empty threats. You're here because you care, and if you release that video, it'll harm Kylie just as much as me. I don't think you have it in you."

Deciding it was time to commit to the bit again, Amara closed the door and started laughing. It started quietly, but she slowly let it overtake her body before she locked eyes with the professor again. "Oh, you stupid little human. You don't think I have it in me? The blackmail was my attempt at doing this quietly, to give you a chance to realize your mistake."

She stepped forward, leaning towards his desk as she locked eyes with him. He was still confident in his position, and she needed to fix that. Her eyes flared, and she urged her inner fire to get excited, to turn up the heat a bit more literally.

"You get one tiny drip of magic, and it all goes to your head," she continued, "but do you know where magic comes from? None of it is yours, humans only get magic by stealing it."

Wave after wave of heat poured out of her body, and before her eyes, Mr. Luxnor started sweating. She knew she had to keep pushing, and with a small flurry of embers, she manifested her tail and sharpened its edge.

"Not me, though. My magic? My fire? It's alive. It's a part of me, and it's hungry. Care to guess what I feed it?"

The teacher swallowed nervously, pulling at the collar of his shirt. "W-what—"

In a flash, Amara's tail swung in front of her, and she cut off his words just as her tail embedded itself an inch into his desk.

"Souls, Garrett. Souls like yours."

The teacher flinched at the tail, his gaze finally leaving her eyes as he started to figure out what she was. Another flash of fire, and her horns appeared, followed by a series of flames around Mr. Luxnor.

"Why do you think you're alive? You think it's because of a tiny man with a control fetish?" She pulled her tail free, then moved its blade towards his throat while she stepped closer, circling around his desk. "Perhaps the goodness of my heart? No. You're alive because it's convenient for me. Because killing you would create more problems than it would solve."

The teacher tried to push away from Amara, but he had nowhere else to go. "S-stop! I'll scream!"

Amara grabbed his collar, pulling him close as she hissed in his ear. "I'm only going to say this once. If you make my life difficult, I'll rip your soul out and throw you into the deepest pits of Hell. You'll spend eternity wishing I'd been kind enough to simply kill you."

Pulling away from Mr. Luxnor, Amara shapeshifted back into Kylie. "I can be anyone I want, Garrett." She shifted her appearance a few more times, cycling through other students she'd seen in his class. "If you ever have sex again, how will you know it isn't me? Do you want to live the rest of your life looking over your shoulder?"

Despite his threats, the teacher stayed quiet as true panic began to set in. "Fine! Okay! I'll quit the cult, I won't tell anyone about you!"

Returning her form to her own, Amara finally pulled her bladed tail away from the professor and snuffed the fire that had been floating around the room. "That wasn't so hard, was it?" After one last flurry of embers, she dismissed her tail and her horns, then happily walked back to the door. "See you around, *Professor.*"

Conveniently, the hallway outside the professor's office was still empty, and Amara began walking as quickly as she could to get away. She still felt her faux cruelty sticking to her, and it made her intensely uncomfortable. Her plan had worked, more or less, but seeing Mr. Luxnor so utterly terrified brought back painful memories of Halloween.

That's not who you are. It was a little heavy-handed, but he's leaving the cult! He's safe now!

With a plethora of information, including a date and location, Amara pulled out her phone to schedule a meeting with Nick and Tessa. She needed to put together a plan for Sunday morning, and she would need all the help she could get.

In the meantime, as she continued to try and run from the cruel persona she'd just invented, she knew it was time to start gathering information on Sebastian Wellington. The most powerful man on the school's Board of Directors, a self-made millionaire, and father to Derek Wellington.

She had a hell of a fight ahead of her.

That night, Tessa and Nick came over for dinner to discuss Amara's interrogation. She explained every detail as best she could, though Tessa was incredibly frustrated to learn that Mr. Luxnor didn't know the full scope of the plan. No one was particularly surprised that Derek's dad was behind everything; if anything, it made his meteoric rise to fortune seem a little too convenient.

"Alright, well, obviously I'm not crashing this meeting, and I don't know anything about magic, but I'll start looking into Mr. Wellington. I'm assuming he's put a lot of money into curating his internet presence, but maybe I can find something helpful, even if it's just an itinerary or something," Nick said, already bookmarking sites on his phone.

"Tess, I'll need you to reveal the secret button in the elevator at some point. Probably better if it's not the night of the meeting, just so we don't risk running into other cult members," Amara said.

The witch was being unusually quiet, all things considered. She nodded absentmindedly before finally speaking up. "So, you seriously had sex with Mr. Luxnor? And recorded the whole thing? Any chance I could get a copy of that?"

"No! I'm gonna delete it so it never accidentally leaks! Mr. Luxnor was completely right, I would never do that to Kylie."

"C'mon, at least let me watch it once before it's gone forever! A hot-for-teacher roleplay where the student is secretly a succubus? Nick, back me up here, doesn't that sound hot as fuck?"

Nick was blushing profusely, clearly hesitant to be dragged into this conversation. "I think that it's Amara's video, and she's entitled to do what she wants with it."

"Ugh, you're all such buzzkills." Tessa rolled her eyes before continuing. "I'll find your stupid secret button tomorrow night. Sure you don't want me to come with to the meeting?"

"Absolutely. I'll be in disguise, and you would blow my cover," Amara said.

"So, I'm researching the leader, Tess is studying the circles and getting you into the meeting. What's your plan?" Nick asked.

"Well, right now it's just to gather intel. Maybe we'll get lucky and Mr. Wellington will finally tell everyone what the goal is at this meeting," she said. "I've been trying to prepare for things going wrong, but I honestly can't think of how they might figure me out. I figure the biggest threat is Mr. Wellington; if he's hoarding the cool magic for himself, who's to say he won't be able to detect me?"

Nick turned back to Tessa. "Is there magic that can do that?"

"There is, but a lot of witches don't get it. Our bodies can only hold so many tattoos, so if you commit space to that kind of detection magic, you're possibly losing out on some of the flashier stuff. Normally covens have one or two witches dedicated to scrying and detection, but they have the benefit of relying on a large group of magic users. Mr. Wellington seems to be keeping everyone in the dark, and I doubt he amassed his fortune by being able to detect if demons are nearby."

"Y'know, speaking of covens," Amara said, "do you have one? Could we ask them for help?"

Tessa locked eyes with Amara, her gaze unexpectedly hostile. "We're on our own, Amara." Her tone made it more than obvious that she wouldn't elaborate, and Amara decided to yield and drop the idea.

So, I have no idea who her parents are, no idea why Raine isn't around anymore, and no idea if she's in a coven... It's like the more I learn, the less I know her.

"Well, regarding the cult meeting, I'm pretty optimistic. I still have the element of surprise, and I can easily overpower a couple random humans if need be. Though, I definitely need to make sure I get laid right before the meeting." Amara chuckled, amused by the thought that getting fucked was the most important part of taking down the cult.

"I call dibs!" Tessa said quickly. Nick looked at her, somewhat surprised, before she continued. "What? You're getting her tonight, aren't you?"

"Speaking of tonight, Tessa," Amara interjected, "why don't you head home? We've got nothing else to do tonight, and I want to make sure I've got enough time to try and practice dreamwalking."

"Or, hear me out, I stay and join in the fun?" Tessa said, a glint in her eyes.

Amara had grown used to turning down her friend's lewd suggestions, but when she opened her mouth to say no, Nick had beaten her to the punch. "As fun as I'm sure that would be, maybe another time? Things are pretty stressful at the moment."

"Ugh, fine. Have fun holding hands from across the couch, or whatever it is you lame boy scouts do for fun." Tessa grabbed her things and turned towards the door, but Amara interposed and demanded that everyone hug goodbye first. After saying their goodbyes, they let the witch head home before retiring to Amara's bedroom.

"Did you seriously just turn down a threesome?" Amara asked, poking Nick in jest.

"Hey, I meant what I said. I'm pretty stressed, and I don't have your abilities or the confidence they bring you. I'm worried about what might happen with this cult, and that's not the mindset I want to be in for my first threesome."

"Typical Nick, always so rational, even when girls are lining up to suck you off."

"There's no way Tessa would wait in a line for sex, and you know it," Nick said. The two of them laughed at the idea, both undressing for the coming activities.

Amara finished first, as she'd gotten quite good at using her tail to help remove everything. As she sat on the edge of the bed, watching Nick finish, an idea crossed her mind. She reached under the bed with her tail, pulling out her box of toys before opening it up.

"Looks like someone has a plan," Nick said, smirking.

"I might," she replied, smiling back, "unless you had any suggestions? You know I love hearing all your dirty thoughts."

"Well, it did occur to me recently that you've been on top the last few times…"

"Ooh is someone looking to be a little dominant? Want to put this slutty little demon in her place?" Amara fell backwards on her bed, wiggling her hips as she taunted her friend.

Now that he was fully naked, Nick crawled towards her atop the covers, their lips meeting. His body pushed against hers, his hardening cock already rubbing against her eager pussy as they started making out. His hands found her waist, holding her tight before moving higher to start massaging her tits.

"Mmm fuck, just like that…" Amara whispered, moaning. His fingers started tracing her sensitive nipples, and after a few moments of teasing, he pinched them hard. She yelped in surprise, loving the sharp sensation, and began giggling once he let go.

Nick's mouth left hers, and soon his tongue was teasing her nipples, alternating between each as his hands moved further down. His fingers teased her entrance, circling around it but refusing to push inside. He redoubled his efforts with her nipples, biting them hard to elicit a reaction.

"Fuck!" Amara screamed. "You've never bitten me that hard before! I forgot how fun this side of you can be..."

"Well, now that we know how tough you are, I don't have to worry about holding back, do I?" Nick smirked as he shifted positions, pushing her arms to her sides and straddling her chest. His hands massaged her neck, then ran through her hair before grabbing her horns tight.

Before she knew it, he had pulled her lips to his cock, and she opened wide. He was already rock hard, clearly excited by the change of pace, and Amara took the opportunity to start feeding.

He started rocking his hips, slowly pushing in and out of her mouth while continuing to hold her horns. He tasted delicious, both his thick shaft and his aura, and Amara felt her strength growing with each powerful thrust he made. As she fed more and more on his aura, she began noticing just how sensitive she was to it. It was obvious that it grew stronger when he was more turned on, but now it almost felt as if she were experiencing his pleasure too.

Amara looked up, locking eyes with Nick as her eyes flared with excitement. She made sure to start gagging, just the way he liked, and was thrilled when her efforts heightened his aura. That sense of shared pleasure grew even more noticeable, and now her hips were squirming in excitement, almost as if he were still fingering her.

He settled into a comfortable pace, continuing to hold her still while pushing in and out of her mouth. As they both moaned in pleasure, Amara snaked her tail higher and started playing with Nick's body, running it over his back and chest to keep him excited. She loved feeling his body when he exerted himself and was thrilled that he'd decided to take charge tonight.

Nick began moving faster, and through his aura, Amara knew he was close to cumming. From experience, she expected that he was going to pull back at the last second, but she was desperate to test her theory. She began moaning louder and louder, gagging hard to keep Nick excited. His grip on her horns shifted slightly, and he started fucking her face in long, deliberate strokes. Barely a minute had passed when her connection with Nick proved too much, and she started convulsing in orgasmic bliss.

Her eyes rolled back in her head, and her hips quaked with pleasure as she came hard. Through Nick's aura, she felt that he was only seconds away from cumming, and at the last moment, he pulled out of her mouth. Gasping heavily from exertion, Amara finally realized just how roughly he'd been using her mouth.

"Fuck!" Nick gasped, "Amara, did you just cum from that?"

They locked eyes again. "Your aura... I can feel all your pleasure, it's incredible! Please don't stop!"

Eager for more, he moved further down on the bed and grabbed her hips. The two worked together, and soon she was lying on her stomach, arching her back slightly to give him access. He lined himself up, then bottomed out in Amara's pussy.

"Fuuuuck yes! Give it to me!" she screamed. Her voice was slightly muffled by the pillow in front of her, which she grabbed hard to steady herself.

Nick grabbed her hips, holding her tight as he started fucking her in long, slow strides. His cock felt incredible, and the feeling was doubled by the connection Amara had to his aura. She pulled the pillow tight, continuing to muffle her loud moans of pleasure while Nick eagerly fucked her.

In her excitement over her new discovery, she'd almost forgotten her first idea. While Nick continued pounding her into the bed, her tail pulled her box of toys closer. "Nick... fuck... use the black one!"

She heard Nick rummage through the box, and soon he'd found her black butt plug. "Are you sure? It looks like you have smaller ones."

"I've been practicing! Just use the lube, and push it in slowly, I'll be fine."

She heard Nick click open the bottle, and a cold sensation covered her asshole. He tossed the lube back in the box, and soon enough, she felt the tip of the butt plug at her entrance. He started cautiously, but as he slowly worked the tip in, he continued slowly fucking her other hole. Each time his cock pulled back, he pushed the butt plug in further, and he kept alternating like this for several minutes.

With each bit of the plug that went further in, Amara felt just how excited Nick was. It combined with her own pleasure, the feeling of both her holes getting filled, to induce another orgasm much quicker than anticipated. Her body shook again, her tail wrapping around Nick's waist and holding him tight as she screamed into her pillow.

When her second orgasm ended, she realized the plug was now completely inside of her. She felt its base sitting comfortably against her asshole, and Nick no longer needed to hold it still. His hand now free, he delivered a sharp slap to her ass before grabbing her hips and starting to fuck her again. His movements were quicker, almost animalistic, and Amara knew he meant business. He was eager to cum, and she was eager to taste his orgasm.

He fucked her hard, both of them moaning loud as he inched closer and closer to his own climax. He changed his grip, one hand now grabbing her shoulder, and after only a few more seconds he finally came. She felt his cock pulse in excitement, and soon his cum was flooding into her. Her butt plug pushed against his throbbing shaft, and when combined with the taste of his aura, she managed another orgasm of her own. The two of them froze with pleasure, their bodies each twitching and shaking as they orgasmed. It would be another minute before they both managed to return to their senses.

Nick pulled out of Amara, falling onto the bed next to her as he tried to catch his breath. She rolled onto her side, giving him space as she did the same.

"Wow, you really enjoyed that, didn't you?" Amara asked, teasing her friend.

Nick laughed, running his hand through his hair. "Look who's talking! You just kept cumming!"

The two stayed like that for another few minutes, and once they had their breath back, it was time to go to sleep. Nick took his shower first, after which he changed into his pajamas and collapsed into Amara's bed. For her turn in the shower, she made sure to take her time. She needed Nick to be asleep for her first round of experiments, and she was pretty sure that after a quick fuck and a hot shower, he'd be asleep any minute. She let herself indulge in her fancy soaps and scrubs, and soon found herself reaching for her razor.

Wait. Do I need this anymore?

Amara paused, razor in one hand, and looked at the small hints of hair that had started growing on her legs. She knew she had to try, and connected with her fire to begin the experiment. She already knew how to shapeshift, but she'd mostly been using it to completely change her appearance or manifest her strange exoskeleton. This time, she tried something small; she tried to envision her own legs, completely smooth, free of stubble, cuts, or razor burn. A small flurry of embers traveled down her legs, and when she ran her hands over them, they were perfectly smooth.

Fucking. Jackpot!

She finished her shower quickly, ecstatic at this new discovery. All at once, the endless possibilities of her shapeshifting became apparent to her, though she refused to try anything tonight for fear of burning herself out.

Back in the bedroom, predictably, Nick had already fallen asleep. Amara moved quietly, trying not to wake him, and slowly sank to her knees next to the bed.

She had no idea what she was looking for, but it was time to try. She manifested her true form and fully engaged her eyes before looking at Nick. She immediately noticed that her vision wasn't quite at the level it had been after fucking Mr. Luxnor. The strange vibrations in the air weren't present, but thankfully this meant falling asleep wouldn't be impossible tonight.

As she looked at Nick, nothing strange stood out to her. His aura was still incredibly vibrant, and she smelled the waves of post-sex euphoria coming off him, but she didn't see anything else. With no idea where to start, she found her thoughts drifting back to the dream where she'd floated up towards the sky. At the time, she'd seen a strange collection of muted colors, all traveling through a grayish-white void, and she wondered if that visual had been unique to her powers rather than Derek's dream.

She reached out, carefully placing a finger on Nick's temple. She tried to envision that same scene, hoping it could be used as a window into her friend's dreams. When she didn't see anything, she closed her eyes, trying to sync her breathing with his. She even connected with her fire, letting it fill her body as she tried to enhance her senses.

Unfortunately, regardless of what she tried, nothing worked.

Frustrated, she pulled her hand away from Nick and gave up. She crawled over him and buried herself under the covers, deciding it was time for her next idea. With any luck, she would find herself in Derek's dream again soon.

Amara leaned in, pushing her lips against her girlfriend's before eagerly grabbing her ass. The two made out for several minutes, slowly grinding against each other, before breaking apart. They whispered for a moment, planning to go somewhere more private to have some real fun, then got in the car. As the sounds of the party faded into nothing, she pulled onto the main street and floored it. Her car was top of the line, the best money could buy, and she loved showing off what it could do.

Wait, I don't drive a Bentley.

Amara shook her head. Something wasn't right here. She looked to her right, watching a gorgeous girl with black hair reapply her lipstick.

That's... my girlfriend? No, I don't have one. C'mon Amara, what's happening?

Her hand reached out, grabbing the girl's leg before daring to push higher. Bright red panties were visible beneath her short skirt, but Amara was looking at something else entirely.

These hands, they're not mine. They're too big, too manly.

As the girl in the passenger seat slapped Amara's hand, she finally understood what was happening. She watched the large, manly hand move away from the girl, instead grabbing a can of beer. Her own hand lingered, now completely separated from the person she'd previously thought she was.

Derek! I'm in his dream!

Recalling the last time she'd been shaken loose from Derek's perspective, she tried to float through the car and into the sky. To her surprise, and absolute delight, her body responded exactly as she wanted it to. Within seconds, she was floating above the car as it raced through the countryside, inching dangerously close to the side of the road. Up ahead, she saw a sizable river, and immediately remembered what was coming.

Okay, the goal is to gain control. What can I do? I need something small to test my abilities.

Amara floated back into the car, unsure what to do. So far, it seemed like Derek wasn't aware of her presence, and she certainly wanted it to stay that way, so she tried to turn herself invisible. As she waited in the back seat for the upcoming tragedy, she watched Derek turn to look at her, throwing his beer can onto the floor.

From her perspective, it appeared as if he'd looked right at her, but he didn't seem to react at all.

Okay, good start. What if I try to make something?

The car started to shake, and Derek's attention snapped back to the windshield. The car had left the road, but his attempts to hit the brakes were derailed by the car hitting a small ditch. The car smashed through the roadside barrier, and within seconds they'd crashed into the river.

She remembered what came next. Derek was going to recover from being stunned, open the door, and swim back to shore. Floating to the outside of the car once more, she focused on the area just outside the driver's-side door. She pictured a small block of concrete, something she'd seen irresponsibly abandoned in rivers before, and tried to will it into existence. Before her eyes, just as she wanted, a tiny slab of concrete appeared in the riverbed, complete with metal reinforcement bars sticking out.

At that moment, Derek returned to his senses inside the car. He tried to push the door open, and Amara watched as the block of concrete prevented him from doing so. He began panicking, pushing against the door harder and harder while the car sank. With her experiment successful, she mentally pushed the slab of concrete further into the riverbed, giving Derek a chance to escape.

She watched as he frantically swam to shore, crawling to safety while Stephanie sank beneath the water. It made Amara's blood boil, but it also gave her an idea. Derek turned back to the car, screaming out his girlfriend's name, unable to dive back in and save her.

Reaching into his pocket, Derek pulled out his phone and began to call his father. Normally, the call would go through successfully, but Amara had other plans this time. When the call connected, it wasn't Sebastian on the other line, but Stephanie. Amara knew what she sounded like and mimicked her voice while projecting it through the speaker.

"Derek? Please, help me! It's so cold, I can't see!" she cried.

"Steph? How are you—can you get out?! Open the door!" Derek shouted, his panic more than obvious.

"I'm scared! I can't breathe!"

"C'mon Steph, you can do this!" he continued shouting. At this time, Amara went silent, watching as he kept shouting her name. After another minute, when it was obvious that Derek was sufficiently terrified, static began to emanate from the phone speaker. It grew louder, and Stephanie's voice echoed through it, now heavily distorted.

"You killed me, Derek."

"No! Please! I-I didn't... I never wanted this!" Derek cried.

Amara cut off the phone line, killing the call as he fell to his knees. She floated under the surface of the river, and changed her form until she looked like Stephanie. She recreated her outfit as best she could, but her makeup was running and her hair was soaking wet. Her eyes were empty voids, and her fingers had twisted into black, gnarled talons. When the transformation was complete, she leapt from the water and crawled towards Derek, who immediately screamed and tried to run away.

His efforts were in vain. Amara warped the sand he stood on, and each step he tried to take failed to find traction. Her clawed hands grabbed his ankles, and she began to pull him towards the water as she spoke once more, her voice still incredibly distorted despite not being filtered through a phone speaker.

"YOU KILLED ME, DEREK!"

Derek continued to struggle, to try and free himself from her grasp, but it was no use. Within seconds, Amara had pulled him under the river, and his strength began to wane as he tried to hold his breath. She began to wonder how far she should push this, if she possibly had any power to hurt people through their dreams, but once Derek opened his mouth to finally breathe in, he vanished.

Amara now floated under the water, her gnarled hands holding nothing, and she quickly reverted to her true form. She rose above the surface, and watched as the sky turned back into the strange, white-washed colorscape she'd seen previously. The dream around her began to vanish, piece by piece, all of it turning into sand before falling into nothingness. The river gave way to the same void she saw above her, and within seconds, the entire scene was gone.

She hovered, alone in this strange void, watching as streaks of color occasionally flew by in the distance. It was oddly peaceful, and she couldn't escape the feeling that she belonged here. Deciding to run one final test, she closed her eyes, pictured the sound of her rain app, and asked herself to wake up.

Amara opened her eyes, awake in the darkness of her bedroom. The transition had been shockingly smooth, almost natural. Beside her, Nick was still asleep, his chest rising and falling peacefully. Looking him over, she still couldn't see hints of any dreams he might be having, but it didn't frustrate her anymore. Even if she hadn't mastered her control quite yet, she was still able to go on the offensive against Derek. Between him, the volunteer effort, and her plan to infiltrate the cult, she was feeling confident.

You're finally doing some good, Amara.

6

CLEANUP

Friday was surprisingly mundane compared to the events of the week prior. Between confronting Mr. Luxnor, cleaning up the Palace, and experimenting with her dreamwalking, a simple day of going to classes almost felt like a waste. Tessa was nowhere to be seen, but a quick text confirmed she was, once again, skipping classes to run tests of her own. This meant most of Amara's day was spent with Nick and Chloé, the latter of whom was preparing for her charity's first volunteer cleanup.

Over lunch, Chloé explained the schedule to Amara. Everyone directly involved in the charity had taken over a specific task: gathering materials, operating the refreshment table, overseeing manual labor, and sometimes minor administrative work. As volunteers showed up, they would be assigned to different parts of the event by Chloé and the other organizers, ensuring everyone a chance to contribute, even those without the desire to sift through burnt wreckage. Amara was to be the event photographer, something she greatly appreciated. Ever since cleaning up a huge portion of the Palace herself, she'd been acutely aware of just how significant her own enhanced strength was. In retrospect, the sheer size of some of the pieces she'd casually flung into the dumpster was surprising.

At the moment, Amara and Nick were making dinner. Determined to keep pushing the limits of her control, Amara was both preheating the frying pan and using her sharpened tail to dice vegetables. She cast her bright, glowing eyes to Nick before asking, "How do I know what's normal?"

The irony of the situation wasn't lost on her.

"Like, if someone challenges you to a push-up contest, how do you know when to quit?" Nick asked.

"Well, nothing that specific, but yeah. What if I accidentally break a door handle when someone's watching? Or someone asks me to hold a stack of books, and I have no idea how much they weigh?"

"I feel like you're overestimating how often people might ask you to perform manual labor. You're not exactly built like a weightlifter." Nick gently placed their dinner on the frying pan, the sizzling sound of oil filling the air as they kept talking. "Plus, guys are the ones that like to challenge their friends to random stuff like that, but all your friends are girls. I think you're safe."

"I still think it's something I should get more practice with. If nothing else, I should know what my upper limits are. Do you still have that key to the gymnastics building?"

"I do! Want to head over after dinner?"

"No, not tonight," Amara said. "I need to pack all my camera equipment for the cleanup tomorrow. Maybe next week sometime?"

"Just let me know, I'll make sure we pick a night when it'll be empty."

Once all the cooking was done, Amara let Nick put the finishing touches on their dinner. While he worked, Amara found herself staring at the frying pan on the stove, an idea forming in her head. Curiosity got the better of her, and she walked over to it before grabbing it with both hands. She took a deep breath, repositioned her fingers slightly, then tried to bend it in half. She'd expected a fair amount of resistance, and was quite surprised when the metal of the pan immediately warped under her touch.

"Alright, dinner's ready to—" Nick looked up, locking eyes with Amara, who was now attempting to twist the pan back into its original shape. "Oh, wow. Everything okay?"

"I wasn't trying to ruin it!" she said in a panic. She adjusted her grip to try and reverse the damage, only to force the pan into a different configuration altogether. After a few minutes, and with Nick's help, Amara managed to return the pan to a halfway decent shape. She groaned in frustration as she set it back on the stove, then Nick pulled her away to distract her with dinner.

"Maybe those tests should come sooner rather than later? Until then, I'd recommend playing it safe. Definitely no heavy lifting at the event tomorrow." Nick playfully scolded her, but Amara had a feeling he'd been caught off guard by her show of strength.

"I'll be good, you don't have to worry about me. I'm gonna be covered in camera stuff anyways."

Dinner was delicious, if slightly overcooked, but Amara was pleased with how much her control had improved in just a few short days. Nick's idea to practice with cooking had been genius, as loathe as she'd been to admit it at the time. They had almost finished eating when Amara's phone went off.

Tessa: u home?

Amara: Yeah, I'm here with Nick. What's up?

Tessa: im coming over, think i figured the circles out

Tessa: so finish up ur fuckin or watever

Rolling her eyes, Amara showed the texts to Nick, and soon enough Tessa was knocking on her door.

"Sorry for the short notice, but I've been working on this all day, and I've finally cracked it!" Tessa said excitedly. She kicked her shoes off before pulling out her notebooks, laying them on the kitchen counter. "Ooh, this smells delicious, are you done?"

Before Amara could object, Tessa had already grabbed her fork and started shoveling food into her mouth. "Um, sure, help yourself. What did you figure out?"

"So, something Mr. Luxnor said really stuck with me. This whole time I've been trying to figure out why the circles exist, why there are so many of them. Witches always use circles to bring magic over, but he's implying that these circles are doing the opposite. Why?" Tessa asked in between bites of food. "According to the cult, this campus is inherently magical, which isn't possible."

"Because... the magic has to come from somewhere?" Amara asked, trying to remember what few magic facts Tessa had explained to her over the weeks.

"Exactly! It has to come from somewhere! It's been staring us in the face this whole time: our campus is a giant soft spot!"

"Hold on, soft spot? What do you mean?" Nick asked.

Tessa spun one of her notebooks towards Amara and Nick, neither of whom understood what they were looking at. "All the planes are separate entities, but in rare cases, the boundaries between them can grow thin, causing them to overlap. Normally, this only happens with one or two planes at once. Like, a small pond siphons some energy from the Plane of Fire, and turns into a hot spring. This campus? It overlaps with *all of them*."

Amara paused, turning over this information in her head before speaking again. "That's why they need so many circles? Each one is trying to keep a specific plane from overlapping with ours?"

"Yes! They're all working together to create, like, some kind of massive planar gate!" Tessa pushed the plate away, having now finished Amara's dinner.

"Hold on," Nick said, holding up a hand. "If they're trying to weaken this gate, doesn't that mean they're trying to bring something through?"

"Bingo. Unfortunately, we still don't know what. They might just want the magic for themselves, but worst-case scenario? They could be trying to summon a creature to our plane, and that's guaranteed to go poorly."

"Why would they want to bring something over?" Amara asked.

"Remember what I said when I found out you were a demon? People want power, money, fame, sex, and sometimes they get in touch with creatures that are willing to trade. Based on Mr. Wellington's suspicious rise to wealth? I'd bet good money he's made a deal with some kind of demon."

The three of them went quiet for a moment. When Amara finally spoke up, her words shook with nervous trepidation. "Demons are a big deal, right?"

Tessa locked eyes with her. "I can't stress this enough, Amara, but you don't make any sense. We don't know why you're here, or how you're even a demon in the first place. You're also a decent person, which flies in the face of everything I've ever been taught. We need to assume that you're one-of-a-kind, for our own safety. If they manage to summon another demon, it could be catastrophic."

Amara pulled her tail close, nervously wringing it in her hands.

Could there be others like me? If there aren't, what does that mean for my future? I still don't know what I'm turning into, what I might be capable of when I'm finished changing...

Seeing that Amara was growing nervous, Nick intervened. "Okay, well, we already have a plan to infiltrate their meeting. Until then, there's no use worrying over hypotheticals, right?" Nick cleared his throat. "On a tangential note, I've been digging into Mr. Wellington recently."

"Oh, how's that going?" Amara asked, eager for a change of topic.

"It's weird, I feel like I've learned a lot, but also nothing at all. Everything I read last time is still there; he was a relative nobody, his parents worked thankless 9-to-5 jobs, and he happened to get lucky playing the stock market. Ever since striking it rich, he's had very few public appearances, and all of them seem carefully staged."

"Well, we're assuming he made a deal with a demon, so chances are he doesn't actually know shit about the stock market. He probably doesn't want people to find out," Tessa said. She was now rummaging through Amara's cabinets looking for snacks.

"I did learn that he's a pretty avid collector of old artifacts and relics. He's had a few interviews focused on his collection, and it's obvious he's really into old-timey mysticism and stuff."

"I see what you mean about pointless knowledge," Amara sighed. "Like, sure, we know more about him, but it's nothing helpful."

"I have a few theories, though whether or not they're of any use, I can't say." Nick waited to get Tessa's attention before continuing. "I have a sneaking suspicion that he only had Derek as an excuse to get on the Board of Directors here. It's small, but he's always been interested in this school, even though he never attended himself. Plus, anyone with his net worth? It's weird that Derek isn't going to Yale or Harvard."

"Okay? How is that helpful?" Tessa asked.

"Like I said, it might not be. But, if Derek is only a pawn in his father's schemes, it just means that we can't try to use him as a bargaining chip down the line. Not that we were planning on it, but... y'know."

"Fair point. You said you had other ideas?" Amara grabbed a cookie out of Tessa's hands, causing the witch to gasp with faux indignation.

"Well, as far as I can tell, he's been making fewer and fewer public appearances recently. Whenever he does show, he has an impressive collection of personal guards, but they try to keep themselves hidden. I noticed them because I was combing through dozens of articles, and I started seeing a couple of familiar faces in the background."

Nick slid his phone over to the girls, swiping through a couple pictures and pointing out the guards in question before he continued talking. "So, when you're sneaking into this cult meeting, I want you to keep an eye out for them. Since we're serious about taking them down, it would be good to know if he's got armed henchmen ready to pull guns on us."

After a few seconds of silence, Amara finally spoke up. "Do you think I'm bulletproof?"

"There's only one way to test that, Amara. Let's hope you never have to find out." Nick stared at her sternly, his fear more than obvious.

She thought back to her time cleaning up the Palace, when she'd covered her wings with her exoskeleton to shield against falling debris, and wondered if it might be worth testing the limits of her chitinous armor at some point.

"Anyways, long story short, hired goons likely means more mundane defenses. If you don't see them, it's safe to assume the threat is more magical, and that's where my expertise ends. Tessa?" Nick asked, looking to the witch. "You say the worst-case scenario is that they summon a creature. What could they be looking to bring over?"

Tessa cleared her throat. "Well, I think a demon is the most likely option, they supposedly love making deals. We also shouldn't assume he got rich from a deal, maybe something else happened. He could just as easily try to bring through a djinn or some kind of fey creature. The list is practically endless; we really have no way of knowing until Amara spies on this meeting."

"So... we wait? It sounds like we can't do much until the meeting," Amara asked, standing up from the counter.

"Certainly seems that way. Go to classes, do homework, pretend our campus isn't hosting an otherworldly demon cult. The usual." Nick smirked, trying to inject some levity into the situation. With the conversation coming to an end, Tessa began packing up her stuff.

"Great! Well, I've got plans with the polycule, and I was only stopping by for a moment. You two idiots have fun!" As Tessa crammed all her notebooks into her bag, Nick and Amara started cleaning up dinner. Soon enough, everyone went their separate ways, with plans to reconvene tomorrow morning for the volunteer event.

Saturday morning proved to be a beautiful day, which had everyone at the cleanup in good spirits. A large folding table sat in the shade of nearby trees, with members of the charity slowly setting up lines of snacks and refreshments. Next to the table sat several small piles of equipment: hardhats, safety goggles, thick gloves in various sizes, and other small necessities.

When Amara arrived, she was pleased to learn that Chloé had designated part of the folding table for photography equipment. Eager to get started, Amara quickly set up her camera before taking test shots of the Palace. Memories of her previous visit here resurfaced, and she forced herself to hide a smile as she remembered just how much she'd managed to clean up. As she scrolled through her test shots, making small adjustments to her camera, Chloé snuck up behind her and excitedly gave her a big hug.

"Thanks again for this Amara! I just know these pictures are going to be great; your original shots of the debris were immaculate," Chloé said. She was wearing faded jean shorts and a gray tank top, which implied she wasn't planning on doing any heavy lifting today.

"I'm more than happy to help, Chloé, you don't have to keep thanking me. How many people have signed up for today?"

"It's a pretty impressive list! I haven't counted recently, but I think we're going to have a healthy turnout for most of the day. Plus, because of the efforts of our mysterious vigilante, a lot of the really hard stuff has already been taken care of. The amount of manpower we need is somewhat secondary to raising enough money."

Amara was about to respond when another event organizer called out to Chloé. The girls parted ways, leaving Amara on her own to start taking pictures.

The first hour was slow, which came as no surprise. Of the many volunteers that had signed up, most had picked later time slots. The turnout wasn't so thin as to prevent any progress being made, thankfully. One of the first to show up was a member of Sigma Alpha Upsilon, and along with several of his friends, they had plenty of muscle to get started. He also indicated that the fraternity had plans to keep someone present at all hours of the event, which Chloé greatly appreciated.

As time went on, more and more volunteers arrived. Amara was happy to have such great attendance, as it made her job as event photographer much easier. Great shots were never hard to find, and nearly everyone happily agreed to have their picture taken. She also noticed a healthy amount of representation from across the student body. Kylie showed up, along with a small collection of cheerleaders, and they were by far the most enthusiastic about Amara's pictures. Closer to noon, a student with short, bright blue hair arrived with several students that Amara recognized as musicians. By the time they arrived, the heavy lifting had mostly wrapped up, and they busied themselves with sifting through smaller pieces of debris.

Amara was in the middle of a small break, posting some pictures on the charity's social media pages, when she heard the heavy crunching noise of a car coming to a stop nearby. Looking up, she saw a frustratingly familiar black SUV, complete with heavily tinted windows. After a moment's pause, during which several volunteers stopped to watch, the back door opened and a large, broad-shouldered man in a dark suit stepped out.

Fighting not to crush her camera in her hands, Amara grit her teeth as Mr. Wellington walked towards the main table. Chloé was currently talking with other organizers, deciding which of them needed to make a run for more drinks, when Mr. Wellington called out.

"Look at all this generosity!" he said, spreading his hands in a show of mock appreciation. "I had no idea today was going to be so busy!"

Amara quickly walked to Chloé's side, hoping to spare her the pain of talking to such a horrid man. "Thankfully, we have a wonderful student body who's happy to help," Amara said nervously. "It's *so* rewarding to put in honest effort for something you want, rather than having it handed to you on a silver platter."

"Oh, I couldn't agree more," Wellington said, forcing a smile that failed to reach his eyes. "I'm a self-made man myself, after all. That's why I want to help." With a snap of his fingers, he looked back at his driver. The man by the car, a younger gentleman wearing ill-fitting khakis and a blue button-down, quickly nodded before turning to the SUV again. From the front passenger seat, he pulled out a massive, stiff white piece of thin plastic, then shut the door to run it over.

Mr. Wellington stepped to the side of the table and began donning volunteer equipment, pulling a high-visibility vest over his suit jacket and then reaching for a hard hat. "I, Sebastian Wellington, head of the Board of Directors, would like to make a humble donation to such a worthy cause!"

Once the younger man reached the table, he turned the thin sheet of plastic around to reveal that it was actually a giant, novelty check. The official name of Chloé's charity had been written on the top line, and Amara saw that he was donating a thousand dollars in total.

That's it? All his money, all his power, and he can only spare a thousand dollars? Ugh, he's probably just here for the publicity.

Chloé and the other organizers spent a few minutes thanking Mr. Wellington for his contribution, praise he eagerly lapped up, and eventually he stepped closer to the burnt ruins of the Palace. Looking around for a moment, he then snapped towards Amara. "You there, with the camera! Come take a picture of this momentous occasion, would you?"

Biting her tongue, Amara forced her own smile as Mr. Wellington ushered the charity members to gather round. They posed for a few pictures with the check, and once they'd finished, Mr. Wellington demanded a shovel from the student with the blue hair from earlier. He ordered Amara to take more pictures of him at the edge of the Palace, the shovel half-buried in soot. Although absolutely convinced that it was impossible to make him look anything but contemptible, she stayed quiet as she snapped her pictures.

"Alright, that should be enough, are we good?" Mr. Wellington asked his attendant, who nodded slowly, then his smile vanished. "Perfect. Camera girl, take

Leonard's information and send him all those pictures, and make sure they get posted to the charity's page, would you?"

Mr. Wellington tossed the shovel to the ground, then did the same with the protective equipment he'd borrowed. He walked away without so much as a glance towards anyone else, and had already started an unrelated phone call by the time he reached the SUV. His assistant hurriedly gave Amara a business card and began to clarify how best to deliver the pictures, but he was cut off by Mr. Wellington's voice booming across the lot from the back seat of the car.

"Leonard! Get a move on, I've got a meeting in fifteen minutes!"

The attendant, fear in his eyes, quickly apologized to Amara before turning to run towards the SUV. Amara was prepared to feel sorry for him, as he clearly had the world's worst boss, but she noticed something as he turned around that changed her mind. Underneath his collar, only visible for a brief moment, she saw the top of a runic tattoo.

"Can you believe him? He's so rude!" Chloé said, stepping over to the pile of protective equipment Mr. Wellington had made. "At least he gave us some money. I'll happily trade a few pictures and some awkward handshakes for a grand."

"Well, he's gone now, and we can actually get back to being productive," Amara said, trying to hide her simmering rage at Mr. Wellington's antics.

"Speaking of money; Connie, how are we holding up?" Chloé asked one of the other organizers. The girl that stepped forward had curly, dirty blonde hair that she'd tied back into a ponytail, and she started scrolling through her phone before responding.

"Not terrible. As little as the money means to that asshat, it'll definitely help us out. I'm mostly worried about the longevity of everything. We've had a lot of earlier engagement, and the mysterious overnight cleanup gave us a ton of publicity, but typically charities like this raise most of their money in the first few weeks. Unless you can conjure up another publicity gold mine, Amara, we might be running out of steam soon."

Amara listened closely to Connie's words, nodding in agreement. Today's pictures would give her plenty of content to post for the charity, but just like their finances, it was a finite well. Connie continued talking, digging into details about their various goals and how they should manage their expectations, and Amara grew more nervous the more she heard.

Amara avoided saying anything, but she found her thoughts preoccupied about money for most of the day. She checked her phone constantly, hoping to keep engagement high with plenty of pictures and status updates. She tagged everyone she could, even cross-posting with some of the school's official organizations, but she feared she wasn't doing enough. Was there more she could offer? Something other than photos and social media?

By the time the sun had started setting behind the nearby trees, she hadn't thought of anything. Thankfully, the ruins of the Palace looked incredibly nice after the hours of hard work, and they'd even found several larger items that had mostly survived the fire. The fraternity had expressed interest in refurbishing them eventually, and Amara made sure to take pictures to eventually put together a before-and-after collage.

Amara's financial musings were put on hold as someone new approached the Palace. The late hour, as well as the stiff nature of his clothes, indicated he wasn't here to help clean up. Instead, he had his sights set squarely on the event's photographer. His short brown hair shimmered slightly in the dimming sunlight, and his cocky grin hinted that he'd overcome his fear of Amara, despite how their last interaction had gone.

"Well, look who it is! I didn't know you'd be working the event!" Brandon said, his voice slightly louder than it needed to be.

She glared at him, unsure what his plan was, but knew she couldn't risk escalating matters. "Well, we're almost finished, I think it's actually time to start putting everything away. Shame you missed it, I guess you can go home now."

She quickly turned away from the cleanup effort and walked back to the refreshment table. As she packed up her camera, Brandon continued the conversation. "You seem pretty invested in helping out here, I wonder why that is."

"A friend runs the charity, Brandon, and I'm helping her out," Amara hissed, wishing he hadn't approached her in public like this.

"You sure about that? Personally, I think you feel guilty." Brandon leaned in closer, his voice much quieter now. "Almost like you caused the fire, and you're trying to make up for it."

Amara froze.

How much does he know? How could he have figured it out?

"You don't know anything about me. Did I not make myself clear last time?" Amara said with a glare, her eyes pulsing slightly.

"Oh, you did, but things are different now. You see, I was taking a lovely evening walk a few days ago, and I happened across something rather strange. I found a demon, all on her own, cleaning up the debris." As he kept speaking, Brandon pulled out his phone and started swiping through his pictures. Amara saw herself, tail and wings out, angrily knocking down a wall of the Palace. "What would people think if they saw this? If they knew their fellow student was a demon, and this fire was no accident?"

She glared at him, her eyes flaring as she pieced together his threat. "You wouldn't dare."

"I absolutely would. Now before you get any bright ideas, know that these pictures are scheduled to go live in a week. If you want to avoid the world finding out about you, I'd suggest you do what I ask."

Amara was seething, her eyes flicking towards the volunteers to see if anyone was listening in. "What do you want?"

"You already know that, Amara. I want you. You're going to show me exactly what a succubus is capable of, however I want, when I want. You're going to be mine." Brandon's smile was infuriating, and she wanted nothing more than to punch it off his stupid face. So long as he had those photos, however, her hands were tied. "I expect your answer in a week. If I don't hear anything, everyone finds out what you are."

He stood up, then pocketed his phone before walking away. Amara watched him leave, seething as she steadied herself on the table beside her. Just as he left the lot, she heard a loud crack, and quickly snapped back to her senses. She'd briefly lost her focus and, in her anger, had snapped part of the plastic. Thankfully, no one else seemed to have heard, and she packed up her camera in a rush before heading out. She hugged Chloé goodbye, made her last post for the charity, and walked home in a daze.

I can't let him do this, but what choice do I have? Those pictures can't get out.

The rest of her evening was incredibly stressful. Her thoughts raced as she tried to think of a way to get out of this twisted deal, but she kept drawing blanks. Once night fell, and it was time to get some sleep, she'd done nothing but stress herself out. Thankfully, she had the perfect way to burn off this frustration, and when she manifested in Derek's dream that night, she did everything in her power to turn it into the perfect nightmare.

The next week passed rather quickly, for better or for worse. Brandon's threat loomed over her head, and although she'd talked it over with Nick and Tessa, they hadn't yet thought of a way out. She'd already tried scaring him away, and apparently that had only pushed him into stalking her. Since fear didn't work, and she knew she didn't have the temperament to pursue a more permanent solution, she was stuck biding her time. Plus, even if Brandon were to somehow disappear, it was obvious he'd set up the pictures to go live automatically in the event something happened to him.

Nick had suggested that she try to use her dreamwalking abilities, but without any control over whose dreams she entered, the idea fizzled out. She was getting better at manipulating dreams once inside them, but her attempts to manifest in other dreams consistently failed.

Still, being able to give Derek constant nightmares had been its own special pleasure. She manifested in his dreams every night that week, and every night she invented new ways to try and push him over the edge. Each nightmare ended the same, with Derek trapped under the water and his dead girlfriend screaming at him, but Amara enjoyed mixing up how exactly it happened.

After the first few nights, she'd enlisted Tessa's help to follow him around campus. Once they pinned down his schedule, Amara started visiting his classes and watching him through the window while disguised as Stephanie. The first sighting caused him to scream and fall from his chair in the middle of class. The second time, and all subsequent appearances, clearly unnerved him, but he'd managed to avoid embarrassing himself any further. The more she followed him around, the easier it was to see him slowly unraveling.

Derek now jumped at the tiniest scare, and often wouldn't pay attention to anyone around him, instead looking for signs of Stephanie. He began skipping classes, and it wasn't long before other students started whispering about his strange behavior.

The entire process of wearing him down had honestly taken Amara less time than she'd initially thought. She suspected that he'd been having those dreams for a while, but with her powers still developing she hadn't been strong enough to pick up on them until recently. It was only Wednesday of the following week when Amara decided to implement the next part of her plan, this time with Tessa's help.

The girls had recently learned that Derek lived close to Amara, on the ground level in a similar apartment complex. They waited until the dead of night, when they knew he would be alone, and got to work.

Amara had purchased an outfit just like the one Stephanie had been wearing the night of her murder. She now stood outside Derek's window, identical to his deceased girlfriend in every way, with Tessa only a few feet away. She'd dressed warmly, in a large black peacoat, and was setting down a large bucket of water and a hose.

"Alright Tess, it's showtime. You ready?" Amara asked.

"Please, I was born ready. I can't wait to go all Ghost of Christmas Past on this asshole." Tessa was practically bouncing in excitement, and squatted down to wait for her signal.

Amara checked her phone, confirmed it was just past 3:30 in the morning, and handed it to Tessa. Based on the last few nights, Derek seemed to wake from his nightmares around this time, only now Amara was waiting outside the dream. She crouched by his window, peeked inside, and waited.

Soon enough, she heard the muffled sounds of someone waking from a nightmare. His room stayed dark, but soon she saw the telltale glow of a phone's flashlight. He was clearly exhausted, Amara saw heavy bags under his eyes, and he stumbled out of his room. When he returned, glass of water in hand, he slowly drank half of it before setting it on his nightstand, hand shaking.

With a flick of her fingers, Amara signaled to her friend that she was about to start. She reached up, tapping and scraping the window lightly to try and get Derek's attention.

"Who's there?" Derek quickly asked, his fear palpable even from outside his window.

Amara kept waiting, knowing she had to draw this out as long as possible. After another minute, she tried again, louder this time.

"I'm serious, you don't know who you're messing with!" he said, his voice shaking. His bravado was nowhere to be seen, a result of the endless nightmares Amara had been forcing onto him. He moved to the window, and with another flick of her wrist, Amara asked for the next step.

Above the window, held aloft by Tessa's telekinesis, the hose turned on. Water rained down into Derek's field of vision, stalling him slightly. He checked the locks on his window, making sure it was sealed tight, and cautiously looked outside.

As soon as he approached the glass, Amara reached up from beneath the window and slammed her hand on the glass. Just as this happened, Tessa emptied the heavy bucket of water, drenching Amara and causing Derek to jump back.

"Fuck!" Derek screamed. "S-Steph? Is that you?" He was clearly terrified, and Amara took this opportunity to move fully into his vision.

"I-I'm so c-cold, Derek..." she whispered, just loud enough for him to hear.

"You can't be here! You're dead!"

"How did I die, Derek? **How did I die?**" Amara's voice distorted, carrying echoes of a dying phone, a shapeshifting trick she'd been practicing the last few days.

"I didn't... I never wanted this! It's not my fault!"

Another signal, and Tessa started the next step. With her telekinesis, the locks on Derek's window unlatched, and the window seemingly opened on its own. Amara crawled into the room, doing her best to make her movements appear jagged and unnatural.

"YOU KILLED ME, DEREK," Amara hissed, her voice even more twisted. She crawled closer, and when Derek tried to run from the room, Tessa slammed his door shut.

"Please, don't kill me! I'm sorry!" Unable to run, Derek turned to face Amara. She reached out, grabbed his ankle, and pulled him to the ground. Despite his best efforts, he was no match for her demonic strength, and within seconds she crawled on top of him, pinning him down.

"TELL THEM WHAT HAPPENED. TELL THEM EVERYTHING!" Her hands closed on Derek's neck, and she carefully started restricting his airflow.

"I... I'll do it! Please, just let me live!" Derek's face turned red, tears streaking down his face as he gasped for air. After another few seconds, his struggles stopped, and Amara immediately jumped off him.

"Tessa! Quick, like we planned!" Amara whispered. The witch peeked through the window, her tattoos flaring up as she prepared to help Amara. The girls quickly moved Derek into his bed, pulled the covers over him, and reset the room to its normal state. Once they were back outside, Tessa closed the window, re-locked it, and they made their escape.

Once they were far enough away, Amara made sure no one was watching, and shapeshifted back into herself.

"Fucking hell, Amara! Is that what you've been doing in his dreams every night?" Tessa asked, clearly excited. "Amara?"

Amara leaned against the outer wall of her apartment, her eyes closed and her breath panicked. Her body shook, tears forming in the corners of her eyes; with the adrenaline rush over, she'd begun flashing back to Halloween. She was suddenly back in the Palace, her twisted talons wrapped around Vee's neck while she begged for mercy.

I didn't do it, I didn't do it... Vee's safe! She's alive! I had to do this for her!

Tessa's hands grabbed her shoulders. "Amara! Calm down, look at me."

The feel of another person's touch shook her back to her senses, but before she mustered the strength to look at Tessa, she first looked at her hands. They were normal, human hands, nothing like what she'd attacked Vee with.

"I-I..." Amara leaned forward, pulling Tessa in for a hug. "I hate how easily being cruel comes to me. I don't want to have to keep doing this, but it keeps feeling like I have no other choice..."

The witch grabbed Amara's neck, looking in her eyes. "Hey, that asshole deserves it. He attacked you! He would've attacked Vee! This is the only way to stop him, and you know it."

Amara nodded slowly, wiping away her tears. After a few more moments, she was able to pull herself together. "Okay, I think... I think I'm alright. Let's head back inside." It only took a few minutes to get back to her room, at which point she eagerly began changing out of her wet clothes.

"So, those are his nightmares?" Tessa asked again.

"Uh, yeah, more or less. Normally I distort Stephanie's body a bit more, but that was the gist of it. Why, you scared?" Amara playfully nudged her friend, doing her best to avoid dwelling on the panic attack she'd just avoided.

"I mean, if I'd been the target of that? I'd have been fucking terrified! I take back everything I said about you not using your powers enough, that was damn impressive, Amara." They both collapsed on the couch, sighing in relief.

"Well, I guess now we wait," Amara said, putting her hair up. "You think it'll work?"

"Are you kidding? With how scared he was, I think you could've talked him into just about anything. Fuck, I should've tried to grab a picture, that would have been hilarious."

"C'mon, you know that trying to take a picture would've—" Amara froze, a sudden idea halting her train of thought. When she didn't finish her sentence, the witch looked over, concerned.

"Hey, Amara? You alright? Demon senses tingling?"

"Taking pictures! Tessa, you're a genius!" Amara ran to her bedroom, a sudden burst of inspiration overtaking her.

"What? I mean, I know I am, but mind explaining what you mean?" Tessa hopped off the couch, following Amara. By the time she entered the room, Amara had already pulled out half of her camera equipment and was setting up her tripod.

"Tess, can you grab my red lingerie set? It's in the top drawer!"

"Alright, I like where this is going, but I'd still appreciate a little context, Amara." Tessa did as she was asked, grabbing the lingerie before handing it over. Amara smirked, meeting Tessa's eyes before finally responding.

"I know how to beat Brandon!"

7
REUNION

Birds chirped outside the window, celebrating the morning light as it slowly filled the sky. A soft breeze rustled the canopy of autumn leaves, shaking some of them loose before they fell to the ground. Inside, a phone prepared to join the morning chorus, but was silenced before it had the chance.

Vee had recently started rising with the sun, and only set her alarm out of habit. Carefully pulling her covers aside, she slid her feet from the bed and sat up. Her toes wiggled amongst the plush carpet, and she allowed herself the simple pleasure of appreciating how much more comfortable she was compared to her apartment back at school. She stretched her arms over her head, sighed in relief as she felt her back crack in several places, then relaxed her shoulders and stood up. Her morning stretches were simple, easy, and felt great. Her hips were still sore from the lack of activity the last few weeks, but that was the worst of it.

The nightmares had stopped shortly after Halloween. Or perhaps they'd stopped before? She honestly couldn't remember, so much had blurred together in the week leading up to that fateful night. With her dreams no longer haunted by visions of demonic incursions, she was finally able to sleep again, and for that she was thankful.

As she finished her more mundane stretches, she sat on the ground and crossed her legs. With a short prayer, she connected with the divine power inside her, and asked it to continue aiding her recovery. Its power traveled through her body, dispelling her aches and pains, drawing on her own natural energy in pursuit of keeping her healthy. This exercise was not only simple, but it also prevented her powers from diminishing while she wasn't actively pushing her own limits.

Of course, it can't heal everything...

Vee touched her forehead, wincing slightly as her fingers traced over the gap in her brow. Her divine magic hadn't been able to restore it, and she suspected it was due to the hellfire that had burst forth from the demon's fists when she'd been struck.

No, not "The Demon." Amara.

She thought back to Halloween, her feelings a tangled mess. For all the time she'd spent reflecting on what had happened, she was more confused than ever.

A knock on her door startled her, and her mom peeked inside. "Morning hun! Whenever you're finished with your morning prayers, breakfast is ready!" The older woman's eyes lingered for a moment, captivated by the magic that pulsed just underneath Vee's skin.

She smiled back, used to her mom being awestruck by her divine abilities. "Of course, Mom, I'll be down in a minute."

Checking her phone, Vee saw it was already seven in the morning. As she looked at her lock screen, she also saw a single push notification; unread messages from Amara. She couldn't bring herself to open them, but every time she tried to dismiss the notification, she hesitated. She stared at the most recent message for longer than she intended, then shook her head to clear her thoughts. This wasn't the time for that.

It only took a few minutes for Vee to get properly dressed. With most of her wardrobe still at school, her choices were slim, but she managed to piece together something cute. Downstairs, she hugged both her parents, giving each a kiss on the cheek before sitting down for breakfast.

"Are you sure you're feeling up to going back?" her dad asked. "If you want to wait another week, you know we won't mind."

"I have to go back eventually; it might as well be now." Vee piled her plate with bacon and eggs before taking a seat. "Besides, it's a nice day, the drive will be easy."

Her mom came closer, cupping the side of Vee's face as she looked down in concern. "We have nothing but faith in you, love, but that doesn't stop us from worrying. I just wish you could tell us what happened."

"You know I can't, mom."

"Oh, I know. 'Official Church business' and all that. You'd think they could make an exception for your parents, that's all I'm saying!" her mom huffed.

The breakfast was delicious, as expected, but soon enough it was time to leave. Vee grabbed a light coat, said goodbye to her parents, and started the drive back to Aurelius University.

It was hardly a long drive; even in bad traffic, it never took more than two hours. She kept the radio off, preferring the silence of her own thoughts. She focused on the road, on the clouds racing just over the horizon as she drew closer and closer to school.

She had no idea what to expect. The events of that night had replayed in her head thousands of times, and she still didn't understand exactly what had happened. For some reason, Amara had let her live, and she didn't know what that meant. Was it a trick? Was it genuine? Even if it was, it didn't change the fact that she'd burnt down the building during their fight. She still blocked off the exits, preventing Vee from deescalating the situation by leaving.

But when we got out, she seemed so worried about me, horrified at what she'd done...

She shook her head. Regardless of everything else, she needed to finish school, and she was trying to focus on doing that one step at a time. Step one was getting back to campus, step two would be to contact all her teachers and ask for the homework she'd missed. Step three, finish the homework, learn the material, prepare for finals. Anything past that didn't feel worth thinking about.

Before she knew it, she was back. She parked outside her apartment, staring up at her window, and walked inside for the first time in weeks.

It was exactly as she'd left it. Scattered, messy, even a little claustrophobic. The blinds were still closed, and she eagerly opened them to let in the sunlight before truly looking around. In the corner, next to the couch, sat a pile of large, plastic empty water jugs. Several unenchanted rosaries lingered on the kitchen counter next to a tiny bag of sulfur that she'd sealed tight. As she nervously wandered through her apartment, it felt as if she were in conversation with a past version of herself. She ended her tour in the bedroom, where her gaze lingered on several large dents in the wall, just above the crumpled mess that was her bed.

Vee sighed.

She took a few hours to clean up, start some laundry, and move the water jugs to the recycling. The sulfur went in the garbage, and she scrubbed the countertop clean just to be safe. She appreciated having busy work, thankful that it gave her a distraction from her thoughts.

Once she'd finished, her stomach began to protest how long ago breakfast had been. Unfortunately, her exhaustive cleaning had included tossing everything in her fridge in the garbage, as none of it had survived the last few weeks without her. With only a single option available to her, she grabbed her keys, left the apartment, and set a course for the cafeteria. The weather was still beautiful, thankfully, but the thought of wading through crowds of students made her sick to her stomach. What would people say when they saw she was back?

Her fears were justified when, from the nearest pack of students, she saw Tania break loose and walk in her direction. This was the same girl that had harassed her over Derek's false accusations, the same girl that had crashed her date with Nick. Whatever she wanted now, it certainly wouldn't be good, and Vee clenched her fists to try and steel her nerves.

No doubt she's going to blame me for the Palace. She already thinks I'm an arsonist.

As Tania drew close, with several of her friends in tow, Vee spoke up. "What is it now, Tania? I'm really not in the mood."

To Vee's surprise, Tania said nothing, instead pulling her in for a tight hug. They stayed like this for a moment before she finally spoke. "I'm so sorry, Vee, I had no idea. I can't believe what that must have been like for you!"

"Um... thanks? What are you talking about?" Vee didn't know what to say, and looked at Tania's friends in confusion as she half-heartedly hugged Tania back.

"You haven't heard?! It's all anyone can talk about!" Vee stayed silent and, in response, Tania pulled out her phone. "Derek confessed to everything! He made a huge post, even turned himself in to the police!"

"He what?!" Vee gasped, hardly able to believe her ears.

"Yeah! He admitted to attacking you, and he admitted that his injuries were his own fault, but it's so much more than that! He's confessed to years of awful behavior, and he's been apologizing to dozens of girls that he's hurt. Apparently, he also got someone killed back in High School? He was driving drunk and crashed his car, and his girlfriend didn't survive."

Vee froze in shock. This wasn't like Derek at all, but as she read the news article on Tania's phone, it was impossible to deny.

"I... but why?"

"Who knows? Maybe he had a change of heart, maybe the guilt was driving him mad, beats me. A whole bunch of girls have started speaking up, it's like the Me Too thing all over again." Tania placed a hand on Vee's shoulder. "Anyways, Vee, I'm really sorry about everything. If there's ever anything I can do to help, to make this up to you, please just ask, okay? I can't imagine what you're going through, with the attack, and then getting caught in that fire..."

Tania pulled away from their hug, her eyes glancing at Vee's eyebrow, then the rest of her friends apologized as well. Soon enough, Vee was on her own again, more confused than ever.

Walking into the cafeteria was a surreal experience. After getting her food and finding the most isolated spot she could, she pulled out her phone and began combing through local news outlets. Every major site in the area had their own article covering Derek's shocking confessions, as did several national papers. Reading through them revealed little new information, so Vee finally took the plunge and opened her own social media feeds. For her own sanity, she'd muted them after Halloween, but now she was ready. Hundreds upon hundreds of messages, posts, tags, mentions, every possible form of interaction directed at her in myriad different ways. Everyone seemed eager for her attention, for a chance to express their sympathy. Some apologized for their own actions, others applauded her for her quiet strength, and she even had several hundred dollars of random donations.

Even now, in the cafeteria, random students and casual acquaintances approached her with their regards. She'd gotten used to the icy stares of people who thought she'd attacked Derek, and this complete reversal was baffling. Before long, the attention threatened to overwhelm her, and she decided to pack up and head home.

She walked quickly, eager to avoid more awkward conversations, but something caught her eye as she left the cafeteria. Towards the center of campus, on the edge of the quad, a crowd had gathered. Curiosity got the better of her, and when she drew close, she was thankful to see this crowd had nothing to do with Derek or his confession. It looked like some volunteers had set up a fundraising campaign for The Jade Palace, and something had everyone particularly excited today.

I might as well make a contribution, right? In a weird way, I'm at least a little responsible for that fire.

She took a deep breath and decided she would brave the crowds to make a donation.

It had taken the entire night and most of the morning for Amara to finish editing her latest photoshoot. With Tessa's assistance, as distracted as she was, she'd spent a considerable amount of time taking pictures: experimenting with new angles, adjusting the lighting, and switching outfits occasionally. Never before had there been so much pressure to truly nail a photoshoot, but with Brandon's threat hanging over her head, there wasn't any room for error.

In the end, she had three professional quality sets of photos that she was extremely proud of. After confirming with Chloé that she could borrow the charity's portable table, she submitted a fundraising application to the school's website, then packed up her things and headed out.

She set up the table first, then integrated her photos with Chloé's app, which ensured that a vast majority of the profits would go to the charity. After the uploads had finished, she sent Nick a flurry of texts to explain her plan, and he managed to join everyone on the quad within minutes. After he arrived, and the crowds started forming for the lunch rush, Amara began posting her big announcement on all her socials.

Predictably, it was somewhat of a slow start. This was a huge gamble, after all, and while she waited for the announcement to gain traction, she nervously paced back and forth behind the table. Thankfully, once there were enough students, she managed to channel her apprehension into extroversion as she tried to drum up more interest.

Amara had never been incredibly popular, but she was far from reclusive. She'd been offering photography services to the student body for a while now, and when combined with her friends' social groups, she had access to a sizable cross-section of the school's population. According to Tessa, her recent debut as a party girl had bolstered her reputation, and her Halloween "costume" had garnered a significant amount of attention. She'd been completely oblivious to all of that, but today on the quad, she began to understand exactly what had changed about her perception in the eyes of the public.

Everyone loved her photoshoot. She'd expected that most of her sales would come from people on campus, and she was surprised to find a significant amount of engagement from random online communities that had nothing to do with Aurelius University.

When she wasn't engaging with the real world at the charity table, she was buried in her socials to attempt to handle another massive wave of donations and excitement. Not only were people predictably thrilled about the photos them-selves, but just as many were eager to compliment her editing skills or the fact that this was all for charity. For a brief moment, the attention brought back memories of how great she'd felt at Halloween just before the fight, but thankfully Nick helped her avoid a downward spiral as she nearly flashed back to the events of that night.

Of course, the other thing propping up her good mood was Derek's big an-nouncement. She'd initially missed it, as she'd spent most of yesterday working on her photoshoot, but Tessa and Nick had blown up her phone in excitement. It was a surreal experience; after so many months living in fear of Derek, the tables had finally turned. He'd confessed to absolutely everything, not just the incident with Stephanie, and there was a faint air of celebration on campus as she talked with everyone that approached the table.

She was in the middle of a conversation with several friends she hadn't seen since Halloween when the moment she'd been dreading finally appeared. From across the quad, she saw Brandon drawing near, his insufferable smirk clearly directed at her. From the look of things, he didn't know what she was up to, and she was itching to wipe that smile off his face.

As he approached, Nick began corralling the crowds to give her some space. Once Brandon closed the distance, he leaned up against the table and pulled out his phone. "Well, Amara, I'm nothing if not a man of my word. It's been a week, and you have yet to give me an answer. Did you think I was bluffing?"

"Oh, I believe you. I just don't care," Amara said.

"I've got it pulled up on my phone right now, one click and you're through!" Brandon was clearly frustrated, his face already turning red.

"But Brandon," Amara said, a smile growing on her face, "don't you want to contribute to our charity first? I'm selling some of my portfolio to raise money!"

"This isn't a joke, Amara. I'm going to ruin you." Brandon was furious now, though he was doing his best to hide his temperament from the nearby crowd. He began typing on his phone, likely setting up what he thought was the final nail in Amara's coffin.

Before he could finish, Amara looked over to Nick and saw one of his friends, Alex, approaching the table out of curiosity. Stepping over to him, she grabbed his arm and pulled him closer to the table. "Oh my gosh, Alex, did you hear the big news? I'm a succubus!" She made sure to speak louder than usual, putting on a show for her blackmailer.

Brandon froze, looking up from his phone in shock.

"Wait, I don't get it, you're a what?" Alex asked.

"A succubus, a demon, whatever you want to call it." As she spoke, Amara scanned a QR code on the table. She angled herself so that Alex and Brandon could see her screen and continued. "I'm raising money for the charity, and since the fire happened on Halloween, I figured I'd do a sexy photoshoot in my costume!"

Amara started scrolling through the photos she'd taken, eagerly watching as Brandon realized what was happening; in every single photo she'd taken the last two days, she'd been wearing nothing but her sexiest lingerie, and her demonic aspects were front and center. Some photos highlighted her horns, some her tail, and her wings had appeared in roughly half of the shots. In one photo she was straddling her tail while moaning, in another she licked its tip while winking at the camera, and each set had dozens more. She'd made the pictures as sultry as possible and had surprised herself at how willing she was to flaunt her body online.

Finally, she showed Alex a picture she'd taken at the Halloween party, one where her tail looked like it was attached with the belt Nick had made. "See, I took all the pictures in that costume, and then edited them to look real!"

In actuality, a vast majority of her photo editing had been to create the illusion that editing had happened at all. She'd subtly altered tiny details to make it look like there had originally been a belt around her waist, or glue residue on her horns. Just like she'd done with her actual costume, the goal was to seed just enough doubt to make people think her true form was nothing but the magic of photoshop.

"Of course, these aren't all of them. The sexiest photos you can only see if you buy the sets, but I'll let you in on a little secret, Alex... I'm naked in some of them!"

Alex, either through legitimate interest or the efforts of a sexy demon hanging off his arm, didn't hesitate to buy all three sets. His eyes were practically bulging out of his head as he started scrolling through them, and after a minute of silent gawking, he finally spoke up again. "Look, Amara, I've been meaning to ask this for a while, but... would you want to go out with me sometime? I-I don't know if I'm necessarily your type, but I think you're really fun, and—"

With a gentle laugh, Amara gave Alex a hug. "You're incredibly sweet, Alex, but I'm not really looking for anything like that at the moment."

Somewhat deflated, Alex quickly backpedaled. "R-right, of course, I knew that!" While he was obviously disheartened by the rejection, he still seemed more than interested in the photos and started up a conversation with Nick about them. With her point proven, Amara turned her attention back towards Brandon.

"Still feel like releasing those photos? It would be a big help for the charity, the more attention the better!"

The two locked eyes, and Brandon finally spoke for the first time in minutes. "This isn't over, Amara. I'll find a way to make you mine. You're going to regret making an enemy of me."

She leaned in, whispering into his ear. "Well, until then? I think you've got an overdue date with your hand, so how about you leave me the fuck alone."

After a final contentious glance, Brandon scowled and walked away from the table. Amara celebrated by running back to Nick, grabbing his arms excitedly. "Nick! It worked! He ran off with his tail between his legs!"

Nick laughed as Amara danced around him, elated to be free of her blackmailer, then returned to chatting with the crowd with renewed exuberance. The line of people wanting her attention seemed endless, and Amara was more than happy to let people openly perv on her so long as it meant more money for the charity. The attention also meant everyone was unusually physically affectionate with her. Everyone seemed to want a hug, and there were more than a few "accidental" brushes against her chest and her ass, but she took it in stride. If nothing else, the rampant arousal of the crowd meant she had a pleasant smell to bask in as everyone showered her with attention.

One particularly enthusiastic student had even managed to print out a copy of one of her photos and offered additional money to have her sign it. Eager to raise more money for the charity, she happily agreed, and grabbed the silver sharpie that Chloé always kept in the charity's supply box.

"And who should I make this out to?" Amara said, doing her best to seem fun and flirty.

"U-um, my n-name's Chris," the student muttered. He had short blonde hair, a matching shaggy goatee, and his deep blue eyes had trouble moving away from Amara's chest as they talked. With a playful giggle, she signed the picture and even kissed him on the cheek as an additional thank you.

The interaction made her consider extending the fundraiser, maybe coming back tomorrow with high-quality prints of her pictures and offering to sign them, but she was forced to table the idea when Tessa pulled her aside.

"Careful, we've got trouble," the witch said.

Confused, Amara scanned the crowd to look for any problems. She was scared she might see Mr. Wellington, or possibly another member of the cult. Both Tessa and Nick had warned her that some people might see through her photo stunt, and she was ready to defend herself if need be. The person walking towards the table, however, was the last person on Earth she wanted to fight.

Vee.

She was wearing blue, relaxed jeans that hugged her hips and ended just above simple, black flats. An oversized, thickly knit green sweater hung off one shoulder, though it was held partially in place by the purse slung across her body. As Amara's eyes traveled higher, she gasped.

Vee's face, previously an impossibly perfect visage, now had two incredibly distinct blemishes. In the middle of her left eyebrow sat a massive scar, at least two or three inches long. The hair hadn't grown back and likely never would. A second scar, slightly smaller, cut through her upper lip on the right side. The scars had clearly been inflicted by a blunt force strike, but the lack of a sharp outline indicated there had also been substantial burn damage.

She held Vee down, clenching her free hand before lashing out. Her bone-covered knuckles, clad in hellfire, struck Vee's brow, a sickening crack filling the air as the angel's head fell to the ground. Amara struck again, furiously, this time connecting with her lip as she felt Vee's body start to surrender.

Terrible memories flooded Amara's head, memories she'd previously failed to recall. She clenched her fists, not in anger, but to try and hold herself together. Taking a deep breath, she attempted to steady her nerves, and watched as Vee walked closer. Soon enough, the girls were standing face to face, neither saying anything before Amara attempted to break the silence.

"Um... Hi, Vee," Amara said nervously.

The blond-haired girl had stopped just a few paces away from Amara. She directed her gaze towards the ground before speaking. "...Amara."

"I, uh... I didn't know you were back. Did you... just get in?"

"Yeah. First day."

The two girls stared at each other in silence for a moment. In the corner of her eye, Amara saw Chloé light up and try to move in, but Nick and Tessa held her back.

"That's... um... It's nice to see you again. Did you... get any of my texts?" Amara asked hopefully.

Vee paused for a moment, pulling out her phone. "...All of them, actually. A hundred and forty-seven."

"Oh, I... didn't realize I'd sent that many. I hope it wasn't annoying, I just... I was worried, and no one knew anything..."

Another round of awkward silence. This time it was broken by Vee, glancing over Amara's shoulder to the pile of QR codes sitting on the charity table. "So, you're fundraising for the fire relief?"

"It was Chloé's idea, since she already had her app and everything. We've actually cleaned up most of the building, so now money is the biggest roadblock."

For the first time since this conversation started, a hint of a smile crossed Vee's face. "That's... really great. I didn't know you guys had put this together! I actually just came into a tiny bit of money I don't need, might as well donate it, right?" She scanned the QR code and started to open the link.

"Wait, Vee, before you—" Amara tried to stop her, but it was too late. A picture of herself appeared on Vee's phone, her demonic features on full display. Vee froze, her breathing quickened, and her body tensed.

"Amara, what the fuck is this?"

"Please, I'm sure this looks bad, but I—"

"But what? You want to tell me that it's not what it looks like?" Vee moved closer, her hushed voice at odds with her furious demeanor. "That's what you said last time, just minutes before you almost killed me, Amara. Or have you already forgotten about that?"

"Vee, I—"

"Is this some sort of sick joke? A victory lap now that I'm out of the picture?"

Amara gasped, the accusation reopening all the pain she'd felt on Halloween. Tears welled in her eyes as she spoke. "...Is that really what you think of me?"

"I don't know what to think, Amara. I have no idea who, or what, you are." Vee didn't give her a chance to respond. She rushed past Amara, shoulder checking her as she left the conversation. The crowd nearby parted to let Vee through, and Amara already heard the onlookers whispering.

Amara stood still, doing her best to hold herself together. After a few moments, she felt a hand on her arm, and she turned to see Nick standing next to her, with the other girls right behind him.

"Aww Vee left already? Is everything okay?" Chloé asked.

"We had a bit of an argument during the... right before the fire started," Amara said quietly, her body tense.

"I had no idea how bad her injuries were! Did you see those scars? Whatever happened must have been really bad... I guess it's lucky you were with her, right?"

The tears in Amara's eyes welled, threatening to break free, and she pulled away from Nick before heading back home. The whispers from the crowd picked up, but she didn't care. Her steps quickened, and before long she was running, desperate to get home. She was suddenly back in the circle, Vee's expression slowly turning to hate before striking Amara, and the pain returned.

When she arrived home, she slammed the door behind her and collapsed on the floor. What little control she had left vanished, and she lost herself to her tears for the better part of half an hour. In time, Nick knocked on her door, and did his best to comfort her as she processed her feelings.

Later that night, after Amara had managed to pull herself together, Nick convinced her to leave the house. They went for a walk around campus, and he claimed he just wanted her to get some fresh air, but she had a feeling he had ulterior motives.

"We're not going to the Gymnastics building, are we? I'm really not in the mood," Amara asked.

"Not tonight, not after all of that. I've got an idea, but I'll fill you in later," Nick said. "I, uh... I'm sorry about what Chloé said. We haven't talked much about Halloween, but I'm pretty sure she thinks you helped Vee escape the fire."

Amara said nothing. Her mind was racing, running through her conversation with Vee for the hundredth time this evening. Could she have said anything different? Are they just inevitably going to end up fighting again?

Ugh, why did she pick today to come back? The very same day I plaster my naked demon butt all over the internet...

"Hey," Nick said softly, prodding Amara with his elbow. She looked over at him. "She was willing to talk to you, right?"

"I mean, sure, I guess."

"What did she say? Well, before she... y'know."

"First day back, she got all my texts, and she seemed happy that I was helping with the charity. At least, until she saw *how* I was helping."

"Presumably she doesn't know anything about Brandon, right?"

"Presumably she doesn't know a lot of things! She doesn't know why I shapeshifted into her, or that Derek attacked me, but so what? The road to Hell is paved with good intentions, right? What if it's like this for all demons? We start as decent people until a comedy of errors traps us in a damnation spiral?" Amara's frustration was clear, and she was having trouble keeping her voice down. Thankfully, it was late, and the campus was mostly empty.

"Hey, no need to jump to conclusions. Try to focus on now, yeah? You raised a lot of money for the charity, you cleaned up the house, and Vee didn't attack you on sight. I think there's a lot to be optimistic about here."

Amara didn't bother responding, instead just grumbling under her breath. The two continued walking for a while, and when she finally looked around at her surroundings, she found herself back on the athletic campus. "Nick, I told you I'm not in the mood tonight."

"And I told you that's not where we're going. C'mon, trust me."

They walked past the Gymnastics building, and soon enough, they were staring at the campus stadium. It was easily one of the biggest buildings on campus, and held significantly more than just the field. The large encompassing structure had tall, spacious hallways, plenty of bathrooms, multiple bays meant to house concessions and merchandise shops, and of course, passages to the many levels of bleachers. One face of the building had recently been redone to add a bunch of administrative space, a project that Amara remembered had taken much longer to finish than the school had initially wanted. There'd been some kind of drama with the football team, but she hadn't bothered paying attention.

In front of the main entrance, leaning up against the doors, was Tessa. She waved as they approached, and Amara was the first to speak.

"Okay, Tess is in on this too? What's going on here?"

"Oh, don't get too excited. Nick asked if I wanted to do some light breaking and entering tonight, and how is a girl supposed to say no to that?" As she finished, Tessa turned towards the stadium's entrance, her tattoos flared, and a few seconds later the doors swung open.

After locking the doors behind them, the trio started weaving through the halls, with Nick leading the way to the field. Now that they were alone, Amara manifested her tail and horns before summoning a few flames for light.

"So, this stadium is one of the tallest buildings on campus, right?" Nick asked.

"Uh, yeah, everyone knows that. What's your point?" Amara said.

"Well, that means the only way to see into the stadium is to be inside it. At this hour, we know the stadium is going to be empty, but even if it weren't, you'd be able to sense other people's auras, right?"

Amara's eyes flared, and she looked around. Tessa and Nick were easy enough to sense; Tessa probably had sex just a few hours ago, and Nick's aura was somewhat muted, as it had been a few days since they last fucked. "I'm not sure what the upper limits on my aura reading are, honestly. If I'm really juiced up, I can see electrical signals, but I don't know if that works through walls."

"Wait, what?" Tessa ran in front of Amara. "You can see Wi-Fi?!"

"Not right now, only when I'm full to bursting. It's only happened once, and I haven't had time to play around with it yet."

"My point is, girls," Nick said, cutting in, "that it's a surefire bet we're alone in this stadium."

As Nick finished talking, they finally walked out into the open air of the main field. It was strange seeing it at night, but there was an illicit charm in being somewhere without permission. Amara hopped over a few barriers and, in just a few minutes, stood at the edge of the main field.

"Nick, do I look like the type of girl that gets cheered up by petty crime?" Amara asked. "No offense, Tessa."

"Psh, I'm having the time of my life. You do you," the witch said.

"The crime isn't the point, Amara." Nick gestured to the field. "Hypothetically, if someone wanted to spread her wings and fly around, wouldn't this be the perfect spot?"

Amara froze, staring at the field in a whole new light. She was so accustomed to hiding her wings that she still internalized the world as a flat, two-dimensional space. At Nick's urging, however, she looked up and realized just how contained the airspace was. The wind would be muted, but it would be infinitely better than flying in the Gymnastics building.

"Nick," Amara said quietly, "I take back everything I just said. This is amazing!"

She ran out into the field, manifesting her wings as she gasped at how big the stadium looked from the field. The entire place suddenly felt like a playground, and she began stretching her wings in excitement. As she did, she ran her eyes over the bleachers, making sure she didn't see any additional signs of people.

After confirming that she didn't see any unfamiliar auras, she took a running start, and leapt into the air.

Her wings carried her higher, one powerful thrust at a time, and she already felt the wind picking up around her. Her horns buzzed, and her wings made minute adjustments as she climbed higher. She decided she would start with a few laps around the stadium, to get used to these new sensations, and then the real fun would begin. As she kept ascending, however, an unsettling heat filled her wings. It felt as if she were being pushed higher by a column of smoke. The air grew thick, soot covered her face, and she heard emergency sirens in the distance. Without warning, she saw Vee, bloodied and terrified, demonic hands wrapped around her neck.

"Amara... please..."

Before she realized what was happening, she felt a sharp pain spread through her body. Hands grabbed her shoulders, then her face, as she heard Nick calling her name.

"Amara! Amara, are you okay?"

"I... what happened?" Amara asked, disoriented.

"I don't know! You started flying, and about halfway up, you just fell out of the sky. We were too far away to catch you, and you just... hit the ground," Nick said frantically.

"I felt smoke, I saw Vee's face and I... I couldn't..." Amara squeezed Nick tight, her breathing erratic.

"C'mon Amara, in for two, out for four, breathe with me."

It took another few minutes, but eventually Nick was able to calm her down. She slowly stood up, stretching her arms and wings to see if she'd hurt herself. Thankfully, while she was pretty sure she was going to be sore in the morning, she couldn't feel any actual damage.

"So, what's the plan? Head home?" Tessa asked.

"No. I want to try again," Amara replied.

"Are you sure?" Nick said. "What if this happens again?"

"Well, it caught me by surprise, but now I'm expecting it. I think I can power through it if I prepare myself."

Amara shooed her friends away, then moved to the edge of the field. She took another running start, jumped into the air, and began climbing higher. Holding any feelings of joy at bay, she tried to focus on her objective.

The party is in the past. You're recovering, Vee is safe, and she's even talking to you again! You can let it go!

The familiar sting of smoke appeared under her wings, and before long, Vee's bloodied face returned. By the time she opened her eyes, she had crashed onto the field again, and Nick was holding her tight.

"Hey, maybe it's too soon after seeing Vee again. How about we play it safe and head home?" he asked.

"No! I can do this!" Amara pushed him aside, immediately jumping into the air again. She beat her wings furiously, desperately trying to climb into the sky, but she kept flashing back to Halloween. She tried again and again, almost a dozen times, and each time she froze up closer to the ground. After nearly half an hour of attempts, as she kneeled in the center of the field, she screamed up into the air. A torrent of fire rose from her horns, echoing her fury as she stared at the sky above her.

When the fire subsided, and her tears had dried up, Nick finally approached her. He was nervous, but it seemed that he was more worried for Amara than himself. He wrapped his arms around her, holding her tight before she finally spoke.

"I... I can't fly, Nick."

8

THE CULT

Several hours after the sun disappeared behind the horizon, Amara was happily relaxing on the couch. She rested her head in Tessa's lap, and some generic action movie was playing on the TV. The two of them had just finished dinner, and were slowly preparing for the main event of the night: Amara's infiltration of the secret cult meeting. It was of utmost importance that she be well-fed, as no one knew what to expect from Mr. Wellington.

Tessa had called dibs on sleeping with Amara before the meeting, and Amara had been teasing her all night in preparation for the fun to begin. She wore thin, stretchy athletic shorts that utterly failed to contain her ass, and the straps of her thong sat high on her hips, far above the waistband. Her low-cut shirt and matching push-up bra helped parade her tits across Tessa's vision at every turn, and Amara took plenty of opportunities to "accidentally" push her tits together and bounce them for the witch's amusement.

Entirely unwilling to help with dinner, Tessa instead relaxed on the couch while glued to her phone. Amara knew her attention was split, however; small pulses in her aura told her that Tessa was constantly staring at her body as she cooked. On several occasions, during stretches of downtime in the cooking process, Amara pinned Tessa's hands to the couch and aggressively made out with her while grinding in her lap. The poor witch was so horny that, even without direct stimulation, Amara had been lightly snacking on her arousal all night. Even now, as they cuddled on the couch, it was easy to tell that Tessa was far more interested in her tits than the train exploding on the television. Amara's tail had been playfully massaging the inside of Tessa's thigh ever since the movie started, and every time Tessa tried to cop a feel, Amara smacked her hands away. By the time the bad guys had been defeated and the credits rolled, Tessa was practically vibrating in anticipation.

"So," Amara started, "should we retire to the bedroom?"

"Fuck, yes! God, you're the absolute worst!" Tessa said, jumping off the couch. "How are you not as horny as me? You're literally a sex demon!"

"Please, I've been feeding on you all night." Amara stood up, stretching her back to continue teasing Tessa. Before reaching the bedroom, she grabbed Tessa by the waist, pushing her against the wall. Her tail wrapped around her leg, its tip brushing against Tessa's sex, and she leaned in to whisper, "Maybe you should learn how to play hard to get."

Tessa whimpered, eager to be fucked, and Amara breathed in her arousal before letting her go. The witch panted in desperation as she jumped in Amara's bed, already starting to undress. "C'mon, haven't I waited long enough? You've been jumping around in that outfit all night, and I know you smell what it's doing to me."

Amara pulled off her shorts and her tank top, but left her lingerie on. She crawled on top of Tessa, pushing her to the bed as her tail started tracing the naked curves on the witch's body. "And you know that I'm doing it on purpose."

When their lips finally met, Tessa moaned in pleasure, and her already excited aura expanded again. Amara's hands joined her tail, exploring Tessa's waist, grabbing her ass and pulling her close. Their legs interlocked, their pussies slowly grinding against each other. Tessa's hands returned the favor, eagerly grabbing Amara's ass and squeezing tight.

In response, Amara shifted downwards and kissed her friend's neck. She treasured every inch, the smell of Tessa's arousal encouraging her to keep going. Creeping higher, she playfully nibbled Tessa's ear before sliding back down and baring her fangs. She licked the witch's neck, then bit down hard, making sure to apply enough pressure to leave a fun mark. There was little Tessa loved more than bragging to her friends about her various sexual escapades.

"Fuck!" Tessa shouted. Her body shook, and her hands moved to Amara's shoulders. She held tight, her nails digging in as she wrapped her legs around

Amara. In return, Amara moved her tail between the witch's legs, circling her pussy slowly with its tip. "Please, Amara, fuck me!"

Amara giggled, continuing to feed on her friend as she teased her entrance. "Not yet, Tessa. You have to earn that privilege."

"Nngh fine! What do you want?"

"Make me cum, and then I'll consider returning the favor," Amara whispered. She pulled her tail away, despite Tessa's whining, and rolled over.

As soon as her back hit the bed, she saw Tessa's tattoos light up. Amara's bra undid itself, sliding off her body before her thong did the same. As they hit the floor, Tessa moved down on the bed and settled between Amara's legs. She began kissing her sensitive thighs, her nails tracing lines in her skin as she crept higher. Before long, her fingers had found Amara's clit, which she massaged gently.

"Mmm there's a good girl," Amara moaned, running her hands through Tessa's hair. Her tail continued teasing the desperate witch, snaking up her back before wrapping softly around her neck. Tessa loved to be dominated, and even the hint of pressure set loose another burst of pleasure for Amara to inhale.

As the witch's tongue found her clit, Amara gasped in excitement. Tessa sucked hard, pulling Amara's clit into her mouth while her tongue circled deftly around it. While this happened, Tessa gently fingered Amara's entrance, coating herself in the succubus's arousal. Amara was already incredibly wet; while she'd played coy earlier, multiple hours of teasing Tessa had her incredibly worked up. Her sex eagerly accepted Tessa's finger, and soon two more had worked their way inside. Amara gripped Tessa's hair tighter, her hips bucking as she moved in time with the witch's fingers.

Tessa's free hand moved higher, grabbing one of Amara's breasts and massaging it. Her fingers circled the demon's nipple before grabbing tight, pinching as hard as she could. Amara moaned in surprise, and Tessa soon did the same to her other nipple, trying to push Amara closer to cumming.

This continued for several more minutes, Amara eagerly feeding off her friend while feeling her pussy stretch around her fingers. She was purposely trying to prolong her first orgasm as long as possible, but Tessa's experience eventually overwhelmed her.

Her body tensed, clamping down on Tessa's fingers as both her hands grabbed her hair tight. She squeezed her thighs, holding Tessa in place as she came hard. Moaning louder and louder, she practically shrieked with pleasure as her demonic senses expanded to fill the room. Her inner fire roared in response to her orgasm, eager to be set free, but she kept everything contained long enough for her orgasm to wane.

As Amara regained her senses, she released her grip on Tessa's hair. The witch pulled back, her makeup running and her face covered with Amara's juices. She wore a look of desperation, eager to see if she'd fulfilled her end of the bargain.

"Mmm fuck, that was amazing!" Amara said. "I think you've more than earned your reward."

She pulled Tessa close, kissing her softly as she let her hands explore the witch again. Tessa's body shook with anticipation, so desperate for release that Amara wondered how fast she could make her cum. She broke off their kiss and their eyes met, Amara making it more than obvious what was about to happen.

Her tail wrapped around Tessa's waist, holding her tight, and Amara pushed her to the side. Within seconds, she had her friend face down on the bed, her arms pinned behind her. As her tail released its grip, she used her feet to kick Tessa's legs open, and soon her tail had gained access to her friend's aching pussy. She circled it slowly, the tip of her tail teasing Tessa's entrance, continuously applying pressure but refusing to push inside.

"Amara... please..." Tessa panted. Her body quivered, and although she was trying to push her hips back against Amara's tail, she was completely powerless in Amara's grasp. One of her hands held the witch down, and the other pushed through Tessa's black hair before grabbing tight. She pulled Tessa's head back, exposing her neck before leaning forward, kissing and biting her once more.

Amara finally relented, her pointed tail slipping inside Tessa's wet cunt. She wasn't at all surprised when Tessa immediately came, her walls clamping down on her tail, and Amara felt her own body shudder in response. As Tessa's first orgasm passed, Amara began slowly thrusting in and out while testing how deep she could go. Each thrust pushed a little deeper, and each time she twisted her tail to massage the inside of Tessa's pussy. As Amara continued to feed on her friend, she carefully watched for any signs of discomfort, but Tessa's body was practically a giant nerve of pure pleasure. The energy she absorbed was delicious, and her vision quickly expanded as she drank more of Tessa's arousal. The colors of her room grew more vibrant, and strange wisps of energy flew through the air above her.

Smirking with satisfaction, Amara refocused her attention on Tessa and her aura. She felt the witch's pleasure through their connection, and she knew it wouldn't be long before they were both cumming.

Her tail started moving faster, pushing as deep as possible before pulling back, her dexterous tip continuing to twist and massage the inside of Tessa's soaking pussy. Amara rocked her whole body in time with her thrusts, pushing Tessa into the bed as she fucked her harder and harder. The witch screamed with pleasure, though with her face buried in a pillow, the sound was heavily muted. Tessa's aura continued to expand, having quickly recovered from her first orgasm, and within seconds Amara had her cumming again.

The energy from Tessa's orgasm surged into Amara, whose own body tensed and shook as she started cumming as well. Her full weight fell onto Tessa, and her tail buried itself as deep as it could inside Tessa's aching cunt. Her tail shook, practically buzzing with excitement, which only served to push Tessa deeper into orgasmic bliss. Both orgasms continued for close to a minute before they finally started calming down, at which point Amara released her grip on Tessa's body.

Amara rolled off her friend, gasping as the last traces of Tessa's orgasm left her body. Tessa, now freed from her demonic grasp, shifted to lie on her side as she slid closer to Amara. The witch laid her head on Amara's chest, settling in between her breasts as she waited for her breath to return.

After another few minutes, Tessa finally found the energy to speak again. "Fucking. Hell. Amara."

"And that's why teasing you is so fun," Amara said, smirking. "Because I know how hard I can make you cum."

"Okay, but seriously? You keep this up, and I'm worried about all other sex losing its appeal in your shadow. Fuck."

Amara's tail snaked behind Tessa, casually tracing circles on her back as they relaxed. The witch moaned with contentment as she settled in, her breath slowing while she wrapped an arm around Amara's waist.

They cuddled for longer than Amara expected. She wasn't used to Tessa being this cozy after sex, and it caught her by surprise.

Well, our first time was under the cafeteria, and we needed to leave as soon as possible. After that, I was trying to buck off Vee's Enochian trap, so I guess there wasn't time to cuddle then either. Maybe I'm just underestimating how good I am in bed.

Amara chuckled to herself before grabbing her phone with her tail. She pulled it close and sighed in resignation.

It was time to get ready.

"Tess?" Amara asked. Tessa groaned, burying her face in Amara's cleavage. "C'mon, you can't fall asleep. I need to get ready to infiltrate this stupid cult."

"Ugh. You suck at pillow talk," Tessa said. She pulled off Amara, then sat up and began tracing her fingers through her short, black hair. She stared at the floor for a few moments before quietly speaking again. "You sure this'll work?"

"It's the best shot we have, Tessa. Besides, as far as we know, they don't have any serious magic yet. If I need to fight through an army of brainwashed teachers, I think I'll be fine."

Amara stood up, moving to her closet and pulling out a pile of clothes. A couple pairs of pants, multiple button-down shirts, all of which belonged to Nick. She took a deep breath, then looked back at Tessa again. "Hey, could you... turn around for this part? It's already kinda weird, even without you watching."

"You never let me have any fun," Tessa said sarcastically. She turned around, now staring at the wall next to Amara's bed.

I guess I'm as ready as I'll ever be. Here goes nothing.

Amara closed her eyes, picturing Mr. Luxnor in her head. Brown eyes, wavy brown hair, and a soft jawline with well-groomed stubble on it. Her inner fire took over, rushing through her body, and she felt a familiar tingle as her form shifted. She was taller now, with a much broader chest. Her breasts had completely disappeared, replaced with defined pec muscles and a small collection of hair. Strangest of all, she now had a dick.

Okay, this is weird.

Her new phallus was soft, and she couldn't fight the urge to explore it, even just for a moment. She flexed it, and watched as it briefly twitched in response. It felt incredibly similar to the pelvic muscles she was used to engaging with her pussy, and the entire thing felt like an extension of her clit. When her hands gently wrapped around it, she felt residual excitement from the fun she'd just had with Tessa. It began to harden, just a little, and Amara got a brief hint of what kind of pleasure a penis might be able to provide.

Now's not the time for an anatomy lesson, Amara, you've got a cult to infiltrate!

She rummaged through Nick's clothes, trying on a few options before finding something that fit well enough. Thankfully, Mr. Luxnor was in great shape, and Nick's clothes provided an adequate disguise. Putting on pants was annoying—she couldn't quite figure out what to do with the thing that now sat between her legs—but eventually she found an acceptable arrangement.

"Um, well... I think it worked?" Amara said, her voice now much deeper.

Tessa turned around, her eyes racing over Amara's new form. "Wow, that looks spot on. For what it's worth, you've got a great eye for shapeshifting. Is that even something you can be bad at?"

"Beats me. Maybe it comes naturally to succubi, maybe it's because I've got so much photography experience? Either way, I'm not complaining. Clothes look good?"

"Looks alright to me. Plus, I'll bet this cult is mostly guys, and they don't give a shit about clothes. You sure you're not supposed to have, like, a hooded black cloak or something?"

"I really hope not. If they call me out, hopefully I can say I lost it. From what we overheard, Mr. Luxnor was already on shaky ground, so maybe it'll be in character." Amara looked over her new form in the mirror, then walked around her room a few times to get used to how this body moved. "So, reminders. I'm not going to bring my phone, I can't risk losing it, or having it give away my identity."

"And I'm going to wait behind the Science Building for you, I know." Tessa half-heartedly quoted their earlier conversations with Nick, when they'd planned out what to do tonight.

Amara checked her pockets one last time, ensuring that nothing on her might reveal her identity. She looked around the room, watching electrical signals bounce back and forth, and took one last breath of Tessa's lingering arousal. Lastly, she snapped her fingers, summoning a small flame and letting it dance between her fingers. With her powers fully intact, there was nothing else to test.

"Alright," Amara said, "let's do this."

It was fortunate that the cult was meeting so late. They obviously picked obscure hours so as to not be discovered, but Amara was thankful that their secrecy made it easy to cross campus without being recognized. The walk also gave her more time to get used to this body, to figure out how men were supposed to move. Her walk across campus took several small detours as she ran up and down stairs, even vaulting several short walls, to adjust to her form.

The entrance to Lysander Hall had already been unlocked, which confirmed she was in the right place. Once inside the elevator, she pressed the secret button Tessa had located earlier in the week, and started descending.

It was immediately apparent that the elevator was going much deeper than the basement. The floor indicator numbers stopped glowing as she traveled, and it took nearly a minute to reach her destination. The elevator dinged, the doors opened, and she took a deep breath to shake off her nerves.

A simple stone hallway stretched out in front of her. Several dim lightbulbs glowed overhead, leading the way further into this strange, underground complex. Down the hall, she saw a large room with several shapes moving around. With one last nervous breath, Amara tried to get into character; she wasn't a hot, young college girl, she was a cocky teacher that was eager for a taste of magic. She belonged here, this was nothing unusual, and she didn't have to worry about anything.

She walked casually but briskly down the hall, soon entering the main chamber. It was bigger than she expected, roughly the size of a school gymnasium or possibly the gymnastics building. She saw entrances to other hallways elsewhere in the chamber, and made a note to explore those at a later date once the facility was empty. Roughly a dozen feet in from each of the corners sat a large supporting pillar, all of them containing strange decorative carvings, and in the center of the chamber a crowd of people had formed into a large circle.

Frustratingly, just as Tessa had sarcastically predicted, everyone present had donned a large, hooded cloak, though they wore red instead of black. Several people turned to look at her, their faces filled with silent judgement, but one person broke from the crowd and walked over to meet her.

"Garrett!" the stranger whispered. "You're almost late, what are you thinking?"

She recognized this man by his voice; he was the second person she'd overheard underneath Brandt Hall. "Phone's busted, I lost track of time," Amara whispered back.

The deeper voiced man grabbed Amara's arm, pulling her to the side. Thankfully, she saw he was leading her to a box of cloaks, and she sighed in relief as she grabbed one from the box. Pulling the hood over her head, she rushed to take her place in the circle.

As she fell in formation with everyone else, she finally got a look at what they were all standing around. In the center of the room, much larger than any she'd seen before, sat another magic circle. It thrummed with power, slowly pulsing with light as she examined it. She also saw heavy traces of some kind of energy leaking from it, as if the circle had its own aura.

When she tore her eyes from the circle, she was able to get a look at the other people present. She recognized about a third of them, and among those, most of them were teachers. Some of the cultists appeared younger, and she suspected they were students; she even recognized one of them. His hair was obscured by the red hood, but Amara remembered his blonde goatee from her fundraising event. This was Chris, the guy that had printed out her picture and asked for an autograph. Before she had a chance to look around at the other students, she heard footsteps echoing out from a side hallway and turned to pay attention.

Entering the main room from a different hallway, carrying himself with far more confidence than he likely deserved, was Sebastian Wellington. Much like everyone else present, he wore a deep red cloak, though his had additional gold lining on the outside. He kept his hood off his head, instead gathering it around his neck, and Amara paid close attention to his features on the off chance she ever needed to impersonate him.

As he approached the circle, an insufferable smile on his face, two cultists briefly stepped back to allow him inside.

"Gentlemen!" Mr. Wellington said. "The time has come!"

Hushed murmurs traveled through everyone present, though they were quickly silenced when Mr. Wellington held up a hand.

"We stand here today, stronger than ever, and ready to embrace our destinies. I couldn't have done this without your help; each and every one of you has proven yourself to me countless times. While there may have been some... setbacks," Sebastian's icy stare settled on Amara, "they are insignificant in the face of what we are about to accomplish."

Amara heard several people chuckle, and she did her best to appear ashamed of her actions.

"However, before we take our next steps, I have an exciting announcement. We have a new member!" His words rang through the large room, and Amara saw another figure leave one of the side hallways, a hood blocking their face. "This young man has proven he has the drive and the passion to further our goals. Even before I found him, he had already begun to unravel the magical secrets of this campus, and his aptitude is without question. I want you all to welcome Brandon Nowak!"

Her eyes wide, Amara watched as this new member pulled his hood down to reveal the same person that had tried, repeatedly, to claim her as his own.

That bitch!

"Thank you so much for your kind words, Sir. I promise to do everything I can to help us take that which is owed to us." Brandon lowered his head slowly, bowing in respect before stepping back and joining the circle.

Would he tell Mr. Wellington about me? He doesn't know we're trying to stop the cult, but there's no way he wouldn't use the knowledge of my existence to try and earn status here...

Fuck!

Amara didn't have time to dwell on the ramifications of this new discovery, as Mr. Wellington had begun talking again.

"Now, with that business attended to, I understand you all have many questions about what we're doing here. I have, of course, given you all small gifts already; enhanced physique, stamina, and mental acuity. However, those gifts are only the first step of your journey. They exist to prepare you for our true goal: ascension!"

Several members gasped, others smirked in anticipation as their leader continued.

"By weakening the seals, we have given ourselves the ability to commune with beings greater than us. They hold wisdom, power, and abilities far beyond your comprehension, and they are willing to share those gifts with us. You see, their presence is limited, and they cannot survive in our world as they are. However, by offering ourselves as vessels, we can combine our minds with theirs, and ascend to a new level of existence!"

Mr. Wellington's voice echoed throughout the chamber, his excitement palpable. Amara was shocked so many people were on board with his claims; did he truly have them so convinced they weren't just sacrificing themselves?

"And to demonstrate my good intentions, I will be delaying my own ascension, giving it instead to the worthy among you. Mr. Roberts, if you could please step into the circle."

Wait, Roberts, where have I heard that name before?

Amara watched as one of the cultists stepped forward, removing his hood. Once the fabric fell from his face, Amara fought to hold back a gasp. In front of her stood Alex Roberts, Nick's friend from high school, the same guy that had been relentlessly flirting with her the last few weeks. His wide smile betrayed his excitement, and he beamed as if he'd just won the lottery.

No!

"It is an honor to be here, Sir, and I welcome this gift with open arms," Alex said.

"After tonight, you will each ascend in turn, and in one week's time I will celebrate our success with an ascension of my own!" Mr. Wellington said. A chorus of cheers erupted, and Amara played along as best she could until the leader finally signaled their silence.

He's going to get himself killed! I need to say something!

But, if I do, I'm completely outing myself. Mr. Luxnor would have already known about Alex's involvement. If I surrender this opportunity, how many more will lose their lives? I don't even know what creatures they're communing with!

Alex centered himself in the circle, and Amara watched everyone present step backwards. With a comfortable amount of space between them and the circle, Mr. Wellington began speaking again, though she didn't recognize the words he spoke. She suspected they might be Latin and, as he spoke, various runes in the large magic circle flared to life. She also saw glowing runes on Alex and Mr. Wellington, though she knew she could only see them because of her enhanced vision; the runes were otherwise completely hidden underneath their clothes.

How have I not seen those runes before? Could I have stopped this if I'd noticed earlier?

The energy of the magic circle continued to pulse, the lights growing brighter and the strange aura intensifying. A soft wind picked up around Alex, causing his cloak to billow and dance. After another minute of chanting, the magic reached a climax, and Amara saw a burst of energy break free from the circle. It flew around Alex several times before ascending into the air and diving down into his body.

Alex gasped, throwing his head back as he floated several feet into the air. Unnatural energy burst from his eyes and mouth, nearly blinding Amara as she watched. When the magic finally dispersed, and the energy in the circle quieted again, he fell back to the ground. The chamber was deathly silent. Several moments passed, then Alex took a breath and stood up. He grinned, an entirely unnatural smile appearing on his face, before opening his eyes and looking up at Mr. Wellington.

His eyes were blood red, and they glowed with ominous intent. Amara watched as his aura came to life, though it didn't resemble Alex's aura at all; in fact, there wasn't a trace of the energy that had once belonged to Nick's friend. This aura felt sinister, malevolent, and most terrifying of all, it felt strangely familiar. Amara stared at this new creature, a horrifying sense of kinship forming in her gut, and she knew without a doubt she was looking at a demon.

Fuck. Fuck! Why would he do this?!

A horrible pit of despair formed in Amara's gut, and it took all her strength to prevent herself from throwing up. Alex had been good friends with Nick for years, and now he was gone. She'd just watched someone die, sell their body to a demon, and she'd done nothing.

"Sebastian," the demon hissed, "it is a pleasure to finally make your acquaintance."

"We welcome you to our world, and rejoice that the ascension ceremony was a success," Mr. Wellington said.

"Indeed it was. I am reborn, I have transcended, and I am eager to see others share in these gifts." The demon's nose twitched, and an uncomfortable look crossed its face. "Although, it appears I was under the wrong impression. I assumed I was to be the first."

Mr. Wellington hesitated, though quickly masked his concern. "I can say with absolute confidence, Alex, that you are. This ceremony hasn't been performed before now."

"Then why do I smell another?" Another pause, and the creature wearing Alex's body began to look around the chamber. "I smell... excitement? No, this is something different, more potent. It reeks of... yes, this is lust. There is a succubus present."

Shit. Not good!

Across the circle, Amara saw Brandon's eyes go wide in surprise. Her body grew tense, and her breathing quickened. She quickly glanced at the hallway leading to the doorway, wondering how fast she could get there. Before she could think of a plan, however, the demon's blood-red eyes met hers. It raised its hand, pointing at Amara as it grinned with sadistic pleasure.

"This one. She wears his face, but she is not him!"

Every face in the chamber turned to face Amara, and she froze. Tension filled the chamber, and she didn't know what to do. Her mind raced through all her options: Run? Fight? Before she thought of anything to say, the person standing next to her grabbed her arm.

The touch shook her to her senses. With her free hand, she grabbed the stranger and pulled him close, throwing him to the ground between her and the rest of the cultists.

"Don't let her escape!" Mr. Wellington yelled.

Amara sprang into action, running for the exit as fast as she could. She felt more hands reach for her, grabbing her cloak to try and hold her back. With a burst of flames, she burned away the ties on her cloak and kept running.

She had no idea how fast everyone else was, or if the demon was in pursuit as well. She only heard the sounds of dozens of footsteps chasing after her. With a flick of her wrist, she summoned a wall of hellfire behind her, filling the hallway with a veritable inferno. She heard several people crash into each other, and when she reached the elevator, she finally dared to look behind her.

No one was foolish enough to cross her wall of flames. To keep them scared, she held out her hand again and intensified the fire, the flames turning purple as she nervously slammed the call button behind her.

Everyone paused, the cultists unable to cross the flames, and Amara unable to leave until the elevator arrived. As she waited, she saw the crowd part, and Mr. Wellington stood just behind the wall of flames. Anger filled his eyes, and he glared at Amara as the elevator door opened. She stepped inside, urging the fire to jump out at the cult leader, but he didn't so much as flinch as the flames threatened to take him.

Their eyes met, and Amara felt Mr. Wellington's hatred. She couldn't bring herself to look away, and after another moment, the doors closed. She collapsed against the back railing, panting in exhaustion, as she waited for the elevator to bring her to safety.

9
TENSE NEGOTIATION

Amara's heart raced as she gripped the railing behind her, and the slow ascent towards Lysander Hall stretched out for eternity as she fought back a panic attack. Could the cult stop the elevator? Call it back? What about the demon, what could it do? Could it sprout claws and chase her up the elevator shaft? She hated the idea of fighting another demon, especially one now wearing the body of Nick's friend.

When she tried to calm her nerves by looking at the reflective metal walls, she flinched in surprise as she saw Mr. Luxnor's face. She briefly considered returning to her own form, but hated the idea of needing to explain her masculine outfit to any potential strangers. Instead, desperate to shake off any association with the cult, she shifted her body into Nick's.

A soft ping punctured her thoughts, signaling the end of the ascent. Breaking into a sprint, she rushed from the building and headed towards her designated meeting spot with Tessa. Breath ragged, heart pounding, she briefly flashed back to the ritual she'd just witnessed. Alex removing his hood, floating into the air, his aura being consumed by the terrifying presence of a demon. By the time Amara finally found Tessa, yawning while she leaned against the back wall of the Science Building, Amara had broken out into a cold sweat.

"Tessa!" Amara gasped, falling to her hands and knees.

"Nick?" Tessa looked up, momentarily surprised, then paused to narrow her eyes. "No, wait, Amara?"

"Yes, Amara! I just escaped the meeting and they're— Fucking hell, Tessa, Alex is— He's not—" Her vision began to blur as she recalled Alex's last moments, and she didn't know how to pull herself together.

Kneeling in front of Amara, Tessa grabbed her chin and brought their eyes together. Amara was tearing up, on the verge of hyperventilating, and Tessa lightly tapped the side of her face. "Hey, pull yourself together, Amara. We're in this together, I'm not going to let anything happen to you, alright?"

Physical touch helped. Having a friend here, someone to ground her, made it possible for her to hold back her panicked thoughts. She took a deep breath, in for two, then released it, out for four.

Amara nodded slowly, then Tessa spoke up again. "Now tell me what happened, okay? What's this about Alex?"

"It's so much worse than we thought, Tess. You thought they might be trying to bring over a demon, but they're not stopping there. They're summoning dozens! Every single member of the cult is going to become a vessel for a demon!" Amara forced herself to take another deep breath, though this one shook with fear. "And Alex, he's... he's in the cult. Well, he was, at least."

"Was? Fuck, are you saying they—"

"He did it willingly, Tessa. He wanted it, he was overjoyed that Wellington picked him first. I-I watched him die, Tess!"

Stunned, Tessa fell backwards to sit on the sidewalk. "That's... holy shit, Amara. I knew this was going to be bad, but I never thought it would be someone we knew. I mean, fuck! Nick's known Alex for years! What the fuck was he thinking?"

"We need to get back to my place, Tess. Nick's smart, he can help us figure something out, and he deserves to... to know."

Nodding, Tessa pocketed her phone before standing up. She helped Amara to her feet, and the two began quickly walking back to Amara's apartment. Tessa seemed unusually quiet, which unnerved Amara. Was she just as shaken as Amara was about losing Alex? To Amara's knowledge, the two of them had barely ever spoken, and Tessa was hardly the type to get emotional over strangers.

"How do I know you're really you?" Tessa finally asked. "That you aren't some other demon disguised as Nick, pretending to be you?"

"Really, Tessa, now? What on Earth would make you think..." Amara paused, thinking over her own shapeshifting abilities. "Actually, no, you're right. That's a terrifying thought. Um, well, you love that thing I do with my tail, you were the first person to fuck my ass, and—Oh! My fire is purple!" Amara held out a hand, summoning a small mote of flame and watching as it danced and flickered with purple edges. She let herself get lost in the flames for a moment, appreciating that Tessa was giving her something to think about other than Alex.

"Good enough for me," Tessa said, shoving her hands in her pockets. "Still, put that shit out before someone sees you."

"How big of a problem do you think that might be? Do you think the other demons will be able to shapeshift the way I can?"

"Again, Amara, we have no idea what you are. I mean, I'm pretty sure you're not a demon inhabiting a human vessel, but we have no way to prove that. I certainly hope no one else can shapeshift, but just in case... what about a code word?"

"A code word? Like a secret call and response or something?" Amara asked.

"Yeah, but ideally something abstract. Something that's never out of place to ask, something that's not obviously a probing question..." Tessa paused, idly playing with her lip ring as she thought. "What's for dinner tonight?"

"Really Tess, now?" Amara asked. After a quick glare from Tessa, Amara pieced it together. "Oh. Oh! That's a good idea! You don't think it'll get confusing?"

"I mean, it would be pretty easy to find other ways to talk about food."

"Good point. Hm." Amara paused, thinking over all the food she'd recently learned she enjoyed cooking, trying to think of something that felt appropriate. "How about hand-seared chicken?" Amara held up a hand, conjuring a few flames to dance across her palm.

Tessa nodded. "I like that. For me, I'll say... lentil soup."

"Short, but to the point. Do you actually—"

"I fucking hate lentil soup," Tessa said. The girls looked at each other, attempting to find some levity amidst this grave situation, but the tension proved hard to break. Once they arrived at Amara's place, and Nick adjusted to looking at a duplicate of himself, he quickly ushered them in before locking and bolting the door.

Over the course of the next half hour, Amara explained everything she'd witnessed at the ritual. She recounted the appearance of all the cultists as best she could, the design of the magic circle, and the surprise appearance of Brandon. She explained Mr. Wellington's goals, the fact that he was hoping to turn everyone in the cult into demons, and his promise that his own ascension was only a week away.

"A week?!" Tessa said. "How are we supposed to stop this in less than a week?!"

"We'll figure something out, Tessa. We have to," Nick said quietly. Although his words were directed at Tessa, he was still looking at Amara with a pointed look. "Amara, was there anything else? You've got that look on your face like you're hiding something."

Amara swallowed nervously as she averted her eyes from Nick's. "Um, well, yeah. There's one other thing. During the ritual, I... I saw Alex there."

Nick gasped, his eyes flicking back and forth as he processed Amara's words. "Alex? No, that's not... that doesn't make sense! He's a great guy, he would never get involved with something like that! Fuck! I'm texting him, I have to talk him out of—"

Reaching over, Amara wrapped a hand around Nick's phone before he had a chance to write a text. "Nick, that's not going to work. He went first."

Another pause. Nick looked at Amara, then to Tessa, then back to Amara as he started panicking. "No. NO!" He jumped to his feet, sending the stool underneath him clattering to the ground. "I just saw him earlier today! We were making plans to put together more pick-up games! Why would he bother if he was planning on throwing everything away?!"

"He didn't know, Nick!" Amara walked over to Nick and grabbed his shoulders. "They don't know what's really happening; Wellington dressed it up to sound like they were joining together with some greater entity."

"Oh God, he's just killing people. He's straight up offering them up to demons and we're just sitting here?!" Nick broke away from Amara, frantically pacing back and forth. "What else can we do? Can we call the cops? If we ignore all the magic stuff, maybe we could pretend that Wellington is holding people hostage or something. Amara, you can pretend like you escaped and lead them right to his doorstep!"

"Nick, I know you're new to all this, so I'll try to be nice; cops and magic do *not* mix well," Tessa said, looking over from her seat at the counter. "On a broad scale, we don't want large institutions learning about magic, and often witches put in serious effort to keep everything hidden from cops and the government. On a smaller scale? We already know that Mr. Wellington has paid off cops in the past, and what if these demons can jump hosts? Suddenly they're armed with guns, body armor, and all sorts of nonsense. Amara and I are the best chance we have at stopping this, we just need to stick together."

"Fuck... Alex, I..." Tears welled in the corner of Nick's eyes, and he moved to the couch before sitting down again.

"Let's focus on what we know," Amara said, hoping to change the topic and give Nick space. "We've completely lost the element of surprise; demons can sniff each other out, and Brandon will have already shared that I'm a succubus and you're a witch. My presence at this meeting also means they know we're trying to stop them. What is our actual goal here?"

"We have to shut down the portal," Tessa said. "I've gotten pretty good at reading the signatures of these circles, and I think I could reverse the changes they made if I had enough time."

"Time is gonna be hard to get. There's no way they let us waltz in there and spend a few hours studying the damn thing. Can you fight at all?" Amara asked.

"Sure, I can fight, but there's a big difference between getting in random scrapes as a kid and fighting actual demons. My telekinesis won't be able to affect them directly, but if I'm forced to defend myself, I have a knife." The tattoos on Tessa's head began to glow, and her switchblade floated out of her bag. It opened on its own, then ominously made a few pretend stabs through the air in front of her. "Realistically? I'm batting way outside my league here. Even if I were stronger, or had better magic, I can't fight if I'm trying to reverse-engineer the circle."

"So, I'd have to keep you safe the whole time," Amara sighed. The task in front of them seemed nigh impossible. "I don't know if I can keep you safe that long, especially against a whole army. I have no idea how strong they are, or if they're resistant to fire like I am. Plus, what if the people are still alive somewhere inside? The thought of turning into a killer, I... I don't think I can handle that."

"They're asking for it!" Tessa shouted. "They're turning their souls over to this stupid cult, and they're doing it happily. Killing them is the kindest thing you can do!"

"But they're people! Living, breathing, people that are trying to find their place in the world!" Amara briefly flashed back to her actions on Halloween, tears forming in the corners of her eyes. "They deserve a second chance. Everyone does."

"News flash, Amara, but they don't give a fuck about you! If you hesitate, even for a moment, they will kill you. Or worse, they'll force you into slavery, just like Brandon tried to do! Have you forgotten that he's in this cult now? Does he deserve a second chance after everything he's done?"

"I'm not a killer, Tessa." Amara locked eyes with Tessa, and doubt crept into her voice. "But... I'm willing to defend myself. If they force my hand... I don't know."

From his spot on the couch, Nick cleared his throat and stood up. He seemed more in control for now, but Amara made a note to check in with him later. "Okay, there's a lot going on. Let's back up, take a breath, and review what we know. A week is better than nothing, and it's safe to assume that everyone in this cult is either a student or a teacher. A few students going missing is one thing, but teachers? There's no way Mr. Wellington can cancel that many classes indefinitely."

"You think demons are gonna wander around campus and teach music theory?" Tessa asked, her voice full of sarcasm. Nick walked back over to Amara and Tessa, a serious look in his eyes.

"I don't know how this stuff works, but wouldn't it make sense if the demons could access the memories of their hosts? Otherwise, a whole bunch of people are going to start looking into these disappearances, and I doubt Wellington wants that kind of attention. But, again, we have a week. If we keep tabs on the teachers Amara saw, and if they're still teaching during the week, that means you two might have a window of opportunity to sneak down there."

Amara thought to herself for a moment, mulling over Nick's idea. "That's a pretty decent plan. We can track their movements, look up their schedules, and see if we can find a time where most of them are busy."

"Plus, that gives me something to do," Nick said. "I'm more than happy to do some social media research while you two handle the fighting and the magic."

"While we're killing time throughout the week," Tessa looked at Amara, "should we start fucking more than usual?"

"That's what you're worried about?" Amara asked, a deadpan look on her face.

"It's a serious question! You get stronger when you fuck, like when you hooked up with Mr. Luxnor and were suddenly able to see Wi-Fi! How do we know that lots of extra sex, or sex with new people, doesn't unlock more abilities?"

"I didn't gain anything new after you and I started fucking," Amara pointed out. "Plus, Nick and I have slept together dozens of times, and my abilities always seem to show up randomly. I doubt there's a lifehack to speeding up this transformation, and we don't even know if there are more changes coming. For all we know, this is the end of the road."

"But we should at least try, right? Obviously I'm willing, but I know for a fact my partners think you're hot. You also just sold a bunch of slutty photos, I'll bet half the campus is dreaming of hooking up with you at this point."

"Excuse me, they were sultry and suggestive, not slutty," Amara said, defending her photography skills.

"Oh, whatever, you know what I mean. We just... we need something more, something to give us an edge."

Amara paused for a moment, thinking to herself. She didn't like the idea of trying to force additional transformations, but she knew Tessa was right. As things stood, their chances of stopping the cult seemed pretty slim. She supposed she could try to get in more fighting practice, but the strength difference between her and Nick would make that difficult.

Suddenly, another answer presented itself. She felt silly for not thinking of it earlier, and she knew Tessa wasn't going to like it. "Tess, there's too much at stake for us to play it safe. I think we need help."

"I'm not disagreeing, but there's no one to ask! What, do you want to give Nick a gun and hope for the best? I told you before, we're on our own."

"That's where you're wrong. We just need someone who already knows about magic, won't spill our secrets, and perhaps, I don't know, has years of experience training to fight demons?"

Tessa glared at Amara. "No. Absolutely not, never in a million years."

"It's literally her life's purpose! She probably knows more about them than both of us combined!"

"She tried to kill you! Does that mean nothing?!" Tessa asked, now angrily pacing around the living room.

"She was confused! She thought I was framing her, purposely manipulating everyone to turn against her! And she was most upset about the fact that I lied, that I kept my identity to myself. If we reach out, we can give her the chance we should have last time!"

"Look, I get you're upset with me for telling you to stay quiet, but it's not that simple anymore. We didn't even know she was an angel back then, and that makes it so much worse! The church is filled with pompous, egotistical maniacs who are convinced they're the only ones that can do the right thing. If we invite Vee into this, how do you know she won't backstab you the instant she gets a chance?"

Both girls were yelling now, and Nick had quietly backed into a corner to avoid getting dragged into the argument. With a deep breath, Amara closed her eyes and quieted her voice. "Tessa, this wasn't a question. Tomorrow, after classes, I'm going to Vee's and telling her everything. End of story."

"You need me to stop the cult, Amara. I'm the only one that can reverse-engineer the circle." The witch's voice was quiet, but intense. The hints of her threat were obvious.

"So, what's more important, Tess? Do you care more about stopping this cult, or shutting Vee out of your life?" When Tessa didn't answer, Amara moved closer and softly grabbed the witch's arms. "Look, this is bigger than both of us. I'm asking you to trust me, just this once. If I'm wrong, well, I already know I can beat Vee in a fight. But... I have to do this, Tess. I have to try."

Tessa stared at the ground, refusing to meet Amara's gaze. "How can you trust her? After what she tried to do to you?"

"I've been friends with her since college started, Tess, and so have you. Do you think that whole year was a lie? That everything we did together meant nothing?"

Without saying anything, Tessa shoved her face in Amara's shoulder and wrapped her arms around her. As they hugged, Amara briefly locked eyes with Nick and smiled. When the witch finally pulled back, Amara couldn't help but notice that tears had pooled near her eyes. "So, what, are you going to make me tell Chloé next?"

"Hey, I understand that you know more about this whole 'world of magic' thing than I do. How about we keep everything a secret, but if someone gets involved, even a little, we tell them everything."

"...I guess that's fine," Tessa mumbled. "Thanks for... I dunno. Talking me down. I'm not used to working with other people like this. It's weird."

Amara smiled, then leaned in to plant a quick kiss on Tessa's lips. "We all want the same thing, right? I'm just glad I didn't have to invoke... *the nuclear option*."

"The what?" Tessa asked.

"Oh, you know... withholding sex until you agree with me."

"You wouldn't dare! You monster!"

With a devious smirk, Amara wrapped her arms around Tessa and picked her up. Both girls started laughing, the witch playfully struggling to try and escape. "C'mon, it's like four in the morning, and I'm exhausted. Tell your partners you're spending the night here; I'm not letting you walk home after that stupid cult meeting. Nick, you cool taking the couch?"

Nick nodded, clearly relieved that the fight had resolved itself. "Perfectly fine by me. Glad we all agree on a plan."

After everyone had plugged in their phones and set their alarms, they settled in to go to sleep. For the first time, Amara and Tessa spent the night together, wrapped up in each other's arms.

The following day was officially Vee's first day of classes. She'd been absent for several weeks, but thankfully she only needed to share half of the real story. She had, truthfully, been injured in the fire, and needed to take time to recover. Dozens of friends and casual acquaintances eagerly chatted her up, talking about Derek's confession and asking about her recovery. Some of them tried to ignore the giant scars on her face, others couldn't resist the urge to try and convince her how much cooler she looked.

She did her best to bury her face in her books, talking with her professors about all the work she'd missed, and most of her teachers were more than happy to give her time to make up all her assignments. The one exception was her music theory teacher, who was normally an incredibly delightful person; he seemed exceptionally rude today, and she couldn't figure out why.

Vee managed to catch Chloé during their lunch hour and did her best to explain why things were so awkward right now; she hated the thought of Chloé getting caught in the crossfire of her fight with Amara. Vee stressed that she needed time to adjust, and hopefully things could go back to normal soon. She had no idea how truthful her own words were, sadly, as she had no idea what she wanted to happen. Her first goal had been to return to school, but that was done now. What was she supposed to do next?

She was currently ignoring the problem, sitting on her couch while organizing her homework. Her apartment had been cleaned to the best of her ability, and most of the traces of her holy crusade had been disposed of. The only thing that remained were her wards, meant to keep her safe should any demons decide to invade. She didn't feel comfortable taking them down quite yet. Besides, they were defensive, right? They would only activate if Amara decided to attack.

Her thoughts were interrupted by a knock at the door. She hadn't been expecting anyone, but with everyone on campus throwing a pity party for her at the moment, she knew of a few dozen people it might be. She was incredibly shocked, then, to find Tessa and Amara waiting on her doorstep.

"I... what do you want?" Vee snapped. She was not ready to have this conversation.

"Hey Vee, I'm... I'm glad you're back!" Amara said. She seemed nervous, and Vee couldn't help but suspect this was more than a casual visit.

"...No thanks to you. Looking for more people to enthrall? Or do you need more hot co-eds for your next porn shoot?"

Why did I say that?

Amara winced; it was obvious how much Vee's words had stung.

"N-no, I just—" Amara started, but Tessa cut her off.

"We need your help, Vee. There's something bad happening on campus, and we're trying to stop it, but we can't do it alone."

Vee bit her lip, her body full of tension as she tried to figure out what was happening. "Why come to me? Why should I trust either of you?"

"Hey, we could say the same about you, but we're at least making an effort to reach out!" Tessa said. She was clearly upset, but Vee also noticed that the argument was making Amara uncomfortable.

With a heavy sigh, Vee kicked open her door and gestured the two inside. "Alright, fine, just get in here."

Tessa walked through first, though not without a heavy glare directed at Vee. Amara, on the other hand, smiled as she approached the door. When her body attempted to cross the threshold, however, the Enochian wards activated. Powerful, angelic energy surged through Amara, and she winced in pain before getting thrown back into the hallway.

Shit, the wards! C'mon Vee, get your act together!

Before Vee could respond, Tessa grabbed her shirt and shoved her against her front door. "Vee, what the fuck?"

"I-I'm sorry! I forgot about my wards!"

"Yeah, likely fucking story," Tessa hissed. She let Vee go, running to Amara's side to help her up.

"Can we just talk about this here? How bad can it be?" Vee asked.

Amara glared up at her, her face still twisted in pain as she fought to regain her breath. When she finally spoke, her words were rushed and bitter. "No, I get it. Tess, you go inside and talk with Vee. I'll just stay out here and keep watch."

"Ugh, fine, but you scream if something attacks, okay?" With Amara now standing, and seemingly recovered, Tessa turned to Vee and grabbed her arm. "You, me, inside. We have a lot to talk about."

If something attacks? What the fuck have they gotten into?

The door closed behind them, and now Vee and Tessa stood alone in the entryway. Vee started talking, still unsure what was happening. "Look, Tess, I'm sorry about the—"

"What the fuck is wrong with you?" Tessa said, interrupting her. "Even setting aside everything you've done, now you're attacking Amara's photography? We both know how much that means to her! And I know, for a fact, that you don't have a problem with sex work. We have friends that run OnlyFans accounts! I've been in their videos! Are you gonna try to kill me next?"

"This isn't about that! I just... I don't know what's happening!"

"Which is why we're here, but apparently you're still out for blood!" Tessa paced back and forth, her anger more than apparent. "That poor girl has been beating herself up for weeks, trying desperately to make up for what happened on Halloween, and you can't even spare the time to talk with her?"

Vee stayed quiet, doing her best to process everything before responding, but it felt like her thoughts were frozen. How could she trust that Tessa was even telling the truth? Before she could think of anything, Tessa continued talking.

"Ugh, I can't believe she forced me to come here. For the record, I don't think we can trust you. You're lucky Amara's a better person than I am."

"Wait, she forced you here? Tessa, I know I've made mistakes, but she's a demon! Can you honestly say that she's in the right, using violence to get what she wants?"

"What?" Tessa asked. "No, not violence. She just threatened to stop sleeping with me."

Surprise crossed Vee's face, and she stepped closer to Tessa. "First Nick, but now you? Tessa, this is what succubi do; they use sex to enthrall people, and you start losing track of what's right and wrong. In the end, you belong to her, body and soul. How do you know you're being objective here?"

"Because there's a fucking cult! They broke the planar seals on campus, and they're summoning a demon army! That's why Amara wants your help, Vee, because we're trying to stop this!"

"Oh, someone's trying to summon a demon? Why should I care? How about I greet them with open arms! Heck, maybe I'll start fucking them, since apparently it doesn't matter!" Vee jabbed a finger to Tessa's chest, her words quiet and furious. "Don't you dare try to convince me that demons are a threat to this campus while also being mad that I tried to stop one on Halloween."

"She's your friend, Vee, and you stabbed her in the back! You try to banish her to Hell, then you try to kill her, and you're mad she defended herself?!"

"You call this self-defense?" Vee pointed to the scars on her face. "I tried to run from that fight, but she wouldn't let me. She held me down, beat me within an inch of my life, and I'm supposed to pretend that everything's fine?"

"She's not asking you to pretend like nothing happened, Vee. She just wants to talk; she wants a chance to fix things." Tessa, surprisingly, calmed down slightly. Vee suspected her two friends had talked extensively about what to say, as this level-headed behavior was quite unusual from Tessa.

"Yet, conveniently, she couldn't do that before? When it mattered most, when I was breaking down in her arms, she lied to me."

"Yeah? And when were you planning on telling us you were an angel?"

"I... that's different," Vee said, caught off guard.

"Why? Because you're better than us?"

"N-no, that's not what I—"

"But you were thinking it, weren't you?" Tessa said, cutting her off. "I've met people like you before, Vee. Nothing is more important than God's plan, and you'll trample over everyone you don't agree with to carry out His will. We couldn't *possibly* understand what it's like to be as special as you."

"Wait, you've met... right. You're a witch."

"I am! You want to say something about that too? C'mon, I'm ready for it, lay it on me. Am I an affront to nature? A blemish on the face of humanity?"

Vee stammered, unsure what to say. Tessa was right, the church loved to paint witches as lost souls, eager to trade their humanity for power, but Vee's training had mostly focused on demons. It was clear Tessa was speaking from experience, the words she used sounded all too familiar.

Tessa collapsed on the couch, burying her face in her hands before sighing heavily. "You want to know why I'm here? Honestly?"

Silence filled the air, and the girls briefly looked at each other before Tessa continued. "I'm here for Amara. I don't think we can trust you, but... she's miserable, Vee. She won't stop beating herself up for what she did, and I think she's too nervous to tell you everything she's done to try and fix things. For fuck's sake, she even got Derek to confess!"

"I... I didn't know that," Vee stammered.

"And you know what else? Every time I argue with her, every time she's defending your actions, she always says you were most upset about the lying, but that wasn't even her fault! She wanted to tell you everything but... I talked her out of it. If you want to be mad at anyone, be mad at me."

Vee went quiet, hesitant to believe what she was being told. She had no reason to believe anything Tessa said, especially after confirming that she was sleeping with Amara. Vee walked closer, sitting across from Tessa before speaking. "Tess... I've studied demons my whole life. My divine purpose is to hunt them down, to protect mankind from them. Yes, they're strong, they can burn down buildings and need to eat souls to survive, but that's not the worst of it. Their biggest tool, the oldest trick in the book, is making themselves look sympathetic. They play the victim, convince you how misunderstood they are, and they prey on our desire to help. The only way to resist them, the strongest defense we have, is to never listen to them, never give them the chance to start spinning their lies. The instant you start to doubt, they've already won."

"You realize how fascist that sounds, right?" Tessa said.

"This is bigger than that, Tess! We have thousands of examples, all throughout history, of people consorting with demons and losing everything! Now you come to my door, you ask for my help, but how can I trust you? How do I know she isn't using you as a pawn in some bigger scheme?"

"What bigger scheme? If she wanted you dead, she would have killed you on Halloween!"

"Just... look at this from my point of view, alright? You're telling me a cult is summoning demons, and Amara just happens to turn into a succubus right around the same time. Am I supposed to believe that's a coincidence?"

Tessa glared at Vee, hatred in her eyes. "She didn't even know about the cult, or the magic circles they're disrupting, until I told her about them. Plus, she can't be the mastermind, because Derek's dad is. All his wealth, all his power? He made a deal with something, and now he's fulfilling his end of the bargain."

"Have you seen this? With your own eyes?"

"Well... no," Tessa muttered. "Amara interrogated Mr. Luxnor, and she was the one that infiltrated the cult meeting yesterday."

"So you have no proof! How can you expect me to go along with this?"

With a huff, Tessa stood up and started towards the door. "This is stupid. I knew you weren't going to help us; I shouldn't have bothered."

"Wait!" Vee reached out, grabbing Tessa's arm. "Just.... give me something, anything. Why should I believe she's different?"

Tessa paused, eventually pulling her hand back from Vee. "You've been friends with her since college started. Do you think that whole year was a lie? That everything you did together meant nothing? She didn't even know she was a succubus until we took her to that party. If you want proof... go talk to Nick. He was there when this all started."

A few seconds passed, and Vee was unsure what to say. She thought back to her first year of college, to all the time she spent with Amara. They'd spent countless nights talking about school, crushes, and hundreds of other pointless things. She'd always valued her friendship with Amara, it had felt so genuine, but Vee had also been hiding her identity. How could she be mad at Amara when she'd hidden her angelic heritage from everyone?

Vee walked to the door, slowly opening it for Tessa. When she looked out, she didn't see Amara, but a quick glance revealed she was waiting at the end of the hallway. When she saw Vee, she quickly jogged back.

"Vee! Are you going to help us?" Amara asked nervously.

With a heavy sigh, Vee answered, "I'll help, on one condition."

"Yes! Anything!" Amara said quickly.

"Just before we fought, I had a large book with me. It's filled with Enochian Texts, and it's an incredibly powerful angelic artifact. If what Tessa told me is true, we're going to need every advantage we can get, which means I need that book. It would have been in the house when it burned down, and I haven't had the time to look for it yet. You give that back, and I'll help you stop this cult."

Tessa pushed past Vee, rolling her eyes in contempt. "Right, the book that lets you banish Amara. How fucking convenient."

"Tessa!" Amara slapped Tessa's arm, glaring at her in disapproval before turning back to Vee. "Vee, I was the first person to clean up the remains of the Palace, and I never saw that book."

"So, what, someone fucking stole it?"

"I-I don't know," Amara muttered. "I'll help you try to find it, but we need to act fast; Mr. Wellington said his big moment is next Sunday."

"Great, there's a time limit." Vee pinched the bridge of her nose, trying to think of where to start. "Alright, tell you what. I have a spell that will help me locate the book, but it has limited range. As soon as I get a ping, I'll reach out."

Amara literally jumped with joy, and seemed ready to hug Vee, but she hesitated. She instead pivoted to Tessa, squeezing her tight as she spoke. "That's great!"

"For now, just... I don't know. I need space," Vee said. As she watched Tessa and Amara turn to leave, she added, "Oh, and... it's nice you're raising money for the Palace. The photos are... very professional."

Vee stepped back inside, closing the door behind her. She heard the other girls slowly walking away, and she couldn't help but overhear what they were saying.

"She's going to help, Tess! Thank you so much!" Amara said.

"Yeah, she also zapped you across the hallway. Were you listening in on our conversation?"

"I heard a couple bits when you were yelling, but I waited down the hall to try and avoid eavesdropping. My hearing is crazy good, remember?"

Their voices grew quieter and quieter, eventually fading altogether. Vee rested her head on the door, almost wishing they would come back. Though, even if they did, would she just snap at them again? Her anger seemed like some uncontrollable viper, lashing out against her will, and she didn't know how to control it.

"If you want proof... go talk to Nick. He was there when this all started."

Tessa's words resurfaced, bouncing around in her head. Vee had, truthfully, never known that she was a witch. Amara had hinted at it just before their fight, and Vee had only pieced it together days later in the hospital. On the one hand, it was hardly surprising; Tessa had always kept strange company, and even stranger habits. On the other, it was yet another secret her friends had kept from her. Why had Tessa told Amara, but not her?

I have to make a choice, I can't keep pushing them away and hoping they wait for me to make up my mind. If I apologize, if I try to make them a part of my life again, will things return to normal? Can we honestly go back to sleepovers and late-night tacos after everything that's happened? Of course, the only other choice is to listen to the Church. Sever all ties, call in reinforcements, and take care of Amara once and for all.

Even thinking it, just for a moment, made her sick. Amara had been so excited that she'd agreed to help! As weird as it was to admit, Tessa had a point; she'd been best friends with Amara ever since college started, was she really willing to throw that away?

Isn't there a third option? One where Amara gets to have a life, but I don't have to turn against the Church?

Vee closed her eyes, and tears formed in her eyes. "What am I supposed to do?"

No one answered, not that she'd expected anyone to. When she was a child, she used to think she might be able to have conversations with her Patron, if she could only grow strong enough. After years of trying, she eventually accepted that she was just as alone as any mortal. She stayed there, leaning against the door, for another few minutes before she made up her mind. Wiping the tears from her face, she grabbed her keys from the counter, and left.

Hundreds of thoughts raced through Vee's head, and she didn't know which ones to listen to. She heard the voices of pastors, first telling her she was an angel. She remembered learning about her sacred duty, being taught the fundamental truths of the universe so that she might enforce them.

She also heard Amara, remembering the sound of her laughter the night of her first party. She remembered how nervous she'd been, and how much everyone had tried to comfort her. Nothing else had mattered that night, they were just four friends dancing their hearts out, and Vee had talked her into going. She'd been the one to pull Amara out of the corner, the one that showed her how to move in time with the music. Of course, that night had been the start of Amara's rebirth. There was so much she didn't know, and it was time to get some answers.

Vee sighed nervously, then knocked on the door in front of her. After her conversation with Tessa, she'd started enhancing her senses again, and she quickly heard footsteps approaching. The door opened soon after, bringing her face to face with the man she'd almost started dating last month. Nick's eyes went wide with surprise, though he tried to stay calm. "Vee! I... wasn't expecting you."

"Well, I didn't tell you I was coming, so that makes sense. Can I come in?" Nick nodded, moving out of the way to let Vee pass. As she entered his apartment, she took a deep breath, wondering how present the smell of sulfur would be. Surprisingly, its presence was lighter than she expected.

"It's good to see you back, Vee. I'm happy you're doing well," Nick said. When Vee turned to face him, she saw his eyes instinctually dart to the scars on her face, but he quickly averted them.

"We need to talk." Vee sat down, her knees curled up underneath her in a corner of the couch, though her body stayed tense.

"I completely agree. I'm... look, I'm so sorry for everything, and if there's anything I can do to help, I want to put things right. For everyone." Nick pulled a chair closer, sitting opposite Vee before leaning in.

"You need to tell me what happened, from the beginning. Tessa tells me you were there when Amara... when she found out."

"It's a bit of a long story; can I get you anything?" Vee didn't answer, instead staring daggers at Nick. With a heavy sigh, he began talking. "It all started at that party, the one everyone talked her into. It started fine, though she was definitely nervous. I checked in on her occasionally, but she wasn't drinking, so I let myself cut loose a little. Eventually, she came up to me with this look on her face, like something was wrong. She pulled me upstairs, and I could tell something was different. She's normally a pretty timid person, but she was moving with this unnatural confidence, it was weird. Still, I was pretty drunk, and before I could ask any questions, she was on top of me. We... slept together, and that was her first time."

"And you just went along with it? What happened to all the times you two agreed to never date? That there was nothing between you two?"

"I don't know, Vee, it all happened so fast. The next morning, I'm freaking out, I'm trying to figure out what this all means, when she texts me. She says she wants to talk, and we do. We agree we don't want to date, but the whole time we're talking, she seems weirdly distracted. Out of nowhere, she jumps me again, and we come to an understanding; maybe we can just be friends with benefits. She had this... I dunno, this odd intensity. So, we hooked up again, and when she stands up, she suddenly has a tail. I point it out, she freaks, and I had to spend the entire day trying to calm her down. You've seen her panic attacks before, and this one was the worst of the worst."

"That... seems like Amara."

"Anyways, we have no idea what's going on, and we agree to try and do some research to figure out what's happening. She starts wearing really baggy sweaters to hide her tail, and I manage to find some leads."

I remember those sweaters. That's what they were for?

"The tail looked kinda devilish, and then I remembered that this all began after she started having sex. We had very little to go on, but succubus seemed like our best guess."

"But you kept sleeping with her? You didn't bother worrying that she was stealing your soul?"

"Are you kidding? I was freaking out! I took a week off school and visited family, just to give myself some space. I've never been a religious person, but suddenly I have definitive proof that it's all real; Heaven, Hell, everything. What if she stole my soul accidentally? I spent that whole week looking for... I dunno, a sign? I wanted proof that I still had a soul, that I was still me."

"Not exactly something that's easy to prove, Nick."

"Look, I'm not an angel, I don't know how souls work. But, fiction tells me that people without souls turn heartless, they stop feeling things, and push themselves further into depravity just to try and feel something again. I spent that whole week doing charity work, helping around the house, playing with the family dogs... and it felt good. I was happy, I felt proud to make a difference in my community. Nothing felt different, so I decided to trust Amara."

"But she's a demon! How are you okay with that?!" Vee hissed.

"I don't know! I can't explain it, Vee, but I've known her for years. We spend so much time together, and the whole time she was transforming, it never felt like she was changing. The only real difference was that she seemed happier, like some veil had been lifted and she could finally see clearly. So, yeah, I was happy for her, and I pushed her into accepting what she was. I taught her how to use her tail, I convinced her to go as herself for Halloween."

Vee went quiet, nervous to change the topic, but she knew she'd regret not asking. "And what about us? Did that mean nothing?"

"Vee, no one was more excited about us getting together than Amara. When I asked you out, I talked with her, and we agreed that we would stop sleeping together if you and I started dating. Neither of us knew you were an angel, and we were just trying our best to find a new normal. I really like you, Vee, I... I still do, but everything is so confusing. After we kissed, you ran off, and I didn't know why. Everything with Derek had just happened, sure, but you also seemed so reluctant to talk about yourself. I assumed you just weren't ready for anything yet."

Silence fell in the room, neither person saying anything as they waited for Vee to think things through. She hated how reasonable he sounded. There had to be more going on, right?

"And this cult? Do you trust that Amara's telling the truth?"

"Without a doubt."

Vee sighed. She'd been studying Nick's face this entire time, looking for any clues that he might be under Amara's influence without realizing it. The entire time he'd been talking, though, nothing had changed; he seemed completely sincere.

It's now or never, Vee. You either help, or you don't.

After another awkward silence, Vee spoke up again. "I can... use magic to enhance my senses. That night, I ran because I smelled sulfur on you. I'd been hunting a succubus, and I thought that, whoever she was, she'd slept with you to send me a message. I thought you'd become her thrall, and were trying to trap me for her."

Nick stood up, moving closer before kneeling in front of Vee. "Vee, I'm just a human. You two are crazy strong, probably more than I know, but if I saw her try to hurt you? I wouldn't hesitate to stop her. I don't know what she's wrestling with, and I don't know what happened on Halloween, but I have to believe that's not who she is." Nick tried to place a hand on Vee's arm, but she flinched and pulled away from him.

Standing up, Vee pushed past Nick and started walking towards the door. "I... I'm sorry things didn't work out between us, Nick." Before he had a chance to answer, Vee ran out the front door. A tear fell down her cheek, and she wiped it off quickly. Her steps grew more determined, and she spent the rest of the night wandering campus, casting her tracking spell.

10

UNLIKELY ALLIES

Chemistry class the next morning proved to be one of the longest hours of Amara's life. She'd spent the entire night glued to her phone and now could barely keep herself awake. Vee was back, after all, and had agreed to help them stop the cult. When they'd last spoken, she'd promised to reach out as soon as she located her Enochian Texts, but Amara had no idea how long that would take. Every time her phone vibrated, she would hastily grab it hoping for a text from Vee, but it always proved to be something else. Another photoshoot sale, a comment on a random post, a text from Tessa or Nick.

Now, as she leaned her face against her hand while the professor explained their lab, she still couldn't resist the urge to check her phone every couple seconds. Her enhanced, demonic hearing made this even worse; she heard every phone in the classroom every time one vibrated, and wasn't experienced enough to differentiate between them.

She was also disappointed that Vee wasn't in class with her. It was her first week back in school, after all, and they'd been lab partners up until Halloween. Amara didn't dislike her new lab partner, a somewhat nervous girl with patchy, bright blue hair, but she wanted everything to go back to normal. Sadly, Vee was nowhere to be seen, and class went on without her. If nothing else, Amara had plenty of time to mope; her lab partner was a very eager student. Amara was practically a glorified lab assistant, doing little more than fetching random items or reading measurements aloud.

"Ugh, Amara, can you light this?" her blue-haired partner asked. She'd been struggling with the Bunsen burner for the last minute, and had finally given up.

With a lazy smile, Amara grabbed the striker and moved it over the burner. She squeezed it half-heartedly, unsure if she'd even made any sparks, and used her own inner fire to light the burner. Once finished, she opened her notebook and started copying over some notes. "Alright, ready to go."

"How do you always get that on your first try?"

"Maybe I'm just lucky," Amara said, chuckling to herself. She spent the rest of class watching her lab partner do most of the work, occasionally lending a hand when asked. Her phone went off exactly six times, though none of the notifications were from Vee.

Hours later, Amara sat down for lunch with Chloé, still having heard nothing. Tessa was also nowhere to be found, but that was to be expected; she'd texted earlier that she was reviewing her notes about the magic circles. Amara tried to pass the time with small talk, letting Chloé talk about her week and her charity.

"What about you? How are classes?" Chloé asked, pushing the remains of her lunch aside.

"I can't complain. They're pretty straightforward, even if it's a little hard to focus right now." Amara sighed, wishing she could tell Chloé more.

"Is that 'cuz Vee's back?"

"...Yeah, pretty much."

Chloé hesitated, looking like she was unsure of something, then continued. "What are you two fighting about? If that's okay to ask, I don't want to step on anyone's toes..."

You know the rule, Amara, only tell people once they're involved. Still, I feel bad leaving her in the dark... maybe a half-truth would be okay?

Amara forced a smile. "Well, kinda a couple things, but mostly... I started sleeping with Nick."

"Seriously?! But you two always said you didn't want to date!" Chloé leaned closer, clearly eager to hear more.

"We're not dating, it's just a friends-with-benefits thing. Vee had a bit of a crush on him, though, and when she found out, things got a little... heated. Then she got hurt in that fire, and we haven't really had time to talk about it."

"That really sucks, I'm sorry. Is there anything I can do to help?" Chloé asked.

"I appreciate the offer, but no. This is something we have to work through on our own." Amara sighed, wishing she could say more. "Could you not tell her I said anything?"

"Your secret is safe with me!" Chloé reached over, squeezing Amara's hand briefly before the conversation shifted to more mundane matters. Over lunch, Amara's phone went off a dozen more times, but still nothing from Vee.

Long after classes had ended, just after dusk, Amara and Nick were finishing up dinner. He'd stopped by after classes, and taken the opportunity to tell Amara everything he'd talked about with Vee. She hung on every word as he recounted their conversation, hoping to learn more about what Vee was thinking. Sadly, the more Nick talked, the more it became obvious that Vee seemed as confused as ever.

"Ugh, I hate waiting! Every time my phone goes off, I think it's her. I wish there was more I could do!" Amara fell onto the couch, pulling a throw pillow over her head.

"I'm sure this isn't easy for her, Amara. We don't know what her childhood was like, but she's clearly known about her heritage for a while. When we had our date, she actually mentioned that her parents weren't entirely hers, but she wouldn't elaborate. I'll bet there's some weird angel magic at play with that."

"Okay? What's that got to do with this?"

Nick pushed Amara's legs aside and sat next to her. "What I mean, Amara, is that she grew up knowing she was an angel. I'll bet the Church has told her a million times how bad demons are."

"That's... kinda what she told Tessa. Something about how all demons are manipulative, and prey on mankind's desire to be good. Stupid church propaganda."

"Are they wrong? The instant you saw another demon at that cult meeting, you were terrified."

"That's different and you know it," Amara said, casting a nervous glare at Nick. She hated the thought of bringing up Alex again, even though Nick had led the conversation there. He paused for a moment, lost in his own thoughts, then appeared to pull himself together.

"Look, she just needs time. I can't imagine what she's going through, but it looks like she's trying to give you the benefit of the doubt. She's helping with the cult, right? She's talking to Tessa and myself about your transformation, she's trying to understand. We can't expect her to shake off years of belief in just a few weeks."

Amara groaned. "Stop being so reasonable, Nick. You're making me feel bad about complaining."

The two laughed, though it was obvious they both carried tension in their voices. After a moment of silence, Nick spoke up again. "Maybe... a distraction would help?" he asked. His hand slid higher on her leg, and he squeezed her inner thigh.

"Ohh is someone feeling frisky?" Amara spread her legs slightly, smirking at Nick.

"Hey, Tessa got you last time, and I seriously considered masturbating for the first time in months earlier today. Plus, you need to keep your strength up."

"You poor thing! So used to having a slutty succubus at your beck and call, however will you survive?" Amara's voice dripped with sarcasm as she sat up, pushing Nick back so she could straddle him.

"Truly no one suffers more than I." Nick smirked as he pulled Amara's shirt off. He undid her bra with a snap of his fingers, a trick Amara showed him that made their constant fucking much more convenient.

"What are you going to do when you finally settle down? How could anyone else possibly compare to having your own personal sex demon?" Amara returned the favor, pulling off Nick's shirt before she started undoing his pants. She leaned in, kissing him briefly before moving to his neck and biting him hard.

"Fuck... someone's awfully full of herself tonight. Do I need to put you in your place?"

"I'd like to see you try, Nicholas." Amara pulled back, her eyes flaring as she stood up. She quickly pulled the rest of her clothes off, but rather than straddling Nick again, she started walking to her room. She flicked her tail suggestively, and made sure to accentuate her hips as she walked.

Nick happily chased after her, undressing as he made his way to the bedroom. His aura continued growing, which brought a smile to Amara's face.

At least this part of my life is simple.

When Nick walked into the bedroom, Amara jumped out from behind the door and grabbed him. "Gotcha! You're mine now!" She wrapped her tail around his torso, took a deep breath, and lifted him clean off the ground. His hands grabbed her arms, and he was clearly shocked by how easily she'd lifted him. Seconds later, she threw him down on the bed and crawled on top of him.

"Fuck, could I get a warning next time?" Nick moaned as Amara bit his neck again, but she quickly backed off and gently kissed him on the lips.

"Aww where's the fun in that?"

The two started grinding against each other, which felt infinitely more enjoyable without clothes in the way. Amara laid on top of Nick, her breasts pushed against his chest as she felt his thick cock throbbing underneath her. His hands brushed against her waist, slowly moving further down until he'd found her ass. He massaged her slowly, digging his fingers deep into her soft flesh. With each gentle rub, her pussy twitched in anticipation.

Not wanting to wait any longer, she connected with his aura and took a deep breath. His excitement was delicious, and it was easy to sense how eager he was to be inside her. She broke off their kiss, smirked at Nick, then slid down the bed until she'd settled comfortably between his legs.

After licking her lips in anticipation, she kissed the base of his cock slowly. Her tongue snaked out, massaging his balls as he started to moan out in pleasure. With each kiss, her mouth moved higher, and soon she'd reached the tip.

"So fucking hot, Amara..." Nick moaned.

"Oh, you like it hot, do you?" An idea formed in Amara's head, and she took a deep breath while connecting with her inner fire. After all her practice, she felt confident enough to try something new. When she breathed out, her breath was much hotter than it had any right to be. She opened her mouth wide, keeping his cock on the tip of her tongue, and spit dripped down her chin as she teased him. When Nick looked down, he saw flames at the back of her throat. They illuminated the inside of her mouth, a soft red glow that made her look like a dragon preparing to attack.

"Shit, Amara, that's... really wild. Hopefully you're planning on putting that out when you actually get to work?"

A giggle escaped her lips, and she felt a few sparks dancing inside her mouth. "Don't worry, Nick, I wouldn't dare hurt this wonderful cock of yours." Amara closed her mouth, made a show of swallowing, and opened it again to show Nick that the fire was gone.

"You'd make a fortune if you ever joined the cir—fuck!" Nick's thought was interrupted when Amara kissed the head of his cock and pushed down, swallowing his entire length in an instant. She let her tongue reach for his balls again, slowly massaging them as her throat constricted around his shaft. His hands reached for her head, grabbing her horns tight as he twitched in pleasure.

Through his aura, Amara felt how much he was enjoying himself, and she started bobbing up and down in long, slow strokes. Before long, Nick's cock, as well as her comforter, were soaked in spit as she eagerly sucked him off. She continued to pick up her pace, keeping tabs on his aura to figure out exactly how fast he wanted her to move today. He usually preferred rough and fast, especially when she gave him free reign to use her horns as handles, but he wasn't in charge right now. She eventually settled on a slower pace than he clearly wanted, which would prevent him from cumming while also keeping him plenty excited.

Her moans joined his, as much as her busy mouth would allow, as she happily shared in his pleasure. After several minutes of this, Nick managed to find the strength to speak again. "I know you can cum from this, but— fuck... I'd love to feel more than just your mouth today."

Letting his cock slide from her mouth, her lips were slick with spit as she responded, "You know, most guys would consider a girl that can cum from blowjobs the equivalent of winning the lottery."

"Maybe you've only got yourself to blame, and your pussy is just that good." With his hands still wrapped around her horns, Nick pulled her close until their lips met again. They kissed slowly, their bodies positioning until Amara's sex hovered over his shaft. Using her tail, she lined herself up, then happily welcomed him inside.

It was her turn to moan, her voice deep and guttural as he slid deep inside her. Once he'd bottomed out, she began eagerly grinding against his crotch, every twitch of his cock making her purr with excitement.

Placing her hands on Nick's chest, she squeezed her legs and began bouncing up and down. She moved slowly, letting the entire length of his shaft pump into her pussy, feeding on his aura all the while. Once again, she found the perfect pace to keep him excited while staving off his orgasm, and happily stayed there until she found her first climax.

Her body shook and trembled as the pleasure raced through her, and she didn't bother quieting her passionate moans. Every muscle in her body twitched, and she fought the urge to squeeze Nick as hard as she could for fear of hurting him. Instead, she channeled her excitement to her horns, an aurora of purple and red firelight cascading across the walls while hellfire danced around her head. By the time she'd calmed down, and checked to make sure she hadn't burnt anything, she felt that Nick had taken control of their pace.

"Now, who said you could do that?" Amara teased.

"Hey, you weren't complaining," he said, smirking.

An idea crossed Amara's mind, and she leaned in to kiss him before speaking. "Do you still want to put me in my place?"

"Absolutely! I've got to get back at you for throwing me across the room earlier."

"Well then, why aren't you bending me over already?" Amara giggled, and within seconds, she was letting Nick pick her up to reposition her. Once she was comfortably on her knees, she reached under the bed with her tail, and soon she'd pulled out her lube. She handed it to Nick, who paused after seeing it.

"Which toy do you want?" he asked, looking down at her shoebox of naughty accessories.

"No toys today." Using her tail, she pulled herself backwards until she was kneeling in front of Nick, and she laid her head on his shoulder. She reached for his cock, slowly stroking him as she whispered, "I want you to fuck me in the ass, Nick."

Nick's aura, already pulsing with desire, doubled in potency at her words. She saw lust and excitement run across his face, but also a flash of nervousness. "Are you sure? I'm definitely bigger than the toy we used last time..."

"I mean, if you don't want to..." Amara teased.

"T-that's not what I said!"

Amara reached up, running her hands through his hair before pulling it tight. "Nicholas, if you're not fucking my ass in the next sixty seconds, I'm pinning you down to see if you like it instead."

The intensity of her words spoke volumes, and Nick clearly got the hint. He pushed her back to the bed, pulled her hips closer, and opened the bottle of lube. A generous amount fell onto her tight asshole, then Nick carefully rubbed a finger around her entrance before slowly pushing inside to warm her up. As his finger entered her, she moaned aloud while squeezing him tightly. Her tail reached for the lube, dribbling several drops across her ass before rubbing them in, giving her entire backside a delectable, glistening visual. Nick took the lube from her, and once his cock was ready to go, he grabbed her hip. Holding himself steady, he lined himself up and started pushing.

It took longer than expected for him to slip inside. He was obviously being cautious, and as much as she wanted to poke fun at him for his caution, she reluctantly accepted that this wasn't an activity to rush. She felt the pressure increase, tried to relax in response, and soon enough her entrance gave.

The head of his cock felt much bigger than it had previously, and it was strange having him inside her ass. Much like with her toys, there was an unusual stretching feeling as he carefully slid deeper inside her, but thankfully she'd come to love that sensation during all her practice. His cock was softer than her toys, which were all various forms of silicone, and she loved how hot his shaft felt. She lost track of time as she waited for him to bottom out; seconds seemed like minutes as she held her breath in anticipation. When his thighs finally met hers, she instinctually let out a loud moan.

"Fuuck! You're so thick, it's so different than my toys..." Amara moaned, her fingers digging into the bed sheets.

Nick leaned forward, whispering into her ear. "Does it feel good?"

"It's amazing, please don't stop. I want more, I want to feel you cum!" Amara pushed back, and the two ground against each other for a moment before she felt Nick pull back. He was upright again, keeping one hand on her hip while the other grabbed one of her horns, pulling her head back sharply. As he held her completely still, his cock started to leave her ass, and her body shook with anticipation. Before pulling out completely, he pushed back in, eventually finding a steady rhythm while he fucked her.

She appreciated his caution; as good as this felt, she knew she needed time to adjust to his cock. Even with her toys, she tended to stop once they were all the way in, and she'd never properly fucked herself with them. Now, with Nick eager to claim her ass, it's like she was rediscovering everything she'd come to love about anal.

Each thrust felt more deliberate, and her confidence grew alongside Nick's as they read each other's movements. He began pulling back even further, threatening to leave her entirely, but he never did. His aura grew more vibrant, and she knew she would have incredible amounts of energy to spare after they finished. She also swore he'd borrowed her shapeshifting abilities, as it felt like his cock grew even larger as he started fucking her harder and harder. His hips bounced off her ass, and he even released his hold on her hips to spank her a few times.

It only took a few minutes for the assfucking to overwhelm her. Another orgasm raced through her body, and now that she wasn't in control, she had no way to steady herself for it. Her eyes rolled back in her head, she lost control of her voice, and she bucked wildly as she tried to throw herself against Nick as hard as she could. This orgasm was wild, chaotic, and she lost track of her body as she grew more and more consumed by the pleasure overloading her senses.

Nick's aura, stimulated by her frantic bucking, pulsed and grew even sweeter. He finally started cumming, both hands grabbing her horns as he bottomed out in her ass. His cock twitched, emptying its load deep inside her, and every few seconds his hips briefly thrusted hard into her. A frenetic, second wave of orgasmic pleasure took hold of her, and her ass squeezed Nick's cock for every drop of cum that it could. Without warning, he pulled her up towards him, their bodies colliding as his arms wrapped around her waist. He bit her neck, harder than he'd ever tried before, and another guttural scream filled her bedroom. They stayed there for another minute, Nick's orgasm slowly fading before Amara's could do the same. When she finally fell back to the bed, and his cock suddenly pulled out of her ass, she gasped in surprise.

Nick joined her moments later, his own breath as haggard as Amara's. She found the strength to look at him, sweat dripping down his brow, and her tail affectionately wrapped around one of his legs. By the time they'd both suitably recovered, something that took Nick significantly longer, they both wore ridiculously large smiles.

"So," Amara started, "think I've been suitably punished?"

"Fuck, Amara, I can't even think of something witty to say. That was so fucking hot."

Amara's tail uncurled from Nick's leg, grabbing a water bottle from her nightstand. She took a long drink, then offered it to Nick as she finally sat up. Just as she'd expected, the bedroom had taken on new life due to her renewed energy. She saw signals bouncing around once more, and was even able to start differentiating them. One errant signal connected with Nick's phone, and she took the opportunity to toss it to him.

"Hey, you're getting a text," she said, taking back the water.

Nick unlocked his phone, his eyebrows furrowing in confusion. "You sure? I don't see— oh, never mind. Wow, you really can see Wi-Fi."

"What, did you think I was lying?"

"Well, no, but seeing is believing," Nick said, pausing for a moment to respond to his message.

Amara took the opportunity to finish the rest of the water, setting it on her nightstand when she finished. She grabbed her phone, which made a familiar tingle when she picked it up, indicating a new text. Used to disappointment, she tried not to get her hopes up, but her newfound self-control went out the window immediately: she had a text from Vee.

Vee: Back of Whitmore Hall, 11 PM. Book is on top floor, possibly the Dean's office.

"Nick! Vee has a lead!" she said excitedly.

"That's great! Where's her book at?"

"She thinks it might be in the Dean's office, weirdly enough."

"That's odd. Why would he have it? Is he a part of the cult?" Nick asked.

"I don't think so, I certainly didn't see him at the meeting. Plus, the cult is trying to summon demons, what use would they have for Enochian Texts? And would they even be able to tell what they were?" As they talked, Amara pulled her clothes back on. "Honestly, right now, I don't care why the book is there. Can we go to your place? I need to steal some clothes."

"Planning on shapeshifting into the Dean? I'll see what I can put together, but I think he's a little smaller than I am. We also have drastically different styles; I certainly don't have any tweed suits."

"It doesn't have to be perfect, just good enough." Amara threw Nick's pants on the bed. "Now c'mon, get dressed."

Soon enough, both of them had finished dressing and left for Nick's place. There, they did their best to pick an outfit that seemed as close to the Dean's fashion sense as possible. By the time they'd finished, Amara decided she didn't want to wait anymore, and left for the meeting spot.

Amara felt silly, waiting outside Whitmore Hall wearing such ill-fitting clothes. She'd considered shifting into the Dean ahead of time, but she didn't want to confuse Vee when she arrived. Thankfully, Whitmore was slightly further away from the busier parts of campus, and the chances of running into any other students were small.

She didn't know what to say once Vee arrived. They'd only talked twice since she'd returned to campus, and both conversations had been incredibly stressful. Amara replayed them in her mind, wondering if she might gain any insight she could use to put Vee at ease, but she kept drawing blanks. She wished she could just sit Vee down and explain everything from the start, but getting Vee to agree to such a conversation seemed like an impossible task, especially given the threat of the cult.

After roughly half an hour of nervous fidgeting, Amara finally saw someone approaching the building. Their aura was incredibly faint, which meant it wasn't Tessa, and it definitely wasn't a demon.

Amara held her breath as Vee approached, wondering what she should say. Should she say anything? Would it be better to focus on the task at hand? Before she could make up her mind, Vee had closed the distance. She paused for a moment, then moved to the brick wall to join Amara in leaning against it.

"...Amara," Vee said.

"H-hey Vee. Thanks for, um... reaching out. Were there any problems finding your book?"

"No."

"That's good! I have no idea how many demons are running around campus right now. The only one I know for sure is Alex."

"Alex is a demon?" Vee seemed genuinely surprised. "Fuck! I ran into him earlier, and he was being a huge creep!"

"Do you think he knows you're an angel? Can demons sense that kind of thing?"

Vee glared at Amara. "Sometimes, it depends on the strength and particular skillset of the demon in question. You can't sense me, can you?"

"Well, I can see your aura, but it doesn't look any different than anyone else's."

"My... aura?" Vee asked.

"That's what I call it, at least. I can sense traces of, I dunno, some kind of energy around everyone? But because of this, I can... well, I can intuit certain things. There's nothing in your aura that seems angelic, or anything like that."

"What do you mean, intuit things? Are you doing something to me?" Vee seemed on edge, and stepped slightly further away.

Ugh, I was hoping to avoid the specifics...

"I'm not doing anything! I just know, like... how horny you are, or when you last had sex..." Amara's voice quieted, nervous to be talking about sex at a time like this; she didn't want to make Vee any more uncomfortable.

"Right. Succubus," Vee sighed. "Should've known."

Both girls went quiet. Amara wished she had something else to talk about, but she couldn't think of anything. It also didn't make sense to talk about tonight's plan until Tessa arrived. Thankfully, they didn't have to wait much longer; Tessa was only five minutes late, practically a new record for her.

"Please, don't stop the party on my account," Tessa said. She looked over at Amara, her eyes running over the clothes she was wearing. "What's with the outfit? You planning on shifting again?"

"That was the plan, yeah. I figured, if we're going to be in the Dean's office, we might as well have the Dean with us."

"In those clothes? He would never wear that," Vee said, rolling her eyes.

"Well, a strange outfit makes more sense than secretly being a shapeshifter. It's just a precaution if we run into a janitor or something. If we find a demon, they'll see through me no matter who I look like."

Tessa stepped between Amara and Vee, changing the topic. "So, what's the plan? Break in and steal the book back?"

"It's not stealing, Tessa, it's mine," Vee said.

"Of course, morality bends to your whims, never the other way around."

"Tessa! Shut up!" Amara said, grabbing the witch's arm and squeezing her tight.

Vee, clearly annoyed, walked over to the back entrance and held her hand up to the door. After a few seconds, a small flash of light burst from the lock, and the door swung open on its own. "I'm not against getting my hands dirty, Tessa. You coming or not?"

A smug look crossed Tessa's face, and she walked past Vee into the building. "Not bad, holy girl."

Amara followed soon after, and when Vee walked inside, she closed the door behind her. "Alright, I should change into the Dean now. I'm gonna duck into that bathroom, gimme a sec." Walking over to the bathrooms, Amara quickly pulled her clothes off, then shapeshifted into Samuel Halsen, Dean of Aurelius University. She didn't like that she had to disrobe to shift, but her shifting always spawned flickers of hellfire, and she didn't want to risk damaging Nick's clothes. She was happy with the face she saw in the mirror, and was pretty sure she'd be able to trick any random students or faculty.

Dean Halsen was a slightly smaller man, with a tendency to hunch forward. He had short grey hair, with greyish-blue eyes that sat comfortably next to his prominent crow's feet. Amara had never seen him in person, other than from a distance at a few large events, but had seen his picture hundreds of times on the campus website. As she walked out of the bathroom, her hands adjusting the last few buttons on the shirt, she saw Tessa and Vee adamantly ignoring each other.

Tessa looked over, examining Amara's new look before whistling. "Nailed it, as always. You wanna give us some light?"

Amara nodded, summoning a small flame to hover in front of them. As she did, she immediately noticed Vee flinch in surprise and take a few steps back. "Fuck, maybe a little warning next time?" Vee said.

Guilt rushed through Amara as she spoke. "Shit, I'm sorry, I didn't think—"

"Yeah, obviously," Vee said, interrupting her. "Just try not to burn the place down, okay?"

Amara stammered, unsure what to say, but ultimately decided it would be best to stay quiet. She walked in front of the others, taking the lead as they started up the stairs. No one talked, and their footsteps echoed off the walls as they passed the second floor, eventually reaching the third.

While they walked, Amara tried to keep an eye out for any unusual electrical signals. She still hadn't found the time to really experiment with her improved vision, but she wondered if she might be able to detect things like cameras or other sensors. To her knowledge, the campus didn't have surveillance equipment like that, but given how many magical secrets she'd stumbled into recently, hidden cameras hardly seemed beyond the realm of possibility.

As they slowly walked towards the Dean's office, Amara felt a strange tingle on the back of her neck. When she turned, she saw Vee had closed her eyes, and appeared to be casting some kind of spell. Although worried it might be something aimed at her, Amara stayed still, and hoped this was just a natural response to being in the presence of divine magic. Her fears were allayed when the spell dropped, and Vee looked up again.

"I'm still sensing the book in the same place," Vee said. "We'll have to go through his assistant's office first."

At the end of the hall, they found a large door that marked the entrance to the Dean's office. A square window sat in the door, the glass clouded to give privacy, and simple block letters said "Samuel Halsen, Dean." As they drew close, and

Amara reached for the handle, she hesitated. She heard something in the Dean's office.

"Someone's inside," Amara whispered. "I'll go first, try to figure out what's happening. You two stay hidden."

Both other girls nodded, and Amara couldn't help but notice that Tessa had pulled out her switchblade. With a deep breath, Amara grabbed the handle and opened the door.

The office she walked into was empty, and the lights were off. A series of filing cabinets sat against the wall to her right, and a few chairs had been placed to her left. The assistant's desk had been set up in the back left corner, and on the far wall, Amara saw the door leading to the Dean's actual office. This door was partially ajar, and a light had been turned on inside.

Amara looked back to Vee and Tessa, signaling that they could enter the assistant's room, and they hurried inside. Trusting they could take care of themselves, Amara approached the door and pushed it open, walking inside.

"Hello?" Amara asked, doing her best impersonation of Dean Halsen.

As she entered the Dean's office, she saw a man rummaging through a large ornate cabinet. He flinched slightly, then turned to look at Amara. His broad, sharp face lit up with a fake smile, and Amara tensed in surprise. She was standing face to face with Sebastian Wellington.

"Dean Halsen! I thought you'd left hours ago!" Sebastian said, his voice calm and confident.

"Why are you in my office, Sebastian?" Amara asked.

I sure hope they're on a first name basis.

"I could ask you the same thing, Samuel."

Amara tried to look past Sebastian, hoping to see what he'd been doing, but he was large enough to block her view. "It's my office, isn't it? I think you're dodging my question."

"You're right, I shouldn't be here, but I have good cause." Sebastian turned back towards the cabinet and pulled something out of it. "In fact, I suspect we're both here for the same thing."

When Sebastian turned back towards Amara, she saw a large book in his hands. It had a magnificently regal, if slightly faded, cover, and she recognized it immediately: Vee's Enochian Texts. "Is that so? What could you possibly want with that?"

"I had the same question, actually. Why would a book like this be in the Dean's office?" Sebastian closed the distance between himself and Amara, holding out the book. "Still, I'm a busy man. How about, rather than bicker back and forth, you just take this book for yourself, and I'll be on my way?"

Amara looked down at the book nervously. She felt intense angelic power radiating from it, and knew she couldn't touch it without revealing her identity. "Just put it back where you found it, thank you."

"What's the matter?" Sebastian asked, a devious smirk appearing on his face. "Afraid to touch it? It's not like there are any secrets between us... Amara."

Amara gasped in surprise. "How did you—"

Before she could finish, Sebastian shoved the book against her chest. Its energy immediately flared up in her presence, but she did her best to hold onto it despite the pain; she needed to keep it safe for Vee. Her entire body felt like it was seizing, and flickers of holy energy leapt from the book as it continued to attack her. Hellfire cascaded down her body, and she unexpectedly returned to her own form, Nick's clothes now mildly singed.

"Don't give me that crap, Amara, I know everything. You do a terrible impression of the Dean, by the way." Sebastian placed a hand on the book, shoving Amara against a wall. "Brandon was all too eager to tell me about you, but even without the hint I would've felt your presence. I've spent years preparing myself, my body has been hand crafted to be a vessel for demonic power."

Amara struggled to stay standing amidst the angelic assault. "Why are you throwing your life away? You'll die as soon as your ritual's complete!"

A deep, confident laugh echoed from Sebastian's throat. "You dare act like you know more than me? You're the one wasting your potential! Why try to stop me? I'm bringing your kin into this world, I could give you power beyond your wildest dreams!" Without warning, Sebastian struck Amara's face, and she fell to the ground.

"You... you can't do anything!" Amara gasped. "This magic isn't yours!"

"It will be soon. I know how to bind the demons, how to bend them to my will. They're blinded by their own arrogance! They think I'm just another foolish mortal, desperate for scraps of their power." Sebastian grabbed Amara's chin, forcing her to look at him. "It's a shame you won't be a part of my future."

Fear flooded Amara, spurring her to action, and she tried to summon her chitinous gauntlets. One hand clutched desperately to Vee's book, refusing to let Sebastian steal it back, and the other erupted in pain as she fought against the Enochian magic. Chitin crawled across her skin, and her clawed hand darted towards Sebastian's neck. The energy from the book, however, slowed her movements, and the mad cult leader managed to intercept her attack, grabbing her wrist tight. Amara's moment of defiance, fortunately, had unwittingly created the perfect distraction; Tessa was standing in the doorway, her tattoos flaring, and her switchblade hurtling through the air. She was clearly aiming at Sebastian's neck, but with a flick of his wrist he managed to deflect the knife at the last second. Rather than burrowing into his throat, as Tessa had likely intended, the blade instead sliced open the side of his neck. Sebastian grunted in pain, releasing Amara as Vee and Tessa ran into the room.

Tessa's knife floated back to her, and Vee brandished the same holy blade Amara had seen on Halloween.

"It's three on one, fucker," Tessa said. "You're not getting out of here alive."

"We all know the succubus is useless now," Sebastian said. He rolled up his sleeves, neck still bleeding, as an insufferable grin appeared on his face. "I can easily take on two inexperienced children."

Tessa attacked first, running at Sebastian as her tattoos flared again. While the cult leader was much larger and stronger than her, she was able to use her size to her advantage, ducking and weaving between his attempts to grab her. She threw a series of quick punches to distract him, then used her magic to slash at Sebastian with her knife. She managed to land several strong hits, but each time he shrugged them off like they were little more than playful slaps.

Vee ran to Amara's side and quickly pulled the Enochian Texts off her body. Amara gasped with relief, the pain receding as she tried to stand up. By the time she'd gotten to her feet, Sebastian had gained the upper hand against Tessa. He shoved her back, her head colliding with a wall, and she fell to the floor.

Taking advantage of the distraction, Vee ran at Sebastian with her sword ready. She fared much better than Tessa, her form practiced and controlled as she managed to land a series of cuts. Sebastian, however, seemed unnaturally fast for a human, and was easily deflecting Vee's sword from doing any serious damage. It only took him a minute to turn the tables, pushing Vee back as he gained ground.

By this point, Tessa seemed to have recovered, and her tattoos flared once more as her switchblade raced towards Sebastian. The cult leader reacted quickly, unexpectedly grabbing the knife out of midair and redirecting it towards Vee. His intent was clearly lethal. He aimed the blade at her heart, but Vee managed to deflect the attack slightly. She screamed out in pain as the knife sank into her shoulder, and she fell backwards onto the Dean's desk.

This whole time, Amara had been trying to shake off the effects of the Enochian magic. Her movements were shaky, her chitin refusing to manifest correctly. Seeing Vee in trouble, a furious anger erupted in her, and she channeled it into a burst of hellfire directed at Sebastian. The flames landed, catching him off guard, and he jumped away from Vee in a panic. He ran to the door, quickly putting out the pieces of his shirt that had caught fire, and glared at the three girls.

"This isn't over! If you try to stop me, I won't hesitate to kill all of you!" Sebastian ran out of the office, his gasps growing more and more distant until he'd vanished completely.

With the fight over, Amara's adrenaline began to fade, and she looked around to see how everyone else was doing. Tessa seemed alright, but Vee was clutching her shoulder, blood staining her shirt. "Vee! Are you okay?"

Amara ran closer, trying to help Vee off the desk, but Vee knocked her hands away. "Don't fucking touch me!" she hissed. "You tried to set me on fire!"

Looking at the injury, Amara saw traces of burn damage on Vee's shirt, and she started panicking. "No! I-I didn't mean to, I was just trying—"

"Enough! Amara was able to scare Mr. Wellington away; he was clearly ready to kill us," Tessa said, cutting Amara off. Vee tried to say something, but Tessa kept talking. "We weren't ready for a fight, and that's not Amara's fault. It's not mine, it's not yours. Besides, we got your stupid book back, didn't we?"

By this point, Vee had crawled to the wall next to the door and leaned against it. She moved her hand, looking at the stab wound, and winced as she pulled her shirt down off her shoulder. "Whatever. We could have done worse, I suppose. This wound isn't as bad as it looks."

Amara sat on the floor, looking at Vee's injury. "Does your book have any healing magic?"

"Thankfully, yes," Vee said. She pulled her book closer, propping it on her leg as she opened it up. After a minute of flipping through pages, she seemed to find what she was looking for. When her mouth opened, the voice that left it was the most beautiful thing Amara had ever heard. It wasn't just her body that was singing, it felt like her soul was joining in as well. Her voice had extra layers that defied the limits of a human body, and the music cascaded off the walls in a way that didn't seem possible.

At the same time, however, Amara started seizing in pain. Shocks traveled through her body, her skin started itching, and an unnatural metallic hum reverberated through her skull. Although her ears enjoyed the singing, it felt like her soul was violently rejecting it. It was as if someone were dragging a cheese grater across her very essence, and she grabbed the sides of her head to try and block out the sound. Still, as painful as the experience was, she couldn't help but look as Vee's wounds slowly began to heal, the skin knitting itself back together in a matter of seconds.

When Vee finished, she closed the book and stood up. Amara fell backwards, releasing her grip on her head as she sighed in relief, the Enochian no longer drilling into her head. Vee moved quickly to the door, not paying any attention to Amara, but stopped after a moment. With a heavy sigh, her eyes glued to the floor, she quietly started speaking. "I guess this adds credence to your claims that Amara's not involved with this cult. It's suspicious that he was here tonight, of all nights, but... he did seem like he wanted to kill you. We have my book back, if nothing else, so we'll need to put together a battle plan. How are we going to stop him?"

Amara stood up, following Tessa and Vee out of the Dean's office before closing the door behind them. "Nick is trying to find a time where all the teachers in the cult are busy with classes. We think we might be able to make a move while they're busy," she said.

"Nick had better not be planning on joining us," Vee hissed.

"Absolutely not!" Amara said. "He's only human, after all."

"Good. Shoot me a text when he's found a time, and we'll figure out the details from there."

The girls walked in silence through the building, and it only took a few minutes for them to find the exit. The cool night air washed over them, and Tessa had to part ways to head back to her apartment. Vee and Amara were left alone, as they lived relatively close to each other, and the awkward silence continued.

"Um... I'm sorry about the fire," Amara said quietly, after a few minutes of walking.

Vee didn't say anything. Another few minutes passed, the only thing filling the silence the sounds of their footsteps on the sidewalk. When she finally responded, her voice was tense, but also strangely hesitant. "Just... don't let it happen again."

Amara couldn't think of anything else that felt worth saying. There was plenty she wanted to say, sure, but she felt like Vee had become a stranger overnight. The Vee she remembered was always smiling, happy to help others, an overwhelmingly positive person. The girl she now walked next to was sullen, cold, and blocked off.

Is this the real Vee? Was everything else an act, and she simply dropped the mask when we learned about her heritage? Or... did I cause this? Did our fight truly break her this much?

Soon enough, the time came to part ways. Amara took a deep breath, did her best to sound sincere, and spoke up. "G'night, Vee. I'm happy you're helping us."

"It's not really something I can ignore, is it?" Vee said. She turned to leave without saying goodbye, and Amara couldn't help but notice the bitterness in her voice. When Amara got home, she briefly texted Nick with an update, and collapsed into bed. Over the next several hours, she barely slept at all, instead tossing and turning as she reviewed the events of the night.

II

PREEMPTIVE STRIKE

The next morning, after scraping together a measly few hours of sleep, Amara joined up with Nick at his apartment before classes began. She collapsed on his bed, eager to vent about how poorly last night had gone, before sharing every detail she could remember. She hoped he might notice something she didn't about her interactions with Vee, and if nothing else, she got to vent about how frustrated she was.

"—and thankfully she was able to heal her shoulder, but even though her magic wasn't directed at me, it still felt awful. How are we going to fight together if being near her causes my whole body to seize every time she casts a spell?"

"I mean, maybe you can talk with her, try to figure out a way for your inherent natures not to interfere with each other? How do you know your hellfire doesn't do the same thing to her?" Nick asked, sitting next to her on the bed.

"Fuck, I hadn't even thought about that." Amara went quiet, wondering what it would feel like if angelic fire had erupted in front of her. "Ugh, I'm the worst!"

"C'mon, try to look on the bright side. Vee's alive, and unharmed. She has her book back, and we don't know how strong that makes her. She wasn't using it on Halloween, right? Maybe, now that she has it, this whole cult business will be a walk in the park!"

"I hope you're right. I'm sick of Mr. Wellington's fat stupid face," Amara grumbled. She buried her head in a pillow, groaning loudly.

"Well, about the cult, I think I've found a window for you all to try and get to the circle," Nick said.

"Really?" Amara sat up quickly, eager to hear the news.

"It's a little short notice, but it's later today. Wednesdays are normally pretty busy, which means a lot of classes are running. So long as all the teachers in the cult don't cancel today's classes, you might have a golden opportunity around one o'clock."

"That's perfect! I'll text Vee and Tessa, and we'll get lunch, then stop a cult! Nick, you're the best!" Amara leaned in, hugging Nick tight. After hearing his back loudly crack, she remembered to loosen her grip slightly; she still wasn't entirely used to her demonic strength. Pulling out her phone, she texted Vee and Tessa the details of the new plan. In just a few minutes, everyone had agreed to meet for lunch at Amara's apartment.

Her sour mood somewhat abated, Amara quickly grabbed her backpack and prepared to leave. Nick, however, stopped her, a serious look on his face. "Amara... look, I know things have been a bit weird recently. Halloween was tough, but that was a fight between two friends. This cult? This is serious business. Mr. Wellington didn't hesitate to try and kill you all last night, and... honestly, it's really hard for me knowing the danger you're throwing yourselves at. I mean, fuck, we've already lost Alex to them. This isn't a misunderstanding, this isn't a mild disagreement, they want you dead. Brandon wants you enslaved. They're going to do everything in their power to take you down."

Amara pulled Nick in for a hug once more, gently squeezing him. "I know, Nick. This isn't how I expected my year to go, and it's not fair that you've been pulled into this. I'm doing my best to hide it, but... I'm scared. Seeing what happened with Alex, it terrified me in a way I wasn't ready for. I'm not brushing off how serious this is. Yes, I want to make things right with Vee, but I could never live with myself if this cult unleashed Hell on Earth. By some crazy stroke of luck, I have the power to stop this, and I have to try."

Nick sighed, leaning against Amara. "I'm not trying to talk you out of this. I'm proud of you, honestly, but it's scary being on the sidelines. If today goes poorly, this could be the last time we—"

"Hey, don't say that. I've got Vee with me, remember? I've literally got God on my side."

"Well, if that doesn't make me feel better, nothing will," Nick said, forcing a laugh. He pulled away from the hug and let Amara leave.

As the clock struck noon, and the school's bell tower rang out across the campus, Amara was pacing nervously in her living room. Vee and Tessa were only a few minutes out, and they had less than an hour to plan their attack and leave for Lysander Hall. Amara fidgeted with her phone, nervously checking her texts every few seconds. She expected Vee to arrive first, and had no idea what to say when she arrived.

Before she decided on anything, someone knocked at her door. She ran to it quickly, then paused. She took a deep breath and tried to open the door at a reasonable pace; no reason to let Vee know how nervous she was.

"Hey Vee, come on in. Tessa isn't here yet, you know how she is," Amara said, forcing a smile.

Vee didn't respond. She set her backpack down on the counter, then grabbed a stool and sat down. After checking her phone, she sighed and finally spoke up. "Did you get my order?"

"Yup, all here. Got Tessa's too; hopefully the food will be here soon." Amara checked the food order on her delivery app, then walked into the kitchen and leaned against the counter. She gave Vee quite a bit of space, and tried not to stare at her as she tried to think of something to talk about. "Um... how's your shoulder?"

"Fine. I heal quickly when there's no hellfire involved," Vee said sharply.

"R-right, of course..." Amara swallowed nervously. "So, when you're using that book of yours, speaking Enochian, I noticed my body reacts weirdly. It's like I'm violently allergic to your magic, and I seize up a little. Do you feel anything similar when I use my abilities?"

"Not to my knowledge."

Out of curiosity, Amara manifested her tail. "How about now? Did you feel anything?"

Looking up, Vee flinched when she saw Amara's tail. "I... no, nothing." Her eyes lingered on the tail for several more moments, but eventually she pulled out her phone and focused on that instead.

An awkward silence filled the room as both girls waited. Amara kept trying to think of something to talk about, but she knew Vee was only here for business. Thankfully, it only took a few more minutes before Tessa arrived. She looked at Vee and Amara, both silently ignoring each other, then spoke up.

"Well, glad to see I didn't miss brooding hour," the witch said, taking a seat at the counter.

"I'm here to stop a cult, Tessa, nothing more." Vee set her phone down, then looked at Amara. "Is the food here yet?"

Amara checked her phone. "Actually, it is. Gimme a sec." She returned quickly, eagerly handing out everyone's food so they could get started.

"So, what's the plan?" Amara asked, happily sinking her teeth into her burger.

"We keep Tessa safe so she can work on the portal," Vee said. "Other than that? Just stay out of my way."

"Shouldn't we, like, discuss what our abilities can do? How am I supposed to stay out of your way if I don't know what you're capable of? You didn't fight with your book on Halloween," Amara said, parroting Nick's thought from earlier.

"Please, like I'm going to give you any details." Vee continued eating, but Amara couldn't help but notice that her eyes kept drifting towards Amara's tail, which was currently wrapped around a drink. "Do you have to keep that... *thing* out? I'm trying to eat."

"What, my tail?" Amara set down her drink. "It's not some fancy accessory that I bring out for fun, Vee, it's a part of me. If I keep it hidden for too long, I get kinda itchy? Like I'm cramping, but existentially. I don't know how to describe it. You want to feel it?"

"Absolutely not!" Vee said, coughing on her drink. "You keep that thing far away from me!"

Tessa, having wolfed down most of her food already, finally spoke up. "Hey, don't knock it 'til you've tried it. She can do this thing with the tip where she—"

"Don't you dare finish that sentence, Tessa," Vee said, glaring at the horny witch.

Amara, having accidentally escalated the situation, decided it would be better to change the conversation entirely. She cleared her throat loudly, then started speaking as she moved her tail out of view. "What about the cultists?"

"The instant someone welcomes a demon inside of them, their soul is forfeit," Vee said, casting another dirty look at Tessa. "The demon can also keep the body fighting past its normal limits, which means killing the body is the only way to ensure the demon returns to Hell."

"I thought demons had to be banished?" Amara asked.

"This is possession, it's different. They're just using the human's body as a vessel. If we destroy it, they have nowhere to go but back to Hell." Vee finished up her food and stood up to throw all her garbage away.

"So... we have to kill them?"

"They're already dead, Amara. Even if we managed to capture them, and set up an exorcism, we wouldn't be able to get them back. They've carved demonic runes into their bodies, and willingly surrendered themselves. If the possession had been forced on them, then an exorcism might work, but that's not the case here. It's kill or be killed."

Amara went quiet, her thoughts drifting back to the upsetting ceremony she'd witnessed in the secret bunker. The whole experience had made her sick to her stomach, and thinking about Alex's final moments again brought the feeling back tenfold. Even knowing that she wouldn't be fighting humans didn't help, they still looked like people. Would they scream in pain as Amara burned their flesh? Would they cry for help if Amara tried to slash their throats? Would she be forced to snap Alex's neck to save herself? Her breathing grew heavy, and embers from The Jade Palace began to fill her nostrils again. Before losing herself further, however, a pair of hands grabbed her shoulders and began to shake her.

"Amara, hey! Stay with me!" Tessa said, grabbing her chin. "You're at home, you're with friends!"

Closing her eyes, Amara focused on Tessa's voice and managed to pull herself together. She found herself staring into the witch's eyes, though it seemed like her vision was slightly blurred. She felt a tear run down her cheek and swallowed nervously. "I-I don't want to be a killer, Tess..."

Tessa threw her arms around Amara, hugging her tight as she whispered back. "They're not people, Amara. You're not even killing them; you're just sending them back to Hell. This is nothing like Halloween." Amara wiped the tears from her eyes and pulled back from Tessa. She nodded slowly, acknowledging the witch's words, even if she didn't fully believe them.

"Look, you all wanted my help." Vee was staring intently at Amara, her eyes unyielding. "But we *have* to kill these demons. So long as their bodies are capable of breathing, they can be used against us. If I can't trust you to do what needs to be done, then I'm out of here."

"Oh, would you rather Amara be a heartless killer?" Tessa said, stepping closer to Vee. "If I remember correctly, you're only alive because Amara is a better person than you thought she was!"

"What, am I supposed to thank her for *only* beating me within an inch of my life? It's easy to sing her praises when she's never done anything but fuck you!" Vee shouted, and Amara felt the back of her neck bristle as angelic energy radiated off Vee.

"STOP IT!" Amara yelled, jumping between her friends. She pushed them apart, looking between them both as she kept talking. "Vee, I'm not saying I won't fight with everything I have. I've just... I've never killed anything before, and it's a big deal for me. And Tessa, Vee's right to be concerned. This is serious business, and she's the only one that's extensively trained for something like this."

Tessa crossed her arms and huffed, refusing to look at Vee, who quickly walked away from them both. She grabbed her bag, then spoke up again. "Whatever. Look, it's almost time to head out, we should grab our things."

Over the course of the next few minutes, all three girls slowly prepared themselves in silence. Tessa pulled out her switchblade, her tattoos flaring as she swished the knife through the air, then pocketed it before packing her magic journal into her bag. Vee opened her Enochian Texts and cast a spell on herself, which caused Amara's body to seize up again. Vee's face scrunched in disgust as the spell finished, then she put her book in her backpack and zipped it closed. Amara, thankfully, didn't need anything; her body was her weapon. She changed into one of her gym outfits, knowing she needed the flexibility, then covered up with some sweatpants and a baggy sweater so as to not draw any looks around campus. Once ready, they closed the door behind them and headed out.

It was time to go on the offensive.

The walk across campus was tense, and the yelling match in Amara's apartment hadn't done anything to calm Vee's nerves. She still didn't trust Amara and Tessa, and it didn't help that the witch was so quick to anger. Though, even with all the anger, Vee found herself continuously replaying one moment.

Amara, her eyes glazed over and staring into the distance, on the verge of a panic attack. Tears forming in her eyes, Tessa stepping in to try and keep Amara grounded.

"I-I don't want to be a killer, Tess..."

This was the person Vee remembered, the kind girl from Freshman Biology that was too squeamish to dissect an animal. Too shy to talk about sex, too nervous to go out and dance with her friends. Vee had always felt somewhat protective of Amara, especially with Tessa taking every chance to try and jump down her pants. This was the same person that Vee had tried to kill, the person Vee had convinced herself was nothing but a heartless demon, reduced to tears over the thought of hurting another human.

How is this the same person that almost killed me on Halloween? Unless... she was just defending herself. Backed into a corner, scared that her friend had suddenly turned on her.

Vee shook her head, shocked at what she was thinking. Amara was a demon, end of story. She'd even been flaunting her tail at lunch, mocking Vee with it. Vee's thoughts drifted back to the mantras she'd been taught growing up.

Doubt is the weapon of the enemy. Doubt can destroy even the strongest faith, and without faith, I am nothing.

Her thoughts continued to wage war with each other as they slowly approached Lysander Hall. She thought about this secret cult base that she'd never seen before, wondering if this was all a massive trap. She thought about Amara, so scared at the thought of being forced to kill. She thought about their fight with Mr. Wellington, who'd suspiciously been in the Dean's office at the same time as them. She thought about the first friend she ever made at Aurelius, desperately texting her day after day, apologizing profusely for her actions.

As usual, there were no answers to be found in the chaotic echo chamber of her mind. She eventually had to silence her thoughts, as they'd found their way into the elevator. Tessa revealed a secret button with her magic, one that led deep underground, and Amara took advantage of the privacy to pull off her baggy clothes.

Vee didn't need to undress, thankfully, but she did have additional preparations to take care of. She opened her Enochian Texts, briefly casting a short spell to magically bind her book to her hand. This particular spell had been born from her perceived shortcomings from her fight with Amara; she couldn't afford to lose the book again. She noticed Amara tense in discomfort as she cast her spell and wondered how much pain she'd been in on Halloween, when she'd been trapped in a banishment circle.

Stop it, Vee. Stay focused.

Next, she summoned her angelic sword, grasping it tight as she felt the elevator start to slow. "Amara, keep them distracted. The more space I have, the more I can focus on my heavy hitting spells."

Amara nodded slowly, her face filled with determination. "We'll come out in a hallway. As soon as we see them, I'll charge in, and hopefully that'll buy Tess some space."

Tessa spoke up next. "Once I've started, I'm going to be pretty oblivious to what's happening. I'll need one of you on me at all times, otherwise I'm done for."

There was no more time to plan. The elevator landed, and a soft ding indicated they'd reached their destination. When the doors opened, Amara stepped out first, her body transforming before Vee's eyes. After a quick flash of hellfire, she now had her wings, horns, and tail ready to go. Her hands were now covered with that strange black substance Vee had seen on Halloween, and infernal flames danced around her fists.

Tessa went next, her switchblade circling her body as she headed down the hallway. She clutched her journal tightly to her chest, nervously looking from side to side.

Vee stepped off the elevator, carefully jogging forward as she held her book in front of her. She didn't want to start casting until she knew what she was up against, so she moved slowly and deliberately as she waited for something to happen. Soon enough, she found herself leaving the hallway, looking into the main chamber of this strange, underground complex.

The room was impressively large, especially for something hidden underneath Lysander Hall. The floor, walls, and ceiling were made of cold, gray concrete, and she saw several other hallways apart from the one they'd entered through. In the center of the chamber, Vee saw the massive magic circle the cult was using to summon demons. It was surrounded by four pillars, each connecting the floor to the ceiling.

Tessa crouched next to the circle, her journal open, her tattoos flaring to life. Amara, her hands still covered in hellfire, slowly paced around the room, her eyes darting to all the different entrances.

"Amara, what is this?" Vee asked, trying to keep her voice low.

"I don't know! I expected there to be guards, or demons, or something!" Amara whispered, moving closer to Vee.

"I don't like it," Vee said. "There's no way they would leave this unprotected. After our scuffle with Mr. Wellington, I expected them to be on high alert."

Vee continued walking around the chamber, holding up her sword to cast light down each of the hallways. Each entrance seemed to fork off in multiple directions, and she wondered what the point of this chamber was. Had it been built to house this circle? If so, it seemed a bit excessive, but she also didn't know much about witchcraft. Perhaps some kind of shelter?

After checking the side entrances, Vee returned to the center and stood next to Tessa. "How's it looking?"

"It's slow, this circle is built differently than all the others. Still trying to make heads or tails of what I'm looking at," Tessa said.

"Well, figure it out, we don't have all day!" Vee snapped. She then moved closer to Amara, taking care to avoid her hellfire. "Can you sense anything? Anyone?"

Amara's eyes flared, and she quickly scanned all the entrances. "Nothing. What are we missing? Where are they?"

A sound echoed out from the hallway they'd entered through. Vee immediately recognized it as the sound of the elevator, and when she looked over, she saw figures stepping off the lift. "Look alive, we've got company!"

There weren't many of them, maybe three or four, but their eyes glowed ominously in the dim light. Vee prepared her book and started chanting in Enochian, preparing a spell for when they arrived. Amara moved towards them, positioning herself between Vee and the incoming demons. Her wings extended, her tail twitched as that strange, bony substance turned it into a small blade, and she leapt at the demons.

Amara met them before they could leave the hallway, which prevented them from surrounding her. Taking advantage of the distraction, Vee finished her spell and watched as motes of holy light appeared around her, slowly forming into arrows. They glowed brightly, and she pointed her sword down the hallway to aim them. The righteous anger of her magic thrummed just under her skin, and she gripped the sword tight as she waited for an opening. She watched Amara's movements closely, trying to find a pattern in her attacks, and soon she found her chance. With one final line of Enochian, she released her volley of angelic arrows.

At the last second, however, she heard a noise from her left. Another cultist had entered the chamber, then snuck up on Vee. He slashed at Vee's stomach with a large knife at the same time she released her spell, forcing her to leap away. From the hallway, she heard several screams of demonic pain, and she redirected her focus on this new cultist.

Brandishing her sword, she quickly disarmed her attacker before throwing him to the ground. She stepped over him, ready to plunge her blade into his heart, when she looked into his eyes. She saw fear, and realized immediately that this cultist wasn't a demon.

She'd been expecting an army of the damned, and froze in surprise. Was she really about to kill someone? The cultist took advantage of her hesitation, kicking her legs out and knocking her down. Within seconds, he'd grabbed his knife again and was trying to drive it into Vee's neck. He threw his entire body behind the blade, and it took all of Vee's strength to hold it back. The tip of the blade reached her neck, and she closed her eyes to ask her magic for more assistance. The Enochian energies pumping through her body intensified, and she shoved the cultist off her. He fell onto his back, and Vee immediately jumped to her feet and drove her blade through his shoulder. As he cried out in pain, she made a fist and struck the side of his head, knocking him unconscious. She pulled her sword free, then heard Tessa speak up from the center of the circle.

"Fuck! The circle's a decoy!" Tessa yelled. "We have to get out of here!"

This whole thing was a trap!

Vee looked over at Amara, hoping to see her cleaning up the remaining cultists. Instead, Vee saw that her arrows had hit one more demon than she'd intended. Several beams of light had embedded themselves in Amara's back, and although she continued fighting, Vee could tell that she was in rough shape. With another few words of Enochian, Vee dismissed the magic, and watched as her arrows vanished from her friend's body. "Tessa, get Amara!"

Running close, Vee pushed Amara out of the way and reached for her own magic. She summoned a burst of light, hoping to blind the demons and give them an opportunity to escape. As the cultists recoiled from her magic, however, she saw the elevator open once more, releasing even more cultists into the hallway.

"Vee, run! We can't get out that way!" Amara said. She was leaning against Tessa, and the two were running for one of the back hallways. Vee quickly joined them, and as she ran, she flipped to a different page in her book and began to cast. By the time she'd left the main chamber, the spell was ready, and she released a thin barrier of light to block off the entrance they'd just taken.

"That will buy us some time, we need to move!" Vee said, pushing past Tessa and Amara. She sprinted down the hallway, exploring the area, looking for any possible sign of another exit. After a brief pause, during which she heard Tessa and Amara talking to each other, they both joined in the search as well.

Vee immediately noticed that, apart from the main chamber, the hallways all looked like maintenance tunnels. They were quite wide, the ceilings crammed full of plumbing, wiring, and air ducts. They found a few different rooms, filled with various storage containers, and even a couple makeshift beds, but no exits. Tessa seemed to be looking for magic, as her tattoos were constantly glowing, but her knife was nowhere to be seen. The girls spent the better part of the next ten minutes checking various hallways, hoping there was another way out.

Eventually, after finding their fifth dead end, Vee groaned in frustration. "What is this fucking place? It's practically a maze, I can't make heads or tails of anything!"

"No clue, but it definitely wasn't built to be a cultist hideout. I saw some magic crap in the rooms we passed, but it looked recent." Tessa walked past Vee, holding out her hand and lightly touching the wall ahead of them. "But... we're in luck. This wall is an illusion."

"Thank fuck," Amara said, gasping. She leaned against a nearby wall, her breathing heavy, and Vee noticed blood dripping down her back.

While Tessa closed her eyes, hopefully trying to clear away the illusion, Vee moved closer to Amara. She paused, unsure exactly what to say, before trying to speak. "Amara, I... I didn't mean to—"

"Likely fucking story," Amara snapped. Her eyes flared, and unnatural heat poured off her body. This was the creature Vee had fought on Halloween, no doubt about it. Was this a fight or flight instinct? Did holy magic cause her to revert to more aggressive instincts? The thought refused to leave Vee's head, making her wonder how responsible she was for Amara's actions that night.

"Got it!" Tessa said, breaking the tension. The wall in front of her vanished, and they saw a staircase on the other side. As Vee ran ahead, she noticed how different the space felt on the other side of the illusion. The area seemed more lived in, as if students visited here regularly, and she even saw a door leading into a small, abandoned classroom. She also opened the door to the staircase, slowly peeking in to make sure they were alone. Content they were safe, she returned to Tessa and Amara, sighing in relief as the illusory wall returned.

"I think we're safe, this looks like a pretty standard basement," Vee said.

"Good. Amara, do you want to recover here, or at home?" Tessa turned to Amara, holding her shoulders gently. Amara looked up, her demonic eyes meeting Tessa's. Her breathing had grown more ragged, and Vee swore she heard growling.

When Amara spoke, her voice was deeper, angrier, and desperate. **"Now."**

Vee watched as Amara grabbed Tessa's waist, pulling her close and kissing her. Amara's tail, no longer covered in that strange material, snaked around Tessa's leg, its tip conveniently stopping at the witch's crotch. Next, Amara's lips moved to Tessa's neck, biting her softly as Tessa looked over at Vee.

"Um, could you take lookout for a sec? We need to— fuck, Amara... we need to take care of this," Tessa said.

Vee froze for a moment, caught up in the novelty of what she was watching. She'd seen Amara get angry before, even been on the receiving end of her rage, but she'd never seen this side of her. She was practically feral, a creature of raw passion, pawing at Tessa as she eagerly started undoing the witch's pants. Shaking her head, Vee realized that she desperately didn't want to watch this happen, and walked into the staircase.

Why are you surprised? You know she's a succubus, you know they're sleeping together. Still, it's weird seeing them just... go for it, out in the open like this. Is that how she heals from her injuries?

Vee slowly walked to the top of the staircase, which seemed taller than usual, before peeking out the door at the top. Thankfully, the hallway on the other side was quiet, and she was able to take a quick look around. It took a minute, but she eventually figured out that this was Whitmore Hall. Most importantly, she didn't see any cultists or demons, so she felt safe returning to the staircase.

She slowly walked down the stairs, finally taking a seat about halfway down. Between the barrier she'd summoned to block off the chamber, and the illusory wall Tessa had found, she'd doubted anyone would be able to find them. Her thoughts returned to that chamber, wondering if there had been anything she could have done differently, but there was only one thing on her mind: Amara had been right. By hiding her abilities, she'd sabotaged their chances of success.

They hadn't expected a trap. They hadn't planned anything. She hadn't expected to find unpossessed humans, and yet fighting one had caused her to freeze up. Amara's words from earlier floated through her head, yet again.

"I-I don't want to be a killer, Tess..."

Vee almost wanted to laugh, but the similarity was eerie.

Maybe I have more in common with Amara than I thought.

She shook her head, trying to dislodge the thought. What would the church think of her now? Working with a demon and a witch, after almost being killed by one of them. Beneath her, just beyond the flight of stairs, she heard excited moans coming from the basement. They were faint, but Vee could tell it was Tessa; she'd always been shameless about her sex life, and this wasn't the first time Vee had overheard the witch in the throes of passion.

Vee leaned back, resting her head on the wall behind her, before sighing in frustration.

All I wanted was to live a simple life, free of all this supernatural nonsense. Her stupid transformation ruined all of that, pulled me back into action, and now they're roping me into this stupid cult nonsense...

Her thoughts spun in endless circles until the moaning downstairs stopped. Vee decided to walk down to the door, then she carefully knocked.

"We're decent, Vee, you can come on in!" Tessa said.

Opening the door, the smell of sex and sulfur immediately washed over Vee. She fought the urge to gag as she looked at her friends, their clothes slightly tussled, but nothing more. Tessa seemed extremely pleased with herself, and Amara was practically unrecognizable from just minutes earlier. Gone was the aggressive, primal demon that desperately needed to get laid; her demonic features were gone, her injuries were healed, and the blood had vanished somehow. Apart from a hole in her sports bra, there weren't any traces of her wounds.

Vee almost wanted to ask, but she couldn't muster the courage. "So, you said the circle was a decoy. What does that mean?"

"I'm not sure how they did it, exactly. Maybe it's an illusion, maybe they just have huge concrete slabs with spare magic circles, but the circle we saw in the chamber didn't actually do anything, which is why I was so confused at first. It was essentially a ball of twine, random magic runes meant to give off signatures without any meaning."

"Great," Amara said. "So, what are we supposed to do? They know we're trying to stop them, so how are we supposed to catch them in the act and find the real circle?"

The girls went quiet, and an unfortunate thought crossed Vee's mind. "Well... we know at least one time the real circle will be out. Sunday, three AM."

"Are you serious?" Tessa said, moving closer to Vee. "That's the worst time to go! They'll have all the demons in one place, and they'll be on high alert! Plus, if we're too late, Mr. Wellington will finish his own ritual, and who knows what kind of demon he'll have inside him!"

Amara placed a hand on Tessa's shoulder, trying to calm her down. "No, Vee's right. What other choice do we have? Hunt down and kill everyone in the cult? I don't know about you, but I'd rather Mr. Wellington not try to frame us for mass murder. We also know from Nick's research that he's a huge recluse; even if we stop this ritual, we can't let him get away. If we attack Sunday morning, we know for sure the real circle will be out, and Mr. Wellington will be there."

"For the record, I hate this," Tessa said, huffing and walking away.

"Of course, this means the fight will be even harder," Amara said, looking at Vee. "We can't afford to go in without a plan. Unless you think I fight better with arrows lodged in my back."

Vee winced. She deserved that, and she knew it. "Amara, I...you're right. I was scared to reveal my abilities, but we can't afford to mess this up. You name the time and place, and I'll be there to start training."

"Great! We have a plan, and I hate it, but I know better than to fight an angel and a demon," Tessa said, playfully slapping Amara's ass. "Could you do me a favor and check the staircase real quick? Just in case holy girl here missed something?"

Amara nodded, then walked into the staircase, her eyes glowing. Vee looked to Tessa, not sure what the meaning of this was, and flinched as the witch charged at her. Tessa grabbed Vee's shoulder, pushing her hard against the wall behind her, and her tattoos started glowing. Her switchblade hovered in the air, aiming at Vee's neck, as the witch spoke. "Listen up, Vee, because I'm only going to say this once.

If this works, and I reverse the circle, there's a good chance I'll be creating a portal into Hell. If something happens to Amara, if you so much as flinch in the wrong direction, I will not hesitate to run this knife through your heart."

"We're on the same side, Tessa. I want this cult finished as much as you do," Vee hissed.

"And, conveniently, Amara needs to be turned into a pincushion in the process? I know how your kind work, and this is your golden opportunity to kill two birds with one stone. If Amara isn't around to go back to school on Monday, I will hunt. You. Down. Even if it takes the rest of my life. Do you understand?"

The girls stared at each other in silence, their anger palpable. Vee slowly nodded, and Tessa begrudgingly let her go. Moments later, Amara returned from the staircase. "Everything looks clear. You two ready to head out?"

Tessa's fury vanished without a trace, and she smiled as she threw an arm around Amara's shoulder. "We're all good!"

Vee watched them leave, eventually remembering that she needed to follow close behind. The last few hours had been incredibly chaotic, and she didn't know how to make heads or tails of it all. As best she could, she tried to focus on the biggest threat: the cult. If nothing else, she now believed that Amara wasn't involved, and she was ready to commit to taking them out.

12

SIMMERING HOSTILITY

Earlier that day

Amara's vision blurred, the edges of her world vanishing in a haze of blood and anger. The fight against the possessed cultists had gone great, in her opinion, until multiple spears of Enochian energy had impaled themselves in her back. Now, as she leaned on Tessa to try and escape the cult's headquarters, it took all of her strength to stay lucid.

"That will buy us some time, we need to move!" Vee shouted.

Amara only briefly paid attention to the words, instead much more focused on the blinding wall of energy that had just sprang into existence next to her. She squeezed Tessa tight, then leaned closer to whisper, "Tess, if I don't feed soon, things are gonna get ugly."

The witch nodded, and soon all three girls were scrambling through the dim corridors in hopes of finding another exit. The hallways seemed to stretch on for an eternity, and Amara had no idea which path they were taking. Her back was drenched in blood, and she barely had the strength to stay close behind Tessa. She heard a few whispers occasionally, the other girls complaining about the circuitous facility, but soon enough they found an illusory wall that Tessa started working on.

"Thank fuck," Amara said, gasping. She moved to a nearby wall, leaning against it for support as she tried to hold herself together. She only barely registered that Vee was moving closer and had started speaking.

"Amara, I... I didn't mean to—"

"Likely fucking story," Amara snapped. She felt the angelic energy lingering on Vee's body, and the smell pushed her closer to the edge. The two girls locked eyes for a moment before Tessa bypassed the illusion, giving everyone a chance to escape. It only took a brief minute for Vee to scout the area and Tessa to restore the illusory wall.

"I think we're safe, this looks like a pretty standard basement," Vee said.

"Good. Amara, do you want to recover here, or at home?" Tessa turned to Amara, holding her shoulders gently. The touch excited Amara, fanning the flames that were already raging inside of her.

"Now."

Amara grabbed Tessa's waist and pulled her close, their lips meeting as Amara's hands started exploring the witch's body. Her tail curled around Tessa's leg, holding it tight as it sought out her sex, eager to start pleasuring her. Amara kissed Tessa's neck next, licking and biting as she felt Tessa's aura start to grow. They both wanted this, and Amara was sick of waiting.

Tessa said something to Vee, who was still standing around for some reason, but Amara wasn't paying attention. She was more focused on undoing Tessa's pants, on tasting her sweet cunt that she smelled growing wetter by the second.

A door closed nearby, and Tessa's hands quickly found their way to Amara's body. "We're alone, finally," the witch said.

"Good," Amara said. She pulled away from Tessa, quickly moving behind her and pinning her to the wall. One hand grabbed Tessa's hair, holding it tight as she kept Tessa's face pushed against the bricks. The witch was clearly excited, her aura growing brighter and brighter, and Amara moaned with delight as she began feeding. Strength poured into her, and she held Tessa tight as she began pulling her clothes off.

Soon enough, the witch's pants were bunched around her knees, along with her panties, and Amara's fingers had found Tessa's sex. There was no time for subtlety, not when Amara was this hungry. She pushed her fingers inside Tessa, feeling her tight walls twitch as Tessa moaned aloud.

"Fuck, Amara, you've never been this rough before!" Tessa said, moaning quietly as Amara began playing with her clit.

"I know you like it," Amara whispered, playfully biting Tessa's ear.

Amara moved her tail closer, slowly circling Tessa's entrance before pushing inside. As her tail began thrusting, Amara stepped closer and pushed her own hips against Tessa's ass. Both of her hands moved down, wrapping around Tessa's hips, and she started grinding against Tessa in time with the thrusts of her tail. Through her connection with Tessa's aura, she felt all the pleasure she was providing, and it made her shudder with excitement.

It was almost like she had a phallus of her own, and was using it to thrust deep into Tessa's eager cunt. The tip of her tail twitched, and Amara's moans joined Tessa's as they continued fucking. Amara was being pleasured both through Tessa's aura and by grinding her own pussy against the witch's bouncing ass.

Tessa's moaning grew even louder, and Amara knew it wouldn't be long before she came. While she regretted not being able to draw this out, Amara knew they couldn't linger in this strange basement. After another minute of frantic fucking, both girls tensed with excitement as their orgasms took them. They both came hard, Tessa's hands forming into fists as she steadied herself against the wall, and Amara pushed her tail even deeper into Tessa while biting the witch's neck. Amara's senses burst outwards once more, Tessa's powerful orgasm restoring all the energy Amara had lost in attempting to recover from Vee's attack. Her wounds closed, and the Enochian energy that lingered on her body dispersed as well.

Amara stepped back, happily running her hands through her hair as she took a breath of fresh air. She felt like herself now, no longer a ravenous beast, and she gently pulled her tail out of Tessa's quivering sex.

"Fuck... wow... Amara, that was... fuck." Tessa was still leaning against the wall, her breathing heavy. Amara stepped to the side, softly tracing her fingers over Tessa's cheek.

"I didn't hurt you, did I? I kinda... let loose a bit," Amara said.

Tessa shook her head quickly. "Only the good kind of hurt, promise." Despite Tessa's words, Amara couldn't help but notice the witch rubbing her neck, rolling her head back and forth as she winced.

Shit, did I push her too hard? The last time I felt those urges take over was back on Halloween, inside Vee's circle. I don't even remember that entire night... At least this time I didn't black out.

With a nervous smile, Amara squeezed Tessa's shoulder before moving towards the open floor nearby. She pulled her clothes off, summoned a small torrent of hellfire, and used it to remove all the blood from her body. The flames also seared away the lingering sweat, the grime, and Tessa's delicious juices that coated her tail. After a minute of bathing in infernal flames, Amara quickly got dressed again.

There was a soft knock at the basement door, and Tessa quickly answered, "We're decent, Vee, you can come on in!"

As Vee walked inside, Amara couldn't help but scowl. Although her injuries had healed, looking at Vee made her back tingle again. The girls took a few minutes to discuss the next steps, the tension in the air obvious. Sure, Vee seemed willing to meet them halfway, but now seeds of doubt had lodged themselves in Amara's mind.

It was late in the evening the following day when the girls found time to meet up again. Amara had borrowed Nick's key to the gymnastics building, as they needed both privacy and a wide-open space to practice. The day leading up to this strange rehearsal had been confusing, to say the least. After so many weeks of beating herself up, convinced that she could change Vee's mind by just explaining herself, Amara was now skeptical. In their very first fight, supposedly as allies, Amara had wound up with a volley of holy arrows lodged in her back.

What if Tessa is right? I've been so focused on proving to Vee that I'm trustworthy, but... I never bothered to ask the same about her. Am I so desperate for forgiveness that I'm blind to what's in front of me?

Amara waited outside the gymnastics building, idly scrolling through her socials as she waited for Vee and Tessa to show up. She wore an outfit similar to yesterday, athletic shorts and a matching sports bra, though this time her clothes were a deep, royal purple. Comfortable sweats covered them, but they were unfortunately not the same sweats from yesterday; those had been a tragic casualty of the fight. She'd briefly revisited the elevator in Lysander Hall, just in case, but her clothes were nowhere to be found.

Vee arrived first, unsurprisingly. "Hey Amara, any problems today?" she asked.

"Nothing really. I don't think they're stupid enough to cause a scene in public. Tess tells me that people who know about magic like to keep it hidden." Amara's words were tense. After being literally stabbed in the back yesterday, she was having trouble extending the same generosity to Vee that she'd mustered their last few run-ins.

"I've heard the same thing," Vee said. They stood there awkwardly for another few minutes before Tessa arrived, and Amara was pretty sure they both sighed in relief.

Soon enough, all three girls entered the gymnastics building, and Amara quickly ran over to the light switches. The bright fluorescent lights took a while to fully kick in, but soon the building was ready for action. Amara started by pulling her sweats off, and she immediately noticed a swell in Tessa's aura. Amara was fully aware that her outfit was pretty revealing, but she needed as little coverage as possible to make sure her wings and tail had room to breathe. Though, she couldn't deny that it was nice to have clothes that so perfectly showed off how athletic her demonic body had gotten.

Remembering Vee's request from back in Whitmore Hall, Amara spoke up. "Alright Vee, I'm manifesting my true form, which means there's going to be some fire. That okay?"

"Sure, go for it."

With a burst of hellfire, Amara's demonic features returned to her. She happily ran her hands over her horns, always happy to have them back, and noticed that they seemed to have grown again recently. They reached further back than usual and angled up more dramatically as they reached the back of her head. A quick check of her tail and wings revealed nothing else had changed, so she started stretching everything out in preparation.

Vee, apparently, wasn't planning on wearing the same revealing clothing. She wore loose, white and gold running pants that cinched at the ankles, and a blue athletic jacket. She pulled out her Enochian Texts and cast a few spells while Amara continued stretching. They were far enough apart that the angelic magic didn't sting too much, but Amara certainly bristled at its presence.

"Alright, what's the plan, you two?" Tessa asked, leaning against a nearby pommel horse.

"What? Why is this on us?" Vee responded.

"You two are our heavy hitters and have the most varied abilities. You want me to explain everything I can do? I can make knives float and try to stab people. There, you know everything you need to know."

"What about when you threw Brandon across the room?" Amara asked. "I know you said that was stressful, but it's an option, right?"

"Not really. See, most magic has trace amounts of psychic energy to it, likely even yours and Vee's. Your hellfire, for example, is an extension of you, but you still have to control it. Think of the psychic connection like a muscle, a necessary part of controlling any magic that's not physically attached to you. Pretty much everyone has a low-level psychic field, which means they can try to resist magical effects. Some people are better than others, but generally, the more resolute you are, the more you can resist most magic directed at you."

"So why did it work on Brandon?"

"Cuz he's a weak little bitch, that's why. He's got no backbone, and he was terrified of me. Fear can be incredibly helpful for bypassing psychic resistance. A roomful of cultists and demons, though? Better to assume you won't be able to just light them on fire. You'll have better luck throwing fire at them, or lighting up your fists and beating them senseless."

"Makes enough sense, I suppose," Amara said. She turned to Vee, who seemed to be looking at Amara's tail again, though she quickly averted her eyes. "Vee, you or me?"

Both girls looked at each other silently, the tension thick. "You first," Vee said.

Hardly surprised, Amara sighed and nodded. "Alright, fine. It's pretty straightforward, honestly. I have enhanced vision, I can see in the dark as clear as day, and I can also see electrical signals. I'm not great at deciphering them, but I'm working on it. I can also see auras around everyone, which tell me if they're horny, who they're attracted to, when they last had sex, things like that. I don't think any of that is going to be very helpful in a fight."

Starting to feel antsy, Amara jumped up on the balance beam and continued warming up while she kept talking. "Physically, I'm much stronger. I can overpower Nick easily, and you both know how strong he is. My shapeshifting lets me grow a chitinous exoskeleton over my body, giving me natural protection, but I can also sharpen it to give myself claws, or turn my tail into a blade."

To illustrate her point, Amara manifested her chitinous gauntlets and sharpened her tail, swishing it through the air as a demonstration. "I can do the same for my wings, and give myself a pretty hefty shield, but it weighs me down. I can summon hellfire and exert my willpower over existing flames. If you see purple fire, chances are I'm the one controlling it. I'm completely immune to fire myself, but as a side effect of that, it's really hard for me to notice changes in temperature, even dramatic ones."

A thought jumped into Amara's head, and she decided to test her balance even further. She leaned forward, planting her hands on the balance beam, and kicked her legs over her head. It was a rocky start, but with the help of her tail, she found the motion came quite naturally to her. "That's about it, honestly."

Vee seemed surprised that Amara didn't have more to say. "That's it?"

"Um... I guess I also dreamwalk, but it's pretty sporadic, and I'm not sure how to control it yet. Even if I could, I doubt we'll need that in a fight."

Amara and Tessa looked at Vee expectantly. The angel let out a sigh of her own, no doubt regretting that she had to give up divine secrets, but she soon began talking. "Alright, my abilities are... complicated. Long story short, angels wield the power of Creation, and our magic can manifest as almost anything we want. However, the more esoteric our desires are, the harder it'll be to control the magic."

"Is that why you stick to making weapons?" Amara asked.

"That's part of it, yeah. Angelic magic can be incredibly taxing, and it takes years of training to prepare our bodies for it. I have an innate well of angelic energy of my own, but it's rather small. That's why this book is so important." Vee tapped her Enochian Texts, which glowed slightly under her touch.

"This book is essentially a battery, a reservoir of holy magic that's been cultivated for generations. These pages contain detailed descriptions of spells, knowledge on how to cast them, and the magic to do it. Traditionally, every angel that inherits this book adds a spell of their own, and future generations continue to iterate and perfect those spells. Those arrows I created came from an angel that roamed the Earth a few hundred years back, and they're one of the most reliable offensive abilities I have."

"You've also got a banishment spell in there, right?" Amara asked.

"I do, but... you saw me try to cast it. It takes a while, and I can't be interrupted. Best case scenario, I can try to trap someone in a circle to buy time, but it's possible to break out."

Amara couldn't help but glare at Vee, watching her recount the events that led up to their fateful fight. "Okay, so you have a lot of options. You've also been training for this your whole life, whereas I'm just some idiot that happened to turn into a demon. Do you have any suggestions on strategies? Spells that might synergize with what I can do?"

"I've certainly been thinking about that, but it's tough. If you weren't a demon, I could probably try to enhance your abilities, make you stronger and faster, maybe even give you weapons of your own, but I think it's safe to assume that my magic will always hurt you, even if it's not aggressive."

"Agreed," Amara said. "Even that healing spell you cast on yourself stung pretty bad. We need something that will let us keep out of each other's way."

"There's another wrinkle, too," Vee continued. "Not all the cultists have been turned into demons yet. I fought one that was still human. Depending on what magic I use, they might be completely immune to it."

"Wait, that's it!" Tessa said, rejoining the conversation. "You can separate the demons and the humans!"

"How would that help?" Amara asked.

"It's simple. On Halloween, Vee locked you inside a circle, right? Well, what if we did the opposite? Lock us both inside a barrier, so that the only people that can get through are humans! That way, Amara can focus entirely on the demons, while Vee can take out any non-possessed cultists that come at us. If I'm inside the barrier, that should buy me enough time to reverse-engineer the circle!"

"That's... honestly a really good idea, Tessa," Vee said.

"What, like it's surprising?" the witch replied, sticking her tongue out.

"Well, there's no time to waste. Let's test it out," Amara said, jumping off the balance beam.

"Fine, just give me a few minutes. I need to figure out which spell would work best for that." Vee sat down, opened her Enochian Texts, and started to flip through them. While she read, Amara busied herself by trying some of the other gymnastics equipment. A few minutes passed before Vee spoke up again. "Got it!"

Amara watched as Vee moved to the middle of the large spring floor, then held her book aloft and started reading. Her hair started billowing and angelic energy swirled around her, the book glowing as its magic activated. Various Enochian runes began to form around her, building in complexity, until they all connected to form a large wall that circled Vee, creating a space roughly fifteen feet across. As expected, Amara's body reacted poorly to the Enochian chanting, but the uncomfortable seizing ended once the spell finished.

"Certainly looks impressive," Amara said. "Tess, can you walk through it?"

Moving closer, Tessa carefully pushed a hand against the barrier, watching as it harmlessly passed through. She then took a step inside, shivering slightly as she did, but nothing seemed to happen. "I think I'm fine. It tingled a little, but nothing else. What about you? That's the real test, isn't it?"

Amara looked towards Vee, who gestured at the wall. "Give it a shot," she said.

With a deep breath, Amara approached the glowing wall. She felt its angelic energy bristling at her presence, and she braced herself for some discomfort as she reached for the barrier. The instant she touched it, her entire body seized up once more, holy sparks surging through her body. It felt like she was holding the Enochian Texts again, the energy making it difficult to move. When she finally managed to pull away, she was panting heavily, sweat pooled on her forehead.

"Fuck, that stings..." Amara said through gritted teeth.

"That's kind of the point, Amara," Vee said. "Do you think you'd be able to break through?"

"Probably, I did it last time."

"I'd like to see you try," Vee said. The two girls stared at each other through the barrier, the challenge obviously more than a simple tactical experiment.

Amara's eyes flared, and she happily manifested her chitinous gauntlets before engulfing them in hellfire. She took a few steps back, crouched low to the ground, and leapt at the barrier. She threw the entire weight of her body behind her first punch, watching as her fist collided with the barrier, holy sparks flying through the air and assaulting her body. The barrier threw her back slightly, but she wasn't done yet. She continued attacking, trying to expand her senses to get a feel for the barrier's limits. She had a harder time reading it than she did on Halloween, presumably because she was on the outside this time, but eventually she started to get a sense of what was needed. With each strike, another barrage of Enochian magic attacked her, and she felt herself getting angrier from its influence. Eventually, just as the holy magic threatened to overwhelm her, she managed to land a strike that sank further into the barrier than before. Her second hand joined in, then her bladed tail. She grabbed the edges of the barrier, let loose an angry shout, and ripped a hole in it.

All at once, the holy barrier surrounding Vee and Tessa dissipated. Amara watched Vee's eyes go wide in surprise, and her own body seemed to recoil as Amara broke through the magic.

The angel and the demon locked eyes, and when Amara finally spoke, her words were surprisingly smug. "Looks like I win again, Vee."

Vee snarled at Amara, pulling herself together before she started pacing sideways, skirting around Amara. "Please, I wasn't even fighting back."

Amara matched the movement, and now both girls were slowly circling the open floor, each waiting for the other to escalate the situation. Out of the corner of her eye, Amara saw Tessa nervously looking back and forth, before deciding to back out and take a seat on the pommel horse.

"Maybe we should throw down, since apparently you're such a better fighter than I am," Amara said.

"Maybe we should. You clearly have a lot to learn." Vee dropped her Enochian Texts to the ground, then kicked them back to keep them out of the way. She unzipped her jacket, throwing it aside as well, revealing a sports bra that resembled marble, with streaks of white, gray, and gold running through it.

"Says the girl that trained her whole life just to lose to a month-old demon!"

"Um, guys? Maybe we should—" Tessa tried to say, but her words were instantly cut off by Vee.

"Shut up!" Vee shouted. She leapt forward, summoning her holy blade with a burst of Enochian energy. She slashed at Amara, who managed to dodge out of the way, but only barely. Vee continued attacking, again and again, trying to push Amara off balance, but Amara continued to evade each attack. This harrowing dance continued until Vee summoned a flash of light from her off hand, which startled Amara and created an opening for Vee to jab the demon's side with the hilt of her sword.

"Your movements are sloppy and unrefined. Your inexperience is obvious," Vee hissed as Amara grabbed her side in pain.

"Yeah? Well you can't handle extra limbs!" Amara's tail darted out, wrapping around Vee's ankle and pulling hard. Vee fell to the ground, gasping as she landed flat on her back. "You only stood a chance because you caught me off guard."

Vee panted heavily, and she glared at Amara before responding. "You're right about one thing, at least." With a quick spin, Vee swung her legs towards Amara, who wasn't ready for retaliation. She fell to the ground herself, and Vee quickly jumped on top of the demon to try and pin her down. "You can't read your opponents! You leave yourself open with every attack!"

Amara's tail lashed out again, knocking Vee's sword out of her hand. Amara thrust off the ground, turning the tables on Vee as she tried to pin her down in retaliation. The girls quickly locked hands as they wrestled, tumbling back and forth as each tried to force the other into submission. This continued for close to a minute, neither one able to cement their advantage. Eventually, the girls began to tire, their actions slowing as they both refused to surrender. Amara, however, had already exerted herself breaking through Vee's barrier, and soon found herself on her back while Vee pinned her hands on the floor over her head.

They both gasped from exertion, sweat pouring down their bodies as they glared at each other. The tension only broke when Amara's nose twitched, and a familiar smell filled her senses. The change in expression threw Vee off guard, and both girls paused as Amara turned her head to look at Tessa.

"Really, Tess?" Amara said.

"What's she doing?" Vee asked, her grip loosening slightly.

"Watching us fight is turning her on!"

"Oh, come on, look at you two!" Tessa said, gesturing at them. Amara looked back at Vee, who was clearly straddling her, her athletic body glistening with sweat. "This is the most homoerotic shit I've ever seen!"

"It is not!" Amara and Vee said in unison. They looked at each other in surprise before Vee rolled her eyes and got off Amara. They both stood up, huffing as they pulled themselves together. Vee picked up her sword before dismissing it, then grabbed her Enochian Texts and her jacket. Amara walked over to Tessa, playfully smacking her with her tail before grabbing her own clothes and starting to put them on.

"I guess we're done?" Tessa said, looking at Amara and Vee.

"For tonight? Absolutely," Vee said. She was clearly flustered, both from Tessa's comments and the tiring fight.

A moment passed, Amara doing her best to calm herself down after the fight with Vee. Enochian magic always riled her up, and she wanted to think about things calmly. "For what it's worth," she started, "I do think we should keep training while we have the time. We've got a couple days, might as well be as ready as possible."

"Yeah? Training? Is that what we're calling this?" Tessa said, the insinuation obvious.

"I'm serious, Tess! Setting aside our... history, Vee's right. I don't have any fighting experience, and she's the only person that can match my strength. If I try to fight you or Nick, I risk snapping you in half."

"Fine by me," Vee said. "I'd like to live past Sunday, so every bit of practice helps."

While it was obvious that Tessa only wanted to make crude jokes, Amara was glad to be on the same page as Vee. She still wasn't entirely sure if the angel could be trusted, but for some reason, their fight had been strangely cathartic. Once everyone packed up their things, and Amara double checked they hadn't scorched anything, she turned off the lights in the building and locked up.

In the chaos of trying to stop the cult, everyone had forgotten about one crucial detail; the following day was no ordinary Thursday: it was Thanksgiving. Amara woke to a very confusing text from her mother, asking when she was planning on driving back, causing Amara to panic and share that she was spending the holiday with Nick. When she ran over to Nick's to make sure they were on the same page, she'd discovered that he'd spun a similar lie.

"Ugh, Nick, I feel so bad lying to her!" Amara complained, falling onto his couch.

"You're not technically lying, we are spending today together," Nick said, cleaning up his kitchen.

"You know what I mean! Not only does she think I'm with your family, but this means she's going to be completely alone."

"Can you remind me why? I always forget. Her family... lives far away? Something like that?"

"She always said they were awful, and she moved to get away from them. Obviously my dad was never in the picture, so there isn't family on that side either. Plus, y'know, since I'm pretty sure he's an incubus, I'm not sure we'd want to hang with his family anyways."

"Well, you can make it up to her on Christmas, assuming there's not a secret second cult somewhere on campus."

With Nick's roommate away for the holiday, Amara was free to manifest her tail, which she immediately used to throw a pillow at her friend. "Don't say that! You're gonna jinx us!"

Nick dodged the pillow easily, laughing to himself as he started pulling bags of food out of the fridge. "Come on, it's just a joke. Now get over here and help me get everything ready."

"Ready for what? It's way too early for lunch," Amara said, sliding off the couch and joining Nick in the kitchen. She was surprised to find a massive spread of food, probably enough to feed a dozen people, including a giant turkey. "Hold on, are we actually doing Thanksgiving?"

"Why not? We're here, there aren't any classes, and it's not like you can spend the entire day sparring with Vee. I heard last night was... interesting."

"What did Tessa tell you? Because whatever it was, she's lying, and that's not what happened!" Amara's face turned red, still flustered from last night's events. She made a face at Nick, who was far too pleased with himself, before diving in to help prepare all the food. The two continued prepping in silence for a few moments before she spoke up again. "Wait, speaking of Tessa, should I tell her about this? There's no way we can finish this by ourselves."

"No need, I already took care of it. You've been busy with Mr. Wellington, and I've been busy making sure we all have a home to come back to."

"Nick... you're such a dork, you know that?"

With a hearty laugh, he turned his attention back to the food with unusual determination. He seemed strangely fixated on keeping himself busy, and Amara knew that wasn't a good sign. She'd been friends with Nick long enough to know when he was trying to bottle something up. Turning to face him, she leaned against the counter and stared at him until he looked up.

"Amara? What's up?"

"What is it?" Amara asked.

"What's what? I... don't know what you're talking about."

"Nick. Come on."

A heavy pause overtook the apartment, and he eventually sighed in defeat before setting down his knife. "I saw Alex yesterday. No, that's not right. I saw... whatever *thing* is lurking inside Alex's body. He ran up to me, excitedly talking about his workout routine and everything he wanted to do at our next freerunning sessions. That demon has his memories, Amara, and I just had to pretend like everything was fine! I had to force myself to laugh, to talk like Alex was still here, but... I could tell. His smile, his laugh, it's just not him anymore. He's gone."

It was rare to see Nick so vulnerable. He had no qualms about sharing his feelings, something Amara had always appreciated about him, but his boundless optimism made it easy to forget that he wrestled with the same doubts and fears as everyone else. When he finally looked up, tears in his eyes, Amara simply opened her arms and invited him in for a hug.

Nick didn't hesitate to accept the invite, pulling Amara close and burying his face in her shoulder. She wrapped her arms tightly around him, her tail joining in as well. Just as she started rubbing his back, his body shook and he began to cry.

Amara stayed quiet. As stressful as this was for her, she wasn't the one that had lost a close friend to this horrid cult. She tried to imagine what it would feel like to lose Nick, and a twisted knot formed in her stomach; even thinking about it made her sick. She couldn't possibly imagine what Nick was going through. She was simply happy to be here for him.

That's why we're fighting. To stop them from hurting more people.

She encouraged him to take long, deep breaths; in for two, out for four. A few minutes later, Nick found the strength to pull away from Amara. With a simple look, she asked if he was alright, and he silently nodded in acknowledgment as he rubbed the tears from his eyes. He even briefly excused himself to go to the bathroom, and Amara heard him splashing water on his face to wash up.

When he came out, he seemed committed to pretending like everything was fine again. Amara wanted to chastise him for putting up an act, but she had a feeling his cheerful façade helped him just as much as it helped her.

The rest of the morning was spent preparing their holiday dinner. Nick blasted music the whole time, singing and dancing like an idiot as he tried to shake Amara out of her malaise. It felt weird, doing something so frivolous after such an intense display of sorrow, but after a while, she let herself get swept up in the holiday spirit and joined in. She even ran back to her apartment to change into a stuffy, beige sweater, one that had plenty of room for her tail to be out.

When she returned, she found Tessa sprawled on the couch, happily recounting the events of last night's tumultuous training session.

"—so they look into each other's eyes, right? Amara's tail is flicking in excitement, Vee is out of breath, and—No! Get away!" The witch, tragically, was unable to finish her story. An enraged succubus leapt onto the couch, pillow in hand, eager to shut her up. Both girls laughed as Amara tried to smother Tessa, who was failing to hold her own. "You can't silence me! The truth will come out eventually!"

By the time Nick needed more help in the kitchen, Amara had pinned Tessa to the ground and was relentlessly tickling her with her tail. Nick's call to action spared Tessa from any further torment, though she seemed to have learned her lesson, and stopped talking about last night. After another few hours, during which all three friends did their best to ignore the impending chaos of the ritual, dinner was ready. It was earlier than usual, but everyone was eager to dig in after spending all day stewing in the delicious smells.

"Amara, where's the oven mitt?" Nick asked, ready to take the turkey out of the oven.

"Psh, beats me." Amara pushed Nick out of the way with her tail, then grabbed the roasting pan with her bare hands and pulled it out.

"I guess that works too. Huh."

"Hey, you're the one that got me into cooking. This is way easier than dealing with that fussy glove." As Amara looked for the tools to move the turkey, it suddenly rose up on its own, floating lazily through the air until settling on the plate Nick had put out. She looked over at Tessa, her tattoos starting to fade, and smirked.

"What? You two have been doing all the work, figured I might as well pitch in a little bit," Tessa said.

As Nick started moving all the side dishes to the table, someone knocked on the front door. Amara quickly looked at him, her head cocked to the side, silently asking who it might be.

"Could you get that, Amara? I'm busy," Nick said, conveniently dodging her question.

Slightly nervous, Amara tucked her tail into her sweater and demanifested her horns before answering the door. Thankfully, there were no cultists on the other side, but instead a girl with bright blonde hair and a serious look on her face.

"I heard we're meeting early for tonight's training?" Vee said.

"I, uh..." Amara opened the door further, looking for answers from Nick, while also revealing the Thanksgiving spread. Nick looked over at the two girls, smiling wide.

"Vee! You're just in time!" he said.

"You... tricked me into coming here for dinner?" Vee asked, refusing to enter the apartment. She looked on in confusion for a few moments before finding something to say. "This is hardly the time, and... honestly, I don't think I'm in the mood. Just text me when you're ready to get some practice in."

Vee turned to leave, walking down the hallway, and Amara quickly glanced back at her friends. Nick had his hands full with dishes, and Tessa seemed to have no interest in helping. Amara ran into the hallway after Vee, the door closing behind her. Amara caught up quickly and grabbed Vee's arm. "Vee, wait!"

Vee spun on her heel, pulling out of Amara's grasp. "Come on, Amara, Thanksgiving dinner? Is this supposed to make everything right between us?"

"I didn't do this! I mean, I helped make all the food, but I didn't know Nick had tricked you into coming over."

"There's always a convenient excuse, isn't there?"

"He's trying to help! We all had to cancel our plans; he just wants to give us something else to think about other than a fight to the death."

"We don't holiday together, Amara. I know you're new to this, but angels and demons don't just... hang out. That's not how this works."

"Yeah? And what if we all die Sunday? Do you want to spend your last days moping around your apartment?" Vee went quiet, her eyes falling to the carpet. When she didn't answer, Amara huffed and rolled her eyes. "Fine, go be miserable for all I care."

Amara turned away, angrily taking a few steps before pausing. She was almost at Nick's door, but she couldn't bring herself to open it. She continued waiting, expecting to hear Vee walking away, but that didn't happen. Vee moved closer, and when she finally spoke, her voice was incredibly quiet, as if she were nervous about someone listening in.

"This... doesn't change anything, Amara." Vee placed her hand on the door, carefully pushing it open before walking inside. Amara followed, almost surprised that she'd managed to talk Vee into joining them. The angel nervously sat down at the table, her posture picture perfect, as Tessa glared at her. Amara unwrapped her tail from her waist and used it to close the front door, bringing her horns back as well. By the time she made it to the table, Nick was finally cutting into the turkey.

"Ah, shoot," Nick said. "This isn't quite done yet. Amara, could you finish it up?"

With a smirk, Amara's eyes flared as she focused on the heat inside the turkey. She stared intently at the oversized dinner, the tantalizing smell filling her senses, and carefully finished cooking the turkey from the inside out. It took a few minutes, mostly because Amara wanted to play it safe, but soon enough everything was ready to go.

As Nick started handing out slices of meat, Amara looked up at Vee only to catch her staring back. Vee immediately averted her eyes, her look hardening as she spoke. "We couldn't have just stuck it back in the oven? You had to use hellfire?"

"I can control all heat, Vee, it's not like I opened up a portal to Hell inside the turkey to finish it. I just tweaked the temperature a bit," Amara said, shoveling sides onto her plate. Her appetite had been increasing in recent weeks, though it was nowhere near high enough to handle the feast in front of them.

"Would Heaven care if it weren't an open flame?" Tessa asked. "At what point does heat stop being associated with Hell? If Amara heats up a room, is the whole room considered evil?"

Vee clearly wasn't amused. "I'm not justifying that with a response. I'm here to eat, not to have my faith ridiculed."

Nick spoke up next, having finally finished cutting up all the meat. "Hey Vee, did they tell you about our codewords?"

"Doesn't sound familiar," the angel said.

"I was planning on bringing it up tonight, but now's as good a time as any." Amara licked some cranberry sauce off her lip before continuing. "I'm a shapeshifter, right? It's probably safe to assume other demons might be able to do something similar, so we all have specific codewords to verify our identities. If you're ever suspicious of someone, just ask 'What's for dinner tonight?' and we'll know what you mean. Tessa's code is lentil soup, mine is hand-seared chicken."

"Mine is pad thai, extra spicy," Nick said.

"That's honestly a good idea," Vee said, almost surprised at the thought. "They shouldn't be able to shapeshift, since they're in human hosts, but I suppose we don't know what the point of the ritual is. I'll say... spaghetti carbonara. I still can't find any place in the states that can compare to when I first had it in Italy." Vee smiled slightly, seemingly lost in her own memories.

"You've been to Italy?" Amara asked, surprised.

"It was a Church thing; angels do a lot of traveling. I had to visit the Vatican."

"No fucking way! Did you meet the Pope?" Tessa asked.

"No, he was busy at the time. I probably could if I wanted to, though…"

"You should totally go back, bring us with, and then we steal the Popemobile and take it for a joyride!"

"Absolutely not!"

"Okay, but picture this. Amara, wings out, crammed in the back of the Popemobile while we're leading a high-speed chase through the Vatican!" Tessa started laughing, her own conjured image clearly too much for her. Her laughter grew more and more intense, and soon she was gripping her sides. While Amara didn't find the thought quite as hilarious, the sight of Tessa losing her shit soon became contagious. She started laughing as well, which led Nick to join in soon after. Vee, unsurprisingly, was clearly annoyed by this, and didn't seem interested in playing along. However, after a few moments, her face softened slightly, and she even started quietly chuckling along with everyone else.

The four of them continued eating for well over an hour, and as much as Nick tried to keep things light-hearted, Amara could tell that Vee was still very conflicted about being here. At times, Vee seemed to be genuinely relaxed, laughing and talking with everyone like everything was back to normal. On several occasions, though, Amara caught her friend staring down at her lap, a strangely mournful look on her face. The look always vanished quickly when Vee realized she was being watched, and Amara couldn't bring herself to broach the topic.

After everyone finally threw in the towel, a mountain of half-finished food in front of them, the sun had set. Amara, Tessa, and Vee decided that they were far too full to visit the gymnastics building today, and Nick tried to convince everyone to move to the couches so they could throw on a movie.

Vee, however, had other plans. As everyone stood from the table and stretched, she spoke up. "I'm going to head out. Thanks for having me, Nick, but… I need to leave."

"O-oh, are you sure?" Nick asked.

Vee nodded. "I'll see everyone tomorrow for practice. We can't lose sight of what needs to happen this weekend."

Nick looked to Amara, silently asking her to say something, while Vee quickly moved to the front door and grabbed her coat. She seemed strangely driven, especially given how much she'd just eaten, and when Amara finally agreed to say something, the door was already closing behind Vee.

Amara ran after her, shapeshifting back into a human form, and finally caught up once they were outside. She ran in front of Vee, stopping her in her tracks. "Vee, what's going on?"

"Look, don't make this any harder than it needs to be, okay?" Vee said, taking care to avoid looking Amara in her eyes.

"Why not? I'm a demon, I'm supposed to make things difficult, aren't I?" Amara said, trying to lighten the mood. Vee didn't seem to appreciate the joke.

"That's entirely the point, Amara, you're a demon! We tried to kill each other! How are we supposed to move past that? We're literally being compelled by forces beyond our comprehension to be at each other's throats, but you think we can just ignore that?" Vee paused, her voice tense as she sighed heavily. "Even... even if I wanted to, I can't. Once this is finished, if we survive... we can't be friends, Amara."

Vee stepped to the side, her pace quickening as she walked away. Amara watched her leave, trying to think of something to say, but nothing came to her. She was never one for big picture arguments or ideas, and trying to picture the will of Heaven was not something she felt prepared to deal with.

She finally walked back inside, her mood soured despite the hours of pleasant company she'd just enjoyed. A part of her had started to wonder if Vee would come around, that maybe they were starting to patch things up, but now she didn't know what to think.

Would Heaven really care if two people happened to be friends? What does it matter to them?

Inside, Amara manifested her tail and horns again, then collapsed on Nick's couch. She rested her head in Tessa's lap as she remained lost in thought.

"I take it that didn't go well?" Nick asked.

"I don't know, Nick. She ate with us, which made me think things were getting better, but then she storms out like that... Why is this so confusing?"

"She's an angel, Amara," Tessa said, starting to play with Amara's horns. "I've dealt with Church people before, and it's like a giant cult. They're all brainwashed into thinking there's only one right way to live, and that they have all the answers. You know all those people that are convinced they're better than you because they happen to be religious? Now imagine how insufferable those people would be if they were literally Heaven-sent."

"Ugh, I don't want to think about it right now. Can we just... put on a movie or something?"

Nick stayed quiet, giving Amara a knowing look, but likely decided that he didn't want to force the issue any longer. Amara ended up falling asleep in Tessa's lap before the movie ended, her thoughts a tangled mess as she tried to make up her mind about Vee.

For better or for worse, the next two days passed without any significant developments. On the one hand, no cultists tried attacking anyone in their sleep, but on the other, Vee seemed determined to keep her distance from everyone. The girls continued meeting up in the gymnastics building to practice, but the Vee that had willingly shared Thanksgiving dinner with them was nowhere to be seen. Still, although things with Vee remained unresolved, Amara was at least happy that she had someone who could genuinely match her strength. She felt her skills improving with each hour that passed, and she had a sneaking suspicion that Vee appreciated having a chance to vent her frustrations.

Tessa continued studying her notes about the circles, and even managed to learn a few things from the decoy circle. While it had been a fake, many of its runes were still demonic in nature to sell the deception, and that proved to be an invaluable learning tool for her understanding of the circles.

Vee spent most of her free time creating small trinkets to help in the fight, all things she'd used against Amara on Halloween. Salt, holy water, rosaries, she even blessed Tessa's switchblade temporarily.

Before long, the night of the ritual was upon them. Amara met up early with Tessa, both girls working out their tension with an intense hour of fucking, which left Amara feeling more than ready for their assault on the cult. When Vee arrived at Amara's apartment, she had a sizable collection of holy items that she distributed between herself and Tessa. She even gave a bottle of holy water to Nick, who had helped finalize some of the logistical planning for the night. If everything went well, they were all hoping to meet up at Amara's apartment after the ritual, where Nick would be ready to help with any recovery that might be needed.

"How's everyone feeling?" Nick asked, clearly nervous about the upcoming fight.

"As ready as I'll ever be," Amara said, warming up as she checked the fit of her current athletic outfit. "Do we all remember the plan?"

"I'm reverse-engineering the circle, Vee is creating a barrier to block out the demons, and you're beating up everything on the outside." Tessa recited the plan half-heartedly, which had been burned into her memory after hours of practice.

"I also need to stop Mr. Wellington as soon as possible. We have no idea what he's trying to bring through, but it's safe to assume it'll be worse than the demons all the other cultists are getting," Amara said.

"I'll be waiting here. I know I can't do much, but when this is all over, I'll do my best to patch up any wounds that need attending to." Nick held up a first-aid kit he'd recently bought.

With a heavy sigh, Amara looked around at everyone. It was weird, finally preparing to interrupt this ritual after so many weeks of sneaking around to figure out what the cult had been up to. She checked her phone one last time, watched the clock turn over to 2 AM, and handed it over to Nick. "I guess it's now or never. Who's ready to kick some—"

Amara was unable to finish the sentence. Her entire body seized unexpectedly while she screamed in pain. Hellfire erupted from her body, growing hotter and hotter until it enveloped her completely. With one last burst, the flames vanished, as did Amara. There was nothing left but a scorch mark on the carpet, leaving her friends to stare at each other in shock.

13
THE RITUAL

"Amara? Amara?!" Tessa shouted, running to the empty space where Amara had previously been standing. Her tattoos flared and she fell to her knees to investigate the scorch mark on the floor, but she didn't seem to be finding anything. After a few moments of panic, she jumped up and ran at Vee, jabbing a finger into her shoulder. "What the fuck did you do?!"

"I didn't do anything!" Vee shouted back. "Why would I get rid of Amara now, when we need her most? Besides, she vanished in a burst of hellfire, that's not something I can do." Vee grabbed Tessa's wrist, throwing the witch back as they glared at each other.

"Okay, okay, let's just stay calm," Nick said, pacing back and forth as he nervously wrung out his hands. "Maybe she's okay! Those flames that surrounded her, they were purple, right? That's her color!"

"How do we know that's unique to her?" Tessa asked. "Maybe all hellfire is purple!"

Tessa and Nick both looked at Vee, who immediately shook her head. "Hey, don't look at me. Amara's hellfire is the only kind I've seen, and I don't remember anyone saying that it can come in different colors."

"Fuck!" Tessa shouted again. "Fuck fuck fuck!"

Vee, rather than joining Tessa and Nick in pointlessly pacing around the room, tried to think of a way forward. Without Amara, it would be nigh impossible for Vee to keep Tessa safe while she worked on reversing the cult's ritual.

"What if the cult has her?" Vee asked. "We know they have ways of summoning demons, and they wouldn't even need to reach into Hell to get her."

Tessa paused, turning to look at Vee. "That's... fuck, that's probably spot on."

"But, if that's the case," Nick started, "then you should be able to find her, right? You know where the cult's headquarters are, and you just discovered a back door. If they're all preoccupied with their ceremony, you might have time to sneak in and free her!"

"Let's quit standing around then!" Tessa did one last check of her equipment, then moved to the front door. "C'mon Vee, it's now or never, and I'm itching to stab some bitches."

Vee took a deep breath, trying to calm her nerves. She couldn't afford to lose her head, her angelic magic worked best when she was calm and collected. She looked at Nick, swallowing nervously before speaking "Nick, if we can't—"

"Don't say it, Vee," Nick said. "I'll see you, all three of you, when you get back. Okay?"

With one last look, and a resolute nod, Vee opened the door.

The Aurelius University campus was deathly quiet, which was hardly surprising given that it was Thanksgiving weekend. While most students were back from the short break already, there hadn't been any parties, and everyone was likely sleeping off their turkey leftovers.

Vee and Tessa ran quickly, making their way to Whitmore Hall as fast as they could. As disastrous as their previous raid had gone, it was hard to deny the good fortune of having a backdoor to the underground tunnels. Tessa was unusually quiet, her determination preventing her from cracking any inappropriate jokes or threatening Vee again. Still, Vee couldn't help but share the same nervous energy.

Despite all their practice, it was hard to deny they were fighting an uphill battle. Without Amara, their plan had no chance of succeeding. Still, Vee continued racking her brain for ideas, trying to think of other solutions to their current problem.

Okay, assume we can't find Amara. I have more powerful spells in my Enochian Texts... but I shouldn't use them, they could rip my body apart. Do I have anything that can disrupt planar magic?

She continued cycling through all the spells in her book, recalling each page in near-perfect detail. She'd spent the last few days memorizing all the magic inside, hoping to find better spells than what they'd been practicing with, but her options were frustratingly few. The only spells that might be able to clear a room of demons would require far too much time to prepare, which in turn would necessitate Amara keeping her safe, but then Amara would also be caught in the crossfire.

Before long, Vee and Tessa were racing down the stairs in Whitmore Hall, and Tessa was bypassing the illusory wall. They decided to leave the illusion down on the off chance they needed a quick escape later and dove into the tunnels once more.

Officially in enemy territory now, the girls started moving slower. Vee summoned her sword, and Tessa's switchblade began circling her body. There was no knowing which hallways might contain cultists, and they also needed time to properly backtrack their steps from last time. In their rush to escape, no one had bothered to chart which paths they had taken.

The flat, gray corridors seemed to stretch on forever, a terrible labyrinth of bland, brutalist monotony. Every turn, every doorway had the potential to hold demons that wanted them dead, but they also needed to search every nook and cranny for Amara.

The two girls fell into a pattern. Vee was the first to check each new hallway and room, and Tessa would hold back until receiving an all-clear signal. At first, their search turned up nothing of note; many of the hallways and rooms were empty. However, as they continued diving deeper into the complex, they started finding signs of life. The occasional small cot, various personal effects, remains of discarded meals; it looked as if some of the cult members had started living down here.

Vee couldn't imagine why they would need to, all these people presumably had homes of their own. She quickly decided against trying to understand them, however; they were also the ones willingly sacrificing their bodies to demons. Presumably they weren't bastions of sanity and reason.

As they pushed deeper, the rooms they found grew more unsettling. In one room, they found a collection of jars filled with suspicious red liquid. A quick investigation confirmed it was blood, and Vee was more than happy to leave that room behind. The next room held a collection of surgical knives, ones that had obviously seen extensive use, and recently. Tessa explained that the cultists were likely carving the runes into their body, rather than using tattoos. Yet another room that Vee was happy to leave.

Back in the hallway, just a few steps after leaving the knife room, Vee finally heard movement ahead. She quietly signaled to Tessa, who nodded quickly before giving Vee more space to maneuver. Stepping quietly, Vee peeked into the next room and saw another space that had been retrofitted into living quarters. A lone man stood in front of a table, rummaging through a bag as he muttered generic frustrations to himself. With his back to the door, Vee knew she had a perfect opportunity: catch him off guard and interrogate him to find where Amara was being held. Stepping into the room, Vee kept her blade behind her back to conceal its glow and slowly moved into position. She crept closer, took a deep breath to prepare herself, and then froze in terror.

Cold, sharp steel had just pressed against her neck.

"Hello gorgeous," a voice whispered behind her. "How about you drop that sword before we hurt your little friend?"

In the corner of her eye, Vee saw Tessa in the hallway. Another cultist had grabbed the witch's knife and now pushed it against her throat. The girls locked eyes for a moment, and Vee finally relented. Her sword dropped to the ground, bouncing a few times before vanishing completely. The first cultist, the one in the room, now turned to face Vee. His face held a horrid, contemptible smirk, and Vee realized this body had once belonged to Nick's friend, Alex.

"My my," Alex said. "Mr. Wellington is going to *love* the two of you."

Earlier that night

Amara's body seized with pain, an agonizing torrent of hellfire surrounding her. She let out a piercing scream, her hands grabbing her head as she tried to block out the pain, when she felt a terrible lurching sensation. It felt like falling, catapulting through space at impossible speeds while also crashing through imperceptible waves of an unknowable liquid. When the spinning stopped and the flames subsided, she found herself on her hands and knees, panting heavily. Every fiber of her body screamed with pain and exhaustion, which didn't make sense. She'd just spent an hour with Tessa, fucking her senseless while feeding on her every desire. How could she be this tired already?

Summoning all her strength, she forced herself to raise her head and look around. She was in a small, dark room, lit only by a series of candles on the floor. She noticed four shapes, all wearing dark cloaks, and one of them began to talk as Amara began moving.

"So nice of you to join us, Amara."

She recognized that voice, it was far too smug to forget: Sebastian Wellington. She glared at him, her eyes trying and failing to manifest hellfire as her anger grew. "What the fuck did you do to me?"

Sebastian smirked, and a pretentious laugh filled the small room. "You know, when your friends show up to try and save you, I need to remember to thank the angel. If she hadn't shot you in the back, this would have been so much harder." He raised a hand, and Amara saw he was holding a small towel covered in her blood.

Without a second thought, Amara leaped at Sebastian, desperate to stop him from using her blood to further bind her. She only made it a few feet before colliding with an invisible wall, one that felt all too familiar. Beneath her, she saw a series of runes and sigils that thrummed with magical power. She was trapped in another circle, and now the cult had her blood. Were they planning on enslaving her? The thought was sickening, and she threw herself at the barrier a second time, hoping to break through.

"You fucker! Give that back!" Amara screamed. She continued attacking, but immediately felt the limits of her weakened body.

"Amara, stop," Sebastian said. As his words filled the chamber, a powerful urge to obey his command surged through Amara. Without thinking, she ceased her assault on the barrier, doing exactly what the cult leader wanted.

No! They already have control!

"Step back, to the center of the circle." Again, Amara's body obeyed. She walked backwards until she was in the center of her prison, but this time she tried to pay attention to the magic. She'd broken through magical prisons before, and if she could find the limits of the spell, she might be able to do it again.

"Now, you may have noticed that we're not alone. These three wonderful gentlemen were kind enough to delay their own ascension in favor of a different reward. You see, I'd prefer my ceremony not be disrupted, and they volunteered to... keep you busy. You'll be a good girl for them, won't you?"

As Sebastian finished speaking, the other people present pulled their hoods down. The first cultist she recognized as Chris, who she'd first met at the fundraiser. He had short, blonde hair with a matching goatee, and his bright blue eyes eagerly ran up and down Amara's body. His gaze reminded her that she was wearing another set of skimpy athletic gear. The clothes on her body didn't feel as snug as they had before her strange teleportation, and she wondered if they'd gotten damaged in the hellfire.

The second cultist had long, black hair that had been tied behind his head. His eyes were brown, and he examined Amara's body with lecherous glee. The last person in the room had short, lightly tousled brown hair, and he was by far the most excited person in the room.

Brandon.

Just like Brandon, the other two cultists were students, and all three of them reeked with arousal. Their eagerness filled Amara's senses, and it only grew stronger with each passing second.

"Now, I've got a date with destiny. You all keep it down, will you?" Mr. Wellington tossed the bloody towel aside, laughing to himself as he left the room.

As the door closed behind Sebastian, Brandon stepped forward to take his place. "I've been waiting far too long for this, Amara. I can finally take what you owe me."

"I don't owe you shit, you pervert!" Amara said.

"Shut up!" Another wave of magic washed over Amara. She focused on how it felt, observed the compulsion that traveled through her and forced her to stop talking. Though she was now quiet, she continued glaring at Brandon. "From now on, the only words that leave your mouth will be to heighten our pleasure. You will also refer to me as Master at all times. Understand, pet?"

She knew what Brandon wanted to hear, and though he didn't outright ask for it, she felt another wave of compulsion pushing her to respond. This time, she briefly tried to resist it, hoping to test its limits. "Y-yes... Master."

The compulsion is strong, but it's not all powerful. I might be able to break it.

"How about we introduce ourselves?" Brandon gestured to the blonde man with the goatee first. "This is Chris. Shake his hand and give him a nice smile."

Amara held out her hand, a warm smile appearing on her face despite her intense desire to punch everyone present in the face. Chris reached out, gently introducing himself before leaning in to kiss her hand. Were it not for the compulsion, she would have rolled her eyes. "So excited to be here. Ever since you signed those pictures for me, I haven't been able to stop thinking about you."

Brandon spoke up again, this time introducing the last cultist, the one with the long, black hair. "This is Mark, greet him the same way."

"You're a real fucking catch, you know that?" Mark said, his grip much more demanding. He openly leered at Amara's breasts, which were still somewhat contained in her sports bra, but she felt the fabric starting to give. As they finished shaking hands, and Amara's fake smile faded, she felt she had a decent understanding of the strength of their binding magic.

It was certainly powerful, leaps and bounds beyond what Brandon had put together underneath the Science Building all those weeks ago. Ever since then, however, Amara had grown significantly stronger; she was no longer a helpless student who didn't understand her abilities. Although she was still weak from the summoning, she was confident she had enough strength to break through the compulsion and free herself from the circle. The real problem would be anything that happened afterwards.

If she exhausted herself breaking free, she wouldn't have enough strength to keep Vee and Tessa safe. A fight with the cult, with hordes of demons, would only end in disaster.

Of course, if I had a way to get my strength back before breaking out... And wouldn't you know it, I've got three horny idiots right here. Is Brandon really that stupid? Would he really repeat the same mistake that gave me the upper hand last time?

"Amara, burn your clothes away, then reveal your true form," Brandon said. She hated how smug he was, but started to take solace in the irony of the situation. The more she could turn them on, the more she fulfilled their sexual fantasies, the easier it would be for her to break out and take down Sebastian.

I'm a succubus, aren't I? A literal sexual predator? Why shouldn't I wring these assholes for every drop of energy I can get?

With a devious smile, Amara summoned a small inferno of hellfire and burned away the last shreds of her clothes. Even this display of strength was enough to tire her out, but thankfully the auras of the men watching her were so strong she had already started feeding. With her clothing gone, she manifested her true form, her wings, tail, and horns returning to her. She stood proud, her naked body on full display. If nothing else, she refused to show weakness, and ever since her photos had started circulating, she'd started understanding the effect her body could have on people.

"Holy shit," Chris said, "your photos don't do you justice. This body is unreal."

"You think she's this tight everywhere?" Mark asked.

Brandon laughed, gesturing to the other guys to wait. "Oh, I have no doubt about it. Before we start, though, we have some ground rules to set up. The first is more of a fun fact, actually: succubi only feel the pleasure of their partners, so we don't have to bother with trying to make her enjoy this."

Only partially true, I could totally cum on my own. Still, he's not entirely wrong, either. I'm more likely to have more fun if they're focused on themselves.

"The other rules, though, are for you, Amara," Brandon continued. "You are forbidden from taking our souls, no matter how many times we reach orgasm. You are forbidden from doing us harm. You may only put in effort if it's in furtherance of our pleasure. Do you understand, pet?"

Ha! I wouldn't be able to take your souls even if I tried. I can't wait to wipe that smug grin off your stupid face.

"Yes Master, I understand," Amara said.

"Now, tell us why you're here. What's about to happen." Brandon's arousal was incredibly overwhelming, and she hadn't even touched him yet. It was almost exciting, thinking about the buffet that was waiting for her.

Amara put on her sexiest voice and did everything she could to play up her own excitement. "I'm here to be your perfect little fuck toy! I'm going to give all of you the strongest orgasms you've ever felt and beg for more every chance I get." As her words ended, she smelled another surge in arousal from the men around her.

This is too easy.

"Well, gentlemen? It would be rude to keep her waiting, wouldn't it?" Brandon began undressing, and the other two quickly followed suit. They were practically tripping over themselves, struggling to get their clothes off as they continued leering at Amara's curves. As she waited, her tail flicked back and forth in excitement. When they had finished undressing, Brandon stepped closer, crossing into the circle. He paused, just for a second, and when Amara didn't do anything, his smug grin returned. "Kiss me, pet."

Leaning forward, Amara threw her arms around Brandon's shoulders and kissed him. Her hands played with his hair, and her tongue pushed into his mouth as she moaned in excitement. His arousal was delicious, and the more she fed, the more she could tell that he hadn't had sex in months, possibly longer. The closest he'd probably gotten was when he'd trapped her under the Science Building, and even then, he'd refused to touch her. Now, his hands eagerly moved over her waist, traveling down before grabbing her ass and squeezing it hard.

She also grew aware of Chris and Mark, who had started moving closer. While Brandon clearly wasn't ready to pass her off yet, the other two seemed more than happy to start inspecting her demonic features. One of them grabbed her tail, fingernails tracing its length as she continued flicking it seductively. The other caressed her wings, squeezing them tight as if to test how real they were.

When Brandon finally yielded, he gestured at his friends to take their turns. Chris moved in first, his approach much gentler. There was a strange hesitancy in his movements, as if he were both scared and mesmerized by her presence. She rather appreciated the awe in his eyes, and she happily pulled him in for a kiss. For her plan to work, she needed him to be more indulgent, and she had to figure out a way to bypass his apparent insecurities. As they continued making out, her tongue reaching deep into his mouth, she let her hands explore his body. The extra attention immediately reflected in his aura, and she had a feeling she knew what he wanted.

Mark was next. His gaze was harsher, more lecherous, and he grabbed her hair tight before pulling her close. When her hands moved to his body, she didn't notice the same excitement she had with Chris, he clearly wanted something else. The hand holding her hair soon pulled back, forcing her to angle her head away and expose her neck. His rough demeanor gave her an idea, and she decided to test her theory; rather than feigning appreciation, she pretended to wince in pain. The instant she did, she noticed an immediate change in his aura, and she knew she'd found his weakness.

He doesn't just like it rough, he wants it to hurt. He's a sadistic little fuck, and I'm going to enjoy breaking him when this is finished.

Now that everyone had gotten a chance to introduce themselves, Amara looked back at Brandon for instructions. She needed to continue selling the idea that he was in control, which was obviously his fantasy.

"On your knees, pet," Brandon said.

"Yes Master!" Amara quickly kneeled, settling on her knees as the three men circled around her. For a brief moment, she reflected on what was happening, realizing that this would be her first time engaging in group sex. It certainly wasn't ideal, and she made a note to put together some proper group fun when this was all over. Still, despite the specific context, it was certainly nice to be the center of attention, and she didn't even have to hide her demonic features.

She now found herself at eye level with three incredibly excited cocks. They were all rock hard, pointing straight at her, and Amara knew exactly how to start. She needed to give deference to Brandon, and she wrapped her tail around his legs to pull him closer. His hands moved to her horns, holding them tight, and she licked her lips while trying to push forward. Surprisingly, Brandon stopped her, holding her back. "Ah ah, my pet. I want you to ask for it. Beg like the servant you are."

"Please, Master! Please let me suck your cock! I want it so badly!" Amara pleaded, her eyes glowing bright. Every chance she had to show off her demonic side would be to her advantage: he loved her inhuman nature.

"Good girl, you can start."

Within moments, Amara had sucked Brandon's cock into her mouth. Her lips wrapped tight around it while her tongue massaged every inch of him. His moans filled the chamber, and he continued holding her horns as she started bobbing up and down on his shaft. Now that Amara had a way to keep him occupied, she let her hands wander to the other men. They were standing on opposite sides of her, just out of reach, so Amara playfully beckoned them closer before grabbing their cocks.

She noticed their auras begin to shift as she started pleasuring them all. Arousal was delicious, and Amara was able to pull quite a bit from it, but there was a different flavor at play once actual pleasure began. It was like the difference between smelling a delicious dinner and taking that first bite, though in Amara's case, she wasn't planning on biting.

Yet.

Knowing how much men liked a good show, Amara made sure to play up how loudly she was sucking Brandon off. She moaned, slurped, spit, and gagged as she did everything possible to keep her guests entertained. Her hands continued stroking the other two cocks, and she even made her tail snake up Chris's body to tease him further. He seemed to enjoy a softer, more intimate touch, and the extra attention was best given to him. Mark, on the other hand, needed to be given opportunities to think he was hurting her.

Thankfully, she knew exactly how to give him that chance. She finally pulled her mouth off Brandon's cock, a long line of spit lingering from its head to her lips. She left her mouth open and her tongue out, knowing how much guys loved that visual, and turned to face Mark next. She looked up at him, doing her best to appear demure and innocent, then pitched up her voice and said, "Please be gentle, Sir."

Predictably, Mark did no such thing. His aura twitched at the opportunity to deny her request, and he grabbed her horns, holding them tight. Without an ounce of regret or hesitation, he pulled her down fast, his cock pushing deep into her mouth and causing her to gag loudly. Her eyes went wide, imitating surprise, and she pretended like she wasn't experienced with deep throating to give him a goal. He started fucking her face harder and harder, desperate to feel his entire cock inside her mouth, and after a few moments Amara relented. Her throat opened up, pulling him deep inside, and she was rewarded with another helping of sadistic satisfaction.

As he continued holding her horns, using her mouth no differently than he would use a cheap toy, Amara started to sense subtle differences in everyone's auras. At the Halloween party, she'd gotten good enough at reading auras to tell where people were directing their affections, but nothing else. She also knew that auras could reveal who was sleeping with who, but this was different. The only aura reflected in the three men standing around her was her own, and there were still more differences to be found.

Since, at the moment, she simply had to let Mark have his fun, she let herself focus on these subtle differences. Mark's arousal felt significantly more aggressive than the others. He was like a storm on the ocean, roiling and thrashing, not caring who got caught in his path.

Brandon's aura was firm and steady, but oppressive. He had taken to calling her a pet, and he clearly wanted to make that a reality. Chris, on the other hand, had the softest aura. He was enjoying himself, obviously, but there was some hesitation. Amara wondered what lies he'd been fed; had they told him she wasn't to be treated like a person? That she would do anything and everything to try and turn the tables? At the end of the day, he was still happily going along with this magically-coerced gangbang, but at least he wasn't treating her like a lifeless doll.

After a few more minutes of letting Mark facefuck her, it was eventually time to switch it up again. She turned towards Chris, his aura jumping in excitement, and she leaned in to slowly kiss the tip of his cock. Her hands wrapped around the base of his cock, gently stroking it, while her tail reached higher to playfully trace circles on his back.

It only took a brief minute of teasing before she sensed that Chris wanted more, and she began sucking his cock in earnest. He seemed to prefer long, steady strokes, her lips traveling the entire length of his cock with each thrust of her head. In contrast to the other boys, when Chris reached for Amara, he didn't grab her horns. His fingers lightly played with her hair, massaging the side of her scalp as she used her tongue to massage his shaft. In his excitement, he almost lost control and started cumming, but Amara was able to pull him back with a gentle squeeze at the base of his shaft.

"C'mon Chris, you're wasting her fucking talents!" Mark said. "Did you see how hard she can take it?"

"I don't know how she's doing it, but she knows exactly what I like. It's unreal, it's like she's in my head!" Chris continued moaning, his hands still playing with her hair as he started slowly thrusting into her mouth.

Before he could continue, however, Brandon spoke up again. "I think I'm tired of waiting. Amara, lean forward and place your hands on the ground. Present yourself like a good pet."

Amara felt another wave of compulsion wash over her, and she immediately noticed how much its effects had lessened. She was already strong enough to resist it, and she hadn't even gotten anyone to cum yet. She had no plans to show her hand this early, however, and let the compulsion guide her movements. She leaned forward, settling comfortably on all fours, and arched her back to show off her perfect ass.

She'd learned during her photoshoot just how much her body had changed. She had never been prudish in her old life and still had several spicy pictures she'd sent old partners, but when she compared the two, the differences were obvious. Not only had her breasts grown slightly, but no matter what she wore, they always appeared as if they were supported by a push-up bra. Her ass had changed much the same way: slightly bigger, but also rounder and more firm. As she presented herself for the lust-drunk cultists around her, she felt their eyes drinking in every inch of her, and she swelled with pride.

That's right, idiots. Worship this body. It's all you're good for.

She watched as Mark walked in front of her, throwing a clean towel on the ground before kneeling himself. Without asking, he grabbed Amara's horns again and pulled her head down, pushing inside her mouth again. He was just as eager to be rough with her, and just like last time, it meant she didn't need to focus on keeping him entertained. Her tail continued flicking back and forth, and she felt Brandon kneeling behind her. He grabbed her tail, wrapping it around his wrist, and pulled it taut while his other hand started massaging her ass. He squeezed her tail tightly, slapped it a few times, and eventually caved to his desires once more. Grabbing her hips, he lined himself up with her pussy and slowly pushed inside her.

Amara made sure to moan loudly as he did. Not only did she need to put on the perfect show, and not only was the attention making her incredibly horny, but her connection to everyone's auras was pushing her overboard. She was effectively feeling the pleasure of three people at once, and Chris was still waiting on the sidelines for a chance to join in.

It proved to be too much, and her entire body shook with pleasure. She had stopped caring about the context, about the fact that they'd summoned her here with the intent of controlling her; right now, she knew she was in control, and she was eager to enjoy her first gangbang. Waves of orgasmic pleasure surged through her, her muscles tensing and relaxing over and over. Both the cocks inside her felt amazing, and she felt her own pleasure reverberating out into the two men fucking her.

When her first orgasm subsided, she immediately noticed that Chris had gotten on his back and moved underneath her. His hands eagerly cupped her tits, softly massaging them as he bit and sucked on her nipples. Amara was genuinely surprised by this, especially after Brandon had told them her own pleasure didn't matter, but Chris seemed to be enjoying himself regardless.

The extra attention felt amazing, and it drove Amara even further into depravity. She began meeting Brandon's thrusts as hard as she could, eager to experience more pleasure, and Mark seemed to enjoy the chance to fuck her throat even harder. She was now bouncing between the two men, frantically moaning as she did everything she could to fuck them harder. It was honestly surprising that they hadn't cum yet, not that she was complaining.

Without warning, Mark pulled out of her throat and began slapping her cheeks, taunting her as he did. She didn't mind in the slightest; he probably thought he was being rough with her, but she barely noticed his strikes. "Brandon, when do I get a turn? I want to feel this bitch's pussy," Mark said.

Amara pretended like she wasn't paying attention, and was busy rolling her eyes to the back of her head to make it seem like she was blissed out of her mind. Her tongue was still pushed out, unchanged from when Mark had been fucking her throat, and she still felt Chris playing with her tits underneath her. With only one cock in her at the moment, she took advantage of the break to test her own abilities.

She felt mostly full, at least in terms of sexual appetite, which wasn't surprising. She'd never fed on more than one person at a time, let alone three, and she felt ready to run a marathon. Normally, she would feel this way after getting Nick or Tessa to cum and would then have at least a day or two before she needed to feed again. Tonight, though? She needed more, she needed to push herself. With her friends, she'd always kept her feeding somewhat in check out of fear she might take too much, but here she had no such hesitation. She had no idea what was waiting for her in the main chamber, and she refused to leave anything to chance.

She felt Brandon push down on her back, then stand up. His cock left her pussy, and she briefly shivered with pleasure at the unique sensation. "Have at her, Mark. It's like nothing I've ever felt before."

In no time at all, Mark was behind her, his thick cock bottoming out in her pussy. He was certainly thicker than Brandon and clearly had every intention to be just as rough as he had with her mouth. He didn't seem to care about her tail and instead slapped her ass with everything he had. They soon found a rhythm, Amara matching his thrusts with her own, her moans echoing throughout the chamber now that her mouth wasn't in use.

As Mark continued fucking her, Chris moved in front of her, and she licked her lips in preparation. However, when he stood up, she noticed that he was still staring at her tits, watching them bounce in time with the fucking. Figuring out what he wanted, she began spitting and drooling on her tits, pushing them together and playing with them. Chris's aura indicated this was the right call, but she had a feeling he might be hesitant to take what he wanted. "Chris, will you please come fuck my tits? They're so wet already, they need a hard cock between them…"

Her suggestion pushed him over the edge, and he stepped closer. Amara happily wrapped her tits around his shaft, and after a few moments to catch her bearings, started stroking his cock. She held her tits up, pushing them together, and continued drooling on them as she bounced up and down.

With Chris and Mark now occupied, she knew she couldn't forget about Brandon and sought him out with her tail. He stood off to the side, no doubt enjoying the show, but her tail pulled him closer. It wrapped around his cock, gently stroking it before surrounding it entirely. Just like she'd practiced with Nick dozens of times, she let the muscles in her tail flex at different intervals, massaging Brandon's cock without needing to stroke it. The novelty seemed to be a good idea, as his aura grew brighter yet again.

Amara continued feeding, now already past her previous limits, and her body began growing hotter and hotter. The candles around the room flickered brighter, and she felt as if her skin were buzzing with untapped potential. She expanded her senses and discovered that all three guys had brought their phones with them; that wouldn't do. Without missing a beat, she summoned tiny sparks of hellfire inside the three phone cases, shorting them out for good. If her control was as strong as she thought, the damage wouldn't be visible unless they opened their phones to look inside.

She saw the signals from the phones die and grinned with excitement. This was almost too easy.

Next, she moved her eyes away from Chris and began staring at Brandon. She continued fucking everyone, taking caution not to show any suspicious initiative, but did her best to make a face that pleaded for more. Brandon, thankfully, seemed to take the hint.

"Alright boys, how about we move on to the main event?" Brandon said. After another surge in everyone's auras, Mark and Chris both pulled their cocks away from Amara. "Chris, lay down, will you?"

The blonde-haired boy nodded, throwing a towel into the center of the circle before lying down. With another look at Brandon, Amara knew exactly what he wanted, and she moved to straddle Chris. She placed her hands on his chest, gently massaging him, and used her tail to line up his cock. After a few playful bounces, she sank down onto his shaft and let out another moan.

"There's a good girl," Brandon said. "Mark, you seem to enjoy her mouth. Make sure you put those horns to good use."

Mark nodded, standing in front of Amara once again. His grip was as rough as ever, and he grabbed her horns tight before pulling her mouth to his cock. She did her best to gasp and gag, making him think he was being too rough with her to keep him excited. Finally, Brandon moved behind her, briefly grabbing her hair and pulling her off of Mark's cock.

"As for me, pet? You've been a pain in my ass for far too long. I think it's time I returned the favor." Brandon released her hair, giving Mark the okay to resume fucking her face. She felt his hands slide down her back, slapping her ass hard before grabbing her tail. He wrapped it around his fist again, then began lining his cock up with her tightest hole. To his credit, he took his time; he valued obedience more than cruelty, so Amara wasn't surprised. After a few moments of careful prodding, however, his cock pushed inside her ass.

Thank goodness I just practiced anal with Nick.

The sensation of having her ass and her pussy filled at the same time was unreal. While previously she'd been able to split her focus, to test the limits of the magic, now she didn't care to try. Every fiber of her being, every thought that crossed her mind, was entirely focused on how full she felt. A second, tempestuous orgasm overtook her, racing through her body as she twitched with pleasure. It felt like being split in two, the sensation amplified by the strange magical buzzing of her body. Every tiny movement was incredible; the cock in her pussy would twitch, and she would feel it reverberate through her ass. When the cock in her ass pushed deeper, it caused her pussy to squeeze the other cock even harder. Time itself seemed to slow, and as she started adjusting to this feeling, she realized that only a few seconds had passed. Her second orgasm started to dwindle, and she knew she needed to keep pushing.

Eager for more, Amara pushed back, and immediately felt both cocks bottom out inside her. She tried her best to moan, to scream out with pleasure, but the cock in her mouth prevented such exclamations. Instead, she did everything she could to start bouncing her ass, eager to feel more. Brandon seemed to sense her eagerness, and he began fucking her in earnest. She met his thrusts with her own, bouncing up and down on Chris's cock as well, both guys starting to moan.

In front of Amara, Mark still eagerly gripped her horns and fucked her face, but she could tell he was getting tired. In fact, it seemed like all of them were. Their auras quivered in anticipation, close to erupting, and she was growing excited to wring their orgasms from them.

Amara found the rhythm she was looking for and began taking all three cocks balls-deep with every thrust. Mark would bottom out in her throat just as the cocks behind her threatened to leave her holes, then she would fall back and reverse everything. She let her wings join in the fun, lifting her up and down, giving her the ability to fuck everyone that much harder. The base of her tail was still in Brandon's grasp, but she had the rest of it snake around his waist, holding him tight. Underneath her, Chris reached up for her tits and squeezed them again, pinching her nipples as he massaged them. Every single guy now had everything they wanted, and they were incapable of holding back any more.

For one brief moment, just before everything exploded, Amara filled with pride as she realized she'd managed to bring three separate men to orgasm at the exact same time.

All three men began cumming, their cocks twitching as load after load filled all three of her holes. She'd always loved the feeling of a hard cock emptying itself inside of her, but three at once? Absolute bliss beyond comprehension. A third orgasm crashed into her, its intensity catching her off guard. This wasn't just her orgasm, it was four at once, and she could barely process all the sexual energy she was absorbing. It raced through her at breakneck speeds, threatening to leave her already satiated body, but she refused to let it go.

Her eyes rolled back in her head, this time not even for show, and her screams of ecstasy filled the chamber. She hadn't noticed before, but after swallowing the first couple bursts of Mark's load, he'd apparently pulled out of her mouth. He was now coating her face with his cum, and she was more than happy to take it. She didn't want him to leave, though, not yet, and she wrapped her hands around his cock to continue pleasuring him. Her body continued shaking, both from her own pleasure and from the excited thrusts of the two men orgasming behind her. She still had a firm grip of their auras, as well as their cocks, and something deep inside her whispered that she wasn't finished yet.

Amara's senses expanded yet again, and she refocused on her connection to everyone's auras. She'd gotten so used to feeding carefully, taking small sips of energy, but could she do more? She reached into those auras, searching for the source of their pleasure, when something strange happened. It felt like grabbing a lightning rod in the middle of a storm; not only was she buzzing with energy, but she had found something deep inside these men, something delicious. She pushed her will through everyone's auras, amplifying the sensation by physically squeezing all the cocks in her grasp. Her pussy, her ass, even her mouth returned to the cock in front of her, and she redoubled her efforts to pleasure everyone.

More. I want more!

Something inside of Amara snapped, as if a dam had been built around her inner fire, and she had finally broken through. She didn't just want to feel everyone cum again, she needed it. She *deserved* it. They needed to pay for what they tried to do to her, and she didn't hesitate to pull more energy through their auras. All three cocks inside her had started fading, their orgasms past, but somehow Amara breathed new life into them. All three began twitching once more, more cum filling her, and she was just as surprised as they were.

A second round of orgasms rushed through her, extending her own pleasure even more. Was this a fourth orgasm? Or had the last one never even stopped? She found it hard to care as her body kept bouncing and twitching, extracting every ounce of cum it could.

Her hair began to float of its own accord, the tips smoldering with infernal fire. All around the room, even outside the magic circle, bursts of purple hellfire appeared, extensions of Amara's will that could no longer be contained. The room grew exponentially hotter, and the heat felt incredible. The robes piled in the corner caught fire, and the door began to burn, its hinges glowing bright as her flames intensified.

Amara rode out the last seconds of her orgasm, focusing on the incredible amounts of energy circulating both through and around her. She didn't quite understand how she was controlling it all, but it felt right. These men had tried to break her; she was merely taking what she was owed.

Her own orgasm finally subsided, and she took advantage of her newfound clarity to look around. Mark, Chris, and Brandon seemed exceptionally exhausted. They were panting heavily, and Amara swore their skin had paled somewhat. Their own orgasms were also starting to fade, and they seemed to be trying to pull themselves back together again.

Amara pulled her mouth off of Mark's cock, craning her neck as she stretched backwards. Her body felt incredible, every tiny movement reinforced how strong she'd gotten from her feeding. She no longer felt like she could run a marathon, she felt ready to run twenty. Her back cracked, and chitinous black claws grew from her hands. Rather than fight this urge, she found it funny. From deep inside her, a place she'd only just discovered, laughter formed. It grew louder and heartier, her rapturous glee reflected in every sweltering flame in the room, and the men around her began to panic.

"What are you doing?!" Brandon screamed. "Stop this! NOW!!"

With a powerful thrust of her wings, Amara jumped to her feet. Her tail twitched towards Mark, colliding with his side and sending him flying against a wall. Underneath her, Chris began panicking and crawled for the nearest corner. Amara then turned to Brandon, the two of them still in the magic circle, and she stared at him. Hellfire danced around her eyes, and when she spoke, an unnatural growl accompanied her words.

"I am no pet, Brandon. You cannot control me!"

She reached out, grabbing Brandon by his neck and pulling him close. He felt so fragile in her hands, and a sinister voice urged her to end him.

It would be so easy.

Her fingers twitched, the hellfire around her surged once more, and a brief moment of clarity hit her. She was still Amara, but something had changed. Was this the creature that had come out on Halloween? No, she was still herself. There would be no one else to blame for her actions tonight. No matter the source of her power, she refused to give in to temptation. Although it took every fiber of her being, she refused to kill Brandon.

But he deserves it, doesn't he? He won't stop unless you make him!

Her head twitched, the war inside her thoughts burning bright. It was like staring into a twisted mirror, every dark thought she'd ever had reflecting back at her.

I won't! I'M NOT A KILLER!!

Whatever power now coursed through her veins, it was both incredible and terrible. She needed to get rid of it, and she knew what needed to happen. She spun on her heel, throwing Brandon through the door behind her. The door, already weakened, shattered from the impact, exposing the hallway outside. Amara walked towards the edge of the magic circle, its energy still trying to hold her, and casually walked through it. The barrier shattered in her wake, and she stepped into the hallway.

Picking Brandon up again, she pinned him to the wall.

"Where is the ritual?!"

Fear filled Brandon's eyes, which quickly glanced down the hallway to her right. With one last smirk, she tossed him aside and started running.

Vee did her best not to panic, trying to control her breathing. She was doing everything she could to keep tabs on the situation around her, but staying calm was difficult given the circumstances. After surrendering themselves, the cultists had taken her and Tessa to the main chamber, where they were being closely monitored. One cultist had even supplied small lengths of rope, which had been used to bind the girls' hands together. Vee heard Tessa muttering under her breath, berating the cultist for his poor shibari technique, but that was the least of Vee's concerns.

Around them, the chamber bustled with activity. Candles had been scattered against the far walls, and the lights above had been turned off. Vee tried to focus on counting all the people present, hoping to figure out how many humans still remained in their ranks. Unfortunately, without expending more magic, it was difficult to tell with just her senses, despite their heightened state.

Her Enochian Texts had been taken from her and were now being kept on a small table closer to the magic circle. Vee knew of a dozen different spells that might be helpful at the moment, especially as Amara was nowhere to be seen, but without her book, she was virtually powerless. Sure, she had a personal well of angelic magic, but she knew she couldn't win a fight against dozens of possessed humans. Best case scenario, she might manage to take down a small handful, and the cult would probably decide she was too much trouble to keep alive.

As much as she hated it, she had no choice but to sit and wait. If an opportunity presented itself, she would be ready, but it was better to make the cult think they'd won.

After a few minutes of waiting, the crowd of cultists began softly chanting to themselves. They formed a large ring, surrounding the magic circle in the center of the chamber, which pulsed with hellish energy. A figure emerged from a side entrance, and he pulled his hood down to reveal himself as their leader: Sebastian Wellington. Though Vee had only seen him once before, during their fight in the Dean's office, it was impossible to miss how exceptionally smug he was.

"At long last, our time has come! We've dispatched those who seek to stop us, and there is nothing left to stand in our way!" The crowd of robed cultists cheered, and Mr. Wellington allowed them several seconds of revelry before gesturing for them to grow quiet once more. He walked across the chamber, carefully avoiding the magic circle, before arriving in front of Vee and Tessa. "We even have the perfect gift for tonight's visitor. I'll admit, I was worried when I realized we had an angel on our tail, but you proved to be horribly inept. Had I known that Heaven's righteous warriors were this pathetic, I would have taken you out back in that office."

Vee glared at the cult leader, refusing to give him the satisfaction of hearing her talk. When the silence continued for a few more seconds, Mr. Wellington clearly got the hint and refocused his attention on the ritual. "Tonight, we take our final steps towards salvation, as we herald in my own ascension! Once my eyes are opened, just as many of you have experienced, we can take the first steps towards our new future!"

With another rapturous cheer, Mr. Wellington took a deep breath and stepped onto the magic circle. Though he was still fully clothed, Vee saw that dozens of magical runes had been carved into his body, and they started glowing. He began speaking in a language Vee couldn't understand, his body producing unholy sounds that defied the limitations of the human body. Underneath his feet, the magic circle glowed brighter and brighter, and the ground seemed to blur as the magic intensified. Waves of hellish energy poured from the circle, and the sickening smell of sulfur assaulted Vee's delicate senses.

The cult leader rose off the ground, now suspended in mid-air as unnatural tendrils of magic latched onto his body. Although Vee had never seen such a ritual before, she'd been exposed to the demons that had previously come through, and one thing was obvious: whatever creature Mr. Wellington was summoning would be significantly more threatening.

Vee began looking around, forcing herself to tear her eyes away from the sickening display of magic in front of her. She was still waiting for a chance to strike back, and this ascension ritual might be the perfect distraction. There were four cultists standing guard around her and Tessa, and she knew they carried lengthy daggers: she'd seen them earlier when they had been moved to this chamber. Two cultists were guarding the table with her book, which also held Tessa's switchblade. Other than that, everyone else present had formed a circle around the center of the chamber.

As she started putting together a plan, trying to find the best way to break free of her guards, she saw something race out of the hallway behind the other group of cultists. It was moving incredibly fast, and before she could identify what it was, it charged the two men watching her Enochian Texts. Some kind of lance burst through the chest of the first cultist, lifting him into the air before throwing him aside. As his body hit the floor, Vee saw a twisted shadow leave him, the demon inside likely being forced back to Hell due to the death of its host.

Whatever creature had killed the cultist then grabbed the small table and jammed it against the second guard. The protective magic of her Enochian Texts activated, sending powerful angelic magic into the possessed body of the cultist.

The creature kept moving, using the table to push the cultist closer towards Vee, eventually pinning him to the ground while he seized in pain.

The table fell to the floor, and before it landed, the creature had leapt at two of Vee's guards, blackened claws digging into their throats. She decided this was her chance to act, but before she started to work on her bindings, they disintegrated under a concentrated burst of purple hellfire. She leapt to her feet, whispering a quick prayer to summon her sword, and plunged it into the heart of the possessed guard next to her. Tessa also leapt into action, her tattoos flaring as she pinned the last of the cultists to the ground, her switchblade forcing the demon inside to retreat to Hell.

The rest of the cult had just started responding to this new chaos, but they hadn't closed the distance quite yet. Vee took a split second to examine this creature that had just freed them and realized she was looking at Amara.

Hellfire leapt from her body as she moved, every feature of her glowing in its unnatural light. At first glance, it looked like she was naked: the athletic outfit she'd been wearing previously was nowhere to be seen. A closer look revealed that, while much of her body was exposed, her most vulnerable areas had been covered by her strange, demonic exoskeleton. Her breasts were held in place by small strips of chitin, as was her groin, as if she were wearing an infernal lingerie bodysuit. The blackened material also formed around all her limbs, giving her feet and hands terrifying claws and her tail a formidable blade.

Fear gripped Vee, as she could sense incredible amounts of energy cascading off Amara. The strength now on display dwarfed everything she'd seen on Halloween, and Vee had no idea how much of Amara might still be conscious inside.

However, at the moment, Amara seemed to be focused on keeping her safe, and Vee didn't dare second-guess her good fortune. She ran for her book, quickly casting another spell to bind it to her hands, then flipped to the necessary page. "I need to cast this closer to the circle!" she yelled. Her words drew Amara's attention, and she turned to look at Vee. The whites of Amara's eyes had gone completely black, and her amber irises glowed brighter than Vee had ever seen. Her gaze was as terrifying as it was awe-inspiring, and she quickly nodded to Vee.

A circle of hellfire erupted around the girls, its heat more intense than any fire Vee had ever felt. When she took a step closer to the magic circle, the hellfire moved with her; Amara seemed to be matching her movements.

"Tessa!" Vee shouted, "Help Amara fend everyone off until I get my barrier up!"

"Finally, some real fuckin' action!" Tessa shouted. Her tattoos flaring, Vee watched the table that Amara had smashed earlier dash through the wall of hellfire. The fire spread to the table, and Tessa took a fighting stance, now armed with her switchblade and a hellfire torch.

A few possessed cultists dared to leap through the flames, and Vee suspected it was incredibly painful. Their bodies were only human, after all, and didn't gain the fireproof benefits most demons presumably called their own. Amara and Tessa engaged everyone brave enough to jump through the flames, doing their best to buy Vee space while she continued her Enochian chanting. As powerful as Amara was, it was obvious that Vee's magic was taking a toll on her, as well as all other demons in the area.

Amara's movements, previously quick and deadly, were growing sloppy, and even the hellfire barrier began to falter. Through one of these gaps, Vee caught a glimpse of the magic circle, and saw they were almost next to it now. Mr. Wellington's body still hovered in the circle, though now he was twitching unnaturally. His skin was darkening, taking on a deep red hue, and Vee swore she saw horns beginning to protrude from his forehead. She had a feeling they didn't have much time left and did her best to refocus on her barrier spell.

A cultist tried to charge her from behind, and Amara appeared out of nowhere to tackle him to the ground. Vee heard a sickening crunch and decided to ignore whatever had just happened.

They forfeit their souls, they're already dead. Don't forget that.

Her Enochian chanting continued, and her words began reaching for the space around her as they sought to establish a protective barrier. Vee could tell that the ritual was nearing completion; Mr. Wellington's transformation seemed to be mostly finished, and she tried not to think about what would come next.

Out of the corner of her eye, Vee saw Amara flinch with pain as the Enochian magic grew stronger. The cultist she was engaged with managed to throw her to the ground, but before he could land a strike with his dagger, Tessa's floating hellfire club shattered against his chest. He staggered backwards, dazed and confused, before stepping into Amara's hellfire and crumbling to the ground. Amara turned to Vee, fury in her eyes, then screamed, **"How much longer?"**

Vee locked eyes with Amara, fighting every instinct that told her she shouldn't trust this monster. Amara's hands, as well as large swaths of her chest, were covered in blood, and again Vee reminded herself of the necessity of their actions. Unable to speak, Vee held up a hand, all five fingers standing tall. One finger fell, then another, and just before her countdown ended, Amara leapt as far away from Vee as she could.

Vee's spell finished, her Enochian magic roaring to life and leaving her body. Amara's hellfire vanished, and the two possessed cultists unfortunate to be close to Vee were catapulted across the room. Vee and Tessa were now the only two people left inside the circle. "Tessa, you're up!" Vee said, turning her attention to the mob forming outside her magic. She saw several cultists attempt to push through only to be violently rejected, but after a few moments of testing, they discovered the trick to the circle. Vee heard them shout at each other, sharing that unpossessed humans could enter freely, and Vee braced herself for a fight.

Amara rolled as she hit the ground, thrilled to be outside the influence of Vee's angelic magic. Despite all the energy she'd accumulated from her gangbang, the Enochian had still been incredibly disorienting. With the barrier now active, she could redouble her efforts to take out the remaining cultists. She leapt at the nearest threat, a shorter man pulling out a dagger, and drove her claws through his throat.

Fresh blood covered her hands, and she watched the cultist fall to the ground before a dark shadow drifted out of the body. She turned her sights to her next target, but before she could close the distance, a massive shockwave threw her off balance. It shook the entire chamber, and it felt strangely familiar. It was like an electrical pulse that induced an intense atmospheric pressure, and it reminded her of the moment before Tessa had accidentally buried herself in vines earlier in the year. When she looked back at the center of the chamber, she saw Sebastian kneeling on the ground.

At least, she thought it was the cult leader. His skin was now dark red, horns had erupted from his head, and a sickening demonic aura surrounded him. When he raised his head, he stared at Amara with glowing, crimson red eyes filled with hate. Before Amara had time to react, this new creature leapt from his place in the circle and charged at Amara.

He moved incredibly fast, and she barely had time to react as she tried to soften his impact. As she caught his fist, redirecting it and dodging to his side, he began speaking.

"How are you free?! That's impossible!" His voice was fractured, as if two creatures were speaking simultaneously.

Amara, her surprise slowly wearing off, jumped to her feet. "Sex only makes me stronger, idiot! Or did you forget I'm a succubus?" She charged Sebastian, trying to land a punch, but the cult leader moved just as quickly as she did. She had gotten so used to the easily-dispatched cultists that it took her some time to get used to this new opponent, one who seemed more than capable of matching her speed and strength.

"We had your blood! The sigils were perfect!" Sebastian shouted, finally beginning to fight back. He landed a series of brutal strikes on Amara, each one threatening to knock the wind out of her. With each attack, however, Amara grew better at reading her opponent.

"Guess they weren't, or I wouldn't be here!" Amara finally caught one of Sebastian's attacks, using his arm to throw him to the ground. She tried to press her advantage, but his speed continued to surprise her. Her bladed tail glanced off the floor as he jumped to his feet, kneeing her in the stomach. The wind knocked out of her, she was unable to stop Sebastian from landing another few strikes. She began coughing up blood, and the edges of her vision turned red. From deep within her, a profound anger began to form, and she directed that anger to fuel her inner fire.

She began moving entirely on instinct, reacting to Sebastian's attacks faster and faster. Soon, she had regained her footing and managed to land her first solid hit on him. Her fist connected with his chest, and a concentrated burst of hellfire sent him flying across the chamber. He slammed into the far wall, and she quickly ran after him, summoning more flames before throwing them at the mad cult leader.

Compared to the cultists she'd fought earlier, Sebastian seemed mostly resilient against her flames. Still, they bought her time to continue attacking, and she managed to land another few strikes with her chitinous fists. Her bladed tail also found purchase, digging deep into his side and causing the scent of fresh blood to fill her senses once again. Strangely, her strikes didn't seem to be fazing him as much as she would have liked. The more they struggled, the more it seemed like she only had a speed advantage, not a strength one.

From behind, she heard the sounds of Vee fighting off the other cultists, and a burst of Enochian magic narrowly missed her. However, it proved to be enough of a distraction for Sebastian to turn the tables again, grabbing her neck and slamming her into the wall. She gasped in pain, trying to pry his hands from her throat as her tail continued to find openings to dig into him. With another thrust, Sebastian slammed her head against the wall, trying to knock her out, but this time she saw it coming. Protective chitin had already crept up her neck, covering the back of her head, and the attack failed. This bought Amara enough time to summon another burst of hellfire, not to burn him, but to explode with enough force to throw him off her.

As Sebastian flew backwards once more, a guttural laugh formed in Amara's gut. The cultists she'd dispatched earlier had been all too easy to take down, but now she was up against a real threat. She wasn't fighting against Nick, who was only human, and she wasn't sparring with Vee, a complicated friend that she was trying to make amends with. Sebastian was evil, plain and simple, and Amara had no reason to hold back.

Blood ran down her face, and her laughter grew stronger as she found she was enjoying the fight. Being able to let loose, to vent all the anger that had pent up since her transformation started, was exhilarating. For the first time since learning she was a demon, she was truly pushing her limits, discovering just how much she'd changed, and she was going to make Sebastian pay for thinking he could force her into slavery. She thrived on the violence, wanted more of it, and leapt at her opponent once more.

Amara lost track of how long they were fighting. They were incredibly evenly matched, and for every third or fourth strike she managed to land, Sebastian would force an opening with his incredible strength and throw her off balance. It was during one of these openings that she saw him look towards her friends, safely contained in Vee's Enochian barrier, and he began ignoring Amara. He leapt at the barrier, throwing himself at it with everything he had, to try and break through. Panic filled Amara, and she tried to pull him away as best she could.

She wrapped her tail around his leg, and with another burst of hellfire, managed to throw him off balance. She put herself between Vee's barrier and Sebastian, knowing she couldn't let him through or their plan would fall apart. Inside the barrier, Amara saw that Vee had almost dispatched the rest of the cultists, and Tessa was still focusing on undoing the cult's circle into Hell.

Sebastian leapt forward again, trying to bypass Amara and attack the barrier directly. Amara stayed in front of him, but the force of his charge was so strong that he was able to grab Amara and shove her against the barrier. Powerful Enochian magic surged through Amara, severely weakening her as she tried to hold Sebastian back. In her vulnerable state, she was unable to stop Sebastian as he repeatedly slammed her against the barrier, and with one last shout, he managed to break through.

Amara fell to the ground, gasping in pain as the angelic magic vanished. She was still disoriented and was only barely aware of Sebastian moving in to continue his assault. Before he reached Amara, however, a barrage of holy arrows flew over her, embedding themselves in Sebastian's body and forcing him to scream out in pain.

Someone knelt next to Amara, grabbing her arm and helping her to her feet. "Amara! We only need a few more seconds!" Vee said.

After nodding in acknowledgement, Amara shook her head to try and ground herself. When she looked up again, she saw Sebastian writhing in pain and holding his head.

"Stop. Fighting. Me!" he screamed, seemingly with two voices again.

Seeing an opening, Amara jumped forward and sank her bladed tail into Sebastian's side, hoping to finally end this once and for all. He began yelling again, though seemingly not in response to her attack, which confused her.

"WELLINGTON! STOP FIGHTING ME!"

Sebastian staggered backwards, and Amara paused to try and figure out what was happening. With a closer look, she saw something new. Instead of a single aura surrounding Sebastian, she now saw two. One was angry, full of hate and ego, while the other had a terrible demonic fury to it. They seemed to be battling for dominance inside the cult leader's body, and Amara shouted out in response.

"Vee, keep attacking! Sebastian is trying to overpower the demon he summoned!"

Amara took a quick moment to look around the chamber to confirm Tessa was still safe. While no cultists were advancing on her, she saw movement from the hallway she'd come from earlier. In the distance, Brandon had reappeared, limping and in pain. He was clearly furious and held a dagger in his hand as he advanced.

Before she had a chance to intercept him, however, Tessa finally spoke up. "I've got it! Brace yourselves!"

Amara turned to the magic circle in the center of the chamber. A crack had appeared in the floor, but it didn't seem to be in the concrete; it looked more like it was in the fabric of space itself. An overwhelming, demonic energy poured from the rift, and as soon as it opened, the bodies of the nearby cultists began moving closer. The portal seemed to be pulling in everything demonic; the cultists and Sebastian were clearly feeling its effect, as was Amara, but Vee and Tessa seemed unfazed.

She watched Vee move to a nearby pillar, grabbing it for support, as Sebastian stepped closer to Amara. He now stood directly between her and the portal in the floor, and Amara watched as Mr. Wellington finally lost his internal battle. The demonic aura took complete control of the body, and his eyes turned black as he stared at Amara.

"What. Are. You?!" he shouted, his body still littered with holy arrows.

"I'm Amara, you son of a bitch! You tell everyone in Hell that this place is protected!" Amara poured all her remaining energy into one, concentrated burst of hellfire, then leapt at Sebastian. With one final punch, she let loose a chaotic explosion that forced the demonic cult leader further back to the edge of the portal that would return him to Hell. His eyes flared, and Amara felt his powerful gaze staring deep inside her, desperately searching for answers, as if he was staring directly into her soul. A horrible smirk appeared on his face, and he began laughing.

"Oh. She's going to *love* this," the demon inside Sebastian said. His laughter grew even louder, and he let himself fall backwards into the portal.

Vee braced herself against the pillar, watching as Amara charged Mr. Wellington. She released a sickening explosion of hellfire that caused Vee's ears to ring, but thankfully it managed to knock the cult leader back to the edge of the portal. By the time Vee's hearing had returned to normal, Mr. Wellington had fallen into the portal, but Amara's attack seemed to have thrown off her balance. Vee watched as Amara lost her footing and began falling towards the portal.

Reaching out, Vee grabbed Amara's arm and held tight, grabbing the pillar to keep them both safe. The pull from the portal was immense, and Vee's body strained as she tried to keep Amara from falling in.

Another shape appeared, seemingly another cultist hurtling through the air. His dagger vanished into the portal, but at the last second, he managed to grab Amara's tail. She winced in pain, and Vee felt her already tenuous grip threaten to give way entirely. She looked down, and time seemed to slow as she locked eyes with Amara.

Gallons of blood soaked her friend's body, especially on her razor-sharp claws. Amara redoubled her grip, her demonic exoskeleton digging into Vee's flesh. Overwhelming anger filled Amara's eyes, fury that had been brought out by the night's events, and it terrified her. She recalled moments from earlier, when she'd caught glimpses of Amara's fight with Mr. Wellington. Amara had been laughing maniacally, completely lost in the carnage she was creating. Was Vee's friend still in there? Or had something finally snapped?

Amara's eyes were still pitch black; her amber irises filled with fire as she stared up at Vee. Behind her, the last cultist was desperately holding on to Amara's tail, doing everything in his power to avoid falling into the portal.

If I let go, not only do I end this cult, but I rid the world of... whatever Amara might become. She's clearly still changing; how do I know where this ends?

As Vee stared down at her prior friend, Amara's eyes changed. The demon's sclera shifted from black to white, and the look of fury in her eyes changed to one of desperation. Tears formed, threatening to fall as she stared back. "Vee... please..."

No. Whatever Amara is, she's trying to be better.

Vee reached deep inside herself, praying for every ounce of strength available, and gripped Amara's chitinous wrist as hard as she could. She nodded slowly at Amara, who smiled back before looking down to start kicking the last cultist off her tail.

"Brandon!" Amara shouted. "Go to Hell, you fucker!"

Behind them, the portal at the center of the magic circle began flickering. The edges of it grew fuzzy, and it started to resemble a skewed, distorted VHS image as it struggled to stay open. Vee had no idea how much longer they had before the portal closed.

The cultist scowled at Amara, his other hand grabbing her tail as well as he started climbing higher. Amara tried to flick her tail, to attack him with its bladed edge, but she seemed to be losing strength fast. Vee tried to think of something to do, but any magic of hers would also endanger Amara.

Before she could think of anything, a switchblade appeared out of nowhere and buried itself in one of the cultist's hands. Vee looked over to Tessa, her tattoos were glowing bright, and saw she was focusing on dislodging this last cultist. The dagger broke the cultist's grip, and Tessa quickly attacked his other hand. The pain must have been too much, as the cultist finally flinched and lost his grip on Amara's tail.

Behind him, the distortion of the portal was growing stronger, its edges scattering more and more. Vee worried the portal might close before the cultist made it through, but thankfully that wasn't the case. Just before the portal closed for good, the cultist fell inside. His screams filled the chamber, he continued reaching for something to grab onto as the portal closed around his wrist. A sickening crack reverberated through the room, accompanied by a strange electrical charge, then all was quiet.

Vee and Amara fell to the ground, gasping from exertion. Once she had caught her breath, Vee slowly stood up, leaning against the pillar to keep steady. Without warning, Amara jumped at Vee, who nearly released a burst of angelic light in her surprise.

"Vee, thank you!" Amara whispered, tears in her eyes. "Without you, I... I would've..."

Vee looked down, stunned by the sudden burst of emotionality. Amara hugged Vee tight, crying into her shoulder. Despite everything Vee had just seen—the blood, the carnage, the terrifying power Amara had unleashed—she was nothing more than a scared college student at the moment.

Beside them, Tessa rolled onto her back, her eyes wide as she gasped for air. She grabbed her legs, her waist, her shoulders, almost in shock that everything was still there. "We... we did it. We survived! Fucking hell! We're not dead!!" The witch started laughing, hugging herself tight in celebration. Her laughter filled the chamber, a welcome reprieve from the agonizing shrieks of demons and cultists.

Vee couldn't help but agree with Tessa's sentiment. She'd been so focused on stopping the cult, on wrestling with her complicated feelings about Amara, that she'd never thought about what might happen if they succeeded. She thought back to the fight they'd just won; how many times had she cheated death? What would have happened had Amara not jumped in to save them? She'd seen the horrible creature that Mr. Wellington had become, and Amara had single-handedly kept him away from her. With the gift of hindsight, she knew that whatever demon the mad cult leader had summoned would have easily killed her.

Whatever came next, whatever tension might still exist between the two of them, Vee was alive. A tear of her own fell down her cheek, and she wrapped her arms around Amara to hug her back. They had been friends once, and that was comfort enough for now.

A few more minutes passed, the girls each processing their victory in their own way. Amara's breathing started to slow, and she whispered, "Vee... you saved my life."

Vee moved her arms off Amara, stammering for a second before responding. "You spared me, I spared you. Just... consider us even, Hellspawn."

Amara pulled back, smirking as she wiped a tear off her cheek. "Right, totally no other reason," she said. She took a deep breath, releasing the last of the tremors that had accompanied her tears. "Could you give me some space? I need to wash this blood off me."

Stepping back, Vee realized just how bloody Amara's nearly naked body was. "Wash it off? How?"

Now several paces away, Amara summoned a torrent of hellfire around herself. For a few seconds, she let the flames circle and dance around her body, and when they finally vanished, it looked like she'd just finished a day at the spa. Her skin was practically flawless, unmarred from the battle, not a trace of blood to be seen. A disturbing thought crossed Vee's mind, and she looked down at her own clothes. As she feared, they were completely soaked in blood.

"Oh, great. You couldn't have cleaned yourself off before you hugged me? How am I supposed to get this off?"

"I'm sure you've got a spell in that book of yours somewhere, right?" Amara said, laughing quietly to herself.

From the center of the chamber, Tessa spoke up again. "Fuck. FUCK!"

Vee just now realized that Tessa had finally stopped laughing and was now kneeling at the edge of the portal. "What happened?!"

"A few things. When I reverse-engineered the portal, I was mostly working to counteract the damage the cult had done. I'd never seen the portal before today, though, so this is my first chance to see exactly what they did. I'm only now seeing that their work was horseshit."

"Okay, so? They're gone, right?" Amara asked.

"Yes, but that's not the problem. If they had been more elegant with their alterations, then my reversal would have restored everything to normal. But, surprise surprise, they were a bunch of fuckwads! They practically brute-forced their way past every protective measure. Previously, every circle on campus worked together to form a kind of Planar Gate. This counteracted the natural soft spot that exists here, making sure that nothing weird came through."

"I don't think I like where this is going," Vee said.

"Well, tough luck. The cult had already done serious damage to the gate, and when I reversed their alterations, I basically blew the door off its hinges. The Gate is now totally inert, and we're completely exposed to... well, anything and everything. At any point, if another plane happens to align with ours... something might slip through."

Silence fell over the group, the girls all looking at each other nervously. Their unspoken assumption was that ending the cult would return things to normal, but apparently that wasn't the case. No one else on campus knew about the cult, the Gate, or this supposed soft spot. If anything else were to pop up, would it be their responsibility to handle it?

"Wait, you said a couple things were wrong, what else happened?" Amara flicked her tail, and after a small burst of fire, it returned to normal.

"Oh, that's the worst part. When I stabbed Brandon, I wasn't able to pull my switchblade out in time. The portal closed on his wrist and severed it, and I was hoping it would be the hand with my knife, but it wasn't."

"Wait, hold on," Vee said, stepping closer. "The worst part of this whole night is that you lost your knife?"

"It was my favorite knife! It had, like, an oily rainbow effect on it!"

Vee rolled her eyes, but stepped closer to examine the circle itself. Just as Tessa had said, there was a severed hand lying on the floor. After everything she'd just seen, all the carnage Amara and Mr. Wellington had wrought, it was easy to suppress the urge to gag, but it was still gross to look at. As she kneeled down to get a closer look, the hand suddenly rose off the floor, its fingers curling into a point. It began moving towards Vee, who fell backwards in surprise.

"Ooooh watch out! Brandon's coming back from the dead to get you!" Tessa began laughing hysterically, her tattoos glowing bright. Thankfully, before the hand reached her, Amara snatched it out of the air.

"C'mon Tess, leave her alone." Amara summoned another flash of hellfire, and after a few seconds, the hand was reduced to ashes.

"Ugh, fine. You're no fun." Tessa stood up, her back cracking as she started walking towards the elevator. "We should probably get back anyways, let Nick know that we fucking kicked ass tonight."

"Wait, that's it?" Vee asked. "We just... head home and go to sleep?"

"That's how this works, holy girl," Tessa said. "Unless you want to start calling in Church officials, the best thing to do is stay as far away as possible. We can't tell anyone what happened, and it's not like there are any bodies to find. Plus, this whole chamber is a secret anyways. Life will go on. It'll be a little confusing for a while, but you either fucking deal with it, or you don't."

Vee almost responded, then hesitated. All her previous work for the Church had been small-scale, usually exorcisms or fighting minor demons that managed to sneak up to Earth. Was Tessa right? Would further action only make people more suspicious of her?

Amara spoke up next, stepping closer to Vee and putting a hand on her shoulder. "Hey, what if we comb this whole compound before heading out? I think there's still two cultists left that weren't involved in the final ceremony. They were trying to keep me busy so I wouldn't intervene, and I never saw them join the big fight."

The idea sounded nice, and Vee certainly appreciated a simpler task that would let her unwind from the chaos of the night. "Actually, Amara, what happened to you? You just vanished on us, and we had no idea what happened."

"Oh, they set up another summoning circle with the blood I left behind from our first raid. Then Brandon and two other guys tried to, um... prevent me from stopping the ritual." Amara looked awkwardly at Vee, likely trying not to upset her.

Vee rolled her eyes as she responded. "Amara, just tell us what happened. It can't be any worse than what we just went through."

With a shrug, Amara responded. "Gangbang. But feeding on all three of them gave me the strength to break out and save you guys, so it all worked out in the end. Plus, honestly? I feel fucking amazing. I've never been that juiced up before!"

"No shit, seriously? 'Atta girl, that's my succubus!" Tessa ran closer, slapping Amara's bare ass while they all started heading towards the back corridors. Amara started sharing details with Tessa, explaining exactly what happened and how she was able to break out. Tessa hung onto her every word, excited both about the fucking and the apparent power spike that followed it.

Great, now there's two of them.

Vee sighed in defeat, listening to Amara recount her sexual adventures while they started clearing out the rest of the compound. She watched them walk away, following a few steps behind, with absolutely no interest in joining the conversation. This meant, however, that she was faced with a very explicit reminder that Amara wasn't wearing any clothes, only covered up by a few strategic plates of chitinous exoskeleton. She'd been so flustered by the blood, and caught up in the excitement of surviving, that she hadn't registered the nudity when they'd been hugging earlier.

Before looking away, for one brief moment, a fraction of a second so infinitesimally tiny that Vee didn't even know it had happened, her eyes lingered on Amara's naked curves.

AMARA'S STORY WILL CONTINUE IN:

PERILS OF PURGATORY

THE AURELIUS ARCHIVES: BOOK THREE

ACKNOWLEDGEMENTS

If there's anything more terrifying than taking one's first step as an author, it very well might be taking the second. On some level, I'm always nervous that whichever muse struck me with the inspiration for Suddenly A Succubus might someday vanish, leaving me with dozens of hanging plot threads and no thoughts for how to resolve them.

Thankfully, this hasn't happened yet.

I'm fortunate enough to have envisioned a story that will span many books, and in many ways, this is only the second chapter of the larger story I hope to tell. As of writing this Acknowledgements page, I'm on the cusp of finishing my first draft of Book Four, and I plan to continue writing this series for many more years. However, as eternally thankful as I am to the muse that gifted me a passion for writing, there are many mortal beings that deserve my thanks just as much.

First and foremost, I'd like to thank my cover artist, Linda Bulickova | Noeran. She possesses a level of talent that's hard to put into words, so I encourage you to instead take another look at the cover to appreciate her skill. Her depiction of Vee takes my breath away every time I look at it, and I can't wait to publish more books so I have an excuse to work with her again.

Special thanks to Jacob Hornstein and Lumi Schildkraut, who worked tirelessly to help edit the final draft of this book. They both possess incredible insight and an immaculate eye for detail, and without them, this book would not have been nearly as presentable.

In no particular order, I also extend my immense gratitude to all my Patrons, beta readers, commenters, and fellow writers. I've found a wonderful community through the experience of writing this series, and I consider myself extraordinarily lucky that I've been able to connect with so many fantastic people.

If you're one of those fantastic people (I mean, *look at you*, of course you are!) and you'd like to join in the fun, I encourage you to check out my Patreon. There, you can find first drafts of future books, behind the scenes thoughts on every single chapter, exclusive story content, and even the chance to join in the creative process! I also have a Discord for everyone that enjoys my work, and it's open to everyone, not just my Patrons.

All that and more can be found by visiting NyxNyghtingale.com.

Last, and certainly not least, I thank my wonderful wife for her undying support of this little writing hobby of mine. She's helped me through many writing blocks and continues to be an inspiration each day we're together.

Until next time! Nyx <3

ABOUT THE AUTHOR

Nyx Nyghtingale is an Urban Fantasy writer who focuses on romance, passion, and self-discovery. After getting her start through online fiction sites, she's very excited to have added self publishing to her list of accomplishments. When not writing, Nyx can be found lurking the aisles of bookstores in pursuit of every sapphic Cozy Fantasy book in existence.